THE LOST GIRL

ALAN JACOBSON

"Jacobson expertly ratchets up the tension and shows us that the most courageous heroes are those with everything to lose."
—TESS GERRITSEN
New York Times bestselling author
and creator of Rizzoli & Isles

THE LOST GIRL

ALAN JACOBSON

Cover Design: Shannon Raab
Cover Photographer: istockphoto.com/ Image Source

THE LOST
GIRL

"A daughter without her mother is a woman broken. It is a loss that turns to arthritis and settles deep into her bones."

— Kristin Hannah, *Summer Island*

"Tragedy should be utilized as a source of strength. No matter what sort of difficulties, how painful experience is, if we lose our hope, that's our real disaster."

— Dalai Lama XIV

"Imagine a future where we could edit a sick person's DNA to make them better...there are a lot of questions about how to use this technology responsibly. But I'm hopeful about the possibilities."

— Bill Gates, *Time magazine*, January 4, 2018

1

The sharp metal shard sliced into her thigh. The passenger side airbag exploded against her body, the steel and aluminum shell of the Mercedes caving in around her. Glass shattered into hundreds of tiny flying projectiles.

Amy Robbins grabbed for something—anything—as the sedan skidded along the wet pavement and then careened to a stop.

Everything went ear-numbingly quiet. She swatted away the deflated airbag but did not spot the truck that had struck their vehicle.

Gone.

Fled the scene.

Pain shot into her left shoulder as she turned her head to check on Dan. He was not moving, his bloody face having left a ghoulish imprint on the crumpled surface of the airbag.

"Dan—*wake up.*"

Amy forced her head around toward the rear seat. "Lindy. Open your eyes!" The little girl's mouth hung open, her jaw slack. "Lindy, look at mommy."

Smoke curled through the interior, the acrid fumes burning Amy's nose. She tried to reach into the back, but the shoulder harness had an iron grip on her torso. She could not unlock the mechanism.

Dan kept some kind of device in the car that had a razor on one end for slicing seat belts and a small hammer on the other for breaking glass.

"Dan, *wake up*," she said as her fingers fumbled for the glovebox. She spread her legs as far as she could, released the latch, and pulled the lid open. Forcing her right hand into the opening, she scraped the skin off her knuckles and drew blood.

"Lindy, can you hear me?"

No reply.

Amy's fingers found the hard plastic of the emergency device's handle. After extracting it—her lubricated, bloody skin sliding out easier than it had gone in—she maneuvered the sharp razor against the edge of the seat belt material and drew its blade firmly across the dense polyester weave. It parted with clean edges.

"Thank God," she whispered into the smoky interior.

As she slammed the compartment shut, bright red blood bubbled from the wound on her thigh.

With a grunt and a yank, she removed Dan's canvas belt, pulled it tightly around her leg, and did her best to knot it. The makeshift tourniquet in place, she set about getting the passenger door open. She repeatedly bashed her right shoulder against it, creating just enough space to push her torso through.

Amy used her arms to leverage the rest of her body out of the vehicle and sprawled face up onto the wet pavement. Rain continued to fall, steadily but modestly.

She struggled to her feet and tried the rear door. It popped open. The odor of gasoline flared her nostrils. Off to her right the orange flicker of a flame danced from beneath the crumpled hood.

A cry emerged from deep in her throat as she cut through the seat belt holding Lindy in place. She pulled the girl's body against hers and shimmied out of the backseat. As she limped away from the Mercedes, she glanced over her shoulder and saw flames slithering from the front of the sedan.

The smoke was getting thicker.

Amy set Lindy's body down thirty feet away, then stumbled

back toward the car. She pulled the front passenger door open a few more inches and climbed inside, checked Dan's pulse, and felt a faint throbbing beneath her finger.

"Danny, wake up! Please, honey..." The words choked in her throat and she coughed hard.

Amy moved the seat as far back as it would go, then sliced through the polyester belt. The interior was getting hotter and the flames were crawling across the windshield. A voice inside her head was screaming at her: *Get out now.*

"Amy..." Dan's eyes fluttered open. "...Lindy."

"Got her out. Help me get *you* out."

"Fire." He coughed. "Hot..." His head fell back against the seat.

"Dammit." She shook his shoulders. "Honey, stay with me."

Amy struggled in the close quarters to face away from him, then grabbed his arms and drew them around her neck. His dead weight draped across her back.

A sharp pain dug into her thigh.

She pivoted forward and half fell out of the Mercedes with Dan dragging behind, his hulk clunking and banging into the door jamb and then his shoes scraping over the wet pavement as she struggled to handle his mass.

Amy pushed herself a foot at a time, exhausted as the rain pelted her face and head. She reached Lindy, fell to her knees—and Dan's body collapsed atop her.

A loud blast muffled her hearing as objects flew in her direction.

Seconds later, billowing smoke enveloped them.

AMY BOLTED UPRIGHT IN BED, her body dripping with perspiration, her breathing rapid and her mouth cotton dry.

She slapped at her clock and silenced the braying alarm.

Amy sat there trying to calm her nerves. She had been through this nightmare many times during the past seven years and had resigned herself to spending the rest of her life—however long that would be—with the memories haunting her sleep as they haunted her waking moments. No matter what therapy she tried,

ALAN JACOBSON

the pain persisted.

She summoned the strength to get out of bed. She had showered...well, she wasn't sure when she last showered. Had to be a couple of days ago.

With stringy hair covering half her face, she padded across the studio apartment into the bathroom. She fell onto the toilet and peed, then washed and towel dried her hair.

Her previously luscious, impeccably styled blonde mane was now brushed back and pulled into a bun. Easy, no work required. No expensive hours-long salon visits. That was in her past. These days, fifteen minutes at Great Clips and she was good to go.

When she looked in the mirror she did not recognize the woman who stared back at her. She still had the youthful skin, but she was getting stress lines. Her smile was no longer radiant. Her sunny disposition had vanished the moment that truck slammed into her car.

She pushed the bottle of Lexapro aside and glanced at the clock. No makeup necessary for this job, so she grabbed her purse and headed out the door.

All told, she rolled into Grand Lake Bakery at 11:05.

"You're late, Amy. Again." Ellen Macafree shook her head. "What am I gonna do with you?"

"Sorry. It's only five minutes."

"Not the point," Ellen said. "You're late every day and every day we have the same discussion about being professional, showing up on time for appointments, and acting like you care."

"I know. Sorry."

"Sorry doesn't cut it." Ellen studied her face. "Do you want this job?"

"Do I want this job?" Amy's gaze found the industrial-chic ceiling, black painted ductwork, and low hanging LED lights. "I *need* this job."

Ellen frowned, then turned and walked to her desk a dozen feet away. "Then act like it. We *need* five dozen baguettes in the oven in the next ninety minutes. And then start on the banana muffins."

14

"Yes ma'am." Amy pulled the netting over her head and slipped on a white apron.

The position had come open six months ago. Amy's brother was a regular customer of Grand Lake Bakery and saw the help wanted sign. His sister needed a job and he escorted her into the shop that afternoon to fill out an application.

All Amy had to do was follow the recipes and operate the machinery. It was rote work. Perfect for her.

"Hey."

Amy turned to see Bobby, a baker who had worked there for twenty-three years, returning from the restroom. He was tying his apron behind him as he walked up to the oven and checked inside.

"You on till closing?"

Amy grumbled. "If I don't get fired before then."

"What now?"

"Nothing."

Bobby laughed. "Lemme guess. Late again?"

Amy busied herself with the dough and did not reply.

Bobby went about his work, using a flat, long-handled wooden spatula to push a tray of sourdough bread deep into the clutches of the oven. A moment later, he glanced in Amy's direction. "How about we catch a movie at the Grand Friday night?"

Amy's hands froze, embedded in thick dough. "What?"

"A film," Bobby said, pulling over a tray. "Friday night, the Grand."

"Yeah, I heard you." Amy resumed her kneading. "This a date?"

"Whatever you wanna call it."

Bobby was a stoner, but at least with marijuana now kinda sorta legal—the wisdom of California voters notwithstanding— he wasn't doing anything wrong. But Amy could not stand the sickly-sweet aroma of pot—found it nauseating—and could always smell it on Bobby's clothes when she went into the break room.

"Thanks," Amy said. "But you're like a gazillion years older than me."

15

"So what?" Bobby put down the wooden tool and looked at her. "Is that an issue?"

Amy shrugged.

"Not like you've got better offers."

Amy froze. "And how would you know?"

"I can tell." He waited a beat, then said, "Am I wrong?"

"None of your business. And no...not interested in the movie." A minute passed. "But thanks for asking."

"Yeah. Whatever." Bobby slammed the oven door shut.

The phone rang and Ellen walked into her adjacent office and picked it up.

Bobby came up alongside Amy. "I didn't mean anything by it. Sorry if I upset you."

Amy nodded—and inched to her right.

"I just...it doesn't take a genius to see you're...I dunno. Lonely, I guess."

Amy stepped another foot farther away.

"No," Ellen said into the phone. "You told me you'd be done with the job a month ago. It's now a month past *that*. I want your men onsite tomorrow at eight."

Ellen's office was about ten feet away and the door was open. Amy glanced over, not intending to eavesdrop yet having no choice but to hear the argument.

"No," Ellen said again, louder. "I want the whole project finished by the end of this month. I've got a wedding in my backyard in five weeks. I can't have any construction going on and I need that deck and arbor finished."

Amy again looked at Ellen. The owner's shoulders were hunched and her left hand was balled in a fist.

"No. No. That's not acceptable, Arturo. You promised me a completion date—that you've extended four times. And you're not any closer to finishing than you were a couple weeks ago."

Ellen listened another moment, then leaned back hard in her seat. "I don't care if you've got other jobs. That's not my fault and it's not my problem."

She dropped the handset away from her mouth. "And what

16

should I tell my daughter?" Ellen disconnected the call and let her head fall backward, her eyes studying the ceiling.

Amy walked over, her gloved hands covered in flour. "So your contractor promised a completion date. Is that written in your contract?"

Ellen chuckled. "Yes. A lot of good that's done."

"Did you have a payback clause?"

She looked up at Amy. "A what?"

"If contractors exceed their estimated time of completion, they have to pay you a set amount per day until they finish. It prevents them from jerking you around. Encourages good behavior on their part, prioritizes your job. It incentivizes them to finish on time."

Ellen swiveled her chair to face Amy. "My minimum wage employee who kneads dough all day is giving me legal advice?"

Amy moved back to her work surface, shrugged, and pounded a fist into the dough. "I...it's just something I happen to know, is all."

Ellen came over and studied her face. "You're serious."

"I'm serious."

She glanced at her watch. "Get that last batch in the oven, then clean up. We're gonna grab a late lunch."

Amy felt a sense of dread descend on her. She should not have intervened like that—now Ellen was going to want to know who she really was. Her right eyelid began twitching, an effect of the accident, or more accurately the stress and emotional trauma it caused.

They walked into Lakeside Grill and a middle-aged woman near the front recognized Ellen. "I've got a table by the window, the one you like."

"Thanks so much, Joan."

They slid into their seats and Joan handed them menus.

Amy looked it over quickly and set it down.

"That was fast. You eat here a lot?"

"First time."

"You hardly looked at the menu."

17

Amy shrugged. "Burger. Fries. Not too hard."

"And not too healthy. How'd you manage to pick the only junk food they serve?"

She bobbed her head disinterestedly. "It's salty."

Ellen scrunched her brow. "Whatever. I'm not your mother."

Joan returned and took their orders.

"You have any beer?" Amy asked.

"Beer?" Joan's eyes drifted over to Ellen. "Yeah, we've got lots. What kind do you—"

"Porter. Anything dark and bitter."

"Sure. How about Old Rasputin Russian Imperial Stout? Made in Fort Bragg and I—"

"Fine."

Joan did not bother writing it down. "Do you want that with your burger?"

"Now. Please."

As Joan backed away, she threw another look at Ellen—which was not lost on Amy.

"You obviously come here a lot," Amy said, rolling her paper napkin between her left thumb and index fingers.

"I've known Joan since I opened the bakery."

"When was that?"

"Twenty-three years ago."

Amy nodded. "Hmm. So Bobby's been with you since the beginning."

"Yeah," Ellen said with a chuckle. "You could say that. He's my ex-husband."

"He's what?"

Ellen frowned and nodded. "Hard to believe. But true." She waved a hand. "Only lasted a couple of years. I still care about him. But I realized he wasn't gonna amount to anything and I cut my losses. I bought him out of his half of the bakery—which wasn't worth much at the time because it was a new business—and I let him stay on. He got into drugs and, well, he needed this. I couldn't stand to see him out on the street. Because that's where he'd have ended up."

Joan set the pint of beer in front of Amy along with a glass.

Amy reached out and took the bottle and looked it over.

"So where'd you learn about contractors and contracts?" Ellen asked. She leaned forward across the table. "I'm not buying the 'just something I happen to know' explanation."

Amy stared at the beer. She abruptly lifted it and drank for a few seconds, draining half of it. She set it back on the table.

"Your employment application doesn't mention anything about being a legal secretary."

"I wasn't." She stole a glance at Ellen, who was looking at her with narrow eyes. Amy gathered up the beer and finished it. She set the bottle down firmly. "I was an attorney. *Am* an attorney. I—uh, whatever." She grabbed Joan's arm as she passed and held up the empty Old Rasputin with her other hand. "Another, please."

Joan glanced at Ellen, whose brow was knitted, her top teeth biting her lower lip. "You sure, miss? I mean, it's only one o'clock."

"Yeah," Amy said. "I'm sure."

As Joan moved off, Ellen touched Amy's wrist. "You still have five hours left in your shift. How are you going to work with—"

"Doesn't bother me."

"Bullshit."

"Hey. You think I'm unfit to work, I'll go home."

"That's selfish. Who am I going to get to fill in for you at the last minute?"

Amy thought a moment, then nodded. "Definitely one of the drawbacks of being self-employed and running a business."

Ellen leaned back in her seat. Amy read her expression as one of disapproval.

Joan appeared with another beer—no glass this time since the first one had gone untouched.

"Don't drink that just yet," Ellen said. "There's a story here. And I want to hear the lucid version. Or...the semi-lucid version."

"Trust me. You don't want to hear either one."

Ellen gave Amy's forearm a firm squeeze. "I do. Really."

Ellen was about her mother's age—or the age her mom would be if she were still alive. Amy stared at her drink. "I was living my dream. And then in an instant, it was gone. Tragic, actually. Because that part of it wasn't a dream. It was reality."

"Tell me more," Ellen said.

"Not my favorite thing to do," Amy said, reaching out and picking up the bottle. "Talking about it."

"When did this...happen?"

"Seven years, two months, and three days ago."

Joan swung up alongside the table with two plates and set them in front of the two women.

"What was this tragedy that changed your life?"

Amy stared at her burger. "I lost my girl. And my husband."

"Lost them? How?"

"Our car was broadsided by a truck. They were killed. I survived."

"I'm so sorry."

Amy laughed. "Yeah." She made eye contact with Ellen. "I've heard it. But no one knows what it's like. No one understands. You *can't* until you've lived through something like that." She dropped her gaze. Grabbed the bottle, put it to her lips, then pulled it away and picked at the corner of the label instead.

"Did you get help?"

Amy canted her eyes ceiling-ward. "Let's see. Depression. Survivor's guilt. PTSD. Destructive tendencies. Yeah, I got help. No—I *went* for help. Didn't *get* any. Lost my family, lost my job, lost my career. Lost my life."

"So you really were an attorney?"

"Partner in the second largest law firm in Boston. My husband and I couldn't get pregnant so we tried IVF. And then we were blessed with the miracle. My daughter. Lindy." Amy stared off at the back of the restaurant over Ellen's right shoulder. Her eye began twitching again.

"You're right. I can't imagine what that was like."

Amy smirked—an "I told you so" look.

"Did you have a support network? Friends? Other attorneys at the firm?"

"Lost it all after having a nervous breakdown. Excuse me. A

severe depressive episode."

"How severe?"

Her right eyelid twitched faster. "Very." Amy took a swig of beer. "Tried to kill myself." She held out her left wrist, displaying a faint transverse scar. "I was bleeding out and a friend found me." She stared at the healed skin. "Spent time on a shrink's couch, my bloodstream filled with all sorts of psychoactive cocktails." She snorted. "*Therapy*." Amy set the bottle down. "They wanted to talk about the accident, about my daughter. About my husband. I couldn't. Didn't want to. So they didn't really have much to offer me. Wasn't their fault. I just wasn't ready. I stopped going and tried to deal with it myself."

Ellen was staring, brow firm with concern.

Amy gestured at her wrist. "Obviously, that didn't work out too well, either. Spent several weeks in an institution on suicide watch. Multiple times." She took another swig. "I needed a clean break, a move somewhere across the country."

"Did that help?"

Amy sighed—a long one, the kind that told you it was not a simple answer. "I was on meds. Lots of meds. Still on some of them. But I had to get a job because I'd eaten away most of our savings..." Amy chuckled derisively. "Funny thing about large gaps in unemployment following a major life tragedy. People can connect the dots. And with a flood of lawyers clamoring for jobs, with no book of business and a sketchy gap on my CV, no way in hell would a firm hire me."

"No book of business?"

"Lawyer speak for no clients." Amy stared off at the table. What she did not tell Ellen was that she had a hard time thinking about returning to that kind of lifestyle. Practicing law would forever keep those wounds open, like a festering bedsore that never healed. Leaving Boston was step one. Leaving the legal profession was a close second. "I finally started looking for different types of work. Minimum wage positions in stable businesses. Do my work and go home. Minimal responsibility. Minimal stress."

Ellen leaned back in her seat. "So everything you told me during your interview—"

"A lie. Never worked in a bakery. Learned it all at YouTube University." Amy forced a half smile.

"I should fire you for lying to me, falsifying your work history."

"And you'd be completely justified. But you won't."

"Why so sure?"

"Because that'd be very harsh. Cold-hearted. And you're one of the nicest people I've ever met."

Ellen's gaze worked its way across Amy's face before she answered. "Fine. Then earn your keep. When we get back, call that contractor and use your attorney tone to scare the living daylights out of him. My daughter's getting married and I need a functional backyard."

2

Amy arrived at the Lake Merritt home of her brother
Zach and sister-in-law Loren. When Amy left Boston
for Oakland—at Loren's insistence—she moved into the
ground floor of their two-story house. She lived there until they
were satisfied she was mentally stable and viably employed—but
after three years, they urged her to find a place of her own to
reestablish her independence and sense of self.

Zach and Loren had two children, which presented both a
challenge and a therapeutic opportunity. At times the two boys,
Devin and Daniel—ten and twelve—filled the void Amy felt in her
life, though it also stirred the deep-seated sense of loss she was
trying so desperately to escape.

Amy sensed that they were now an age where Loren and Zach
could tell them what had happened to their uncle and cousin—but
if the boys *had* been told, they were obviously instructed not to
ask her about it.

"I brought a loaf of olive and walnut sourdough," Amy said as
she gave Loren a hug and a peck on the right cheek.

"My favorite," Loren said, gathering up the white bag. "Did
you make it?"

"I did."

"Zach will be up in a minute. He's doing some research for tomorrow morning's trades."

Zach had been a successful Wall Street investment banker, but when the recession hit his firm suffered lightning quick losses that put them in liquidity hell—they did not have enough capital to survive, so in a matter of days they unloaded tens of billions of dollars in subsidiary lines of business to generate the funds needed to hold off the blood-smelling foreign sharks. The firm made it through—but Zach's division, and thus his position, did not.

Truth was, he and Loren had been discussing an exit from the insanely stressful, cutthroat world. The work was destructively competitive and took its toll. Corporate politics made it worse and kept him looking over his shoulder.

Wanting to raise a family, he realized that he needed to be more accessible, and toiling away with a Wall Street firm was less than ideal for fostering a healthy family life. Loren's stable job as an FBI agent afforded him the flexibility to work for himself as well as the ability to move anywhere in the country she was transferred.

He was confident he could make enough money from home to supplement Loren's salary. Although he had done well on Wall Street, he refused to blow it living the high life, unlike many of his friends. As a result, he and Loren were able to pay cash for their two-million-dollar Lake Merritt house—and have four times that in reserve. If he could earn enough to cover their monthly expenses, the dividend payouts from their portfolio provided plenty of free cash. Loren's job supplied the family medical insurance while her salary would more than fund the boys' private schools and college educations. If they were smart about their finances, they were financially set.

"I wish my brother would get out of that business."

"Day trading?" Loren pulled out a platter from the cabinet. "I'd hardly call it a business. I mean, I guess it is." She shook her head. "But yeah, me too. He's better than that. He could've gotten a job with a San Francisco firm doing institutional investing."

"That'd be a good idea if he didn't hate anything to do with 'institutional' and corporate."

Loren chuckled. "And he's none too happy to have a spouse who works for the FBI."

"Oh yeah? You never mentioned that before."

"It's a bit of a sore point between us. Dirty laundry."

"He thinks it's too dangerous?"

"Yep."

"Hey, it's steady work. With full health care and retirement benefits. The kind of things he can only get with the institutional and corporate bodies he rails against." Amy glanced around. "Where's Coco?"

"The boys took her for a run around the lake."

"They don't run."

"They're riding their bikes. Coco's the one running. She got hold of an entire bag of dehydrated chicken strips and needs to burn it off."

"Exercise? Or punishment?"

Loren laughed. "A little of both. Problem is, Coco loves to run. Mostly while chasing after the two cats next door."

A German shepherd mixed with the thick undercoat of a Husky and the disposition of a Labrador, Coco was eighty pounds of lovable, food-scavenging lapdog. Loren and Zach adopted her from a rescue organization when she was about four months old. Coco had been found by a vet when she was a young pup, ridden with fleas and ticks. It was a miracle she had survived. After Dr. Johnson nursed her back to health, Coco was placed with the Robbins.

"Told the boys to be home at six." Loren removed the loaf from the waxed bag and set it on a cutting board. "So what's new? How's work going?"

Amy squinted and scratched the back of her head, tussling her dirty blonde hair. "I had an interesting discussion with my boss today."

Loren selected a knife and held it against the crust. "'Interesting' can be taken a lot of ways. Is this good interesting or bad interesting?"

Amy thought a moment, then moved behind Loren and opened a cabinet, removed the olive oil and vinegar bottles. "I told her about what happened."

Loren stood there, the blade still resting on the hard exterior of the bread. "You told her?" She shook her head. "I mean, that's great. I—I didn't realize you were, you know, comfortable doing that."

"It kind of...came up." Amy explained how the discussion originated.

"Not sure it was such a good idea to drink a couple of beers at lunch. With your boss, no less."

"Probably not. But I needed it. I knew she was going to ask and I had to give her an answer. An honest one." Amy's eyelid began twitching. She looked away. "Anyway, can't take it back."

Loren began sawing away at the sourdough, slicing thick pieces, before answering. "How did it make you feel? Telling her what happened."

"Exposed," she said without hesitation. "Naked."

"Do you like Ellen?"

Amy nodded slowly. "Yeah. A genuinely good person. Honest. Real. Always straight with me."

Loren placed the bread on the platter and set it on the dinner table. "Being able to talk about it, that's a big deal. I'm not a shrink, but I think this was a good thing." She turned to Amy and studied her face. "Don't you?"

"I guess. I think so. Yeah. I'm just still not real comfortable with exposing myself like that."

Loren gave Amy a hug. "I'm proud of you. I think it's another important step. I know it wasn't an easy thing to do, but you can build on this."

Amy took a deep breath, then moved away and gathered up the oil and vinegar and a bottle of za'atar spice Loren had bought in the shuk, or the outdoor market, during a trip to Israel. Loren told her it was supposed to give strength and clear the mind. Amy had eaten a lot of it the past few years. She wished it would work faster.

The door to the downstairs office swung open.

"So did it feel good playing lawyer again?" Loren asked.

"Whoa. What?"

They turned in unison to see Zach standing there. His head was canted left and his gaze was riveted on Amy.

"Just some advice I gave my boss. It was nothing." She glanced at Loren and tried to signal her, without alerting her brother, to not make a big deal out of it.

But Zach advanced on her nevertheless. "Sis, I've been through hell and back with you. And discussing *anything* involving the law has been off base for you. Not just off base. Forbidden."

Amy looked away and pulled some dishes out of a cabinet. "It just kind of happened. I overheard something and had to speak up. It's not like I was trying a case."

Zach took his sister's shoulders in his hands. "Don't get me wrong. I'm not upset. I'm really, really happy."

"Let's not make more out of it than it was." A grin teased the corners of her mouth. "But it did kind of feel good. To be able to help someone with...well, something I know about."

"I bet." He started to help set the table. "So if you can't catch on with a law firm, maybe you should open your own practice."

Amy laughed. "Even if I wanted to, that's a huge leap from helping out my boss. I'd have to take the California bar—and pass it after not practicing law for several years—and then start from scratch to build a business. Oh—and I've got no assets. No collateral. No goodwill."

Loren and Zach shared a look. Amy had the feeling they were about to offer her a loan—or worse, a monetary gift. Seed money.

"It was just some commonsense advice I gave my boss, that's it. Really, let's just drop it."

"No," Zach said, "I'd rather not drop it. You did a great thing today, made important strides toward coming out of your shell, getting your life back together, and I—"

"Zach," Loren said. "Don't. This is probably not the time or—"

"And when would the time or place be? Huh? My sister's been

sleepwalking through life. Time to wake up. She's a Stanford-educated lawyer. To throw that all away—"

"I'm standing right here," Amy said. "No need to refer to me in the third person."

The garage door rolled up, vibrating the walls as it rumbled along its track. Coco's barking echoed as she ran the stairs.

"Kids are home," Loren said. "This *really* isn't the time, Zach."

The young men came running up the steps and tossed their helmets on the sofa.

"Hold on a minute," Loren said. "Is that where your stuff goes? On our nice couch?"

Coco ran over to her water bowl and began slurping.

"Hey Aunt Amy," Daniel said, wrapping his arms around her.

"Hey back." Amy brushed the hair out of his eyes.

Devin likewise greeted her warmly and, at Zach's direction, they ran off to wash their hands, Coco turning and dashing after them, a trail of water following her.

Once they left the room, Loren, Zach, and Amy were left to themselves, setting plates of grilled shrimp and crab cakes on the table and killing time until the children returned.

Amy went through a difficult time when Devin turned eight, roughly the age Lindy would have been had she not died in the accident. She felt resentment toward her nephew and jealous of her brother and sister-in-law. She successfully fought those emotions over the years but had to admit it probably had more to do with the passage of time and Devin getting older.

When Daniel and Devin reentered the dining room, Amy remained silent, withdrawing back into the world she thought—hoped—she might have started to escape.

At the moment, however, she felt like no such progress had been made.

3

Amy and Loren made plans to go running the next morning, a Saturday. Amy had to be prodded, but Loren made the case that she should build on the positive development she had at work. Amy again downplayed its significance.

"Small victories," Loren said. "Sometimes the Bureau can't go for big scores. That's actually how it is most of the time. We may only be able to take down a bit player, but we can make that guy turn on someone else, who helps us put the screws on a guy who's higher up. By the time we're done, we've gutted the organization and shut down their operation. But it all started with that first low-on-the-totem pole knucklehead."

"Fine, I'll go. Haven't put my running shoes on since..." She shook her head. "Well, since *then*."

"The fresh air will do you good. There's a nice breeze coming off the lake. We're on a roll, sis. Let's keep it going."

LAKE MERRITT WAS A THREE-AND-A-HALF-MILE heart-shaped tidal lagoon in the heart of Oakland surrounded by parkland and city neighborhoods. It began as an arm of the San Francisco Bay before becoming the city's main sewer, but as the surrounding community grew, the stench of human waste became unbearable.

In the late 1860s, the body of water was dammed off from the bay, the lake was cleaned and turned into the nation's first wildlife refuge. The centerpiece of Oakland, it now featured paved jogging trails, grassy shores, bird refuges, a children's amusement park, and rowboat and canoe rentals.

Amy and Loren started out near the pergola and made their way past a bicycle stand. They jogged clockwise around the large lake toward the aviary, passing a circle of Acro yogis.

"Yoga," Loren said. "You should try that."

Amy slowed and veered left. "Now?"

Loren laughed but didn't break her stride.

Next to them, on a large, expansive lawn that abutted a main street about fifty yards away, a flock of geese stood grazing. People sat under mature oaks eating muffins and drinking coffee, taking in the sun, or reading books and Kindles.

As they passed a couple of boys playing ball with their dog, Amy's gaze caught a blonde girl with ponytails sitting with a woman in her early twenties. They were lounging on a blanket and eating sandwiches.

The girl was strikingly beautiful, with light, clear aquamarine eyes. Amy found herself headed right for them. A few strides later, she was standing five feet away.

"I—I'm sorry." Amy laughed to mask her odd behavior. "Your daughter is just gorgeous."

The woman grinned. "Thank you—but she's not my daughter. I'm the au pair."

She had a thick accent—German, Amy guessed—but she spoke nearly flawless English.

"Those eyes," Amy said. "They're magnificent."

"Amy."

She turned to see Loren jogging over. "What happened? I was talking to you and all of a sudden realized I was blabbering to myself."

"Sorry. I, I just..." Amy could not pull her gaze from the girl. Her right eye twitched.

"Beautiful day," Loren blurted. She looked at Amy, then the

child, then the au pair. "Sorry to, uh...sorry to bother you." Loren took hold of Amy's left elbow and tugged.

Amy nodded good-bye and started jogging away, glancing over her shoulder as they got back on the path.

"What was that?" Loren said.

"She looks like Lindy. Did you see—"

"A normal person glances over and keeps running. You don't walk up to a stranger and stare."

The comment was like a wet towel slap across her face. "I'm not normal. We already know that."

"Not what I meant," Loren said. "I'm only saying that you're not...the acute pain hasn't gone away completely. You're still grappling with this."

Amy stole another peek over her shoulder. The blonde girl was tossing something—probably pieces of bread—into the lake for the ducks. Just like Amy used to do with Lindy. She felt a whimper of sadness in her chest. *Lindy is dead.*

Amy turned back to Loren and said, "I can't see that pain ever going away."

4

The following Monday, Amy returned to work. It was as if nothing had happened. Ellen greeted her as she always did—on those rare occasions when Amy was on time—with a smile and a nod. Amy wanted to ask if her discussion with the contractor had spurred him to action...but realized it was better if she did not know. She did not want to get dragged back into it.

That said, she had to admit that resuming her role as a lawyer, even if only for a few minutes, felt good. In control. Knowledgeable. Worth something. And it also scared the crap out of her.

As she kneaded the dough, she glanced up at Ellen—but averted her eyes when Ellen looked in her direction.

The morning skipped by, but other than some work-related banter with Bobby, she kept to herself. She wondered if Ellen had said anything to him about Amy's past—or her previous career. If she had, Bobby did not mention it. Ex-husband or not, she did not know how close they remained.

Amy removed her apron and hairnet, then grabbed her lunch bag from the staff refrigerator and walked down the block to Lake Merritt. She tried to get there a few times per week to clear her head and breathe some fresh air. It did not always make her feel better, but Loren and Zach insisted it would help her and, in theory, she knew it *should*. With nothing better to do during lunch, she stuck with the routine.

As she padded along the path around the lake, she finished the sandwich, crumpled the empty paper sack into a ball—and realized she had walked in the opposite direction than usual. While in the past she preferred to vary her route, after the accident she found comfort in rote tasks and patterns. It required less effort, less thought.

A few yards later, she realized why she had subconsciously started in this direction: she had gone to the location where she had seen the au pair. And the girl.

Like yesterday, they were camped out on the grass on a colorful blanket, a wicker picnic basket set out between them.

Amy tried to make her feet carry her past them, but she felt an overwhelming draw toward the girl. "Hi again."

The woman looked up and shielded her eyes from the glare of the bright sky.

"Oh. Hi." Her eyes made a quick assessment of Amy's clothing. "You're not running today."

Amy laughed. "No, I'm on lunch break. I work right up the street."

"I'm Giselle."

"Amy." She set her knees on the edge of the blanket. "And you are?"

Those crystal-clear eyes locked onto Amy's. "Melissa," she said, singing it and drawing out the sound of the *s*.

"Melissa. Very pretty name. And you've got very pretty eyes. I bet lots of people tell you that."

Melissa grinned broadly and looked down, turning away and clasping her hands in front of her body.

"So you guys like spending time at the lake."

"Melissa's favorite place," Giselle said, her accent permeating each word. "Well, second to Disneyland."

"You enjoy feeding the ducks?" Amy asked.

Melissa nodded and looked away.

"Use your words," Giselle said. "Do not be shy."

Melissa swung her gaze back toward Amy. "Yes. I like feeding the ducks. They eat my bread. But I like bread, too. So I don't really want to give it to them. Giselle says I can't give them peanut butter."

Amy laughed. "Peanut butter may be kind of difficult for them to swallow."

"I like ice cream too. And the ice cream man comes three times." She held up three fingers.

"Monday, Wednesday, and Friday," Giselle explained. She cupped a hand and shielded her mouth from Melissa. "Weekends too," she mouthed, then winked.

Amy stifled a smile. "So, Melissa, what's your favorite flavor?"

"Strawberry."

"Strawberry? Really?"

Melissa animatedly nodded her head up and down.

"Mine too. I used to pick strawberries when I was your age."

"*Pick* strawberries?" Melissa scrunched her nose.

"Yes, they grow on little plants." She pulled out her iPhone and found a picture that supported her claim.

"I want to pick strawberries too."

"Maybe Giselle can plant some with you. In a pot at your house." She turned to Giselle and shrugged.

"We can try. I am not good with plants. I mostly kill them. What is it you Americans say? Green thumb?"

"Yes."

"I have a brown one."

They both chuckled.

Amy bent forward to engage with Melissa. "So you said you like bread. What's your favorite kind?"

Melissa shrugged.

Amy tilted her head. "How about pumpernickel?"

"I don't know."

"It's brown bread. Kind of sweet. It's delicious. Would you like to taste it?"

Melissa nodded.

"Well you know what? I work in a bakery. I make bread all day long. Would you like me to bring you the absolute *bestest* pumpernickel in Oakland?"

Melissa looked at Giselle.

"That would be fine. But I do not think we should feed it to the ducks."

"We've always got some day-old loaves that don't sell. I'll bring one of them too. You can give that to the ducks." Amy caught the time on Giselle's watch and jumped up. "Whoops. Gotta get back to work. Will you be here tomorrow?"

Giselle canted her head toward the gray sky. "Unless the weather's bad, we're here every day for lunch."

"Great," Amy said as she backed away. "See you tomorrow. With some delicious brown bread." She gave Melissa a wink and headed off down the path.

5

"You okay?"

Amy turned to face Bobby, her hands still moving, massaging the dough. "Huh? I'm fine. Why?"

"You're working about twice normal speed. And you're singing."

"What? I'm not singing, Bobby."

"Humming. Whatever. You never hum. You're always...you know."

Amy's hands stilled. "I'm always *what*?"

Bobby looked at her a long moment, then turned his attention to the oven on his left. "Nothing. Forget it."

Amy tossed the dough onto the counter and rubbed the flour from her hands as she advanced on Bobby. "No, it's not nothing. What did you mean?"

He shrugged. "Well...like there's a black cloud hanging over you." He pulled open the oven door. "You're kind of, I dunno, depressed."

Amy frowned. "There's more to it than that." She headed back to her workstation. "And I wasn't humming."

"That song from *Something Rotten*."

Amy had to fight to keep herself from smiling.

"Yeah, I see that grin. I'm right, aren't I?"

"Yes."

Bobby laughed boisterously. "So...what, did you meet someone?"

I did, but it's not what you're thinking. "No."

"But something happened at lunch. You were real quiet this morning, you leave for a half hour and you're humming Broadway tunes."

Amy punched her fist into the mound—one of the things she enjoyed about her job. Controlled aggression. "Whatever."

"Yeah," Bobby said with another laugh. "Whatever. But whoever it is, I'm happy for you. Even if I wanted it to be me. I'm happy for you."

"I didn't meet a guy."

"Hmm. Then I still got a chance."

"You know, Bobby, that's true. You do. Just like winning the lottery."

6

"Did you say two billion dollars?"

Angelo Lira chuckled lightly and flashed a left-sided grin. "Don't give me that crap, Brandon. You knew this was possible."

Dr. Brandon Ellis, CEO and founder of LifeScreen Genetics, absolutely knew it was possible. Lira had sat down with him four years ago and planted that seed in his mind over a steak dinner at the tony Boulevard restaurant in San Francisco. Seed is right—as in seed money Lira and his AIL Venture Capital partners poured into Ellis's company, buying out the initial "angel" investors for a fifty percent profit. Then AIL stepped in and dropped two million for equipment, then another three for staffing and expanded lab space and computers, and finally another four million to facilitate the development of branding and marketing.

Now the seed had sprouted and grown into a promising plant that would bear fruit for many years to come. That is, once the IPO, or initial public offering, launched.

The short and stout Ellis had been an exceptional student in medical school but never showed any business acumen. However, that didn't matter when he joined a successful practice because all aspects of what happened outside the treatment room were handled by his office staff and then the large health care organization that purchased the medical group.

The field of reproductive medicine was burgeoning—but it lacked something. For him. The creative spirit he had enjoyed as a boy, and then a teen, was stripped from him during the rigorous rote memorization of medical school, then the rules governing proper standards of care, insurance codes, management procedures, and malpractice guidelines.

Despite the monotony, he took to the material and became an excellent diagnostician because of his ability to see the big picture and think outside the box. He became adept at solving the puzzles of tough cases.

But the part of his brain that thrived on creativity was atrophying. Although he was aware of what was happening, he did not know how to arrest it.

He tried sculpting for an hour or two on the weekends, but as the demands of practice grew, he had less time to himself. After meeting Christine—a fellow reproductive physician he had shared lunch with at a medical conference—their relationship fast-tracked to cohabitation and then engagement within nine months. His isolated recreational hours shriveled to nothing.

The tipping point arrived on an unassuming spring morning. Ellis was asked to consult on a dispiriting case that gripped him like scar tissue around a nerve causing unrelenting pain: a child born with a horrible genetic disease that was incurable. It would shorten the boy's lifespan to single digits.

After that young patient left his office, Ellis took a walk in the brisk air, wondering why his profession had not devised an effective method of genetically screening fertilized ova before the embryo could develop into a mistake of nature that caused endless pain to all involved—including the physician who presided over the initial spark of life and burgeoning pregnancy.

While researchers had developed preimplantation genetic diagnosis, or PGD, and preimplantation genetic screening, or PGS, these tests could detect only a limited number of conditions. The technology that would later form the basis behind LifeScreen went a magnitude further—at substantially lower cost—and without the need for invitro fertilization.

The concept of fertility doctors being able to select certain desirable characteristics and reject "bad" ones was not new. But it was fraught with moral and ethical questions. Although Ellis could not deny this, he was able to see beyond the criticisms, media sound bites, and naysayers. The image of that young child remained fresh in his mind.

It was one of those times in life where something moves you to action, the type of thing that changes your viewpoint, the way you look at things—at *everything*, really—and forces you to put all the controversial issues aside and find a solution. To think outside the box.

As he walked, the cool breeze invigorating his face, an idea began to form. He stopped and stood there for minutes—ten, thirty, he did not know—working out the broad strokes of what could be done. It was pie-in-the-sky stuff, a wish list of *what if* scenarios that could not be solved in one night.

It took two.

However, having an idea of how to do something and seeing it to fruition were different things. He understood that intellectually, but as he dove deeper into the details of his plan, it became more apparent. What he needed to do would take time and money—neither of which he had.

None of that mattered at first. He continued seeing his patients but was distracted. Sleep was fitful and he would awaken in the middle of the night with ideas. He started keeping a notebook on his nightstand and jotting down his thoughts in the dark so as not to disturb Christine.

Each morning he would run his ideas by her and together they would refine them. Christine's business sense was a great deal more acute than his, and her aggressive, competitive nature drove him to think harder.

As the weeks passed, he realized he had reached the point where he had to make one of those life-altering decisions. He quit his medical practice and began attempting to cobble together the monetary resources he would need to make his idea become reality.

John Hutchinson, his longtime childhood friend and medical school roommate, connected him with Angelo Lira, a friend of his in Silicon Valley—a wealthy man who now had a nephew because of Hutchinson's expertise in helping his sister get pregnant. Lira owed Hutchinson, he told Ellis.

"Will that get me an investor?" Ellis asked.

Hutchinson chortled, a hearty belly laugh. "No. These venture capital types are tough negotiators. But it'll get you a sit-down dinner with him. Pitch him your idea. Face to face. He bites, *then* you'll have an investor."

"Maybe Christine should go."

Hutchinson screwed his mouth into a frown. "Yeah, maybe *not*. This kind of meeting requires tact. A softer approach. If you get what I'm saying."

Ellis laughed—and then Hutchinson joined in. The adjectives gentle, sensitive, or subtle would never be used to describe Christine.

Ellis did as suggested and set up a dinner with the entrepreneur—alone.

When Ellis landed in San Francisco, a place he had never visited, the allure of the city hit him. The weather was brisk and the green hills picturesque. The streets were full of life, a cauldron of couture and culture, diversity of race and gender, a spectrum of wealth and poverty: stately Victorian mansions a block away from homeless encampments on the sidewalks.

When Ellis walked into Boulevard, the maître d' escorted him to a table in the back. The restaurant was noisy and candlelit, and the artfully presented food on the oblong plates that he passed looked both delicious and expensive.

Angelo Lira stood as Ellis approached. The two men shook hands and sat simultaneously. "Welcome to our wonderful city."

"Thank you, Mr. Lira. I blocked off a day to sightsee tomorrow."

"On your own?"

Ellis smiled. "I have a map in my pocket and Google on my

phone."

"Nonsense. My driver will take you around. Born and raised here."

Ellis unfurled his napkin. "Not necessary."

"Of course it isn't. But I insist."

"Okay." Ellis pursed his lips. "Thanks."

"So John tells me you need an angel investor."

"Actually, I don't know what I need. Well, that's not true. I need capital to purchase equipment, lease space, hire a couple of research assistants." He explained a little more as the waiter brought a bottle of sparkling water.

"Yes, angel investors are where you want to start. If things go well..." Lira shrugged. "We can sit down and talk some more. If your prospects are promising, we'll buy out the angel investors at a hefty profit and start pumping money into your business. Millions. For a percentage of the company, of course."

Since Ellis was not much of a businessman, Christine had given him her input and did some research. He at least arrived in San Francisco equipped to ask a few pertinent questions. "What percent?"

"Can't say at this point. But VC takes a big enough chunk to make our investment pay off. Otherwise, if the ROI, or return on investment, isn't sufficient, there are other places we could be deploying that capital. There's gotta be enough in it for us. You understand."

Ellis did not like it, but he understood. As a neophyte small business owner, profit and loss were concepts he was becoming all too familiar with. If he didn't make money and watch his expenses, he would not be able to keep his doors open very long. That much was simple math.

"How do I find these angel investors?"

"A guy I know focuses on health care and medical device companies. Is there technology involved in your business?"

"Yes. A lot."

"Even better. I'll set you up." Lira pulled out his iPhone and a moment later was chatting with someone he appeared to be very friendly with. He handed the device to Ellis, who answered some questions, set an appointment for the next day, and then ended the call.

"Thank you."

"Thank me after they decide to invest. Until then, I didn't do you any favors except make a phone call."

EVERYTHING HAD GONE AS LIRA had described. Lira's company, AIL, had bought out the angel investors two years into the venture and promptly provided, in addition to expertise and cash, a credit line that Ellis tapped as they expanded and hired a consultant to take the product through the process to obtain FDA approval.

The credit line expanded as more capital was needed to market LifeScreen to the medical practitioners who would either sign on for the genetic screening service or purchase the equipment and computer software that would assist in the analysis, identification, and filtering of the most disease-free and genetically "normal" embryos a couple could implant.

"This has the potential to revolutionize health care," Ellis told Lira when they were ramping up for the IPO process. "Think about it. How much society pays for the care and support of people with genetic diseases—it's a staggering sum."

"And we own the patents."

"One thing, though. I've heard some grumbling from a couple of friends, liberal types, who feel this will only benefit those who can afford to have the tests run."

"How's that different from, say, cancer therapy?"

"Well, a lot of cancer therapies are covered by insurance. In a lot of states, IVF *isn't*—so who knows if LifeScreen would be, either. I've got some people working on that, a lobbyist in DC who's making the pitch to several members of Congress, showing how it'll dramatically reduce health care costs. But we had another idea."

Lira leaned back in his leather chair. "And that is?"

"We take one percent of our net profit and put it into a beneficiary fund. We dole it out on a first-come-first-served basis.

We let someone from a federal agency make the distribution so we don't have any liability for who gets the grant and who doesn't in case the money runs out in a given fiscal year."

"One percent of net." Lira rocked in his seat, mulling the idea. Finally he nodded. "I like it. It neutralizes the argument before it becomes an issue—before it becomes a *political* issue."

"Exactly. And it gets us some terrific PR—completely free— that we'd otherwise pay millions for. Not to mention the goodwill it'd generate."

"Brilliant, Brandon."

"It was mostly Christine's idea."

"Let's build it into our presentation. I'll have my marketing guys coordinate with yours, make sure the message is properly conveyed."

IN MANY WAYS, FOUR YEARS passed quickly. But at other times it crawled by with the alacrity of a tortoise.

"So," Lira said, "this begins your last two weeks as a well-to-do citizen. At the end of the month, you'll join the exclusive ranks of billionaire entrepreneur."

Ellis shook his head in disbelief. "I always figured I'd do well in reproductive medicine. But this is way beyond anything I thought possible."

Lira consulted his watch. "I've got a roomful of people waiting to walk you through what's going to happen during the next couple of weeks. You ready?"

Ellis rubbed his palms together. "Let's do it."

As he entered the conference room, Ellis was surprised that every seat was taken. Since starting the company, he had sat in dozens of meetings, but during the past month they had intensified in frequency and in the number of individuals attending. Still, this was the first time the large oval table was packed shoulder to shoulder. All were in custom suits, the women among them wearing exquisitely tailored business attire.

He recognized about a third of the people in the room. Lira had told him to expect representatives from the investment banker, Soliman Perkins, AIL Venture Capital, their underwriters, law firms representing all three entities, and support staff.

Christine was not present, by design. As they had decided early on, Ellis possessed the better constitution for serving as the inspirational figurehead.

"Good morning," Ellis said. "It's been a marathon, but we're incredibly close now. I want to thank every one of you who's been involved in the process, and all those behind the scenes who've made this a reality. We're going to enrich ourselves, yes—but we're also going to enrich the lives of each and every one of those parents and parents-to-be who come to us hoping to avoid the scourge of horrible, painful genetic diseases that, up till now, were largely left to chance.

"We've almost completely eliminated that randomness—and with it, cut the risk of contracting a debilitating condition by sixty-nine percent." Ellis waved a hand. "I know many of you in this room have seen the statistics. Some have parsed the research data. But for those who haven't, this is going to be an exciting day for this country. And eventually all developed countries *in the world*."

"The cost savings to health care will be enormous," Lira added, "the strain on governments running national health care programs reduced considerably. For those of you not on the analytics or marketing side, that's a prime reason why we've been so successful in gaining relatively swift FDA approval and the endorsement of medical organizations in over a dozen countries."

Lira continued speaking, then called on each of those attending to provide status reports.

Todd Soliman, sporting salt-and-pepper hair and wearing a red power tie and navy pinstriped suit with a white pocket square, looked the part of a successful entrepreneur. "Some great news. In the past hour, we've gotten buy ratings from Citigroup, Morgan Stanley, JPMorgan, and Bank of America. We're expecting UBS to fall in line as well, tomorrow at the latest."

A round of applause broke out—which surprised Ellis. He felt overwhelmed by the swell of excitement—and surge of adrenaline—in his chest. If he didn't know the cause, he would have suspected the tightness was the onset of a massive heart attack brought on by the stress of taking the company public. He allowed a grin to spread his lips.

Securing the buy ratings was a significant development, one that Lira had predicted just prior to the "road show" portion of the IPO process, but could not guarantee. Now it was in the bag, substantially improving their ability to score a huge payday.

AIL would be cashing out upon the IPO launch, its job done, profits booked, and the funds reinvested into another private company's efforts to take its organization public.

"We have fourteen days until we launch," Lira said. "You're all professionals in this room, but I feel better saying it nonetheless: we're still in the quiet period. Most analysts will respect that. But if you get a call from some up-and-comer looking to make a splash, just say, 'No comment' and hang up."

A woman raised her pen in the air.

"Yes." Lira pointed at her.

"Nora Dickson, marketing. I've got a request from *Vanity Fair* to do a personal interest story on Drs. Ellis and their daughter, Melissa. It's a soft promo for LifeScreen and because of the IPO's quiet period, it'll only make peripheral mention of the company. This'll focus on your personal lives, to show the people behind the venture. That Melissa is your only living relative makes it even more of a human-interest story. It's for their next issue. Cover story. Coming on the—"

"No." Ellis's face had flushed. He turned to Lira, then swung his gaze back to Nora. "We discussed this. Privacy is very important to both myself and Christine. Using our daughter's face to promote LifeScreen is one thing, but talking about her, our lives, any of that, is just off-limits. I mean, Melissa just turned five years old. Jesus Christ."

"Dr. Ellis, my job is to promote your company and maximize its value. And in turn enhance *shareholder* value. This feature would be the lead in a top ten periodical with a solid web property. Hitting so soon after the IPO would give us a tremendous boost and second wind at a pivotal mo—"

"No." His gaze bore into hers.

"Where do things stand with Melissa?" one of the senior bankers asked, breaking the tension in the room.

"The photos were taken a week before the road show," Nora said. "The videographers finished shooting their B-roll and worked through the night to assemble the promo piece and sizzle reel."

"It helped a lot with the investment bank pitches," Lira said. "For those of you who haven't seen it, Melissa's a beautiful girl and her wholesome looks drive home the emotional aspect of what LifeScreen is all about. She is, after all, a product of LifeScreen's technology."

Nora nodded. "A long-form version is being put together as well as various shorts for Facebook and Instagram ads that'll be demographically targeted to all women of child-bearing age."

"About the *Vanity Fair* piece," Soliman said. "I appreciate you wanting to maintain some degree of privacy, Dr. Ellis. But does privacy really exist anymore?"

Nora spread her hands. "Even if it did, didn't you give it up when you made Melissa the poster child for LifeScreen?"

The muscles in Ellis's jaw contracted. "No."

"I can make sure we guide the quest—"

"I don't know how else to say it, Nora. We. Are. Not. Doing it."

"Okay," Lira said, holding up his right hand. "Let's all take a deep breath. Dr. Ellis and I will discuss this—in private—and we'll get back to you, Nora, on potential options. Maybe the editor would be open to a different angle. Meantime, let's not take any action."

Nora turned away and bit her bottom lip. The others in the room did their best not to make eye contact, studying their pens, tablets, and laptops.

"Excuse me," Ellis said. He turned and reached the door in two strides, slamming against it with his left forearm and continuing down the hall.

LIRA CLEARED HIS THROAT. "We've all seen this before, people. The final weeks and days before an IPO are incredibly stressful for everyone—no one more so than the company's founder. He had the vision and the idea, and he shouldered the early risk. It's his baby and he's now getting ready to send her off into the world.

"That's stressful enough, but he and Dr. Ellis have a lot riding on what happens during the next couple weeks. Do it right and they'll become billionaires overnight, wealthy beyond anyone's dreams. Do it wrong, fuck up in any way, and they'll be facing a depression the likes of which they've never experienced. It could rip apart their marriage, destroy their family."

Nora nodded but did not make eye contact, her gaze fixed on her iPad as she scribbled a note.

"I know how hard it is to get these features. I'll talk with him. We'll work something out."

She glanced up and Lira gave her a reassuring wink before turning his attention to the large screen behind him.

7

Ellis walked into his office, his blood pressure still elevated, his jaw still clenched.

Christine was sitting at his desk. "Well?"

He looked at her.

She studied his face. "What's wrong?"

Ellis took a deep breath and shook his head. "Everything's fine. I'm—I'm just on edge. They want to do a—" He waved a hand at the dead air. "Never mind. Not important."

Christine pushed out of the chair and stepped in front of Ellis, gave him a hug. "We're in the home stretch. It'll be over soon."

"I know. I just have to get through the next two weeks."

"Is Lira causing problems?"

Ellis leaned away. "Why do you say that?"

"Because they're vultures. They've taken half our company. For what? It was all our idea, our hard work to make it a reality. The eighty-hour work weeks for the past seven years. The stress we've been under, what that's done to us. Our marriage. Do I have to go on?" She dropped her arms and walked away from him. "Their price is too high. Greedy bastards."

"Without their capital we'd have nothing but a great idea," he said to her back. "No way to execute. You know this. Nothing's changed."

"What's changed is that they are about to reap a financial windfall—from *our* idea and *our* hard work."

"I didn't want to give away the store either. But there was no choice. You had no idea how to develop the product, build the business, or even fund it. Neither did I. And I sure as hell didn't have the contacts to get us to—and through—each phase."

Christine shook her head. "I knew it'd come back to bite us in the ass. I told you when you first signed on with that angel investor."

"It was our only way to make it work." He walked over to her and gently turned her around. "They're not the only ones who are going to reap a financial windfall. We're going to be billionaires. Whether it's one or two, three or four, what does it matter? It's more money than anyone needs in a lifetime. Ten lifetimes." He shook his head. "I mean, it's a *thousand* million. Or two thousand million. Either way, that's...it's an inconceivable amount of money."

Christine scoffed. "You've always lacked drive, Brandon. Ambition. If it wasn't for me pushing you, lighting the fire every step of the way..." She put a hand on his chest and drove him back. "You never were a good negotiator. I told you: you had to be prepared to walk away from the deal and tell them no. Remember?"

How could he forget?

"But you didn't even make a counteroffer."

"That wasn't the right call at the time."

"Maybe we could've found a way to do it without Lira and his conspirators. You could've brought me into the negotiations. I'd have put them in their place."

He had no doubt she would have. And it could have blown the deal apart before it got off the ground.

When he was negotiating their first office space lease, Christine did not like the conditions the landlord put on them—in the eleventh hour—and told the guy it'd be the original deal terms they agreed on or they'd find another medical building. The man told them to take a hike. They spent three months finding a suitable location—and ended up paying *more* per square foot. In standing their ground, Christine thought they had won but they had really lost, something she refused to admit.

"Look," Ellis said, choosing not to dredge up old arguments. "How about we focus on the good this screening technology will do for millions of people?"

"After all we've been through, the sacrifices we've made, the only *millions* I'm concerned about are the ones this deal will be netting us. In our brokerage account."

"And you call *them* greedy? I wish you'd open your eyes and appreciate what you've got. Your dear departed daddy always made sure you got whatever you wanted. You have no idea what it's like to do without."

Christine reached back and slapped his left cheek.

It caught him off guard and he felt his jaw clunk. The skin tingled and burned simultaneously.

It was not the first time she had done that. It was not the tenth.

Ellis clenched his molars, walked past her, and sat down at his desk. "I've got work to do. Please close the door on your way out."

8

Amy walked briskly toward the large plaid flannel blanket stretched across the grass a few dozen feet from the lake's edge. The noon sun streamed through the tall trees and a cool breeze rippled across the leaves.

As Amy crossed the street, she saw the ice cream truck that Melissa had mentioned was at the curb serving children and adults out of its large side window.

Giselle turned to see Amy approaching. Amy held up the waxed white bag containing the heavy pumpernickel loaf and smiled. Giselle tapped Melissa's arm. The girl spun on her tiny rear and clapped when she saw Amy.

"You knew I'd keep my promise, didn't you?"

Melissa jumped to her feet. "Is the brown bread in there?"

"It is." Amy took a seat between the two of them and unrolled the top edges of the bag. She held it up for Melissa to peer inside.

"It *is* brown."

"Of course it is, silly. That's why I called it brown bread. Actually, the real name is—"

"Plum," Melissa said, bouncing up and down on her knees. "Plum-something."

"Pumpernickel." Amy reached in and removed three paper plates and a compostable knife, then cut into the loaf. "I know, it's a strange name."

"Actually," Giselle said, "it's German. Pumper means breaking wind."

"A fart?" Amy said with a chuckle.

"Yes. And nickel means devil. So a bad fart!"

Giselle and Amy giggled hard.

"I haven't laughed like that in a long time," Amy said, regaining her composure.

Melissa took her portion and looked it over suspiciously, tilting it to examine it from all angles.

"It's still warm," Giselle said.

"Right out of the oven. I just made it."

"Mmm," Giselle said as she chewed. "And so good." She nodded at Melissa, who took a bite.

"Yum. I like *plumnickel* bad fart bread."

"Better not tell your mom about that," Giselle said.

"I won't."

Giselle gave Melissa a sideways look. "And what do you say?"

"Thank. You," she said coyly. "What's your name again?"

"Amy."

"Thank you, Amy."

"Oh." Amy put her plate down and reached into the bottom of the large bag and pulled out another, smaller, loaf. "For the ducks."

"Yay! Can I feed them, Giselle? Can I?"

"Go on. Little pieces, okay?"

"Okay." She took the bread and skipped to the lake's edge.

"That's close enough," Giselle said. She glanced at Amy. "You showed up at the right time. She was bugging me for ice cream. I told her after lunch. That didn't go over well—until she saw you."

"She's adorable," Amy said.

"And she knows it, too."

Amy laughed.

"She actually did some modeling recently. Some kind of promotional video. The photographer and producer were very impressed with how poised she was."

When Lindy turned three, Amy and Dan were approached by a talent agent about her doing a photo shoot and possibly even television commercials. They went so far as making a portfolio, but once they heard about the schedule she would have to keep, they decided it was not in Lindy's best interests. Although it paid well, they passed.

"Do you have any children?"

"Me?" Amy placed a hand on her abdomen, thinking about the silvery stretch marks that remained after her pregnancy with Lindy. "No."

Watching Melissa toss pieces of bread into the water—and then jumping with joy and clapping when a duck would gobble them up—made the pain in her heart sting. She pulled out her phone and shot ten seconds of video of Melissa interacting with a few large geese. It was something she would do with Lindy when they would play at the park. Lindy loved showing the "movies" to her father later in the day.

Amy shoved the handset in her pocket and watched Melissa. *I should implant the frozen embryos, have Dan's baby. Maybe Zach is right. Time to get on with my life.*

"You okay?"

Amy shook her head. "Huh?"

"You got real quiet, like you spaced out or something."

Amy checked her watch. "Oh—you know what? I've gotta get back early today. Big order of cupcakes for a party and my boss only gave me half an hour for lunch."

"Thank you so much for the bread. You made Melissa's day."

Amy found herself grinning broadly. The feeling was mutual.

"Maybe you can come by tomorrow. I'll bring sandwiches."

"That'd be great," Amy said, stealing one more glance at Melissa. "I'd like that."

AMY ENTERED HER APARTMENT. She tossed her keys on the counter and fell into the kitchen chair. Exhausted from baking three dozen cupcakes and a large chocolate raspberry tart for a couple's sixty-fifth wedding anniversary, she just wanted to sit for a while before making dinner.

She opened her laptop and launched iTunes—but it had been such a long time since she had been in the mood to listen to anything that she wasn't sure what music she still had on the hard drive. It immediately asked her to update the program—no surprise there, her version was years old—and suggested she install the new app, Apple Music. She clicked yes and sat back while it downloaded.

She thought about her visit today with Melissa and Giselle. Did she have the courage to go through with IVF? She and Dan had frozen several embryos that they had not used when she got pregnant with Lindy. Would it still work? Were they still good? Theoretically, yes. At least, that's what her doctor had told her. But could she get through a pregnancy alone?

She would not be alone. Loren would be there. And Zach. Could she handle being a single parent?

Maybe it's what I need. Maybe it'll help me get past this. Shit, nothing else has.

She glanced at the large framed photo that hung on the wall of her kitchen nook...happier times...Dan and herself, Loren and Zach, their two infant boys...and Lindy in Dan's arms.

She rubbed at her twitching right eye, hoping to make it stop—though that never worked—and decided that she would call the fertility clinic tomorrow morning before she left for work. It would be three hours later in Boston, which would be perfect.

After Apple Music had finished loading, she selected "Hold on Tight" by Electric Light Orchestra. The guitars and upbeat keyboard rhythm started thumping from the laptop's speakers. After the tune ended, she thought about the song's theme of holding on to one's dreams.

"Yes," she said aloud. "That's exactly what I'm gonna do."

She felt better already.

9

Amy awoke to the chime of her iPhone alarm and swung her legs out of bed. After showering and dressing, she actually had the urge to put on some makeup.

She found the phone number for Boston Fertility Clinic and asked to speak with the office manager. The woman had just left for an early lunch but would be back in about an hour.

"Should I have her call you back?"

"You can probably help me. I'm a patient of Dr. Hutchinson's. My husband and I—" She choked on the words. "Sorry." She cleared her throat. "Allergies are bad this morning. My husband and I froze the fertilized ova that we didn't use for our last round of IVF and I'd like to make an appointment to find out what I have to do to start the implantation process."

There. She said it. She had lain awake for two hours last night trying to convince herself this was the right thing to do. Once she decided she was going to make the phone call, she was not sure she could get the words out without breaking down. So far, so good. If she got this far, she might be able to go through with it. Small steps.

"Your name?"

"Amy Robbins. Amy and Dan Robbins." She heard some clacking of keys.

"Right. Oh, it's been a while since you've been in. Dr. Hutchinson will need to do a complete exam and..."

Amy waited, the silence making her think the line had dropped. "And what?"

"Um, I think it'd be best for you to wait and talk with Jane. Like I said, she'll be back in about an hour."

"Why? What's wrong?"

"Well, your account is, um, well, there's a note that I'm to refer you to the office manager."

"Really? What kind of note? I mean, that sounds strange. I—just tell me what's going on. I have to leave for work in ten minutes and I'm in California, so you'll be gone by the time I can call back."

The woman sighed. "Okay. Well, a few years ago there was a fire in the clinic and they lost dozens of embryos."

"Lost?" Amy felt dizzy. She felt for the chair and sat down hard. "What does that mean, lost? How?"

"Well, I wasn't here back then, so I don't know the details but your account has a note on it because, well, it was one of the ones whose embryos were..." She cleared her throat. "Lost in the fire."

Amy's field of vision went snowy gray. She grabbed the edge of the table and steadied herself. *Think, Amy. Focus.* "You're saying my—our—embryos were...they were destroyed?"

"Looks that way, yeah. You and some others. But like I said, I wasn't working here back then. Your account is, um, flagged."

"Are you absolutely sure?"

"Unfortunately, yes. I'm very sorry, Mrs. Robbins."

"How—how'd it happen? What kind of fire?"

Amy knew none of this mattered. But she had to keep the woman talking to get as much information as she could while fighting through the fog that was clouding her thinking.

Zach had been after her for years to use the frozen embryos and have another child—not to replace Lindy but to help her heal. She had much to offer as a parent, he told her. It would be a shame to dwell on the past and sacrifice her future.

His words had been heard but not listened to. She had finally made the decision to move forward, prepared herself for having Dan's baby again...and now she felt like her chance at bearing a child, watching her or him grow up...was ripped away from her.

Again.

"As I said, I wasn't working here at the time. But really, this should be handled by Jane. And our legal counsel."

Amy laughed animatedly—as if that were a ridiculous statement. "Fires are a fact of life. I'm not looking to sue, I just want to know what happened."

"I wish I could tell you more, but I'm not authorized to talk about it. All I know is that your embryos were being stored in that room where the fire broke out. And like I said, there's a note in the computer. Although...I do see that a guarantor on your account, a Zachary Robbins, has still been paying the cryo storage fees via EFT on his checking account. I'm sure Jane will send out a refund in arrears. That should've been taken care of. Again, my apologies."

Amy took a deep breath. She was out of questions. All she wanted to do was crawl into bed. After thanking the woman, she hung up. And started to cry.

10

The morning dragged on, Amy sleepwalking through work. Several times Bobby asked her what was wrong. He was speaking but his voice was somewhere in the distance. She finally realized she had been ignoring him.

Amy tossed a handful of dough onto the counter and walked over to Bobby. "I'm sorry. I—I'm kind of out of it today. On autopilot."

"Yeah, no shit. What's going on? Past couple of days you were like a kid with a new toy and then, we've got the old Amy back."

She looked at him.

"Sorry." He lifted both hands, palms out. "I didn't mean that. I just—well, it was nice to see you happy for a change and then..." He sighed. "I'll shut up now."

"No, you're right, Bobby. I got some bad news this morning and it's gonna take some time to sink in." She walked back to the dough and scooped it up off the counter. "And no, I don't want to talk about it. Maybe tomorrow or the day after. Maybe never."

Bobby nodded slowly. "I get it. Well, Ellen may tell you otherwise, but I'm a pretty good listener. If you want to get a drink after work..." He shrugged.

"That's sweet. Let me—just give me some time."

AS LUNCHTIME APPROACHED, Amy considered blowing off her visit with Giselle and Melissa and going to a bar instead and downing a couple of beers to blunt the depression. But she was thinking clearly enough to know where that path led, and it was best a road not traveled.

She opted instead for a walk in the fresh air, one that would happen to take her to the lake. And to Melissa. Maybe seeing the girl would do her some good.

Or would it send her into a deep, spiraling darkness?

Trying not to overthink it more than she already had, Amy pulled off her apron and hairnet and marched toward the door. Ellen called after her about a pending order, but Amy was determined not to let anything stop her. She told Ellen she would be back soon and take care of it when she returned.

The sky was overcast, gray with a dense humidity that threatened precipitation. In reality, it was just the marine layer—low hanging fog coming off the bay. That the weather mirrored her mood was not lost on her.

"Hey," she said as she approached.

Giselle and Melissa were wearing stylish coats and cute knit caps.

"Right on time," Giselle said with a smile.

Amy did her best to adjust her emotions, to relax the tension in her face. Kids were perceptive and Melissa might pick up on her melancholy.

"I forgot to ask you what kind of sandwich you wanted, so I made you two—a grilled veggie and a turkey club. That okay?"

"Wow, sorry you went to so much trouble. The turkey would be great."

"I have PB and J," Melissa said, holding up the wrapped lunch.

"I love PB and J," Amy said. "My d—" She stopped herself. "My dog does too."

"You have a dog? What kind?"

"*Had* a dog. A standard poodle. More like a person than a dog."

"Do you have a picture?" Giselle asked.

"Not with me." A lie—she did have one on her phone, but it was a family photo with Dan and Lindy. As she unwrapped the foil, Amy changed the subject. "So you're from Germany?"

Giselle laughed in mid-chew and covered her mouth. "What gave it away? My accent?"

Amy chuckled. "Afraid so. I had a few European friends in college, so I developed a good ear. One was from Berlin."

"I *like* the way Giselle talks," Melissa said, rocking on her knees.

"Me too. Is she teaching you how to speak German?"

"Hello is Hallo. And good-bye sounds like a dog barking. Ruff."

"Ruff?"

"*Auf*," Giselle said. "*Auf Wiedersehen.*"

Melissa smiled and nodded shyly, took another bite of her sandwich.

"Where'd you go to school?"

"Harvard for undergrad," Amy said. "Stanford for law school. You?"

"That is *amazing*. I went to Goethe University in Frankfurt am Main. Haven't finished yet. I needed the money—and a break from my family."

"Oh," Amy said. "That bad?"

"Bad enough. But it also gave me an excuse to see America. When I got here I took a cross-country tour by bus. Saw all the tourist traps. But it was a lot of fun. Met some nice people. I am thinking of staying here. I would miss my grandmother, and she is not well, but...other from—other *than*—ehm, I think you say *other than that*—it would be hard going home."

"You're what, twenty-three?"

"Twenty-two."

"*I'm* five," Melissa said, holding up a hand and twisting it side to side.

"Such a big girl." Amy shared a smile with Giselle. "She's got a Nordic look. Is her mom from out your way? Or maybe northern Europe?"

"Christine? She's a local. Born in Los Angeles but grew up

around here somewhere. Brandon—Dr. Ellis—he's from New Jersey. They met in medical school."

"They're doctors?"

"Not practicing anymore though."

"Retired?"

"They're involved in some kind of company. A start—can't remember what it's called. A new company. Start something."

"Startup?"

"I think so. I do not understand financial things. They do not tell me much. Just what I overhear. Something is happening very soon. Selling it maybe, the company. That is why Melissa was modeling. Had to do with their business."

"Well she certainly is a beauty." Amy turned to her. "Aren't you?"

Melissa grinned, then looked away coyly. "Yes."

A strong breeze blew off the lake and tossed Melissa's hair across her face. She wiped at it sloppily with her hands. Amy reached over and brushed it away with her fingernails.

"Turkey okay?" Giselle asked.

Amy held up the last quarter of the sandwich. "Not just okay. You should open a café in town. You've got a knack for flavor. What kind of mustard did you use?"

"Red pepper and mushroom. Something Christine gets in Napa. And I added lemon balsamic she has delivered from the Carmel valley. An olive oil club they belong to."

"What's she like?"

Giselle's eyes flicked over to Melissa, then back to Amy. "Kind of intense," she said in a low voice.

Amy scrunched her brow. "Problems?"

She busied herself with the lunch basket. "A lot of stress with the business." Giselle nodded at Melissa and then shrugged. Amy got the hint: she did not want to talk in front of the girl. "Anyway, I have always been a good cook. The only decent thing my dad did for me. He is a...what do you Americans say? A creep?"

"Creep works. Is that why you don't want to go back?"

"Big part of it."

"How 'bout your mom?"

"Passed away five years ago. Breast cancer. Life's not fair, you know? My grandmother took it hard. Outliving her child. She kept saying, 'Not the way it's supposed to be.'"

Amy's eyes teared up. "No, that's not the way it's supposed to be." She sighed deeply, then noticed the time. "Gotta get back." She stroked Melissa's chin then rose from the blanket. "Thanks for lunch. It was the best meal I've had this week. Breakfast, lunch, or dinner."

"Come by tomorrow. I'll make you something else."

"And I'll bring some delicious cupcakes." She looked at Melissa. "Sound good?"

"Sounds good!" Melissa said.

"You know what? If you guys come by the bakery at noon tomorrow, I'll show you how we make bread. I can even show you how we make bad farts. I mean pumpernickel."

Giselle laughed. "That would be great. I had great-grandparents in Poland who owned a bakery. And their parents were bakers before them. It's a lost art in our family."

"Then maybe I can give you some insight into your family history." She chuckled. "Baking hasn't changed much the past century." Amy gave her the address and bid them good-bye.

She glanced over her shoulder to see Melissa waving at her. Amy turned and walked backward, smiling broadly and wriggling her fingers in response. She swung around and trudged along the grassy parkland, tears rolling down her cheeks.

Reality hit her. Hard, like a slap to the face. Frustration and anger alternating with intense sadness.

Goddam clinic. Maybe I should sue.

11

That night, ten minutes before closing, Loren stopped by the bakery to pick up an olive and walnut sourdough loaf for garlic bread she and Zach were making with dinner. She waited until Amy clocked out and got her coat on.

"What's wrong?" Loren asked.

"See?"

Amy turned to find Bobby behind her.

He shrugged. "It's not just me." He held out his hand. "Bobby Macafree. I work with Amy."

"Loren Ryder. Amy's sister-in-law."

Bobby gestured at Amy. "She's not been right. I mean, 'not right' more than usual." He snickered, then stepped around Amy. "Good to meet you, Loren. See you tomorrow, Amy."

Amy rolled her eyes and waited for Bobby to walk out of earshot. "Nice guy, but he can really grate on you."

Loren gestured with her chin toward the door. "Let's step outside for a moment."

Amy pulled off her apron and hairnet, then followed Loren outside.

"He's right, Amy. I can see it on your face. What's going on?"

Amy shook her head and began walking. "Nothing. Just having

a tough day."

"Bullshit." Loren grabbed Amy's arm.

She turned and faced Loren. "Nothing I feel like talking about. Okay? Can you respect that?"

"Actually, no. You've been doing better. I don't want you crawling back in your hole again."

Amy took a deep breath, as if it took all her effort. "That girl. Melissa. I—"

"What girl?"

"From the lake. Our run."

"You know her name?"

"She and her nanny go to the lake to feed the ducks and geese. I've met them a couple of times during my lunch hour."

Loren waited a moment, but Amy was lost in thought. "And?"

"And—well, she reminds me so much of Lindy and I—I just feel great being around her."

"Good. I mean, I'm not a shrink, so I don't know if it's a good thing or not. Maybe you're just torturing yourself, not letting yourself move on."

Amy nodded. "I've thought about that. But I can't help myself. I haven't felt good in years. I'm never excited to wake up in the morning. Now I am."

Loren looked at her a long moment. So long that Amy became uncomfortable and turned away.

Loren buttoned her coat. "Let's just say for the moment that you're right, that this is a positive in your life. Why the long face and slumped shoulders?"

Amy closed her eyes and put a hand to her forehead. "You know how Zach is always telling me to go back to Boston and have those embryos implanted?"

"He and I disagree on that."

Amy drew her arms around her torso, warding off the chill. "Yeah, well, seeing Melissa, feeling happy again, it made me think that Zach was right. So I called the clinic. And..." Tears pooled in her eyes.

"And what?"

"And there was a fire. Took out part of the clinic and the embryos that were stored there. Mine and Dan's were destroyed." Her lip quivered and she began sobbing.

Loren drew her close and hugged her, gently stroking her back. "I'm so sorry, Amy. Oh, sis...I'm so sorry."

AN HOUR LATER, AMY SAT alone in her apartment, having cleared the dinner plate and washed the pots and pans.

Before leaving Loren, Amy had made her promise not to tell Zach about the fire. She needed to process it and let it sink in before her brother got on her case. He would probably make some comment about her waiting too long to implant the embryos; if she had done it years ago when he told her, it never would have been an issue. She did not want to hear it.

For that reason, she declined to go home with Loren. She would not be able to disguise her state of mind. Zach would pick up on it and refusing to tell him what was bothering her would only result in an argument, even with Loren urging him to back off.

Amy sat down in a recliner in the living room and pulled out her iPhone. She watched the video she had taken of Melissa. First she laughed. And then she cried.

Seven hours later she awoke where she had fallen asleep, her cell just about out of charge and her mouth dry as cotton.

Amy plugged in the handset and got ready for work. It was six in the morning, so she was in no rush, although she felt excited about the prospect of seeing Melissa later at the bakery.

She had thought many times about the days when Lindy would be old enough to go to the office to see what she did, and then to the courtroom to watch her try a case. And then there would be career days at school, where she would get up in front of the class as her mom, a physicist, had done for her.

Growing up, Amy was very proud of her mother. She used to think she was the only female physicist in the world, and when she got older and realized that was not the case, she still considered her the smartest...even though she had not met another before, or since.

Amy wanted to *be* her mother, and she would have—if she had liked science. She discovered in junior high that she did not. Chemistry and calculus bored her. But standing up against an injustice, and holding the power to correct a wrong, that was something she salivated over. It was also a talent of her father's. When she tried her first case he sat in the gallery beaming with pride.

She smiled at the memories.

Friends and colleagues encouraged her to run for office—and it was in her long-term plan. Ten years of practice, she figured. Sock away enough money, make partner, and then run for the state legislature. She was a good speaker—honed from law school and later pleading her case in front of juries, reading body language and faces, playing to the crowd. She learned to think before she spoke. She knew how to answer questions without answering them.

More important, she had no problem going toe-to-toe with anybody who stood in her way.

She had wanted to do all that, and more, for Lindy. That dream died, just like her daughter and husband.

Damn car accident. Damn fire.

Amy started to tear up again, then grit her teeth. "Stop it," she said aloud. "Enough."

She went about making coffee, then scrambled eggs and sautéed onions. Thinking as she went. She turned off the stove and scooped the food onto a plate. As she chewed, an idea began to form.

She set her fork aside and pulled open her laptop. Launched the browser and began googling for information. There was an article in the *Herald* detailing the extent of damage to the fertility clinic. And a quote from the lieutenant and supervisor of the Fire Investigation Unit—nothing significant, but now she had a name. A few keystrokes later and the Mass.gov website gave her the man's contact information.

I need some reason for him to talk to me.

She thought a moment longer, then dragged a chair close to the wall where her iPhone was plugged in.

As the line rang, she debated whether or not to use a fake name. Her caller ID likely displayed "Amy Robbins"—or did it merely show a phone number? At least it was a Boston area code.

"Fire and Explosion Investigation Section."

"Yes, this is Ada Robinson and I'm calling from Equity Insurance. Can you put me through to Lt. Peter Gilbert?"

"I think he just left. Shift's over. But hold on, I'll check. Can I ask what this is regarding?"

"The fire at Boston Fertility Clinic a few years ago."

"I'll see if I can catch him."

A long moment later, a deep-voiced man took the call, his accent bringing a sense of familiarity. Amy had consciously lost hers—but could bring it back as needed. This was one of those times. Familiarity for her might mean the same for the lieutenant.

"How can I help ya?"

"Thanks for taking the call, lieutenant. Shift's over, so I won't take much of your time." She told him the fire she was calling about—and he recalled it, having worked the case and filed the report.

"I'm doing some follow-up for Equity Insurance. We're a secondary carrier, and the original carrier has made a subrogation claim, and—"

"Sub-what?"

"Sorry, industry speak. When an insurance carrier pays out on a claim, they pursue reimbursement from another carrier. So if there's secondary insurance, we can make a claim and get a portion of our money back. Kind of boring stuff, lots of red tape and paperwork...but money is money so, I've gotta run through the paces."

"Hate paperwork. Love my job, but—"

"I hear ya," Amy said. "Look, I know you're off the clock, but one thing isn't clear on the carrier's documentation. I need to confirm that the clinic's cryo storage rooms were affected. They're making a claim for frozen embryos. Fertilized ova. And

I just have to cross all the T's. You know how this business is."

There was some clacking on a keyboard—it sounded like the old IBM kind that made loud noise with each click—and then he grunted. "Got it. Oh yeah, right. Lucky bastards. Minimal damage to a storage room and uh, the break room."

"Storage. You mean *cryo storage*?"

"Uh, nope. Office supplies, that kinda stuff. Old files waiting to be entered into the computer, from what I remember." More clicking. "Yep, looking at my photos. No high-tech equipment there—which obviously means no embryos. According to the plans we pulled from the city, the liquid nitrogen cryo storage freezer units were in a different area of the building. Another floor, actually."

"Are you sure?"

"Lookin' right at the report, floor plan of the building 'n' everything."

"Hmm. Interesting." *Not interesting. Odd. Strange. Fishy, even. But definitely* not *interesting.*

"Surprised your company's even bothering with that subtraction claim."

She let the flub go. "Well, you investigated it. Clearly, it was big enough to get your attention."

"Had nothing to do with the amount of property damage. Onsite lieutenant thought it looked...ah...questionable."

"Questionable? How?"

"Kinda like he thought it mighta looked like it was deliberately set. That's the only reason we investigated."

"According to my paperwork," she said, crumpling some pages of her legal pad for authenticity, "it was *not* classified as arson. Otherwise the original carrier wouldn't have paid the claim. And I'm not seeing a police report in the file."

"Yeah, well, we couldn't find any definitive proof. Actually, no real proof at all."

"But..."

"But my lieutenant at the time, he and I been doin' dis twenty-five years, ya know? You get a sixth sense about these things.

Nothin' that can be proven."

"Obviously—otherwise the carrier wouldn't have paid out."

"Sometimes makes more sense to pay a small claim than to lay out the big bucks to do up a full engineering and fire analysis, ya know?"

"Can't argue that. But what was it that set off your alarm? Your sixth sense?"

"Fire was supposedly started by a cigarette in the storage room. But smoking's not allowed in any building these days. Especially a medical clinic. And it shoulda set off the smoke alarm. But the one in that room wasn't working. The *only* one that wasn't working in the whole building. Get my drift? Best I could tell, it wasn't tampered with. So my antennas were up, ya know? But couldn't prove nothin'."

"Thanks for your help, Lieutenant. Appreciate you filling in the blanks for me. Hey, can you email me a copy of the report? Just for my file so I can submit paperwork on time."

"'Course."

"Company email's been down past few days. Never seen anything like it. Mind sending it to my Gmail address?"

After they commiserated over tech snafus, he told her he would get the document to her as soon as possible.

Amy hung up and sat there staring at the desk. Things were not adding up. But what *were* they adding up to?

12

The morning lumbered by. Amy was lost in thought, repeatedly having to stop and refocus on her task. Bobby finally nudged her.

"Hey, I can cover for you here and there, but you're really off your game today." He nodded at the cake batter. "You forgot the sugar."

"Huh?"

"Birthday cakes have sugar, Amy. Kind of a necessary ingredient."

She looked down at her countertop and began to cry.

Bobby drew his chin back. "I'm sorry. I—I didn't mean to upset you. It's just sugar. We can mix it in now. Here, let me help." He reached up to a canister, but Amy grabbed his forearm.

"I've got it. Sorry, I'm—" She sniffled. "I'm just having a tough time."

"No shit. You wanna talk?"

She dabbed her eyes with a sleeve, taking care to keep her hands away from her face.

"Not really. I've got friends coming by at noon. I'm going to show them how we bake bread."

"You clear it with Ellen?"

"Of course. But I need to get this cake done and in the oven so you can decorate it."

"You've got plenty of time. C'mon, Amy, talk to me. It'll help. You'll feel better."

She did want to tell him all about what she was going through. But it was more than a quick conversation. And when you shared your problems with someone you worked closely with five days a week, when you opened your soul and exposed your fears, there was no going back.

Bobby was the closest thing she had to a non-family friend in the Bay Area—which was not saying much—so if she were going to spill her guts to anyone, it made sense it would be him. Then again, it should be Loren. Loren was her relative, but more than that, she was her best friend and confidant. She could be trusted not to share it with Zach unless it was okay to do so.

An argument could be made that her confidant should be Zach. They had been there for each other through some tough times growing up. But her depression had dragged on so long that their relationship had become strained and he had reached a threshold of sorts. Her inaction or apathy or fear or sorrow or melancholy—the list was too long, and that was the problem—it all frustrated him greatly. He lost patience with her.

By the time Giselle and Melissa walked in, Amy had composed herself and was ready for their visit. Amy took their coats and hung them on hooks in the break room. She handed a hairnet to Giselle and helped Melissa fold her thick blonde locks under the elastic band.

"Ow," she said.

"Sorry. Did I pull your hair?"

But then Amy saw a bruise on the back of the girl's neck—two, one purple and one light brown. Amy turned to Giselle.

"Melissa was playing in the kitchen and a bowl dropped from the cabinet," Giselle said.

Amy pursed her lips in sympathy then led them on a brief tour through the modest-sized facility that occupied a quarter of a block—land Ellen and Bobby had purchased before Bay Area property made like a NASA rocket rising into the stratosphere.

"And this is where I work." Amy took Melissa by the hand and led her to the area where all her baking supplies and equipment were located.

"What's that?" Melissa asked, pointing at large canisters filled with powders that ran the color palette from bright white to wicker and chocolate brown.

"Those are my ingredients. Oats, brown sugar, confectioner's sugar, white flour, almond flour, wheat flour and—"

"Can I make something?"

Amy brought both hands to her cheeks. "What a great idea. Why didn't I think of that? Would you like to make pumpernickel or cupcakes?"

Melissa put an index finger to her lips, then jumped a couple of times in place. "Um...cupcakes!"

"Chocolate?"

"Yes please."

Amy brought over a step stool as Giselle helped Melissa put on thin clear plastic gloves.

They went about mixing the ingredients, spooning the batter into the baking tray and pushing it into the oven.

"That's gonna take a little while. Bobby here will take them out at the right time. Right?"

Bobby grinned and gave a thumbs-up. "I won't let you down."

Amy untied her apron. "Let's go eat lunch."

As they neared the area where they usually set up camp, an older woman came lumbering by on a red electric scooter. Her scarf was flapping behind her in the breeze and a teen was standing on the rear, along for the ride around the lake.

Giselle and Amy unfurled the blanket and set out the picnic basket. "Can I feed the ducks?"

"Of course." Giselle handed her a bag of food and Melissa skipped about fifteen feet away, tossing seeds as she went.

"She's precious. Is her mom as beautiful as her daughter?"

"Christine's attractive, but no—she looks nothing like Melissa. I overheard them talking one night. They were arguing about something. I got the impression Melissa was adopted."

Amy watched as Melissa tossed some food at the ducks. A flock waddled over to scoop up the morsels. The girl cackled and threw another handful. "Looks like she lives a charmed life. I'm guessing her parents are well-off."

Giselle harrumphed. "I think the Ellises are going to make a lot more money very soon. I heard them talking in the kitchen one night. But about Melissa being lucky..." Giselle shrugged.

When she did not finish her sentence, Amy swung her gaze to Giselle. "What?"

She hesitated a long moment. "Nothing."

"Does this have to do with the bruises on her neck?"

Giselle looked out at the lake.

"Do you know how she really got those marks?"

"I only know what Christine told me when I asked."

"About the falling bowl? Did you believe her?"

Giselle continued to stare out at the water. "Christine doesn't cook. She *has* a cook. So that, plus some other things...no, I do not believe it."

"Neither do I. Do other accidents like that happen often?"

Giselle nodded.

"Have you reported it?"

"Reported *what*? I have not seen anything. Just bruises. I do not know how it works. I googled it. I read that American police won't do anything unless they have proof. Or a witness. Or if there are more serious injuries, like broken bones. And Melissa will not talk about it. I asked."

"Who's doing it?"

"Christine can be a bitch at times. Hard to work for. Last few months it's been worse. She is under strain. I think you call it 'stressed out.' If I put two and two together, I am sure it is from that business deal."

Amy knew that "stressed out" and "difficult to deal with" were generic traits. Most people could be described as such in various settings. They certainly were not behavioral descriptors that supported accusations of child abuse.

"Not an excuse for hurting a child," Amy said, "physically *or* emotionally. You see anything, if Melissa tells you anything, let me know."

"What would you do?"

Good question. "I have a...friend who'll know how to handle it." Loren's work with the FBI dealt with crimes against children but she did not think that included local cases of abuse. That said, Loren probably had contacts or friends at the Oakland Police Department who would know what to do about it or who to speak with. "Meantime, see if you can get Melissa to talk about it."

Giselle chewed on the side of her bottom lip. "If Christine finds out, she will fire me."

Amy understood that Giselle was perhaps more afraid than most people about losing her job. She might have to return to Germany if her work permit was terminated. Amy was not an expert on visas but she could probably dig around for some information—if it became an issue.

Amy gave her a weak smile. "Then don't let her find out."

13

After dinner, Amy sat at her kitchen table, staring at the blank laptop screen.

She had been thinking about everything Giselle told her the past few days. She pressed the power button and her desktop instantly appeared. Her fingers paused over the keys, then she opened her browser and searched for information on the clinic fire. She copied and pasted salient facts into a Word document.

Next came the notes she had taken from her conversations with the receptionist at Boston Fertility and the Fire Investigation Unit supervisor.

Amy sat back and looked at what she had assembled. She highlighted a few points with her stylus, then returned to Google.

She typed in *Brandon Ellis MD* and pulled up a slew of information on his professional career as well as his company, LifeScreen Genetics. An IPO was due to launch in fewer than two weeks. There was a downloadable PDF on its website, which featured a large, full color close-up of Melissa's innocent face.

After reading through the promo piece, she determined that the technology behind LifeScreen—intriguing and filled with enormous promise—faced a tangle of ethical problems akin to unraveling a ball of knotted yarn. That was of course not addressed in the pamphlet, but she knew that it would be questioned by people of religion and science alike. Like drones, autonomous cars, internet-connected refrigerators and insulin pumps, and AI-infused robotics, technology was marching us into the future, whether or not the public was ready for it—politically, emotionally, or morally.

The cost/benefit analysis laid out in the PDF was strongly positive toward wide-scale implementation of the technology. Because of that, she figured that any obstacles would be favorably addressed by the courts, assuming it was challenged.

She scrolled down and saw that Brandon Ellis went to medical school at Tufts University—the same college John Hutchinson, her fertility doctor, graduated from. She grew up not far from the school and discussed the area with Hutchinson during their initial IVF consultation.

Amy leaned back in her chair.

She googled *John Hutchinson MD Brandon Ellis MD Christine Ellis MD.* She found a photo taken at a medical symposium fifteen years ago of the two men with their arms around each other's shoulders, mugging for the camera. Another one featured Christine, John Hutchinson, and his wife Virginia.

A few links later, she discovered the two men were in the same fraternity at Boston University.

Amy reclined in her seat again and stared straight ahead, seeing nothing but her mind swirling with a web of thoughts as she fought to reject the revelations forming in her mind. She began typing:

- *The fire was real. But it was arson. A ruse to create the lie that her and Dan's embryos were destroyed?*
- *Her embryos were not really burned up in the fire.*
- *Her physician was buddies with Brandon Ellis.*
- *Brandon Ellis is Melissa's father.*
- *Melissa looks nothing like her mother.*
- *Melissa is really her daughter. Hers and Dan's.*

She cupped her mouth. Rather than anger, she felt sheer elation that—if true—she had been spending time with her own little girl.

The last vestige of her and Dan.

Wait.

This is what I want to believe.

But is it the truth?

She needed proof. Not legal proof, at least not now. But what would she do if Melissa turned out to be her child?

14

Amy hated doing this, but she had to know.

She laughed at Melissa's blonde locks and tousled them playfully. "Oh my goodness, girl. Your hair's all tangled again."

Giselle rummaged around the lunch basket. "It's the wind. I usually fix it when we get home."

"No need to wait." Amy reached into her purse and pulled out a small brush—which she had purchased this morning at Walgreens on the way to work.

"Here." Amy dragged the bristles through Melissa's jumble. "Ow."

"Sorry. The wind did a good job." She finished combing it out and gave the bristles a quick glance. Perfect. It looked like she had gotten several strands by the roots—more than adequate samples for DNA testing.

Amy pulled out a doll she had as a child and handed it to Melissa. "You like Barbie?"

"Mommy won't let me have one."

She looked at Giselle. "Body image?"

Giselle hesitated. "I'm not sure what her reason is."

Amy thought Giselle knew what the problem was but would

not say. If it was not the controversy surrounding body type perception and young girls, it could be something simpler, as in basic cruelty. Although merely a supposition, given Amy's suspicions regarding physical abuse, it made sense that there could be an emotional component as well.

When she returned to the bakery, Amy carefully extracted several hair strands, prepared the package, and asked Ellen if she could take fifteen minutes to run something down the block to FedEx.

She struggled to concentrate afterward, trying to determine when the results might hit her mailbox.

After slipping a batch of walnut cookies into the oven, Amy texted Loren and asked if she could join her and Zach for dinner tonight. Loren replied immediately:

seriously sis? youve got a standing invitation

If nothing else, it would help occupy her thoughts for a few hours.

The coming days would be a sign of how effective her antianxiety meds were. She would have to take it an hour at a time.

As she kneaded another batch of dough, she wondered what she wanted the DNA report to show. Was it better for it to be a match, that Melissa was really her daughter? Or would it be preferable, in the long run, to finally put that part of her life behind her—if that were even possible—and turn the page, get on with *living*—something she had not truly done since that fateful evening?

Amy now knew that what Zach and Loren had been telling her for years was true: she was sleepwalking through her days, weeks, months.

Years.

THE FOLLOWING NIGHT, she walked into her apartment and put her keys down on the dresser. Staring at her was an eight-by-ten photo of better days: Dan and Amy, Lindy, Loren, Zach, and Coco. Taken in a park in Boston during one of Loren's and Zach's visits, they were all dressed in white shirts and jeans.

She remembered that day as if it were a month ago. Lindy came down with the flu that evening and Amy and Dan followed the next day.

That was a week before the accident.

Amy stood there looking at Lindy. She sure did look like Melissa. They definitely could be sisters—physically *and* genetically.

Amy pulled up the photos of Melissa on her iPhone and studied them. Watched the video.

She had to be her daughter. Had to be. And the DNA would confirm it.

Tears rolled down her cheeks—tears of joy. She sniffled as the video ended. Reality began creeping in, her euphoria evaporating like an eraser wiping away markings from a whiteboard.

Amy stood up from the table and began pacing her apartment. What if the lab returned with a positive result? Was there a legal basis for her to wrest Melissa from the Ellises?

How would that play with Melissa? Christine and Brandon were her mother and father.

But they're not.

Yes they are.

Amy continued pacing. Melissa doesn't know me, not really. What damage would it do to her if she were forced to leave her family, the *only* family she's ever known?

But the abuse. She trusted that Giselle was telling the truth—she had no reason to lie. Amy's trial lawyer skills, though eroded, were still worth something. And the years spent learning how to read a jury told her that the young woman was being honest with her.

While no one would dispute that getting a child out of an abusive situation would be in the girl's best interests, Amy could not prove it. Without conclusive evidence, what court would give her custody even if it were to Melissa's benefit?

What about the fact that Amy had her offspring stolen from her—shrouded by a deliberately plotted scheme to make her think that her embryos had been destroyed? That was conspiracy to commit kidnapping. And kidnapping was a federal crime. Right in Loren's wheelhouse. But was it kidnapping? Did embryos count as a life, or was it considered simple theft of personal property? Probably the latter.

From what she recalled, her fertility contract referred to the frozen embryos as her and Dan's property and their rights were forfeited only if they no longer desired to use them to initiate a pregnancy—because the whole idea behind their involvement in the fertility program was to return the embryos to her and Dan via an IVF procedure.

She could not recall, however, her rights—and their responsibilities—relative to storing unimplanted embryos. She did not think she still had a copy of the agreement, but she was confident the terms absolved Boston Fertility of any liability should the embryos become lost or damaged. That was how lawyers worked—the contract always favored the organization that wrote it.

But if the embryos were lost or damaged during the commission of a crime...

Again, though, could she prove a crime had been committed?

Amy stopped and leaned on the back of her wood kitchen chair. *Dammit.* There had to be a way of hurting these people, a way of proving their egregious behavior, a way of getting Melissa released to her custody.

She kicked the chair. More than anyone else, as an attorney she knew there did *not* have to be a way of obtaining justice. The law could be like that...more than she wanted to admit. Sometimes things were inherently unfair and people got away with crimes.

Amy pushed the chair under the table and started pacing again, mentally reviewing what she knew: Ellis and Hutchinson were well acquainted with each other. More than that, they were longtime friends, fraternity buddies, and classmates. Colleagues. No question about that.

And no crime in that.

Three significant questions gnawed at her as she walked her apartment: What now? Why her? Why her embryos?

The lieutenant had already told her they were not able to prove the fire was deliberately set, which is why the insurance payout was made. If there was any way of denying the claim, a carrier would have found it and refused to release the funds.

Amy divorced herself of emotion and tried to view the case impartially. And she saw the stark reality: her case against the Ellises was circumstantial at best as it currently stood, with little chance of succeeding. She could hope to influence the jury by emphasizing the emotional impact of her loss, but such cases needed a solid foundation or they risked being overturned on appeal.

That had not stopped her before. It just meant she had to think outside the box.

She could hire a private investigator to dig around, unearth compromising information on Ellis or Hutchinson and attempt to turn one against the other. If either talked in exchange for a light prison sentence, or none at all, the odds of an almost sure defeat would drop significantly. Prosecutors searched for such levers to pull all the time, especially in big cases. It was a tried and true tool of the trade.

Or Amy could find a news outlet and tell them about Ellis and Hutchinson. Maybe an employee who was on the inside would see the report and come forward. That could complicate things for the IPO. She was not a securities lawyer, but her efforts would be about public opinion, not the law. *If* the media would be willing to run her story without proof. They used to fact check things from at least two sources before going live with an article, but these days the tenets of good journalism were not practiced by any but the more reputable outlets.

If she could find one willing to broadcast, the Ellises would do whatever they could to shut her up. But would they hand over custody of their daughter, the girl on their company's glossy brochure? No, people like that would offer money. Pay her off. It would be a tidy sum, but Amy was not after money. She wanted what was hers. Her child.

Amy again traced the stretch marks on her abdomen. Her eyelid began to twitch.

And she returned to the original question: what now?

She could go to Loren, but Amy already knew what she would say: there was nothing she could do without proof. And it was not like she could open an investigation because she wanted to. She needed approval from her superior. And when Loren disclosed that the reported victim was her sister-in-law, how would that play out? It would undoubtedly work against her. Even if her boss gave the go-ahead, he or she would assign it to another agent. She knew the Bureau was steeped in process and procedure and there was no way they would allow an agent to work on a case involving a family member.

Amy yawned long and wide. She trudged into her bedroom and collapsed onto her bed. There was time before the IPO to try to find the leverage points she needed...maybe even hire a private investigator and send him in search of information—dirt—that could threaten to derail the IPO. Or she could contact CNBC, Yahoo Finance, Bloomberg, and the *Wall Street Journal* and see if any of them bit. Then there was social media pressure: some sort of Facebook campaign to spread the story and gain national attention.

But she knew her case would be that much stronger if she waited until the DNA test results came back. That would prove the core of her allegations. Combined with the suspicious fire and the relationship of the two physicians, it could be enough. Should be enough.

But if the IPO happened before she received the genetic report, she would lose much of her leverage.

As she reasoned it through, she drifted off to sleep.

15

Amy woke with a start. She had slept through the night in her clothes, but fortunately her alarm was set for the same time every weekday morning.

She swung her legs off the bed and shuffled into the bathroom. She showered, dressed, and ate a protein bar while sitting at her laptop. She had ten minutes to make a list of private investigators. Although she had decided to wait for the DNA test results, there was nothing wrong with gathering information. When the time was right, she would be ready to pull the trigger.

During her break she would make some calls and see what kind of questions they asked. The easier approach would be to spend her lunch hour conducting the search, but that meant missing her time with Melissa. As it stood, she had no way of seeing her if not at the park.

She desperately wanted to continue building their relationship. Somehow, even if only peripherally, Amy needed to be a part of Melissa's life. But she had to tread carefully. If Amy asked Giselle to give her their home address or set up specific times to meet aside from their park outings, it would seem odd.

Maybe in a week or two the familiarity, and their relationship, would develop further and getting together at a restaurant, a blues club, a bar, would be a natural progression. Although it would build trust, Melissa would accompany Giselle to none of these. However, a BART ride into San Francisco to catch a show like *The Lion King* or *Beauty and the Beast*—something age-appropriate for Melissa—could then seem normal. Slow steps were best.

The sky was overcast but it was warmer than usual for this time of year. Amy strode across the lawn toward the blanket where Giselle was seated, watching Melissa feed the geese.

"Your timing is impeccable," Giselle said.

"Ice cream truck again?"

"I really need to talk with that guy, ask him to come an hour later."

Amy chuckled. "Or you could eat lunch earlier. Problem solved."

"Except that if we ate earlier, you would not be able to join us."

Amy felt a surge of warmth in her chest. "That's so sweet."

Melissa came running over. "Hi Amy. Did you bring us bread today?"

"I sure did." She held up a white bag. "Wanna see?"

Melissa knelt beside Amy and peered in. "What is it?"

"Well it's not pumpernickel, right? Because it's not brown."

"Then what kind is it?"

"Sourdough. A specialty of San Francisco." Amy reached in and tore off a piece. "Try it."

Melissa took it and bit into it—and made a face. But she kept chewing.

"What do you think?"

"I think I like it."

Giselle dug around the picnic basket and handed out their sandwiches. Ten minutes later they were collecting their garbage.

"That was delicious," Amy said.

"I don't think—" Giselle was interrupted by her cell phone ringing. She pulled it out of her purse and looked at the screen. "Oh. It is my aunt. From Germany. Do you mind?"

"Are you kidding? 'Course not."

Giselle answered and listened a moment. "Oh my god. *Ist sie in Ordnung?*" She sat there, her gaze roaming the area.

"'Selle," Melissa said. "Can I have ice cream now?"

Giselle, wearing concern on her face, glanced at Amy. "Can you?" She spoke into the phone then twisted the handset away from her mouth. "They took my grandmother to the hospital. Can you go buy Melissa some ice cream? I need to deal with this. I'll pay you back."

"Nonsense. Take care of your grandmother. I've got this covered."

"C'mon," Amy said, "let's get you a strawberry cone."

"Yay." Melissa jumped up and clapped, then walked alongside Amy toward the truck. She reached over and took Amy's hand—which was the best, and worst, thing she could have done.

Her eye began twitching. Tears started flowing. Her breath got short. She focused on putting one foot in front of the other.

As they approached the vendor, Melissa started running toward the truck. Amy arrived a few seconds later, in time for Melissa to face Amy and hold her arms up.

Amy hoisted her higher, onto her hip, so the girl could see inside.

"Strawberry cone." Melissa said, eyes wide with anticipation.

The man pointed at her. "I know. Same thing every time. Strawberry cone, chocolate sprinkles."

Melissa nodded.

Amy paid the man as Melissa stuck out her tongue and dug in. Amy walked past the truck, turned left, and headed in the direction of the bakery.

She was not sure where she was going or why, but twenty-five yards later she was standing in front of her car, just outside the parking lot.

"Where we going?" Melissa asked, pinkish red covering her lips, nose, and cheeks.

"Uh...nowhere, honey. I—I'm—I, uh..." She looked down and realized she had her keys in her hand. The doors unlocked and she was pulling open the rear door. "Let's go for a quick ride around the lake. I can show you where there are lots of birds and ducks."

"What about Giselle?"

"She had a very important phone call. We'll come get her a little later."

She put Melissa in the back and reached for the restraint.

"I don't have my car seat."

"Uh—right. I, uh, I know honey."

But Amy did not know anything. She had no idea what she was doing. She was outside her body, watching from above. No control, no thoughts.

Swung the door shut, then ran around to the front of the car. Got in, turned the engine over, and yanked back on the gear shift.

16

Amy drove with no particular destination in mind.
She looked in the rearview mirror and saw her daughter—
Lindy—years earlier, staring back at her.

"How's the ice cream, honey?"

"Gooood." A few seconds later: "Where are the birds?"

"Oh. The uh...the birds weren't there yet."

My god, what am I doing? I'm kidnapping a little girl. This is wrong. This is wrong. Head back to the lake. Turn around.

But she could not bring herself to stop. She continued in a straight line, down Bellevue.

Stop, Amy. Think. As soon as Giselle realizes you're gone—with Melissa—she's going to call the police.

And the police would figure out where she worked, what her name was, what car she drove. And then they would realize Loren was her sister-in-law and she would be called. Loren would call Zach.

Amy, what the hell are you doing? Turn around.

An APB would be put out on her car. An amber alert would be issued. And then everyone's cell phone would ring a shrill alarm. The color of her beat-up Subaru, its model and license plate number, would be displayed.

She would be pulled over before she made it to the freeway.

How would Melissa take all this? Once she finished her cone, she would start asking questions. Where are we going? Why? Are we going home?

And Amy had no answers for her. Would she start crying? Would she willingly go along with her?

At the next red light, she pulled out her cell and paged to the settings menu, then found the ringer samples. She pressed one and it sang its tune.

Amy pushed the handset against her ear. "Hi Giselle. Oh, I'm so sorry. Yeah, Melissa and I are in the car, going for a ride. The zoo? Great idea. Okay, I'll take her there. No, no, don't worry about it. We'll have a great time. Take care of your grandmother. I hope she feels better. I'll call you later."

She stuck the phone in her purse and looked up at the mirror. "Okay, honey. Giselle is still helping her grandmother so she wanted me to take you to the zoo. We'll see all sorts of animals. Have you been to the zoo?"

"Once."

"Once? Only *once*?"

"I like the animals. Elephants and the scary birds."

"Scary birds? Like crows?"

"Like batman."

"Oh, bats. Okay, we'll go see the bats."

"Yay!"

Yeah. Yay.

Amy glanced in the mirror again and saw the excitement on the girl's face. Her daughter's face.

Oh my god, what am I doing?

17

Brandon Ellis glanced at the iPad Angelo Lira was holding and nodded. "Okay, I'll take it."

"Good decision, Brandon."

Ellis sat down at his desk and lifted the handset to answer the call on line two.

But as he reached for the button, his office door swung open and Giselle ran in, her hair a tangled mess, her face streaming with tears.

"Giselle." Ellis set the phone down as he rose from his chair. "What's wrong? Where's Melissa? Is Melis—"

"I—I got a phone call. My grandmother's taken ill, went to the hospital. I was talking to my aunt and—and—Amy said she'd help."

"Who's Amy?"

"A woman—a friend. She works at a bakery a few blocks from here, right near the lake."

"Giselle," Ellis said firmly. "Is Melissa okay?"

"I don't—I don't know. I lost her."

"Lost? What the hell do you mean?"

"We have to call the police. When I started looking around for Amy and Melissa, I—I must have dropped my phone. I wanted to find someone who would call the police but I was so close I thought I should come right here instead."

"No police," Lira said.

Ellis turned. He had forgotten Lira was in the room.

Lira shook his head emphatically. "No police."

"What are you talking about? My daughter's gone missing." Ellis swung back to Giselle. "Are you saying this Amy woman kidnapped my daughter?"

"No. Yes. I mean, I don't know. She's so nice. She would not *kidnap* her."

"How well do you know her?" Lira asked.

Giselle started crying again. "We met a few days ago."

"A few days ago? And you trusted her with my little girl?"

Giselle fell to her knees. "I'm so sorry. I'm so sorry." She looked up with a tear-stained face. "We have to call the police."

"What does this Amy look like?" Lira asked.

"Blonde hair. I think you call it dirty blonde. About five foot nine. She's thin. Blue eyes. Pretty."

"You have her cell phone number?" Lira asked. "Home number?"

Giselle averted her gaze. "No."

"Angelo," Ellis said, "we're wasting time. We've gotta call the cops."

Lira handed her his business card. "You think of something—anything—call my cell. I don't care what time it is. You call."

"Okay. But—but what do I do now?"

"Go home and wait. We may have more questions for you."

"But the police—"

"Go home, Giselle. We'll call them. We'll take care of everything from here." Lira said it firmly, then shooed her away with his hand.

She backed out and closed the door behind her. Lira immediately pulled out his Pixel and started dialing.

Ellis realized Lira had touched too many numbers for 911. "Angelo, what the hell?"

He faced Ellis and held an index finger over his lips, then

rotated the handset back to his mouth. "Bill Tait, please. Tell him it's Angelo." He waited a beat then said, "Bill. I need help with a situation...No, like right now. Immediately. And I want Mickey." He recapped what they knew—and the situation surrounding the IPO. "Whoa. That's kind of steep...No, no. I need him...Fine, I'll pay it. How soon can he be here?" He listened a few seconds, then said, "Fine. Call me right back."

"Angelo, what are you doing?"

"What needs to be done."

"That's not an answer."

Lira frowned. "Look, I know you're under a lot of stress and this is the *last* thing you need, but we'll deal with it."

Lira's phone vibrated. He held up his left hand to keep Ellis quiet as he answered.

"Mickey. Been a while." He listened, his gaze canting toward the ceiling. "Yeah, that's the gist. When can you get here?" He closed his eyes. "Not fast enough. Go to Van Nuys airport. I'll have the private jet fueled and ready."

He hung up and dialed again. "Bruce, this is Angelo. I need a flight plan up to Oakland International. Twenty minutes. Can you do this for me?...Of course. I'll make it worth your while." He listened, then said, "Name's Mickey Keller...Yeah, Mickey. Forgot you've met him. Thanks, buddy."

Ellis's face was flushed—he could feel it—and his entire torso was damp from perspiration. "Angelo. What the hell are you doing?"

"Got a guy flying up from LA. He'll find her. I'm meeting him in ninety minutes."

"Ninety minutes? No, no. Too long. I'm calling the cops. This is *Melissa* we're talking about."

"What's going on?"

Ellis turned to see Christine standing in the threshold to the room. She closed the door behind her and marched in. "What's the problem with Melissa?"

Lira and Ellis shared a look. Ellis was not sure what Lira was thinking but he, for one, did not want to tell Christine what had happened.

"Melissa's gone missing from the lake," Lira said. "She was last seen by a friend of Giselle's. We think she's safe—but we don't know where she is."

"Brandon." Christine stepped closer to her husband. "How could you let this happen?"

"How could *I* let this happen? What are you talking about?"

"You hired Giselle. This is your fault."

Lira held up a hand. "Look, you two can argue later. Right now I've got an expert on a private jet on his way from LA. He'll be here soon and he'll get Melissa back for us."

"We need to call the police," Ellis said, moving toward his desk.

"You can't do that," Christine said, grabbing his arm. "Are you crazy?"

Ellis yanked himself free. "Am *I* crazy?"

"You call the police and this will become a major news story," Christine said. "We want to be in the news for the IPO, not a kidnapped little girl. We need to get people excited about investing in us. Billions are at stake."

"Our daughter's *life* could be at stake."

"Brandon." Christine shook her head, as if pitying her husband for being so stupid. "When a child goes missing, you know who the police suspect? The father. You'll be interrogated, maybe even arrested. How will that play with investors? Wall Street will run as far away from LifeScreen as they can get—and they'll *never* come back. Because once a suspect, always a suspect. Your career as a physician will be over—not to mention your career as a CEO. Everything you've worked for—*everything*, gone."

They were all quiet.

"She's right," Lira finally said.

Ellis dropped into his chair. He closed his eyes. "How good is this 'expert' you've summoned?"

"The best."

"Retired cop?"

"Mickey's done it all. Decorated Special Forces. Purple Heart.

Cop. Detective. Fixer. And some other stuff."

"What other stuff?"

Lira pursed his lips and shrugged. "He's the right guy for the job. Maybe the only guy. That's all you need to know."

"Great," Christine said as she turned and headed for the door. "Keep me posted."

As it clicked closed, Ellis sat back in his leather chair. "This guy really that good? Or was that fluff for Christine?"

"He's really that good. You want to check him out, google Bill Tait Protection Service. That's the company he works for. I need something done, they're the ones I call. Tait's the best. And Mickey's the best he's got."

Ellis heard Lira, but he was physically exhausted from the stress of the sprint to the IPO finish line. Now Melissa was gone.

"Brandon. Look at me."

Ellis opened his eyes and focused on Lira.

"Bill Tait has never let me down. Mickey's never let me down. You hear me?"

"There's always a first time."

"This is not gonna be that first time. I'm paying five million dollars to get this taken care of. It'll be taken care of."

Ellis swallowed deeply and again closed his eyes. "How long till he gets here?"

"Get yourself a drink, Brandon. I'll send you a secure message on WhatsApp when he lands."

18

As Amy made a pit stop at Walmart in San Leandro to buy a car seat, she tried to clear her mind. The adrenalin in her system had faded a bit, allowing her to gain some perspective on what she had just done.

Beyond the act of kidnapping a young child, she now knew she should have waited until she received the DNA results. Then she would know, without any doubt, that the girl sitting in the back was hers...at least genetically. But would that really matter?

Melissa was not actually her daughter, even if, on a biological level, she technically was. Assuming the test confirmed it, Melissa was her offspring, the genetic mixture of hers and Dan's genes.

Yet what if she wasn't? What if she was just a sweet little girl who *looked* like her own sweet little girl?

No. Melissa was hers. She could feel it.

But was Melissa actually alive as a frozen embryo? Or did Christine Ellis give her life?

What if the fire in Boston was real and the friendship between Ellis and Hutchinson had nothing to do with her or her destroyed embryos?

There was no valid explanation for Amy's behavior should the police arrest her. A good defense attorney would claim that she was mentally ill, or whatever psychiatric diagnostic code they could conjure, according to the medical expert they would hire to describe such irrational and immoral behavior.

But if I know it's immoral and irrational, why did I fake the call to Giselle? Why aren't I headed back to the lake?

The drive to the zoo after Walmart was no better. She engaged in chatter with Melissa about birds, ducks, and geese, but Amy was distracted. She finally fell silent, once again perseverating on the fertility clinic fire. Could it have been real and she was imagining some criminal act that did not exist?

"Are we there yet?"

Melissa's comment jostled Amy from her fugue. "Sorry, honey. Yes. We just need to park."

Amy found a spot at the far end of the Oakland Zoo lot, sandwiched between two oversized SUVs. A cop would have to drive right up to her Subaru to get a look at the license plate.

Melissa unbuckled her seat belt and turned around onto her knees to peer out the rear window. "I don't see any animals."

"Silly girl. They're inside. C'mon, let's go get tickets."

They made it through the admission booth without incident. Amy was half expecting cops to surround her—at any time, in any place. She found herself constantly checking over her shoulder, then realized that even if no one was suspecting her of a crime, they would soon start because of her odd behavior.

She admonished herself and readjusted her thinking. She was spending time with her daughter, and if she was going to be arrested, she would at least have these few hours with her girl. After all she had been through, she deserved this. She had gotten a second chance at something she never dreamed could happen.

Appreciate it. Live in the moment.

But had she really done anything wrong? She had merely taken back something that had been stolen from her. And removed the girl from an abusive environment.

Cut it out, Amy. You're writing your opening statement at your own trial. Enjoy the time with your daughter.

Her twitching eye was driving her crazy.

"Look Amy. Elephants!" Melissa started running down the path where the massive beasts roamed freely. It was an expansive exhibit, one that allowed the animals the ability to live as close to their natural habitat as possible while in captivity.

Amy smiled. Lindy had loved the zoo, too—and she had been to the one in Boston more times than she could count.

"Look at the way they curl their trunks around the dirt and mud and toss it onto their backs."

Melissa laughed. "Silly elephants. Why are they throwing dirt on themselves? Mommy would get very mad at me if I did that."

"If you want to throw dirt on yourself, that's okay with me."

Melissa looked at her as if that were a revelation.

When she and Dan took Lindy to the beach and Lindy tossed sand all over herself, they let her do it because she was having so much fun. They had to shower to get the sand out of Dan's beard and Lindy's blonde locks, but it was worth it because of the joy Lindy had.

"Look at him now," Amy said. "He's playing with that big ball."

She jumped in place. "Can I pet him?"

Amy chuckled. "I have a better idea. You like to feed the ducks and geese. Should we go see what time they're going to feed the elephants?"

"Yes!"

She took Melissa's tiny hand in hers and they walked back down the path. Amy scraped a fingernail against the right side of her neck. It hurt—and served as some kind of proof that she was not dreaming.

19

Mickey Keller was a wiry man skilled in a variety of martial arts, including krav maga. Although not physically imposing, he was the model of health: he worked out regularly, snacked on nuts, fruits, and vegetables, eschewed red meat, and preferred fish. He never smoked and drank moderately—primarily red wine—although craft beers were catching his interest.

A mutt of Polish, Greek, Serbian Jewish, and Venetian Italian heritage, he felt like a man without a past—it was too much diversity to embrace any single one. He considered himself an assimilated American and tried—often unsuccessfully—to convince himself that was enough.

Keller stepped off the Gulfstream V and jogged along the tarmac to the black Lincoln that was waiting for him. He punched the keyless entry code into the window pillar and slid into the sedan. A moment later, he was on the road. Twenty minutes after that, he arrived at a nondescript bar off Embarcadero West and bypassed the elevator, taking the stairs—just as his grandmother had done for nearly all of her 104 years—to an abandoned artist's loft.

He found Angelo Lira standing at the large picture window

that had a decent, though obstructed, view of downtown Oakland, and sidestepped small talk. Lira gave him his mission briefing, highlights of which were simultaneously delivered to his iPhone in an encrypted Word document.

"Bottom line," Lira said, "your number one priority is to retrieve the girl."

"And this Amy woman?"

"She's the one who kidnapped the kid in the first place. She'd be stupid to go to the cops. Get the girl and get out of there."

"Okay," Keller said. "Got it."

"No complications, Mickey. I want this done quick—and clean. Under the radar."

"Cops on the case? Who's the dick?"

"Haven't been called."

Keller tilted his chin back in understanding. "Okay."

Lira worked his jaw. "We're on the verge of an IPO with the parents. The girl's the face of the company. If word gets out that she's been kidnapped, and they give the media her photo—she'll forever be associated with a kidnapping, not a revolutionary change in health care and genetics testing. At best, it'll divert investor attention away from the IPO and toward the search for the girl, endless stories about the woman who took her, the police investigation—everything but what we want. A kid in danger gets people's hearts racing. At worst, the father will be questioned, if not suspected of conspiring with his hot young au pair. Too much at stake."

Keller nodded. "That's why I'm here."

"No cops, no media. No one knows. Except you, the nanny who let it happen, the parents, and me."

"Where can I find this nanny?"

Lira gave him the Ellis address.

"This is an important case. Important to me. Personally."

"Bill said there's a lot riding on it."

"That's an understatement. Don't fuck it up."

20

Fifteen minutes later Keller was knocking on Giselle's bedroom door. He held up a brass badge then dropped it back in his sport coat pocket. It was an authentic replica made by a European foundry that specialized in creating collector's editions of those brandished by many US law enforcement agencies. The workmanship was extraordinary, with very little difference between the real detective's shield he had earned with the LAPD and the inauthentic one he now carried.

Keller asked her a few generic questions, then said, "What else can you tell me about Amy? Anything. No detail is insignificant."

Giselle's gaze roamed the carpet before she lifted her head. "She is—she's a runner. She runs with a woman who looks like her. Maybe her sister. How do you say? A brunette. And Amy works at a bakery near the lake. I was there. It's uh, Grand Lake Bakery." She gave him the cross street and described the place. "There is a guy there. He works with her. Um, Bobby or Billy. He's older, maybe fifty?"

"This Amy. Is she married?"

"No. And no kids."

Keller nodded, knowing there had to be a reason why a woman would kidnap a young girl. It was unusual. There had to be a trigger of some sort. "You get any indications—before she

101

kidnapped Melissa—that something was off about her?"

"Off?"

"Like something wasn't right."

"No, she seemed normal. Very friendly."

"Did she act strange around Melissa? Say things that were maybe a little odd?"

Giselle shook her head. "She seemed completely at ease around her. Like..." Her voice trailed off.

"Like what?"

She shrugged. "I don't know. Now that I think about it, maybe she was too much at ease around her, like she was a natural. She knew how to relate to Melissa." Giselle shook her head. "Maybe she has a young niece or a cousin."

Keller absorbed that. These were certainly possibilities.

"There is one thing." She bit her lip but did not continue.

"Go on."

"I, um...I don't want to get anyone in trouble."

Keller leaned forward and placed both forearms on his knees. "Giselle, a young girl's life could depend on what you do or don't tell me. We need to find her before she's harmed."

"You really think Amy would harm her?"

"No idea. Do you?"

"I—" She sighed. "She may have taken her because she wanted to protect Melissa."

Keller sat back abruptly. "Protect her. From who?"

Giselle's lips quivered, then tightened. "I do not know for sure."

"But you have suspicions."

"If I lose my job they will send me back to Germany. And my—I am much happier here. I do not want to go home."

"I'll keep what you tell me between us."

"Promise?" She looked deep into his eyes.

Keller froze. Her face oozed natural beauty. And innocence.

His attraction to women was not just sexual: he loved spending time with them, chatting with them. That presented a problem, as he tended to talk too much—and that sometimes included mission details. If such behavior occurred with an off-duty law enforcement officer, it would've been disastrous. When he went to work for Bill Tait, Tait told him that if his cadre of employees could discover this weakness in their vetting, others could, too. Under the threat of losing his lucrative career, Keller agreed to work with a counselor.

"Yes," Keller said, clearing his throat, "I promise."

Giselle leaned forward and lowered her voice. "I have seen bruises on Melissa's body. Her arms, her neck. And red lines on her back."

"She's been abused?"

"I think so. How else does a little girl get bruises like that?"

"Did you ask Melissa what happened?"

"She won't talk about it."

"Who do you think is hurting her?"

Giselle bit her lip.

"C'mon, Giselle. This is important."

She put her chin down and whispered, "Christine."

Keller tilted his head back. "Really," he said under his breath. "Christine Ellis? The mom?"

Giselle nodded silently.

"Did you ever *see* anything that—"

"No. Nothing. It is just a guess. I have no proof of anything. I never heard anything. Never saw anything."

"I'll handle it," Keller said. "So you spend a lot of time at the lake. You happen to see any surveillance cameras in the area?"

"I do not know. There could be. I—I do not really notice those things."

"Anything else you can tell me?" Keller asked.

"I, I don't think so."

He gave her his card. All it had on it was a phone number and above it the words, "Call with information."

Giselle inspected it. "Sorry. I did not get your name."

He chuckled inwardly. *That's because I didn't give it to you.* "Carr." He pointed at the card. "You think of something, call me. Immediately."

IT WAS DUSK AND KELLER needed to get to the bakery before it closed. When he walked in, he did a quick survey of the place and took mental notes.

"Can I help you?"

His attention, and gaze, were drawn to a middle-aged woman with shoulder-length hair.

"Looking for Bobby. Or Billy."

"Bobby. He's in the back. He's one of our bakers."

Keller removed his badge and held it up, his fingers conveniently obscuring key information on its face...the product of practice and long, slender digits.

"I need to ask him a few questions."

"What's this about?"

"One of his coworkers. Amy."

Her brow crunched. "I'm the owner. I can answer your questions."

The door swung open and two women walked in. Another employee stepped forward from a back room and greeted the customers.

"Come back to my office. I'm Ellen Macafree," she said as she swung open a half-door beside the cash register to allow Keller to pass.

"Thanks. Sorry to drop in on you like this. I appreciate your time." As they entered a modest-sized room that was filled with stacks of papers, Keller was quick to begin talking. "Do you have a personnel file on Amy?"

"I do, but I don't think I should give it to you without a warrant."

Keller pursed his lips and nodded, then took out a pad and pen to look official.

"Is she okay? Did she do something wrong? Why are you here?"

"Can't discuss it," Keller said. "Ongoing investigation."

"Something I should be concerned about?"

"There's a detective sitting in your office, Ms. Macafree. That should be your answer. When was the last time you saw her?"

"Today. She came in for work and left at lunch time. But she hasn't returned. No phone call. Not answering her phone at all."

"That unusual?"

"Very. Aside from occasional lateness, she's been a responsible employee."

"What's Amy's last name?"

Ellen's eyes narrowed. "You don't even know her last name?"

"I was just handed this case. Literally thirty minutes ago."

"Robbins."

"Phone number?"

Ellen jotted it down on a piece of paper and handed it over. "You can't tell me anything about what the problem is?"

"Sorry, I can't. Have you noticed any behavior lately that, well, seemed out of the ordinary?"

Ellen hesitated. "If anything, I'd say she seems happier."

Keller harrumphed. That could indicate that she identified a target she found appealing, was planning to abduct the girl, and was confident in her plan. Or it could indicate nothing of the sort. Pedophilia among women was rare.

"Home address?"

"That you could get from your department, I'm sure."

"Right you are. What about friends? Family?"

"I've never seen her with friends. But she has a brother in town. I honestly don't know a whole lot about her."

Keller sensed some evasion but decided not to ruffle feathers. He might have to return for more questions and if he pushed Macafree too hard and she called the station to complain, she would discover there was no case and no detective. It would cause a boatload of problems for him. He rose from his chair. "Thanks for your cooperation."

He walked out before she could ask him any questions—like what his name was—and drove his Lincoln around the block before pulling out his phone and starting his search for an Amy Robbins in Oakland. There was nothing—no LinkedIn profile, no Facebook, Instagram, or Twitter accounts.

But then he found an old article from the *Boston Herald* covering a tragic car accident. It was only a brief piece, a filler in local news. But it provided some important information.

Keller took a screenshot, which included a grainy photo of the Robbins woman, and securely WhatsApped it to Lira with a message to show it to Ellis. Maybe he knew her.

A few clicks and the picture was on its way. In the meantime, Keller continued to poke around to see if he could locate a current address for Amy Robbins.

21

Ellis and Lira were still at the office, navigating a difficult conference call with one of their banking analysts.

Lira glanced down at his Pixel as the photo hit his inbox. He held it up to show Ellis and shrugged.

Ellis took a moment to study the screen, and then his jaw dropped open. "Oh shit."

"Excuse me?" the analyst asked.

"Uh..." Lira read Ellis's reaction and inched forward in his seat. "Listen, Rhonda, we need to call you back in a few minutes."

"Everything okay?"

"Everything's great," Lira said, knowing it was likely the opposite. "Brandon just got some news about his dog. I'll get back to you within the hour." He disconnected the call. "Who is this woman?"

Ellis swallowed. "It's a bad picture. I, uh...I can't be sure."

"Bullshit. You're sweating. Who is she?"

Ellis stood up and ran his right hand through his hair. He turned away, toward the window, and looked out at the city of Oakland as darkness descended and pinpricks of streetlights began to appear.

"Brandon. Talk to me."

"Where'd you get it? The photo?"

"My guy. Don't know where or how. This is the woman who took Melissa. Amy Robbins." He studied Ellis's face. "Is there a problem?"

"No, all's good. I'll—I'm...I'll handle it."

"Handle what?"

Ellis cleared his throat.

"Brandon, if there's something you know about this, you need to tell me. Do you or do you *not* know who this woman is?"

"I—I'm not sure. The photo—"

"We're talking about your daughter here," Lira said.

"I may know who this woman is." He swallowed hard. Ellis bowed his head. "It looks like someone I know. Well, not someone I know. Someone I know *about*."

Lira waited a beat but Ellis was not forthcoming. He came up alongside Ellis and looked at his business partner's face. "I really need you to start talking, Brandon. And fast. I can't help you—and my colleague can't help find your daughter—if you keep stuff from us."

"She looks a lot like the woman whose embryos we used for..." He cleared his throat. "For Melissa."

Lira canted his head. "I'm not clear on what you're saying. Or not saying. So have a seat and take a breath and start from the beginning. I need to know what the hell's going on."

Ellis bit his bottom lip. He pulled his hands from his pockets and sat down heavily on the sofa along the left wall of his office. "Shut the door."

Lira did as instructed and moved in front of Ellis but remained standing.

"Melissa possesses an outstanding genetic profile."

"Of course she does. That's what LifeScreen does. I don't und—"

"We didn't use LifeScreen."

"Yes you did. We've been discussing this for years."

Ellis closed his eyes for a long moment, then started talking. "Melissa is not our biological child." He swallowed deeply.

"Christine and I used another couple's embryos."

"So you lied to us—to get funding?" Lira's cheeks flushed the color of a blood red orange. "That's securities fraud."

"We'll have to deal with that later. If anyone finds out."

"Why would you do this? Why not use LifeScreen?"

"Because Christine and I had multiple failures with IVF. Couldn't get pregnant. Turns out I have an absent vas deferens— I'm missing the tube that carries the sperm—so without that you can't impregnate an egg. And Christine had some scarring. She was raped as a teen and the doctor who did the abortion was a hack. The malpractice settlement covered her medical schooling, but we knew conceiving might be a problem." He cleared his throat. "This couple my colleague found for us were exceptional individuals. Bright, high achievers. Unusually clean genetic profile free of most diseases that we tested."

"But that's what LifeScreen is supposed to do. Unless you're saying that LifeScreen doesn't really work?"

"It wasn't that."

"Better not be, because if that's the case you'll be spending the rest of your life in federal prison. You'll lose everything. And I personally, together with my investors, will be the ones taking it from you."

Ellis gathered in a deep breath. "The algorithm was having issues back then, and I couldn't afford to continue work on the code. Remember when I told you I needed another infusion of cash? And you told me the well had run dry until I demonstrated concrete results for the board?"

"*That's* when you did this?"

"Christine and I didn't have a choice. We were on a very tight development deadline. Before we met, you our home was underwater from the recession and we'd burned through all our investments. When you said no—"

"You're blaming me for this?"

"Just stating facts. Bottom line was, Christine and I had too much invested in this. We couldn't lose it all. What we did, we did for everyone. Me and Christine, you and all the investors. I knew the algorithm would work. I knew we had a viable product. But reality collided with theory. We needed more time to fine-tune it." He rubbed his eyes. "I found a couple who were as genetically clean as you can be. Christine was implanted with their embryos. It was a difficult nine months. We needed her to go to term without complications and we needed Melissa to be the perfect little girl we hoped she'd be."

"This couple—" Lira consulted his Pixel. "Amy Robbins? And her husband?"

Ellis nodded.

"And let me guess. Your colleague didn't ask permission to use their embryos?"

"How could they? No one could know."

"Jesus Christ."

"It's not like you think. We had reason to believe it'd never become an issue."

"It's become an issue."

"I get that. But back when we...did this, it seemed like they'd never be having another child. They had to use IVF to get pregnant. Their extra embryos were cryogenically stored. Frozen in time, for lack of a better term. They were fortunate. Mrs. Robbins got pregnant on the first round. The rest of the embryos were never used. A few years later her husband and daughter were killed in a car accident. The mother—Amy Robbins—went into deep depression, lost everything. Her job, her career, her...well, her sanity. She was in no condition to even consider having another child."

"But time passes. Wounds heal. What if she got her life together? Did you even consider that?"

Ellis nodded absentmindedly. "That was always possible. Unlikely, we thought, but possible. So Christine...made sure that was not going to be a problem."

Lira furrowed his brow. "What the hell does that mean?"

"A fire. Confined to a specific area of my friend's lab. Nothing that would affect his business. The appearance, and fire marshal report, would state that it destroyed a portion of the lab. A storage area. And some embryos. Including the Robbins embryos."

Lira turned away. "And now Amy Robbins is convinced that Melissa is her daughter."

"Apparently."

"How—how'd Robbins find her?"

"I don't know."

"Does she know about the fire?"

"I have to make a call, let my friend know what's going on."

"Your friend's name?"

Ellis hesitated. He looked away.

"Brandon, is there a problem?"

He stood there, sighed deeply, then met Lira's eyes. "It's John."

"John. Can you give me a little more? John is a pretty common—"

"John Hutchinson. In Boston."

"You're not serious."

Ellis averted his eyes. "Christine asked John not to say anything to you about it. She didn't want to jeopardize the deal. She said that if we told you we had a problem, well, we didn't know what you'd do, how you'd react."

"This isn't happening." Lira's cheeks reddened. He shook his head. "Don't assume anything. Don't *do* anything. We have to keep the press—and the police—away from this. No one can know. If it hits Facebook or—CNN, for Christ's sake—"

"I understand."

"Can this Giselle woman be trusted?"

"She's a good kid. And it's obviously in her best interest to keep her mouth shut. She's the one who let this happen."

"Nice of you to shift the blame. Let's not forget you were the one who stole this woman's embryos and committed arson to cover it up."

Ellis swallowed hard.

Lira thought a long moment. "You did eventually get LifeScreen squared away?"

Ellis rubbed his face between two open palms. "I know, this

looks bad. But I'm telling you, it's just a technicality—"

"There are no such things as technicalities in an IPO. Perception is everything. If it looks like we're doing funny stuff behind the scenes, manipulating data, or using embryos that were not screened using LifeScreen's technology, if the government launches an investigation, who's going to invest with us? We stand to make billions of dollars. Everything needs to be above board."

"I know. It was a mistake. I—I'm sorry."

"Sorry." Lira laughed, then shook his head in disgust. "LifeScreen works? Yes or no?"

"While Christine was pregnant with Melissa, I put in a lot of long nights and saw patients in a colleague's fertility clinic to get some cash together to pay the programmers and researchers to fix the algorithm."

"And?" Lira asked, his voice rising. "Did you? Yes or no?"

"Took longer than I thought it would. Than it should have. But yeah. Yes."

Lira breathed a deep sigh of relief. "Thank God."

Ellis chuckled sardonically. "I think it's safe to say that God has nothing to do with this."

22

Keller hung up from a call with Lira and now had a more complete picture of what was going on. He located Robbins's address from leasing records and headed to the apartment. It was around the perimeter of the lake, in the Ivy Hill neighborhood on the southeast side.

It was 11:00 PM and although Ivy Hill was a safe area of Oakland, it was not far from the sketchier locales. At night, a block or so in the wrong direction, and violent crime and armed robberies were the order of the day.

Keller parked fifty yards or so from the complex. He seated his compact SIG-Sauer and checked to make sure the folding Tanto was within reach, protruding slightly from the small pocket of his black 5.11 tactical pants. He grabbed a few small electronic devices, shoved them in his jacket, and headed out.

Upon arriving at Amy Robbins's apartment on the third floor, he took a swift accounting and saw no security cameras—not even ghost cameras...those that looked like functioning devices but in fact were empty—no electronic guts. Cheap, but effective, deterrents.

Keller found number 52 and put his ear to the door. Nothing. He pulled out his lock-pick kit and five seconds later entered the place, ski mask pulled down over his face. Thin black gloves were stretched tightly over his fingers. He had bought them in Venice, custom made by a man who had operated a kiosk near the canals for thirty years, a master craftsman who took precise measurements of both hands. Keller wanted them to hug his digits to allow for maximum dexterity, the finest supple, sheer, and formfitting Nappa leather that would allow for breaking and entering, operating a firearm, strangulation—anything that might arise. Admittedly, he did not mention the strangulation requirement to the artisan.

With his phone flashlight, Keller did a quick search, then went back to the kitchen. He opened Robbins's laptop and expected to find it password protected—but it was not. That made his job easier—and less risky.

He inserted his high capacity USB flash drive and launched the AllClone imaging utility. Robbins had a 125GB SSD, so he figured the time to copy her computer's contents would be around twenty minutes. The tool confirmed his estimate. While he waited, he resumed his search, looking for information he might be able to use to locate Robbins should she not return home...checking the refrigerator for notes, business cards lying around, opened mail, and credit card statements. He found each of these and took photos.

By the time he was finished, the cloning app had just about completed its task. He unplugged his device, shut down her laptop, and left the apartment.

He peeled the backing from an adhesive sticker on a miniature sensor and reached to the top of the door. He pushed it against the metal surface of the jamb and affixed its magnetic mate an inch to the right.

Keller walked thirty feet away to the stairwell and checked the app on his phone. The cellular signal was strong. When the magnetic seal was broken by Amy Robbins entering her apartment, he would be alerted immediately. It would take him less than a minute to get there from where he was parked.

Back at his car, he gave a look around, taking in his surroundings. He got in and made himself comfortable, reclining the seat and keeping his right hand on the SIG's handle. The Lincoln's windows were tinted a shade darker than what was legal, making it difficult to see in, particularly at night.

Practicing a skill he had mastered in the military, he fell asleep within minutes.

23

Amy had faked another call to Giselle around dinner time, then told Melissa that Giselle was still busy helping her grandma, and that her parents had late meetings for work.

"That happens a lot," Melissa said. "'Selle and I eat apple—um, it sounds like a doggie. A poodle."

"Strudel?"

"Uh-huh. And we put on our PJs and watch movies. Or read books."

"Would you like me to read a book to you?"

"In the car?"

"No, silly. Later, after dinner. Once I figure out where we're going to sleep tonight, we'll read one of my favorite stories."

"We can go home. You can sleep in the guest room. We can have a pajama party when 'Selle's done with her grandma."

Smart kid.

"They didn't want to be disturbed," Amy said. "Their work is very important and the meeting's in the house."

Melissa fell quiet. Processing all that? Amy wasn't sure—but if she did not have to field any more difficult questions—for which she did not have adequate answers—that was fine with her.

On the way to dinner at Zachary's pizza in Berkeley—Zach liked to joke that he was an early investor in the restaurant, and its name was proof—Amy debated whether she should call him and Loren. But what would she say? *I've kidnapped a little girl and I need your help?* There was no way her sister-in-law could get involved. She'd be fired at best—and thrown in jail alongside Amy if she helped in any way. And endangering Zach, leaving the kids with no parent...no, she could not place them in danger for her stupidity and irrational behavior.

Am I being irrational? Melissa might be—probably is—my daughter. Is she?

Amy almost screamed in the middle of the restaurant. She rubbed her twitching eye.

"Amy, I have to go potty."

She shook her head and focused on Melissa. "Sorry. Let's go do that. Leave your napkin on the table."

By the time they returned, their pizzas had arrived. Melissa saw them a dozen yards away and ran to the table. She put her nose above the pies, taking in the aroma, then bobbed up and down in her chair. "Mommy doesn't ever let me eat pizza. But Giselle sneaks me some on Special Fridays."

"Special Fridays?"

"Pizza and ice cream for lunch."

Oh yeah. The ice cream truck. Amy cringed.

After serving a plain slice for Melissa and a deep-dish spinach and mushroom piece for herself, Amy started thinking again about what her next moves would be. As a litigator, she always prepared a game plan, along with contingencies depending on what actions her opposing counsel could take. But now she felt like she was flying by the seat of her pants.

Because she was. And that had to stop because she had committed a serious crime. She knew that now. And if Melissa was not her genetic progeny, stolen from her in a criminal act... Amy was in a heap of trouble. She would have to find an attorney who could negotiate her surrender. And if Melissa *was* her child... Amy shook her head. Either way, what would happen to Melissa?

If Amy had any say in the matter, putting the girl back in an abusive environment was not an option.

They finished their pizza and Amy left cash on the table to cover the bill, then led the way back to their car. It was dark, nearly 9:00 PM by the time they got to her Subaru, and almost certainly past Melissa's bedtime.

A few minutes later, with the heat blasting, Melissa was asleep. Amy used the quiet to think. But she had an ongoing sense of unease. She could not work things through as she used to—her sense of reason seemed obscured by fog.

Hard to believe several years ago she was a high-powered attorney, mind as sharp as anyone's, quick of wit and even faster with a comeback argument. She felt like a shell of her former self.

In so many ways.

After driving around Berkeley and Piedmont for a couple of hours, she decided she could not wait any longer. She needed to know where she stood—what her future, and Melissa's, was.

Amy pulled into her Ivy Hill neighborhood and circled the block a number of times to look for police or unmarked cars surveilling the area. Waiting for her.

Seeing nothing out of the ordinary, she pulled into her complex and gathered Melissa in her arms.

"Shh," she whispered in the girl's ear. "Go back to sleep."

She held Melissa close to her body as she yanked the mail from her box and then made her way up to the apartment. Amy struggled to fish out the key from her wool coat and unlock the door while supporting the girl in her left arm. She stepped inside and found that all was quiet. No police waiting to arrest her. Everything the way she left it.

Amy leaned backward slightly to keep Melissa against her torso as she dropped her purse and keys on the kitchen table. She stood there a moment, the smell of the girl's hair strangely comforting, the slight rhythmic rise and fall of her chest taking her back in time to her rocking chair in Lindy's room: reading books and gently gliding to and fro until she fell asleep. Amy would stay there another ten or fifteen minutes cherishing the closeness, those special moments when a mother marvels at the gift she holds against her body—which grew *inside* her body.

Melissa's weight roused Amy from the memories. She swung toward the living room couch when the front door popped open. A man stood there, dressed in a dark sport coat and turtleneck.

"Who are you?" Amy asked.

Police. Had to be.

Amy swallowed hard, adrenalin pouring into her veins, sending her body into a frenzy.

The man flicked his foot and the wood door arced closed behind him. "Oakland PD, Ms. Robbins. Slow and steady, now. Show me your hands."

Amy fought to compose herself. She gripped Melissa tightly and backed away but hit the kitchen chair. "ID?"

He reached into his inside pocket and held up a shield, then quickly put it back from where it came.

"I didn't see it."

"Didn't see what?"

"Your shield."

The man eyed her. "Amy Robbins, you're under arrest for kidnapping a minor."

"No," Amy said, her voice rising. She shifted Melissa's body in her arms—but no way was she handing her over.

"No?"

"You don't understand."

"Nothing to understand. Put her down on the couch and put your hands on the back of your head. Interlock your fingers and—"

"No." Amy's tone—and volume—were getting harsher, louder. "*You can't have her.*"

Melissa stiffened, waking up and squirming—which made it difficult for Amy to hold her. She dropped to a knee and pulled the girl against her body.

"Ms. Robbins. Don't make this more difficult than it has to be. I need you to do what I said."

"Get out!"

The man drew a handgun from beneath his sport coat. "Back away!" His tone had changed. Anger, frustration. "Now. Back the hell away from Melissa."

Amy stiffened. "You're not a cop, are you?"

"Don't make me do something we'll both regret."

Amy's jaw tightened. "You're not gonna shoot me while I'm holding Melissa. You won't."

KELLER STEPPED FORWARD. He had misjudged the woman's resolve. Her courage and resilience.

"I'm only interested in the girl," he said. "Put her down and I'll let you go, talk to the DA, have him go easy on you."

"Like I said, you're not law enforcement."

How was she so sure?

The question must have registered on his face because she said, "The DA is a woman."

Keller squinted. *Amy Robbins works in a bakery. What are the odds she would know the gender of the district attorney?*

"Give me the girl."

"No."

Dammit. I'm not in control here.

He reached behind his back and pulled out a set of handcuffs. "You have the right to remain silent."

"You're not taking her from me. She's mine, she's my child!"

Keller advanced on her, now three feet away, SIG in his right hand and handcuffs in his left. "What the hell are you talking about?"

"I told you. You don't understand. She was stolen from me. I'm her *mother*."

Melissa started to cry.

"It's okay, honey. It's okay. Don't worry. Everything's going to be fine."

"But you're not my mommy."

"Enough," Keller said firmly. He shoved the cuffs in his pocket and grabbed Melissa by the arm, but Amy maintained a vise-like grip on the girl.

Amy cried—wept—repeating "No, no, no," over and over.

Keller was about to use force to end the stalemate when his gaze caught a photo on the wall a few feet away across the table. He recognized one of the women: Loren Ryder—former colleague, longtime nemesis. And Amy Robbins, standing beside her holding a girl, a little younger than Melissa. Who looked very much like Melissa.

What the hell's going on?

Keller shoved his pistol against the back of Amy's neck. "Who's in that photo behind you?"

"What?" Amy struggled to compose herself and speak clearly.

"That photo. Is that you?"

"Yes. And my—my daughter. And my brother and sister-in-law."

"Your daughter?"

"Lindy. She and my husband were—" Amy swallowed deeply and whimpered as she fought to form the words. "They were killed in a car accident. Melissa's my daughter. The Ellises took her from me. Stole her. Please don't take her. Please don't hurt me."

AMY'S HEART WAS POUNDING so hard she felt it physically striking her chest wall. She struggled to think clearly while cuddling Melissa beneath her. The child was shaking in fear, not moving. Not saying a word. Amy was using all her motherly strength to form a protective shield.

She braced for—well, she did not know what.

But there was silence.

And then she felt a draft of cold air slither around her neckline. She lifted her head slightly and peered through perspiration-soaked strands of hair. The front door was swinging slowly open.

What just happened?

She started to get to her feet—but Melissa grabbed her shirt. "Don't leave me."

"I'm not, honey." Still on her knees, Amy helped her up and gave her a hug. "I'm not going anywhere. I'm just—I'm just closing

121

the door." *And locking it.*

"Who was that?"

Amy knelt in front of Melissa. *Good question. Another one I don't have an answer for.* "I don't know."

"Was he a policeman?"

"He said he was. But I don't think so."

"You mean he was lying?"

"Yeah."

"'Selle says people who lie are bad."

Amy found it hard to argue with that but knew that in an adult world the issue was a great deal more complex. After all, she had been lying to Melissa all day. "It depends who they are and why they're lying. Sometimes you tell a little fib because it'll make someone feel better. Because the truth might hurt them."

Melissa looked at her. Amy knew it was probably a concept with too many gray areas for a child to be able to process effectively.

"Like you don't tell someone they're fat because it'll make them feel bad. That's what 'Selle said. A really fat girl at the lake has a fat dog and 'Selle said I should say the dog is cute."

Amy lifted her brow. "Exactly."

She helped Melissa to the couch. They both sat down and fell silent. Melissa took Amy's hand.

Her touch felt good and natural—but at the moment Amy had to figure out who that man was. He had obviously come to take Melissa back to the Ellises. So he was working for them. A private investigator. But then why lie about being a cop? Why go through the charade of arresting her?

And why didn't he take Melissa—after all that trouble to find her, and the girl, why would he leave without her?

Did he believe me, that Melissa was my daughter? Felt sorry for me?

He saw the photo. That's when everything changed.

Why?

It did not matter. They knew who she was and where she lived. The guy might come back—or someone else could be sent in his place. Either way, she was not going to hang around to find out.

Every minute they remained there, they were in danger.

"We have to go," Amy said. "Give me a minute to get some things together. Okay?"

Melissa looked up and nodded, her grip tightening around Amy's hand.

24

Keller needed a place to stay for the evening and booked a motel online. Low-key was best, one less likely to monitor his comings and goings. He could put a DO NOT DISTURB notice on the knob, slip out the door, walk a few steps to his car, and be gone with few, if any, people being the wiser.

He opened his laptop, turned on the VPN to mask his internet address, and started poking around to see what he could learn about Amy Robbins—and Loren Ryder, her supposed sister-in-law.

He should have done this before diving in head-first, but that was the job, handed to him at the last minute with the orders to hit the ground running. But after what he had seen, he needed to take a step back. And a deep breath.

Keller knew Ryder going back almost fifteen years when he was a detective with the LAPD and she was a relatively new agent stationed out of the Wilshire Boulevard federal building. They collaborated on a number of cases—or, rather, *clashed* over a number of cases. Although they had their share of disagreements, he respected her and her integrity. And he got the sense she respected him.

Ryder was one of those women he found himself attracted to and had a tendency to open up to more than he should.

That relationship took a turn for the worse when Keller got

involved with a Russian mobster. Not him, per se, but Bill Tait. Tait took the man on as a client to broker an under-the-radar arms deal and Keller was assigned the case to make it happen. The NSA caught some chatter about it, turned it over to the CIA—until a connection was made to an American player—and then the FBI stepped in. Loren Ryder was one of seventeen agents working it.

As (bad) luck would have it, she ended up following her gut and finding a thread that led, unfortunately, to Keller. But she did not have enough to charge him with anything.

When he had first seen her walk into the interview room, he professed surprise—which was genuine because he had no reason to know she had been transferred from the Bureau's Los Angeles field office to San Francisco's.

"I've heard some things about you," Loren had told him.

"Oh yeah? Like what?"

"Like you're now involved with some bad actors."

"Don't believe everything you hear."

"Of course. Except that the people telling me this are people I trust. Like I used to trust you."

"Past tense?"

Loren shrugged. "Like I said. I've heard some things."

"You know who I am. That Tarzana case? We trusted each other, depended on each other. For our lives."

"I remember. And I also remember that you had my back and got me out of a jam."

Keller nodded, maintained eye contact with her. "That bond is deep, Loren. I'd never do anything to hurt you."

"Hurting me includes breaking the law. Did you break the law here?"

"We've already been through this. I'm up here meeting with a company in Silicon Valley."

"My partner's making that call right now, checking it out."

"Good. Then maybe we can get back to trusting each other again."

Loren frowned.

"I'm sorry we lost contact."

Loren looked at him. "Me too. And I hope to god the rumors I've heard aren't true. Because you were a damn good detective and a really nice guy. You're no longer a cop, but I sure hope you're still a good person. Because it'd piss me off big time to have to arrest you. Ex-cops don't do well in prison."

"No, they don't." He smiled and winked at her—the same wink he had given her on more than one occasion when they had worked together.

The door swung open and Loren whirled. Her partner nodded his head. Keller's story checked out.

"Okay then," Keller said as he held up his handcuffed wrists. "I'll be going. I don't suppose you're available for a cup of coffee?"

"Maybe next time I arrest you."

"There won't be a next time."

Loren frowned. "Let's hope not."

Before leaving, Ryder did her best to make him feel shame at "going over to the dark side," as she had put it, and Keller had to admit—to himself, at least—that he did feel shame. She was right. He had become one of the perps he had chased as a detective. And for what?

Well, for the money.

It really was that simple. He rationalized it well enough—as a public servant he was paid poorly and he was not getting any younger. He had made a bad investment with a friend and he ended up losing his house in the Great Recession. He needed a job with a robust salary where he could right his financial ship as quickly as possible.

Enter Bill Tait and Tait Protection Services. Tait served under Gen. Lukas DeSantos, a decorated war hero who, like Keller, had served his country. Though Tait and Keller were in the same outfit and became fast friends, they chose different paths upon leaving the Army and entering the private sector. Tait started a company and found enormous financial success. Keller joined the police force and that did not go as smoothly for him.

He enjoyed the work and did well organizationally, making detective—but living in Los Angeles in a decent neighborhood that did not require a two-hour commute left little in his bank account.

Tait checked in on him one day when he was in town on business and read Keller's face perfectly. He offered him a job that Keller initially declined—but ultimately accepted after falling behind on his new mortgage. Walking away from the loan was not his preferred way of doing business. And it would have damaged his credit substantially.

At first, Keller refused to work a case for Tait where he did anything illegal or caused harm to others. Tait accepted that arrangement for a while. But when a couple of Tait's key employees left and started a rival firm, Tait took on some marginal clients who paid exceptionally well.

He needed someone he could trust to handle the case professionally and responsibly, so he turned to Keller.

That meant Keller needed to modify his code of conduct a bit, moving it farther from his comfort zone. His edict of not doing "anything illegal that caused harm to others" became "not doing anything illegal that caused *direct* harm to others."

For his part, Tait understood and was selective of the cases he gave Keller. But after the third year, Keller having repeatedly proved he was better than most of Tait's other fixers or cleaners or wet operatives—whatever it was they were called that week, depending on the job—word got around and requests for repeat business started coming in from Tait's less legally inclined clients.

Keller thought long and hard about his personal conduct code when he was given more complex (or "murky") cases, where it was not entirely clear that the client was involved in a criminal enterprise. But like a skilled defense attorney, you did not have to ask—and often did not want to—to know your client was guilty.

By year four, it got to the point where he had direct contact with the client, and any pretense of only working with law-abiding citizens on legal cases evaporated. After one particularly difficult case where Keller could no longer look the other way, he took an extended vacation and told Tait he was not sure if he was coming back.

Tait the businessman took this to be a shrewd negotiating tactic. The ploy-that-wasn't worked, however, and Tait tripled his salary to seven figures. For someone who had earned $95,000 as an LAPD detective, it took him 144 months to make the base pay of $1.5 million Tait offered him in a single year. It was a dream, like flying to the moon. You might fantasize about it, but you could never see a viable way of making it happen...so it did not occupy your thoughts for more than a fleeting moment.

The lifestyle Mickey Keller never envisioned for himself—which he thought he was incapable of having as a public servant—was providing him almost anything he wanted, whenever he wanted. Financial stability. Two impressive homes, one on each coast, a Tesla in each garage, and most important, peace of mind relative to his future...if he continued to work for Tait.

Tait had identified Keller's price for willingly, though reluctantly, compromising his morals. They had come a long way from their days eating MREs and lugging gear around in desert-hot Middle Eastern locales.

Keller told himself he would only do it for a few years and then quit and find something else to occupy his time.

But the trappings of wealth were difficult to give up. And a million dollars did not go nearly as far as it used to. He decided not to get ahead of himself. Take it a day at a time, don't worry about making big decisions. And in the meantime, do as little damage as possible. Break as few laws as possible.

He knew this was one oversized rationalization, but it enabled him to wake up every morning and look himself in the mirror.

Working for nefarious individuals, however, did take a toll. He would grit his teeth, remind himself he had made a commitment to his former unit mate, and fool himself into thinking he was taking one for the team.

When Tait told him about the case in which he was to track down and recover a kidnapped young girl, he jumped at the opportunity to do something wholesome, to again be the champion of the right side of the law.

He would be able to feel good about himself for a bit.

But.

Now he was not sure what he had gotten involved in.

He took a drink of high octane cold brew and tapped his screen. The link opened and told him that Loren Ryder was still in the Oakland Resident Agency of the FBI working in the Crimes Against Children Squad. He found a photo of her. She looked good. A little more mature, a little older than he had last seen her...than the photo hanging on Amy Robbins's kitchen wall.

He scanned a couple more articles, then shifted to Amy, her sister-in-law. He read a couple of news pieces about a fatal motor vehicle accident involving Robbins, her husband, and daughter.

Keller leaned back to think. *Why would a woman whose relative is involved with crimes against children kidnap a young girl? Was it as she had said—that Melissa Ellis was really her daughter?*

Keller was staring at the screen but seeing nothing. Could he take Robbins at her word? She could be delusional. If she were mentally unstable, she could believe the child was hers and that people were conspiring against her. She endured a terrible tragedy, if true.

It was true. That newspaper article mentioned their deaths...

He huddled over the keyboard and found something mentioning a trial for the truck driver who had struck the Robbins' vehicle. This provided a little more background: they had used IVF to get pregnant. Robbins took their deaths very hard, suffering from severe depression and leaving her lucrative law practice.

He kept reading and compiling information. Finally he sat back and thought for a few minutes, absorbing what he had put together.

She said the Ellises stole her daughter. Why would she say that? Why phrase it that way?

What did he know about the Ellises?

He took a long drink of coffee then hit the keys again. An hour later, he glanced over his notes. The photo of Melissa Ellis, the girl he was supposed to recover and the one he had seen in the apartment, stared at him from the screen.

Keller thought a moment, then opened a picture of Christine and Brandon Ellis from the LifeScreen promotional brochure. Then he located a better image of Lindy Robbins and arranged it alongside the one of Melissa. The girls were fairly close in age. The resemblance was unquestionable. And uncanny.

Sisters. Lindy—and therefore Melissa—bore a strong likeness to Amy Robbins. And other than blonde hair, Melissa looked nothing like Christine—a somewhat attractive, though awkward-featured woman.

Robbins claimed the child had been stolen from her. An adoption by the Ellises, if legal, would not be considered theft... unless Robbins was emotionally damaged and viewed anything that "took" her child from her as a criminal act. Accessing adoption records would be near impossible, especially when up against the clock.

But Amy Robbins had IVF.

A medical clinic was a soft target. He could more easily get at that information. If it did not bear fruit, he would have to find an illicit way of getting at the protected custody data he needed.

He could go to Lira, but not without explaining why he was asking such questions rather than focusing on tracking down the girl.

Taking the path of least resistance, Keller started calling fertility clinics in the Boston area, where Amy and Dan Robbins had lived at the time of the accident. There were three, but one was not in existence when the couple sought treatment.

THE FOLLOWING MORNING, Keller dialed Boston Fertility.

"Yeah, this is Dan Robbins. My wife and I were patients there several years ago, and we had a beautiful daughter—but I need to know the last date Amy was seen there. I'm having an issue with the insurance company."

"I can give a look," the woman said, the sound of keys clacking, "but if it was more than three years ago, the files will be archived. Last name again?"

"Robbins. Dan and Amy."

"Which doctor?"

Keller laughed. "Signs of age. Can't remember. Nice guy, though. Spent a lot of time with us going over all our options. Made all the difference in convincing us we were in the right place. A positive attitude—well, I'm rambling. Sorry. We were just so happy with the results."

"No, no, I understand. But all I have are dates of service. The file was purged a couple of years ago."

"Dates of service are all I need."

"Oh." The woman fell silent. But the keys were clacking rapidly.

"Problem?" Keller asked.

"There's a note on the file. About the fire. Is that what the issue is with the insurance company?"

Fire? "Yeah, afraid so. If you've got the date of the fire, that'd be helpful, too."

"All I see here is November 19. But I really need to transfer you to our office manager."

"Yes—November. I remember now. My parents were in town for Thanksgiving and—well, anyway, all I needed was the last date of service."

"You sure? Because I can see she's—"

"Nah, we're good. Gotta run to a meeting. Thanks for your help."

He cut off the call and sat back. He confirmed that they did have IVF, and it was done at Boston Fertility.

But how does a fire figure into this?

He did a quick search and found only a mention of the incident in the *Herald*—and a comment from Lt. Peter Gilbert, supervisor of Boston Fire's Fire Investigation Unit.

Keller dialed, then easily worked his way to the lieutenant.

"Now that's the second call I've gotten on this old fire," Gilbert said. "In the same week."

"Really," Keller said.

"Yeah, some insurance adjuster. Hang on a sec." He put the phone receiver down with a clunk, then the sounds of sliding and shuffling. And then he came back on the line. "Ada Robinson from Equity Insurance."

Keller jotted the name down. *Ada Robinson. Amy Robbins. Subterfuge.* "My questions aren't insurance related. I just want to know if there was anything unusual about the fire."

Gilbert snorted. "Dis is like déjà vu all over again, ya know? I had dis conversation with that adjuster. Yeah, there *was* something weird about it. Looked fishy, but I couldn't prove nothin'."

"What didn't look right?"

After explaining his observations, Keller knew that Gilbert was probably right.

"Hey Lieutenant, I appreciate your time. And candor. If I find anything out, I'll share it with you."

"Please don't. I mean, I'm curious now what the hell's going on. But if it really was arson, you know how much paperwork that's gonna make for me? On an old case?"

"Sorry, I won't—"

"I'm shittin' you. 'Course I wanna know what you find."

"Will do. I'll keep you plugged in."

Keller rose from his chair and stretched, then pulled out his phone and called someone he had not talked to in about five years.

"Bureau of Alcohol, Tobacco, Firearms, and Explosives. This is Regina. How may I direct your call?"

"Agent Richard Prati, please."

"One moment." She put Keller on hold, then returned: "Oh—Agent Prati is now at headquarters. He's, um, now an assistant special agent in charge. Would you like the number?"

"That'd be great."

Keller lifted his brow and took a deep breath. Did he really want to reinitiate contact with Prati—now an ASAC at the ATF? Doing what he did now...it put him closer to the crosshairs of federal law enforcement. Not the greatest of ideas he'd ever had.

But he found his fingers dialing, his subconscious already having made up his mind.

"And who may I say is calling?"

"Mickey K. A friend."

"Are you with an agency?"

"Tell him Detective Mickey Keller, LAPD." Prati would know who he was—but he had to get past the secretary. And having an agency title was the way to do that.

"Hold, please."

A moment later, Prati came on the line. "Well I'll be damned. Mickey K, how the hell have you been? What are you up to these days?"

"Kind of retired, poking around here and there."

"I can't see you retired, let alone 'kind of' retired. You gotta be doing things. Boredom is your enemy."

"You know me too well, Richard. What about you?"

Prati laughed. "You got an hour? If this job doesn't kill me, some perp with a gun or a bomb will. I was over at DEA for several years, handled some tough cases in counterterrorism and cartel stuff, but now I'm back with ATF."

"Never heard of that happening, switching agencies back and forth like that."

"Me either. For all I know, I could've been the first. They hired me away, made me an offer I couldn't refuse."

Yeah. I'm familiar with that scenario. "Similar thing happened with me, with my boss. Couldn't say no."

"Yeah, I wasn't buying the *kinda retired* bullshit. Can't bullshit a bullshitter."

"Doin' private stuff. Pay's way better."

"I get it. Friends of mine are starting to retire after they get their twenty, going private and collecting their pension."

"I didn't make twenty, but, well, it was time. Sometimes you just know. Better to leave on your own terms than make a mistake that costs a life."

"I admire that. So was it a good move? Sometimes the grass looks greener but when you get there, it's all weeds."

"Not what I was expecting, but like I said, pay's pretty damn good. Next time I'm in DC I'll give you a shout, we can grab a beer or dinner. Or whatever."

Prati laughed. "I'm gonna hold you to that."

"So I got a case I'm working and things don't look right. And it's in your wheelhouse. Maybe you can take a look and give me your opinion?"

"My opinion?"

"If it's kosher or not. If everything's cool, I'll look elsewhere."

"Gimme what you got."

"Fire at a fertility clinic in Boston. The Fire Investigation Unit supervisor had some questions, things didn't add up. But nothing he could put down on paper." He told Prati the rest of what he knew.

"I'll poke around, look over the file."

"How long?"

"If you're asking, it's time sensitive. I'll do my best."

"Do me a favor, text me on your mobile so I don't have to play games with your gatekeeper."

"Soon as we hang up."

He gave Prati his cell number. "Hey. Appreciate this. Dinner's on me when we get together."

Prati laughed. "Yes it is."

25

Giselle heard the front door chime. She hurried down the winding wood staircase and saw Christine Ellis setting her purse on the entryway cabinet.

"Anything?" she called down to Christine.

Christine jumped, but quickly recovered and squinted up at Giselle. "Anything what? What are you talking about?"

"Melissa. Any news?"

"We've got people working on it. It won't be long now."

"You know where she is? Have the police found her?"

Christine hung her keys on the rack and headed down the hall. "You don't need to worry about it. We're taking care of it."

Giselle reached the last step and spoke to Christine's back. "I *am* worried. I—I need to know that she's safe."

Christine wheeled on her. "You should've thought of that before you put her in the hands of a kidnapper."

Giselle took a step backward. "I—you're right, Dr. Ellis. I'm sorry, very sorry this happened. I don't know what to say."

"Make yourself useful. We've got some guests coming by at five for a meeting. Jennifer will need your help in the kitchen." She turned her back, indicating it was time for Giselle to leave.

Hours later, Giselle recognized a few of the people seated around the table. She was tempted to approach Angelo Lira, or even Dr. Ellis, to see if either of them had information on Melissa. From her point of view, it did not appear that Christine cared about whether or not Melissa was found. Perhaps that was harsh, as she was busy with the deal they had been working on, but Giselle believed that a good mother would be an emotional wreck worrying about her child. Conduct business? She did not think it possible. Still, Giselle was a young woman and Christine a seasoned adult, so perhaps with age and wisdom came the ability to compartmentalize.

When dinner drew to a close and the people retired to a private room for a confidential discussion, Giselle sensed that the time was less than ideal to broach the topic with either of them.

As Giselle helped clear the table, she decided she would walk over to the office tomorrow and try to grab some time with Dr. Ellis. As far as she could tell, he seemed to have a better relationship with Melissa, and a father's bond with his daughter was special—or at least it should be.

26

That evening, as Keller was working his keyboard, his cell phone rang. His brow rose as he glanced at the caller ID. "Richard."

"Got something for you," Prati said.

"It's late back in DC."

He yawned audibly. "Sorry. Yeah, it is. But you said it was important and once I saw what I was dealing with, I didn't want to wait until morning."

"I appreciate that. What'd you find?"

"I had one of my agents touch base with Lieutenant Gilbert at Boston Fire. He sent the file over and we did some preliminary analysis. And you were right. Doesn't add up."

"How so?"

"Fire was contained to a room that was used for storage. But it wasn't storage of patient embryos. It was storage of files and supplies."

"So whoever told the investigator it was 'storage' was being disingenuous."

"Possibly." Prati yawned again. "Could've been subterfuge, but that'd be conjecture at this point. Doesn't look good—which means it warrants further investigation. I've assigned it to a case agent in Boston. It's old, yeah, but it's a federal crime to commit insurance fraud, if that's what we're dealing with here. But who knows, there could be more to it. A smokescreen."

"And where there's smoke, there's fire."

"Leave the fire jokes to me, okay?"

"Right. I'm sure you guys have tons of 'em."

"I did some poking around myself and looks like the clinic's owner, John Hutchinson, doesn't have a record. No evidence of financial distress—but I only grabbed a quick look. My people will dig, go back several years. Follow the money, right?"

"Always a smart strategy," Keller said. "Hey, keep me posted on what you find?"

"I will—what I can. If this *is* something, I'm gonna be restricted in what I can share. You know the deal."

"Whatever you can give me, even if it's some innocuous suggestions of things you 'recommend' I check out..."

"Yeah, yeah, yeah. Gotta get to bed. Talk soon."

27

Giselle woke up early and went for a brisk walk around the lake to clear her head, try to cast off some of her guilt into the water, and do some yoga on the grass. It was a beautifully sunny day, with a gentle breeze and crisp air.

She wished her mood matched the weather. But whenever she passed an area where she and Melissa had spent time, she teared up and started to cry. If anything happened to that sweet little girl, Giselle knew she would never get over it.

How does someone go on from there?

She bought a coffee at Starbucks on Lakeshore Avenue, then walked over to the LifeScreen offices several blocks away.

Giselle took the elevator to the third floor, then stepped up to Dr. Ellis's office. She was about to knock when she heard a voice behind her.

"Can I help you?"

She turned to see Angelo Lira.

"Giselle," Lira said. "You need something?"

"Yes. I—I need to talk with Dr. Ellis."

Lira chuckled—but it was not a friendly laugh. "He's a very busy man." Lira took Giselle by the shoulders, turned her gently, and led her away from the door. "What can I help you with?"

She stopped and eyed Lira carefully. "It's—I want to talk to him. I *need* to talk to him. It's important."

Lira gestured with his head, getting her to walk again, away from Ellis's office. "Tomorrow might be better."

Giselle stopped again. "It can't wait."

Lira's eyes narrowed. "What's so important? Is it about Melissa?"

Her gaze darted around the hallway. "It's—yes."

"I'll relay the message. And if it's anything that'll help us find her, I'm the one you need to talk to anyway. I'm the liaison on the search."

She shifted her feet.

Lira glanced at his watch. "I've got a meeting in a couple of minutes. What's the problem? Remember something about the woman—Amy—that you'd like to share?"

"No, I'm...no. I don't remember anything. I just have to give him some...information."

"Go ahead. Just tell *me*."

"I'd rather not."

LIRA EXAMINED HER FACE. He grinned slightly, trying to appear nonthreatening. But his thoughts were moving in a different direction. This woman was now a liability. They had no idea what she was going to do—or say—and to whom she might say it.

"I'm glad you found me, actually," Lira said, feigning a disarming grin. "The Ellises asked me to get you a plane ticket back home."

"Home?"

"To Germany."

The young woman's face dropped faster than a steel hammer. "I—I do not want to go back to Germany. I want to stay. Here. And—and the Ellises still need me. When they find Melissa—"

Lira laughed. But it was devoid of humor, a fact he did not attempt to hide. "Do you really think they're going to trust you again with their daughter? You let her be taken—by a stranger."

"I—I am sorry. I did not..." Her voice trailed off and she seemed to shrink into herself.

"Go home and pack. I'll tell Dr. Ellis you came by and that you've gone home to gather your things. I'll have the ticket and confirmation number emailed to you. My driver will take you to the airport."

Giselle stared at him, disbelief etched into her face.

Lira checked his watch again. "Oh. What was it you wanted to tell us about Melissa?"

Her eyes darted left and right. "Just—just that Amy, the woman who took her, she cared about her. I don't think she would hurt her."

Lira studied her face. He did not think she was being truthful with him. There was something else she wanted to say. "We're way past that. We know a lot about her and what her intentions were. She's a troubled individual, a history of mental illness. Tried to kill herself. But the good news is that we've made a lot of headway in locating her."

Giselle's eyes widened. "You have?"

He patted her on the back. "Don't worry about Melissa. We've got it covered."

The woman should have looked relieved, but the hope immediately dropped from her expression. She was not buying what he was selling.

"Trust me, Giselle." He placed a hand on her left shoulder as he started walking again, guiding her toward the elevator. "We want the best for Melissa. And despite what I said about the Ellises being angry with you about what happened, they're relieved we're making progress in the investigation." He stopped by the polished stainless steel doors and pressed the down button.

"Now—go home and get ready. My driver will be at the house to pick you up three hours before departure."

28

Keller stood in the building's parking garage, behind the large pillar in a dark alcove—exactly where Lira told him to meet.

The click clack of Lira's dress shoes got louder as they approached Keller, five minutes late.

"I got detained," Lira said in a low voice. "The au pair is becoming a potential liability. I may need you to deal with her."

Keller, whose back was to the wall, glanced around over Lira's shoulder. There was no one nearby. "What kind of liability?"

"She feels guilty about the kidnapping. I don't want her to do something stupid if she gets too anxious."

"Stupid like...what?"

Lira shrugged. "Who knows? Talks to people. Walks into the *Tribune*. Or goes to the police."

"She thinks the cops are already involved. Want Investigator Carr to pay her another visit, tell her we've made progress and that we're negotiating her release?"

Lira considered that a moment. "I want you focused on finding Melissa. I'm sending Giselle home to Germany in a few hours. If she doesn't get in the car with my driver or refuses to get on the plane, yeah. Go see her. But if she doesn't bite, you're gonna have to make her disappear for a couple weeks, until after the

IPO launches."

Keller absorbed that without comment. That was certainly possible—but not easy to pull off. He would need to bring Tait into it and have another operative dispatched to drug her and transport her to a black site. They could even sedate her and fly her back to Germany on a private charter. If it became necessary, they could keep her drugged and at a secure location for a month. He would have to do some research on Giselle, but if the Ellises were onboard with the plan, and no one back home would miss talking to her, they could pull it off. When she was finally released, she would be so afraid of the people who abducted her, she would keep her mouth shut.

Keller glanced around, ever vigilant. "Keep me informed."

"Will do." Lira shoved his hands into his wool overcoat pockets. "What did you want to talk about?"

"Trying to get a complete picture of who this Amy Robbins woman is and why she'd want to kidnap a young girl."

"Why's that important?"

"Get to know the person you're looking for, what her motives are, you can get a line on where she is, or may be headed. I've done some poking around and it seems that Robbins's husband and daughter were killed several years ago in a car accident."

"Okay."

"And she and her husband needed help to get pregnant. They went through IVF at a Boston fertility clinic. That clinic had a fire a few years ago and—"

"Let me stop you right there, Mickey. I'm not paying you to ask questions. I'm not paying you to play detective. I *am* paying you for one thing right now. Get the girl back. Help me manage this situation without the cops or media getting involved. Pretty fuckin' clear. You going to do that? Or do I have to call Tait and tell him this isn't working out?"

"Nothing's changed, Angelo. I just wanted to let you know what I'd found in case it mattered to you. I know you've got a business deal in place and, well, things may not be kosher. This could cause some problems, so I wanted you to have a heads-up."

Lira yanked on his tie and opened the top button of his dress shirt. "Okay. Fine. I appreciate the tip. Meantime, find the girl. Let me worry about the details."

"Got it. Keep you posted."

Keller waited a couple of minutes after Lira left, then walked out of the garage and headed to his car, which he had parked on the street. It gave him some time to think.

He could not pass up the payday. That was clear. But despite his expectations when he took this case, he again found himself on the wrong side of the tracks, propping up the bad guy and contributing nothing to society.

How much longer he could do this, he was not sure.

29

Giselle walked out of the LifeScreen offices, headed home as Lira had instructed her to do. But it was no longer *home.* That word had taken on a different meaning the past couple of years. The Bay Area, the Ellis house, was her safe place, her sanctuary, where she felt like an adult. She was able to shed the bad memories of her childhood, of a failed family life.

And now? She was headed to the airport in a few hours to fly across the world to a place she did not want to be. Tears began forming in the corners of her eyes. She felt lost. Afraid.

Giselle turned left and headed toward the lake. She crossed the street and stood on Lakeshore in front of a tailor shop that featured antique clothing irons in the window. She remembered one from her childhood—her grandmother's sat on a cabinet in a hallway in their house.

But as she stepped closer for a look, she saw her reflection in the glass: tears streaking her face, bloodshot eyes. She took a deep, uneven breath. Perhaps returning to Germany would give her an opportunity to exorcise her demons, help her decide what to do next with her life.

As she swiped away the tears, behind her, in the reflection, she saw a little girl walk by with her father. Giselle turned and watched them pass. For the next few hours, she was still in the

United States. In California. She needed to do whatever she could to help find Melissa. Knowing she did everything possible might make the long trip, and transition, easier.

And if they found Melissa, the Ellises would need her, just as they needed her before Melissa was taken. Whether or not they would still trust Giselle was a legitimate question. But it was not one she could answer—nor would it even be asked—if Melissa was not found.

Giselle started walking, thinking about what she could do. With no resources, no authority, no car, and no experience in tracking down missing children, she needed help.

The swing of the Grand Lake Bakery door jarred the bell and it jingled and clanked as it rattled against the glass. Other than knowing this was where Amy worked, she hoped that the people there might have some ideas where she went. However, she had to think that the detective who spoke to her had already talked with Amy's friends and fellow employees. Still, she didn't know where else to start.

The sweet smell of baking pastries caught her off guard—and triggered a rumble of hunger in her stomach. The older woman—Ellen, if she recalled correctly—was behind the counter ringing up a customer.

"Can I help you?"

Giselle hesitated. "My name is Giselle. Amy's—Amy's friend. I was here last—"

"Yeah, I thought you looked familiar," Ellen said. "Amy's not here. We don't—"

"I know. That is why I am here. Um..." She looked around at the two customers who had walked in behind her.

"You want to talk in private?" Ellen pulled open a swinging half-door beside the cash register and motioned Giselle to follow. "Vicky, can you take the front counter?"

They sat down in Ellen's small office.

Giselle glanced around, not knowing where to begin.

"You're here about Amy," Ellen finally said.

"Yes. I, um, they are sending me back to Germany and I do

not want to go."

"Who's sending you back?"

"The Ellises."

Ellen shook her head. "I'm sorry, I have no idea what you're talking about."

"If I can find Melissa, maybe they will let me stay here."

"Who's Melissa?"

"The little girl, that's who Amy kidnapped."

Ellen swallowed noticeably. "Kidnapped?"

"I thought you knew."

"Look," Ellen said, leaning back in her chair. "Amy's just an employee. All I know is that she didn't return to work after lunch. Then a detective came around asking questions about her."

"A man about six feet, short dark hair? No beard or mustache. Forty years old, maybe? Middle—how do you say it?"

"Middle-aged."

Giselle nodded animatedly. "Yes. Athletic."

"That describes a lot of men, but yeah, that's what he looked like."

"Wait, he also had a small scar in his left eyebrow."

"I didn't notice that," Ellen said.

"And he said his name was Carr."

Ellen chuckled. "That's more than I got."

Giselle cast her gaze to the floor, thinking.

"There's something bothering you. About Detective Carr?"

Giselle sighed. "I am, um...I do not think things make sense."

"Because?"

"They told me they did not want to call the police, then there is a detective asking me questions. And he gave me a blank card with his phone number. No name. Nothing about the police department where he works."

Ellen looked at her, in thought.

"Detectives have identification. Right? And business cards with their photo on it. In Germany they do."

"I—um..." Ellen looked up at the ceiling. "I only dealt with the police once, in San Jose. The officer gave me his card in case

I remembered something." Ellen absentmindedly shook her head.

"Why would Amy take Melissa? She was so nice. I do not think she would hurt a child. Do you?"

"Wait a minute. Is Melissa the girl you brought here the other day?"

Giselle nodded.

"Oh my god. Bobby!" Ellen cupped her mouth, then stood up. She led the way into the production area, where Bobby was moving quickly, hands busy with automated mixing bowls and trays. "Bobby." Ellen spoke louder, over the din of the machinery.

He looked up, saw Ellen and Giselle, and made his way over. They were not properly attired, so they could not enter the food prep room. He slid his mask down to his chin and nodded at Giselle. "You were here with Amy and that little girl making cupcakes."

"That's what I wanted to ask you about," Ellen said. "Amy apparently abducted that girl and took off."

Bobby's jaw dropped open. His gaze shifted from Ellen to Giselle. "That doesn't make any sense. I worked alongside Amy for months. She'd never do something like that."

"Maybe," Ellen said.

Bobby contorted his face. "What's that mean?"

"Something happened to her several years ago. Her husband and daughter were killed in a car accident. Amy survived. She hasn't gotten over it."

"Holy shit," Bobby said. "She never said anything to me about that."

"Me either," Giselle said. "She told me she did not have any kids."

"She doesn't, not anymore." Ellen massaged her temples. "And Melissa—the girl she abducted—is around the same age as her daughter was when she was killed, if I'm remembering right."

Bobby repositioned his hairnet. "When'd she tell you about this?"

"Last week. She used to be a partner in a law firm. Lost everything after the accident."

He shook his head. "I had no idea."

"My point exactly," Ellen said. "We think we know someone, but do we really?"

Bobby frowned and looked away. Giselle got the feeling this had meaning to them beyond the current situation with Melissa.

"You know," Bobby said, "there was something. A week or so ago, Amy seemed to be in a totally different mood."

"What do you mean?" Ellen asked.

Bobby wiped his hands on his apron. "She was happy. Humming a song. That doesn't sound like a big deal, but for Amy, I don't know, she's been friendly and all, but I never saw her, well, happy. Lighthearted, having fun. Laughing. I even kidded her. I thought she'd met someone, a guy. She said she didn't. I thought she was bullshitting me. Sounds like she met someone all right—Melissa."

Ellen pulled out her cell phone.

"What are you doing?"

"A detective came by asking questions. I'm calling the police, checking some things out." Ellen poked at the screen and put the handset to her ear. "How old is Melissa?"

"Four," Giselle said. "No, wait. She just turned five."

"Yes," Ellen said, shifting back to the call. "Can I speak with Detective Carr?" Her gaze roamed the ceiling a few seconds—then she drew her chin back. "Giselle, you sure that was his name?"

Giselle nodded. "I remember thinking it was easy to remember because, well, it is like a car."

Ellen turned her attention back to the phone. "That's what he said." She listened a moment. "It's about a missing child case. She just went missing a—" Ellen nodded, rolled her eyes. "*Investigator.* Not detective. Got it." To Giselle: "Did he say he was with the Special Victims Section?"

"No, nothing like that."

"No," Ellen said, "he didn't...Okay. Kidnap suspect is Amy Robbins and the girl's name is Melissa—" She motioned to Giselle.

"Melissa Ellis."

Ellen repeated it. "Yeah, I can hold." She put a hand over

the microphone. "Something's not right. They don't have any record of Carr. And in a—" To the call: "Yeah...No, no, that's okay. Thanks."

"What did they say?" Bobby asked.

"In the department that handles child abductions, they're officers or investigators, not detectives. Either way, they don't have a new case involving a missing five-year-old child."

The machine droning in the background stopped. Bobby checked over his shoulder. "So what the hell's going on?"

Giselle watched both Ellen's and Bobby's reactions.

"Yeah," Ellen said. "Good question."

30

Keller went to the lake and stood at the water's edge for ten minutes, sorting out his thoughts. As he watched a western gull glide through the air looking to snatch a fish from a pelican's mouth, he realized he was not unlike that predator: he had a job to do. And a vital part of that job was to put his personal feelings aside and carry out the task with efficiency and professionalism.

His particular fish was Melissa Ellis.

He went back to his room and opened the USB flash drive on a virtual machine he set up on his Surface tablet. While the app installed the cloned copy of Robbins's computer, Keller spent some time doing traditional investigative work, knowing there was a low chance of success because Amy Robbins was not the typical missing person or kidnapper. She had gone through a tragedy that caused her to withdraw from just about everything. She had no friends he could find. She had no Facebook, Twitter, or Instagram accounts where he could grab a location...or even photos from which he could glean information on places she had recently, or frequently, visited.

When he had finished recreating her hard drive, he checked her email messages to see if there were any of significance. Amy

Robbins was perhaps the only individual who had fewer than fifty sent entries in the past year. It seemed unfathomable in the twenty-first century. As he had figured, she had no presence on social media and almost no current photos—another perplexing finding in today's environment, where just about everyone had a quality camera in his or her pocket at all times. There was one exception, however: she had a few pictures and a video of Melissa Ellis and several old ones of her daughter, Lindy, and her husband Dan. No documents of any significance: a few recipes and a copy of her job application for the bakery.

He did find a Word document containing notes from a conversation she had with Boston Fertility and fire marshal Gilbert. It was the same information he had learned on his calls.

Keller then turned to Private Investigation 101 and tapped the usual databases at his disposal, including TracersInfo, Accurint, and TLOxp, which processed trillions of records at sub-second speeds.

Not surprisingly, he got very few hits—and those he did get spit back material he, again, had already procured.

Finally, he called the Tait cyber technician and set things up. Having gone cold on Robbins's trail—where she could now be anywhere within a twelve-hour-plus radius—he was going to need some help. This was not a legal case, so the data he was looking for would not be used in a court of law. That gave him tremendous latitude...including resorting to pretexting—illegally impersonating someone else to obtain protected information—as he had done with his call to Boston Fertility.

An hour later, his satellite phone rang. As he pulled it out and moved to the window, he hoped it was a lead on Robbins's whereabouts.

"Yeah."

"It's Bill. Give me a SITREP."

He was not keen on having to give his boss an update until he had something productive to report.

Keller cringed as he spoke: "Almost had her at her apartment, but she got away."

"Got away? How the fuck does that happen?"

"Sometimes shit happens."

"Mickey." Tait hesitated as if shaking his head in disappointment. "I'm not sure that's an acceptable response. Did she see you?"

"No," he said without hesitation. He hated lying to his friend. "I'm not compromised."

"You want to tell me what happened?"

No. Keller definitely did not want to relate the sequence of events. "Bottom line, I had her. She came back to her place but when I approached the apartment her neighbor came out and I had to wait—"

"All right, all right. Shit happens. I know. I get it. But Lira's very concerned."

"Yeah, I spoke with him. He worries a lot."

Tait snorted. "Mickey, this is a two-billion-dollar deal for him, if not more. He's got a hundred million, at least, invested in this company. I were him, I'd be a fucking basket case. All you gotta do is bring that girl home safely."

"I get it."

"Compared to what you've done these past several years, not to mention what we had to do in Iraq, it's pretty simple shit. You can do this in your sleep."

"I know."

"Don't forget we've got five mil riding on making sure the IPO comes off without a hitch. So concerned? Lira *should* be concerned. And so should you, buddy. And properly motivated."

"I am, Bill. I am."

"You'd better be."

Keller opened his mouth to speak but Tait had already hung up.

31

Amy took Melissa to Avila Beach in San Luis Obispo County, a three-and-a-half-hour drive from Lake Merritt.

Amy had vacationed in the Napa Valley a year after getting married when she and Dan were having difficulty becoming pregnant—and getting on each other's nerves as a result. They thought a relaxing wine country trip would give them a chance to escape the stress and reenergize their efforts.

After spending four days in Napa, they drove down the coast and stopped at Paso Robles, a burgeoning wine-growing region all its own, and then hit some of the nearby cities. One was SLO, or San Luis Obispo, a charming college town with art galleries, ethnic restaurants, bookstores, coffee shops, and local music venues. They stayed at the Apple Farm Inn, a Victorian-style boutique hotel that was still there, looking much the same, when Amy and Melissa drove by it on the way to a market to pick up food for lunch.

Very few people knew of their trip, let alone remembered it now, with the obvious exception of Loren and Zach—who had known but might not recall it. At the time, they were living in New York—Loren's first Bureau assignment.

Amy and Melissa left the downtown area and drove to the

beach, where they played with the dozens of dogs that ran toward the water when the waves went out—and away from it when they rolled in. A golden retriever decided to buck the pattern and went swimming, much to his owner's consternation. Melissa found it all too amusing.

Sometime past noon, they picnicked on the sand farther back from the ocean's reach.

It was sunny and the weather was a pleasant sixty degrees—much more palatable than a typical Massachusetts winter.

Before leaving her apartment, Amy took all the cash she had there, enough to cover two days in the motel she had found down the block from the Apple Farm, not far from the Cal Poly university campus. It was reasonably priced and clean. Basic stuff—a couple of beds, a bathroom, a TV.

Melissa had kept her busy since they left, except for a nap in the car while they drove. It gave Amy some time to think, but it only reinforced her sense that she had a mental block that prevented her from properly evaluating the situation. She was not thinking clearly—an ongoing problem during her years of depression. This was different, though. Despite the mental fog, she felt...alive. Energized. As if her life had been on pause and she finally found, and pressed, the PLAY button.

She had purpose again.

But what was that purpose? *That* was where her mind refused to go.

Melissa had asked about Giselle a couple of times, but not her parents. Despite the abuse, Amy figured that a young girl would want to go home. Or at least ask about it. She would yearn for familiar surroundings rather than living on the road, without structure, filled with uncertainty.

Melissa clearly felt comfortable around Amy. Safe. Amy was keeping her entertained, doing fun things, and making it a memorable time.

Was she making it memorable for Melissa or for herself?

They gathered their picnic trash and headed back to the car. Amy used the last ten dollars she had to put a few gallons of gas in the tank, then drove back to the motel.

Upon arriving, she reserved the next two nights with her credit card. There was risk in doing that, but she asked if the front desk attendant could refrain from charging the room cost until she checked out. The man said he could but that he would need to at least verify her card, which registered a minimal charge of around a dollar that would then be immediately credited back.

"Any way around that?" Amy asked, her eyes pleading for consideration.

"Sorry." He was no older than twenty, she figured, and was quoting his manager's payment rules. "I'm saving for grad school. Need the job. Gotta follow procedure."

Amy nodded resignation. However, she was fairly certain the police were not on the case. She would have seen amber alerts on the freeway signs and it would've been all over the news. She saw nothing on TV—or in the local papers.

"What about an ATM?"

"Um..." He glanced up at the ceiling. "Couple blocks away, at the gas station. Might be one closer, don't know."

"That's fine. Walking is good for us."

"I'm tired," Melissa whined.

"Okay, honey. We'll drive over."

As Amy stood at the ATM plugging in her PIN, she wondered if this was any less risky than using a credit card. Probably not. But she would only have to do it once because she could withdraw a couple hundred dollars. That was nearly all she had left, anyway, since she was due to be paid next week and she was living paycheck to paycheck.

Amy grabbed at the bills rolling out of the machine's mouth, thinking about what she might have set in motion. While she did not know who had burst into her apartment the other night, she figured he was a private investigator working for the Ellises. Unless the laws had changed in the past few years, she did not think PIs had the ability to trace her electronic transactions—at least, not legally. Regardless, she had no choice.

But how long could she keep this up? And, again, to what end?

She kicked at a rock in the parking lot, frustrated at her inability to reason this through.

32

Having exhausted all known avenues for locating Robbins and the girl, Keller began thinking outside the box when his sat phone rang.

"This is Martinez in cyber. Got a twenty for you. Sending it through now."

Keller plugged the address into Google Maps and zoomed to the location, then switched to Street View.

"ATM," Martinez said. "Positive ID."

"I see it."

The line went dead.

Keller was looking at a town in central California, between three and four hours south of Oakland. He reconnoitered virtually, orienting himself. It was a town he had never visited, so before he started driving he wanted an idea of what he was getting himself into.

Robbins had withdrawn a hundred and eighty dollars. There had been no other known uses of her debit or credit cards, so he reasoned the cash was needed for gas, food, and a place to sleep. The odd amount suggested it was all the money she had left.

He switched to satellite view and saw what he was looking for: two motels in close proximity to the ATM. He jotted down the information and a few minutes later he was tossing his tablet onto the passenger seat of his town car. He merged onto the 580 freeway, then dialed a number on his mobile.

A woman answered the phone and Keller chuckled. "I feel like a dope making a call like this, but my wife and daughter might've checked in recently. I mean, she told me where they were staying, but...well..." he laughed again... "guess my wife's right. I don't listen so good sometimes. Too busy with the football game, but...sorry, I'm rambling here. I know it's either your place or the Sands. You got them there?"

"Name?"

"Amy Robbins. Daughter's Melissa. Cutest little thing, five years old with the prettiest blonde—sorry, rambling again."

"I don't have anyone by that name registered."

Maybe she didn't use her real name. I might've really freaked her out. He shook his head. *Of course I freaked her out. I held a gun to her head.*

"Sorry," the woman said.

"You don't remember seeing them around though? In the office or—"

"I haven't, sorry."

Keller tried the other number, hoping he had guessed correctly.

"Sands, this is Ted."

Keller went through the same spiel with Ted.

"Yeah, yeah. I've seen them. But I...I don't think she...you said the name's Robbins?"

"Well, she's a little strange. Sometimes she uses her maiden name when she travels. Security thing. We had an identity theft ten years ago and she's worried about her credit." That did not make sense, but the idea was to keep talking until the person stopped listening. Once the guy got enough details he could relate to, he often did not continue the effort to reason it out. Unless it violated company policy, he would accept what you were telling him and comply with your request.

"That's okay," Ted said. "Doesn't matter what name she used. I've seen them."

"Good. It's Amy's birthday and I want to surprise them. I was supposed to be out of town on business, but the trip got cancelled and I figured, what the hell, it's only three hours. I should make it a birthday she'll never forget. Show up unannounced."

"They're in 124. We've got some balloons in the back room. You want, I can hang them on her door."

"No—no. I don't want to do anything that tips her off. I'm on my way. It's her thirty-fifth and I bought her a ring."

"That's gonna be such a surprise."

Keller laughed heartily. "Exactly."

"No worries, Mr. Robbins. Your secret's safe with me." Ted chuckled. "Freshman year, I flew home to Texas and surprised my mom. She had no idea I was coming. It was awesome. Anyway, wish I could see Ms. Robbins's face. She's gonna be shocked."

Keller grinned as he pressed the accelerator a little harder. "You have no idea, Ted."

33

Ellen and Giselle got in the car and drove along Bellevue Avenue, a tree-lined street that fronted the northern side of the lake.

Giselle pointed to Ellen's left. "Melissa and I eat lunch every day over there."

A playground with swings and a climbing structure was a few yards farther along a footpath that snaked along the water's edge.

"Lovely setting for lunch."

"I hope we find her," Giselle said.

"*We* won't. But I'm hoping the FBI will."

"FBI?"

"I watch a lot of true crime shows on TV. The FBI's in charge of finding missing or kidnapped children—if what I've seen on television is right. If not, I'm sure they'll tell us. I looked up their office before we left. It's nearby. Right off Webster."

Giselle shook her head. "I still can't believe Amy would do this."

Ellen looked over at her. "You're young. When you've lived a few more decades, you'll start to believe anything can happen."

They drove another minute in quiet. When they turned onto 21st Street, Giselle said, "I'm worried about Melissa."

"I'm obviously not a psychiatrist, but like you said, I don't think Amy's going to hurt her. She probably sees her own daughter and in some twisted way believes Melissa's her dead child. There's some psychological term for it."

"I cannot imagine what Amy went through. If she thinks Melissa is hers, she will take good care of her. She would not hurt her own daughter. Right?"

"Not purposely." Ellen was quiet for a moment, then said, "But Amy's not acting rationally. She could unintentionally put Melissa—and herself—in bad situations."

Giselle absorbed that.

"Even if she's safe, I'm sure this is very upsetting for a five-year-old. To be separated from her parents." Ellen found a parking spot on Webster in front of the building that housed the FBI office—tough to do during the work week. "Melissa's probably having a very hard time."

"Maybe."

Ellen glanced at her. "What do you mean?"

"She does not have much of a connection to either of them. Her father, maybe, but she hardly sees him. And Christine, her mother, I think she may be abusing her. I *know* she's abusing her."

Ellen shoved the gearshift into PARK. "Tell me."

Giselle related what she had described to the fake detective.

Ellen's face turned hard. "Did Amy know about this?"

Giselle bit her lip. "Yes. Some way—somehow, she knew. She said I should tell the police. But I never saw Christine hit her so what would the police do? And then nothing would happen and I would lose my job. Instead I lost Melissa *and* my job."

"We should tell the FBI. I don't know if they handle child abuse, but they need to know everything."

They entered through the Webster Street doors then walked beneath a humongous blue, red, and yellow abstract mural that spanned the width of the lobby and continued a hundred feet to the large security desk. Ellen explained why they were there and the guard told them to go up to the fourth floor.

The Bureau shared the twenty-story building with City National Bank, the Small Business Development Center, Pandora

Media, AT&T, and a number of other tenants.

Ellen and Giselle exited the elevator and were met with a blue and white FBI logo hanging on the wall, another for the FBI National Academy, and an oversize three-dimensional gold mockup of the Bureau badge. They turned right and saw a large sign that read, "OAKLAND FBI RESIDENT AGENCY." Walking up to the metal door, they were met with a wall-mounted camera and keypad. Ellen pushed a large red button and a buzzer sounded.

They entered a modestly sized rectangular room. To the left was a magnetometer, which they walked through after emptying their pockets into a plastic bin and stepped up to the bulletproof glass.

"We need to report a kidnapped girl," Ellen said.

The woman in the office leaned closer to the pass-through at the bottom of the window. "Let me have your photo IDs."

They slid their cards through and she wrote their names down on a steno pad. "I'll have an agent with you in a moment."

Seconds later, a man in his mid-thirties walked through a door on the far side sporting a large '70s-sized afro. "Special Agent Jimmy Hill. Crimes Against Children Squad. You're here to report a missing child?"

"Kidnapped," Ellen said. "She's not missing."

"Follow me." He walked across the room, directly opposite the security window, and tapped his key card against the lock. He opened the door, revealing a modest eight-foot by seven-foot room with a metal desk, three chairs, a wall-mounted stainless-steel handcuff bar, and a conspicuous surveillance camera on the ceiling.

They took seats opposite Hill, who sported a broad nose and assorted espresso colored moles on his milk chocolate complexion.

He pulled over a yellow pad and clicked his pen. "So tell me about this girl. How do you know her?"

"I'm her au pair. The Ellises—her parents—told me they were going to handle the kidnapping themselves, but then a detective came to ask me questions. I mean an investigator."

"Wait—back up a second. The parents *did*, or did not, report her abduction?"

"I'm pretty sure they did not. Their business partner said, 'no police.' He said they would take care of it. But then a police officer came to talk with me."

"That was a hoax," Ellen said. "I don't think he was really a cop. He came to talk to me, too."

Hill cocked his head. "And you are?"

"I own Golden State Bakery."

"Oh," Hill said. "My wife loves your walnut cranberry bread."

"Yeah, well, it may've been made by the woman who kidnapped Melissa."

Hill shook his head. "So you're here because one of your employees is the person you think abducted this girl? Melissa?"

"Yes. I mean, we know it was her. Giselle saw it happen."

Hill swung his gaze back to Giselle. "Start from the beginning."

Giselle took a deep breath and recounted the events.

Hill sat back in his chair, rocked a moment, then nodded. "Okay. First thing I'm gonna do is call Oakland PD and see if I can get to the bottom of this. Maybe you misheard the name. He had an Oakland Police badge?"

Ellen and Giselle shared a look.

"He had a badge," Ellen said. "All I can tell you. Looked real. I don't know what an Oakland badge looks like."

Hill asked them more questions—including a description of the man purporting to be Detective Carr—and took meticulous notes. He set his pen down and glanced at his pad, paging through the information. "I'm gonna give Oakland PD a call. If they're not involved, they should be. We work with the locals as a rule. If they want us to take the lead, we will. Sometimes they want to work it. Either way, we'll be involved. Give me a few minutes."

"Wait," Ellen said. "What are we dealing with here? I mean, Amy doesn't seem to want to harm the girl. She's just a little psychologically unbalanced. Because of what happened to her family."

"At this point we can't really say what she's thinking. Or how healthy her thinking is, for that matter. She may be delusional, thinking that Melissa is her daughter. How dangerous is that? I don't know. And at this point, even a psychologist couldn't tell us because he hasn't examined her, or even talked with her. Anything we think may be wrong."

Ellen placed a hand over Giselle's. Giselle wiped tears from the corners of her eyes.

"What we do know," Hill said, "is that this appears to be what we call a non-family child abduction. Term is self-explanatory. Some agencies may narrow this down more to an 'acquaintance kidnapping' because Robbins obviously knew Melissa—not well, but well enough to identify her as a target. She spent time with Melissa." He paused. "This situation is a little unusual because her parents aren't the ones reporting the crimes. We're going to be bringing them into this. Interviewing them."

"They never met Amy," Giselle said.

"That we *know*." Hill made eye contact with each of them. "There could be more to this than either of you realize. Not saying there is. But what appears to be true on the surface could run much deeper. Things could be going on behind the scenes that you don't know about. Relationships between each of the people involved have to be looked at." He turned to Giselle. "And that includes you."

Giselle recoiled a bit. "I've told you everything."

Hill nodded thoughtfully. "No offense, but an hour ago I didn't know you. I still don't know you. So I can't take your version of events as the truth until I verify it for myself. Follow?"

Giselle nodded.

"Good. That's a tough concept for some people. They think we're being hard asses. We're not. We're just doing our jobs. Looking at everything objectively so we don't get led down the wrong path. You could be telling us the truth, but her father might not be—in which case we wouldn't know, unless we checked it out."

"I understand."

"One other thing. Until we get things squared away, you'll

need to stay in the area. Accessible to us."

"The Ellises are sending me back to Germany tonight. I think they are angry at me for letting this happen. I do not blame them."

Hill lifted his brow. "Regardless of how the Ellises feel, I'm going to have to ask you not to leave the country. At least not until we've got a handle on what's really going on."

"I do not want to go back to Germany."

Hill pushed away from the desk. "Time is of the essence, so sit tight for a bit and I'm gonna call Oakland PD."

Hill returned six minutes later. He sat and laid one hand over the other on the table. "You were right. The police have no record. No officer took a report and no investigator was assigned. The man you spoke with was an imposter. Why, we don't know—yet. But with the descriptions you've given us, we've put out a BOLO notification for both Melissa and the man who interviewed you."

"BOLO?"

"Stands for Be On the Lookout. Exactly what it sounds like. Most likely scenario is he's a private investigator hired by the Ellises. There are a number of reasons why they wouldn't call the police. So let's not jump to any conclusions. And I'd appreciate if you didn't talk to the media or post this anywhere on social media. We need to control the release of information to things we *want* circulated. Certain details we'll withhold to identify the offender when we catch her." He glanced at both of them. "Can we count on your cooperation with that?"

Giselle and Melissa nodded.

"Those photos you gave me from your iPhone are extremely helpful, Giselle. That alone may be the single most important tool we have in this search. That and bringing this to our attention. Just remember that sometimes bad things happen. Blaming yourself won't help us and it won't help Melissa."

Giselle looked down at her lap.

"I want you both to stay positive," Hill said. "Out of every 10,000 missing children reported to the local police, 9,999 are found alive."

"Those are incredible odds," Ellen said.

"We'll have law enforcement officers across the state looking for her very shortly." Hill handed them each a card, embossed with a gold FBI shield and emblazoned, SAN FRANCISCO DIVISION.

"Is there anything we should do?" Giselle asked.

"Go home. We'll contact you if we need more information."

"But the Ellises bought me a ticket to Germany. I'm supposed to leave tonight."

"Well," Hill said, "you can tell them that until we get this sorted out, you're not going anywhere."

Ellen gave Giselle's hand a squeeze. "You can stay at my place."

Giselle bit her bottom lip. "Thank you so much."

"Very good." Hill shook their hands. "You two think of anything else, call me."

34

oments after Keller spoke with Ted, the motel clerk, Martinez at Tait Protection called to tell Keller that he picked up a temporary credit card authorization at the Sands. Keller chuckled to himself and told him he had already figured that out.

Keller exited Freeway 101, marveling at the beauty of the region's mountains and green rolling hills. He had passed the Paso Robles wine country twenty minutes back. Had this been a vacation, he would have loved to stop and spend the afternoon. Or two.

He knew of the area because of the fruity Zinfandels, full-bodied Cabernets, and Bordeaux-style blends he had consumed over the years. But other than driving past central California en route to San Francisco from Los Angeles along the inland Interstate 5, Keller had never visited the Golden State's heartland. While this lack of familiarity would normally put him at a disadvantage, the most important thing was getting near Amy Robbins and the girl. He would figure it out from there.

He passed the parking lot of the Sands Motel in San Luis Obispo, a town known for the highly regarded Cal Poly, the California Polytechnic State University that graduated top engineering, agriculture, and animal science students.

He drove a half-mile circumference around the Sands property, getting a feel for the area, including routes of ingress and egress.

He pulled into the lot and found a parking spot a dozen yards from Robbins's room. The place was an older structure, well maintained but tired. Wrought iron staircases led to a second story. Small planters here and there softened the hardscape.

Fortunately Robbins was on the first floor. But the main entrance to the grounds was narrow and fixed on both sides by buildings. There was a secondary exit around back but getting there was convoluted and equally confining. Bottom line, it was a bad place to get trapped.

After checking that the parking lot was clear, he pulled an attaché out of his trunk and chose a fake mustache and goatee, Dodgers baseball cap, and a pair of black-rimmed glasses. Though not a foolproof disguise, it should prove sufficient for a person unaccustomed to the tradecraft of playing fugitive. Robbins probably figured that putting three hundred miles between herself and her pursuer was a safe buffer.

Keller did a pass of 124, pausing to look through the white window curtains. They were room darkeners, but no lights were visible below the bottoms of the drapes. The TV was off and a second with his ear to the glass told him no one was talking. The lock used electronic key card access. While that was not insurmountable by itself, the location was in clear view of everyone in the parking lot. Breaking in was a poor option.

He took a circuitous route and returned to his car, where he spent the next twenty minutes studying maps of the area on his Surface, trying to get a better picture in his mind of the town. A short time later, with the suggestion of dusk on the horizon, Robbins's Subaru rolled into the lot.

As she and the girl parked, Keller sat up and partially covered his face with his left hand, not taking a chance that the tinted windows and/or disguise provided insufficient. While Robbins had only seen him once—and in a moment of extreme fear, at that—he did not want to give her any unintended advantage.

After the door to their room closed, a few other vehicles pulled onto the property. He waited for an opening to act, but before anything presented itself, Robbins and the girl left and got back in their car. He started his vehicle—and they started theirs.

They were on the move. And so was he.

35

Melissa laughed.

"What's so funny?" Amy asked, looking in the rearview mirror.

"The leopard joke."

Amy smiled. "I like that one, too."

"Can you tell me again?"

"You sure? Last time you couldn't stop laughing for five minutes."

"I'm sure."

"Okay. Why couldn't the leopard play hide and seek?" She glanced over her shoulder at Melissa. She saw anticipation and joy.

"Why?" she asked, already grinning.

"Because he was always spotted."

Melissa cackled—as did Amy, until tears flooded her eyes and she had difficulty driving.

"You know, Missy, it's just not that funny."

"Yes it is," Melissa said. "It *is*." She laughed again.

"Okay, okay..."

Amy found a parking spot and turned off the engine.

"Where are we going?"

"I already told you, silly. We're gonna do some shopping at the farmers market."

"Are we going to buy a farmer?"

Amy turned to look at her. "That's funny."

"I made a joke."

Amy nodded admiration. "That wasn't bad."

"It can't be bad if it's funny."

Amy pulled the door open and helped Melissa out. "Actually, it can be both bad *and* funny."

"It can?"

"Humor is a complicated thing sometimes."

Melissa seemed to accept that—or was trying to understand how something that's funny could be anything more than that.

They crossed to Higuera Street, where the farmers market was located. People milled about, parents toting their children and vendors selling their wares along the curbs under blue and white tented canopies. Fresh, organic vegetables and fruits were piled in boxes exuding a spectrum of colors from luscious burgundies and deep greens to summer yellows and earthy browns. Music played from down the street. Teens rode bikes and adults pushed strollers.

"What do you feel like eating?"

Melissa looked at the pile of fresh-picked radishes as she walked by. "I dunno."

"Let's look around. We'll find something yummy."

KELLER PARKED AND watched as Robbins and Melissa got out of their car. He was surprised Robbins had chosen this location, as a vacant police vehicle sat at the curb two car lengths in front of her Subaru. Most likely, she had not seen it.

His preference was to wait until they returned, and then take the girl. But the proximity of the cruiser greatly increased the risk.

Keller moved on to plan two: he followed them on foot at a discreet distance, attempting to blend in with the people drifting from vendor to vendor.

Dusk moved on as night arrived in the eastern sky. While there was still a hint of cobalt blue brightness in the west, and although the streets were fairly well lit, it still presented a better environment for doing a snatch and grab than during the day, as there were a substantial number of mature oaks obscuring the reach of the streetlights. Along with the vendor canopies, blind spots were present on each block.

Keller tailed them as they purchased some fruit and a couple slices of pizza from one of the area restaurants that had a portable oven set up under its tent.

Robbins and the girl passed someone dressed as a giant brown bear with an orange scarf and a permanently gaping mouth emulating a smile. Melissa pointed at it and the "animal" interacted with her, animatedly touching the girl's nose and telling her how cute she was.

Keller passed a few uniformed baseball players at a booth teaching kids how to hold a bat; a bit farther down the street, fire fighters in near-complete turnout gear were taking turns hoisting boys and girls into the cab of their engine, giving each an opportunity to sit behind the wheel and "drive" it.

Keller kept updating his planned route of egress after he secured the girl while taking an inventory of the police presence in the area—he saw none on foot, though because of the cruiser he had seen by Robbins' car, he knew they had to be around. This was a safe neighborhood, with the worst offenders likely being drunken college students leaving a bar or club in the early morning hours.

But Keller was pragmatic. Although he knew his secondary plan was less than ideal, there did not seem to be a better way of securing the girl and making a clean getaway. No matter what he did, there was risk. With so many people in the area, however, he was counting on them fomenting confusion, allowing him to blend into the masses.

To prevent any chemical odor from alerting anyone in such close quarters, he had a BetaSomnol-soaked rag sealed in a Ziploc in his pocket. Once he got Melissa to a secluded area, he would inject her with a longer-acting dose to induce sleep and reduce anxiety. When she awoke, she would be home in her own bed. No drama. And she would have no recollection of the ordeal.

If he was corralled by law enforcement, he would attempt to ditch the baggie containing the rag. If questioned, he was a private investigator hired to find and retrieve the abducted girl.

But doing his job properly meant zero contact with the police.

Keller decreased his following distance, creeping closer while maintaining awareness of Robbins's state of mind. As of now, based on her body language and the casual nature of her movements, she had no inkling she was being followed.

After eating, Robbins and Melissa stood in line at an ice cream vendor. Keller gave a final check of his surroundings and liked what he saw.

This was his chance.

He moved swiftly but carefully—to avoid bumping anyone, getting into an argument, or drawing attention to himself—and within several seconds was standing a few feet behind Amy Robbins, Melissa to her right and slightly behind her hip.

Keller glanced at the people gathered around the stand. He figured he would grab Melissa and clap the soaked cheesecloth over her nose and mouth as he carried her away. Her fear would cause her to suck the BetaSomnol deeply into her lungs and hasten its effects. Robbins would be looking around, wondering where Melissa had gone. If he timed it right—and executed it well—she would not know there was something wrong until she turned around to hand the girl her cone.

He was not concerned about anyone identifying him. His disguise, combined with poor eyewitness reliability and the paucity of security cameras that could capture his likeness, was sufficient to keep him out of the crosshairs of law enforcement.

Keller moved in as the line brought Robbins closer to the attendant. As she gave the man their order, Keller walked up to an area in Robbins's blind spot, directly behind her.

As Robbins pointed to the tub of strawberry ice cream, Keller opened the bag and closed his fingers around the rag in his pocket.

36

A dog barked.

It was close and loud and angry—followed immediately by another responding in kind. Everyone turned—and Keller did the same, not to see what the ruckus was but to shield his face from Robbins.

Keller moved away, heading past the canine altercation and melting into the crowd of bodies. His heart was pumping harder than usual. Despite having mastered the skill of lowering his blood pressure and slowing his breathing before engaging an enemy, the close call caused an uncharacteristic adrenaline dump into his bloodstream.

He stopped thirty yards or so away and swung back, picking up Robbins and the girl as they licked their ice cream cones. They had no idea how close he had come to securing Melissa. How close he had come to securing the five-million-dollar payday.

He needed a few minutes to regroup and try again.

He reassessed the area, going through his check-downs like a skilled NFL quarterback. If one receiver was not open, look for your secondary targets. It was frustrating to start back at square one, having been on the cusp of success...but sometimes that's how it went. He had been involved in many such scenarios while in Delta, so he knew how to turn off the emotions and focus on mission objectives.

Right now, that was exactly what he needed to do.

AMY LICKED HER ice cream. "This is really good. Sure you don't want to taste it?"

"Uh-uh. I don't like that flavor."

"Good rum raisin is heavenly. Haven't had it in years. Haven't had ice cream in years."

"How come?"

Amy thought about that. She knew the answer but was not sure how to explain it. "Wasn't in the mood."

Melissa stopped eating and turned to Amy. Her brows lifted. "I'm always in the mood for ice cream."

"I used to be."

They came upon a booth for the Cal Poly university band. They had brass instruments of all types—saxophones, tubas, trumpets...even a set of cymbals.

Two college-age men and one woman were coaxing passersby to pick one up.

"I'm Kathy. Have you ever played?"

"When I was a kid," Amy said. "I took lessons for a couple of years."

"Which instrument?"

"Believe it or not, the tuba. I was barely big enough to hold it."

"Well then," Kathy said, taking the large contraption from her colleague. "Have a seat." She gestured to the folding chair to her right.

"Oh no. I can't. I haven't played in years. A lot of years. Too many years."

"It'll come back to you." She held the instrument out, nearly pushing it into Amy's chest.

"Play it," Melissa said. "Play it, Amy!"

"You can do it," said a man to her left holding a trumpet. "We'll do this together. Then no one'll realize it's me stinking up the place."

177

Amy glanced over and saw three people in chairs, all looking at her. Apparently they were going to play as a mock band. *This is going to be ugly.* "Fine."

"Remember how to hold it?" Kathy asked.

"Yeah, I think so." She placed her fingers and Kathy fine-tuned her grip. A couple of minutes later, after doling out instructions, Kathy brought her hands up and then down, conducting the worst ragtag group of musicians west of the Mississippi.

They blew and made horrendous noise for about fifteen seconds, at which point they all burst out laughing, none of them able to keep the seal on their mouthpieces.

Amy looked over at Melissa to share the fun—but she wasn't there.

She stood up quickly, nearly dropping the tuba—Kathy grabbed it before it hit the ground—as Amy sucked in a deep breath, hyperventilating, swinging her head left to right and back. "Melissa? Missy, where are you?"

She pushed her way through the crowd into a small clearing in the street and saw what looked like a man carrying a girl—a girl wearing Melissa's shoes.

"Oh my god," she mumbled. "Melissa. Stop him!" Amy took off in a sprint, bumping into people and pushing others out of her way. "Help, police—he's kidnapping my daughter!"

KELLER HAD DONE as planned, plucking Melissa away when the Robbins woman's attention was diverted. He clamped his hand over the girl's nose and mouth, the rag giving her a strong initial dose of BetaSomnol and making her body go limp. He had about a minute, give or take, before she would awaken. He needed to get her somewhere secluded to inject her with the drug.

He refrained from running—people rushing somewhere carrying a limp child attracted unwanted attention. Instead, he turned her so that she was facing him and rested her face on his right shoulder—making it appear as if his tired daughter did not want to walk anymore and was taking a nap.

That worked well until a woman—Robbins, no doubt—started

screaming.

He resisted the urge to react and kept walking, eyes darting around, trying to find a place where he could quickly disappear. An alley would be terrific just about now. A dark area where a streetlight was burned out would be a decent alternative. His car was still blocks away. Truth was, he was not entirely certain where he had parked. He needed a moment to get his bearings and compare his location to the map he had memorized.

But he did not have a moment.

Keller heard Robbins behind him—not nearly as far away as he had hoped.

"He's kidnapping my daughter!"

In his peripheral vision, he saw people looking at him. And he realized he could no longer hide by acting innocent. He started jogging, squeezing Melissa against his torso, his right hand cupping the back of her head to keep her neck from whipping around each time his heels struck pavement.

He cut right, down Broad Street, but the screaming continued.

Heavy footsteps behind him. Men were after him.

This was not going as planned. If they made any further gains, he might have to turn and confront them—and plead his case. Then the police would arrive and he would have to attempt to turn the table on Amy Robbins.

Pretty damn smart on her part. A woman screaming that her daughter was kidnapped and pointing at a male carrying a young girl was powerful. Who wouldn't help? Never mind that the situation was the complete opposite—*she* was the perpetrator and on the wrong side of the law. He was acting in the girl's best interests.

Keller heard a noise to his left and twisted to get a view—and saw two men approaching, one with a bat. The other—outfitted in firefighter turnout gear—was carrying an ax.

This had gotten out of hand.

Before he could react, he saw a blur in his peripheral vision and collided with something or someone. Melissa flew from his arms as he slammed into the asphalt, his left shoulder absorbing the impact and his temple striking something hard.

Keller shook his head and got to his feet, a bit woozy but mentally intact enough to be oriented to time and place.

Melissa! He swung his gaze around—causing some dizziness— and saw her on the ground, a couple of men attending to her.

He started in her direction but was sucker punched from behind. He swung an elbow blindly, hitting something squarely, before repeating the move toward the other side and rotating around, hands fisted and ready for battle.

People grabbed at the back of his jacket, but he yanked himself free, only to have others latch on. He twisted, dropped, and rolled, then got to his feet again and saw a mass of bodies approaching. He knew when the odds were getting insurmountable.

"My baby," Robbins screamed.

No one was going to believe him. Sorting this out would require time and extensive explanation, identification and background checks. And when they examined the girl, they might detect remnants of BetaSomnol, a controlled substance he had secured without a prescription. It was time to retreat, regroup, and live to fight another day.

He half ran, half lunged down the street, hoping to find some darkness where he could hide—or, better yet, get back to his car.

He glanced over his shoulder to check on Melissa's status, but all he could see was one large male pursuing him—and a crowd surrounding the girl.

Dammit. He hoped she was okay. He thought of an acronym every military person knew well: FUBAR. Fucked up beyond all recognition.

At the moment, as much as he hated to admit it, that description was spot-on.

37

"Oh my god."

Amy came upon Melissa, laid out prone on the ground. "My baby. Is she okay? Is she—"

Amy's voice caught. She could not go through this again. *Please tell me she's alive, please tell me I didn't kill her.*

Did I just say that out loud?

"You her mother?"

"I—yes. Yes. Is she okay?"

It was one of the firefighters. A woman. "She's breathing. We need to stabilize her spine. I called an ambulance. It'll be here in a couple of minutes."

Amy's vision closed in around her. Her head got heavy. And she crumpled to the ground.

She felt someone sitting her up. She was on the asphalt in the middle of the street, a crowd surrounding her. A police officer was making his way toward her.

"What happened?" the cop asked.

"Man tried to kidnap her daughter," the firefighter said. "Someone tackled him, the girl flew from his arms, hit her head. Ambulance is en route."

He asked Amy if she was okay, then gathered more information from the woman tending to Melissa.

The cop turned to those surrounding them. "Anyone see this guy, the kidnapper?"

Amy got to her knees and moved to Melissa's side. Felt her face. Still warm. Saw her ribcage moving. Breathing. *Thank God.*

Multiple people began rattling off physical characteristics of the kidnapper. Some could only provide details of his clothing.

It was dark.

It all happened so fast.

Too many people got in the way.

I was scared and worried about the girl.

Not surprisingly, some of the descriptions were contradictory.

The officer absorbed it all, then grasped the microphone clipped to his jacket to call it in. "Suspect is about six feet with a brown goatee, wearing a dark jacket. Black or navy. May be leather but could be wool like a pea coat. Glasses. Dark-colored baseball cap. No identifiable logo but someone thought it could be the LA Clippers." He swung the transceiver away from his mouth. "Anyone see a weapon of any kind? Knife or gun?"

All indicated they had not.

"Does fighting experience count," one of the men asked, "like maybe martial arts?"

"Why do you say that?"

The guy shrugged. "Just, I dunno. Had a confidence about him. A purpose to his movements. And he seemed to drop and roll to give himself some space from the people closing on him. Kinda like he had practice."

The officer relayed that information and recorded the names and contact information of the witnesses.

Amy wanted to speak up, to tell the police she had seen him before, at her apartment, almost four hours north of here. But she could not. She needed to be gone from here as soon as possible—without answering too many of the officer's questions.

"You're the mother?"

Amy looked up and nodded. She got to her feet, but before the cop could ask any follow-up questions, a siren blared in the near distance.

"Okay, everyone," he said, turning around, "let's open up the street for the ambulance to get through."

Two female paramedics jumped out and began assessing their patient. A spine board was brought over and an IV started. They loaded Melissa into the back.

"Can I ride with her?" Amy asked.

"Of course," one of the women said. "Climb in."

"I've still got some questions," the officer said. "And I need your contact information."

"Can we do this some other time?" *As in, never?* "I can drop by the station tomorrow."

The officer frowned. "Meet you at the hospital."

Amy grabbed the side rail handle of the ambulance and lifted herself up.

Can't wait.

38

Loren Ryder was sitting at her cubicle in C15, commonly referred to as Child Crimes—or the more formally named Violent Crimes Against Children Unit—of the FBI's San Francisco Division. She worked out of the Oakland Resident Agency, a satellite facility across the Bay Bridge that, despite its name, employed a whopping two hundred federal law enforcement officers. Some RAs, as the resident agencies were known in Bureau-speak, were home to a single agent, while others had five or even ten. The expansive territory covered by the Oakland RA's jurisdiction, however, necessitated a substantial complement of men and women occupying more than three full floors of the large office building.

Loren found herself staring at a photo from her San Leandro case: a missing three-year-old, his beautiful nutmeg complexion contrasting sharply with the bright yellow background. She shook off her funk and completed the FD-302, a form used for recording interviews and other investigative activity.

She realized it was getting late—Zach would be starting to make dinner about now so that when she walked in, she would have enough time to wash up, set the table, and corral the kids into the dining room.

The sun had set a while ago and some of the agents were preparing to wrap things up for the day. Loren was always one of the last to leave. Not because she loved her office—she cared for and respected most of the people there, even though the work itself was emotionally difficult—but she felt a certain level of responsibility to do everything she could to find the missing children. Knocking off before six seemed like giving them the short stick. All in her squad felt the same way.

As she set the photo back in the San Leandro file, she heard her colleagues, Jimmy Hill and Tran Minh, welcome an investigator from Oakland PD's Special Victims Section, part of the Vice/Child Exploitation Unit.

Another new case. Another missing kid. Does it ever end?

She knew the answer to that question, and it was not anything she wanted to think about.

"Elvis Courtland," a man with a moderately deep voice said.

"Elvis your real name?" Hill asked.

"Actually, it is. Parents were fans."

"Have a seat," Minh said with a chuckle. "You're new to Oakland. I know a lot of the investigators. Never seen you before."

"Moved from Nashville. Worked there fifteen years, then the wife got a job at Facebook. Bam. Life turned upside down."

"I'll give you what we've got," Hill said.

Loren spaced out, her mind periodically picking up a detail here and there...

Young blonde girl about five years old

Loren pulled out a report from the investigating San Leandro detective and re-read the original complaint.

Au pair from Germany befriended thirty-something woman

Loren logged onto her system and pulled up the case.

Abducted from Lake Merritt area

She opened the photos of the street where the child was last seen and clicked through them, hoping to catch something she had not previously seen.

Suspect met au pair at the lake

Loren made a note to re-interview the contractor who worked

on the house prior to the child's disappearance.

Suspect identified as Amy Robbins

Loren sat up straight. Suddenly all nerve endings were awake, her hearing tuned to what was being said in the adjacent cubicle.

"What do we know about this Robbins?" Courtland asked.

Hill: "Haven't had a whole lot of time to drill down. Suffered a tragedy years ago. Child and husband killed in a car crash. Deceased daughter fits general description of abductee, Melissa Ellis."

Loren closed her eyes. *Jesus Christ, Amy.*

"I don't know if your lieutenant told you, but complainant said an OPD detective came by asking questions. Didn't get his name. But the au pair said he visited her too, and said his name was Carr. About six feet, athletic, had this scar that cut through his left eyebrow, causing a small bald spot there."

Loren's jaw dropped. That description sure sounded like someone she knew. The general physical characteristics could describe millions of men but for the nearly unnoticeable facial blemish. Still, was that possible?

"Parents were not the ones to report the child missing," Hill said.

"You're kidding."

"Suspicious," Hill said, "I know. Got a list of questions for the Ellises. Wanna come along with us?"

The creaking sound of a chair moving. Then Courtland's voice: "Hell yeah. They know we're coming?"

"No." Hill laughed. "Absolutely not. Something's off if they don't call the police when they realize their daughter's missing. Au pair thinks there's child abuse. Mother."

"Let's do it," Courtland said.

"Gotta grab our jackets and we can head out."

Loren pulled her phone from her pocket. She brought up Amy's number, then stopped with her finger poised over the green CALL icon. *Is this the right move? What the hell's going on here? Doesn't sound like Amy. Gotta be mistaken identity.*

And then it hit her. The au pair, the blonde girl at the lake.

Loren was there when Amy met them.
Holy shit. This is not good.
Amy, what've you gotten yourself into?

39

Keller walked into the Starbucks off Morro. The café was a large open space, and as he entered and took in the layout, he realized he would have been better served by going into the two-story bookstore across the outdoor mall.

He ditched his hat, fake beard, and glasses—which were now bent and scratched—then turned his coat inside out, transforming the brown exterior into a blue shell...chosen specifically for reasons such as this. He grabbed a copy of *USA Today* off a nearby table, ordered a tall coffee, and casually sat with his back to the windows thumbing through the business section.

As he sipped his drink, he considered his options. The safest move would be to leave town and reduce the odds law enforcement could locate him. Explaining and proving that he was not the criminal party would take time—time he did not have. What's more, the girl was injured after he drugged her and ran through a crowded street. An argument could be made for reckless child endangerment.

Alternatively, he could attempt to obtain a status on Melissa. He only got a glimpse of her before he had to flee, but she was still and lying face down. Not good, and that concerned him...not only because he was responsible for bringing her home, but because she was in his arms when she got injured. He failed to protect her. He had her against his body. A helpless little girl. He found himself shaking his head and clenching his right fist.

Keller took a deep breath, closed his eyes, and cleared his mind. He needed to let it go, focus, and figure out a path forward.

A moment later, he heard a commotion outside when a patron opened the door and a cool breeze rushed in. He looked up and saw two of the men he had fought with, looking for him, rubbernecking their heads with a cop following closely behind them.

Keller was confident he no longer fit the description of the perpetrator they were looking for, but he had to busy himself to maintain his air of confidence. He pulled out his phone and began a search of area hospitals.

He had a job to do and retreating—playing it safe—was not a viable option.

40

The siren rose and fell in a rhythm as the ambulance raced through the streets en route to the hospital. Amy held Melissa's hand as the paramedics took her vitals and completed their assessment.

"Is she going to be okay?"

"I'm going to leave that to the doctor to answer," the woman said as she placed a stethoscope on her chest. "Your daughter took a nasty blow to the head. Vitals are stable, but she's in shock. Possible concussion. More than that, the doc's gonna have to determine."

As they approached the emergency room entrance, Amy realized she was going to need a plausible story. Who was she? Christine Ellis? Amy Robbins? Someone else altogether? Melissa did not have any ID, and Amy could claim she had lost her wallet in the pursuit. They had no reason to search her. She could create an alias and hope that they did not have time to figure it out before Melissa was discharged.

The last time Amy had seen the inside of an ER, it was in a state she cared not to revisit. This was a different magnitude—she had not been through a trauma herself, her daughter and husband were not seriously injured...but a little girl she cared about deeply, who might *be* her biological daughter, was in this facility because of actions Amy had taken. That weighed heavily on her. She had to make this right.

To do that, she would have to lie and deceive and keep her distance from law enforcement.

As the ambulance's rear doors opened and Melissa was offloaded, Amy reached into her purse and yanked all the ID and bank cards from the zippered compartment, then shoved them into her underwear. There were only two dollars left in her wallet, which she ditched in the ER waiting room trash can.

Amy was mesmerized by the sudden, orchestrated activity surrounding Melissa. Doctors and nurses moved in coordinated chaos. She was drawn back to that rainy, fateful Boston evening. And as hard as she tried to push the memories away, they kept dominating the scene in front of her, like a sheet draped over the stage play unfolding before her. She sensed her grip on reality slipping away.

Amy fought to stay in the here and now, to see Melissa and not Lindy lying helpless on the bed. White coats moved in and out, orders given, and instruments and devices passed about.

A bloody sponge dropped to the floor.

Amy's gaze dropped as well, watching as a shoe stepped on it. Red liquid pooled beneath it on the tile, running slightly toward her.

"Miss," a woman said by her ear. "Come with me. Let the doctors do their thing."

"No," Amy said automatically, the words not truly registering.

"C'mon." A tug on her shoulder. Gentle, nonthreatening.

Amy allowed her torso to be turned. She headed away from Melissa, swinging her head to give a final look as she trudged away.

"I'm Catrina. I just need to get some information while they work on your daughter. That is your daughter, right?"

"Huh?" Amy took in her face: creased and lined, a middle-aged woman staring at her, awaiting her response. "Sorry. I'm..." She looked back over her left shoulder but could no longer see the area where Melissa was being treated.

"Let's start with something easy. Your name."

"My..." She turned again and glanced back from where she had come.

"Your name. First name?"

"Um...sorry. I'm not...not feeling so good. Can I..." Amy took a seat where she was, on the floor.

"Miss? Are you okay?"

Amy lay back and rested her head on the ground. Staring at the ceiling. She just wanted to close her eyes and go to sleep. The stress of the past few days, the guilt and emotions of the past hour...

"I need help here," the nurse yelled into the hallway.

Amy let her lids shut and she heard voices but was not able to respond. She let things happen somewhere in the background, off in another room. For now, she just needed to rest.

41

L oren sat there a long moment after Hill and Courtland left. The man that the au pair and bakery owner described sure sounded like Mickey Keller.

And that was not a good development.

Loren had worked with Keller when he was an LAPD detective and she was a new agent assigned to the FBI's Los Angeles Division. She found him a skilled investigator but had handled only a couple of complex cases with him. They had a solid professional relationship based on mutual respect. He saved her bacon on one occasion and never made a big deal out if it—which she appreciated.

After he retired from the force, however, things got murky. As time passed, she heard rumblings about, and was briefed on, cases where he appeared to be involved in suspect business dealings linked to sordid individuals.

Keller did not appear to be initiating illegal or criminal behavior—as far as she could tell—but his name seemed to be turning up more frequently in recent years associated with oligarchs and drug lords and corrupt foreign presidents.

The Bureau had never been able to amass sufficient evidence to arrest him, but after a while, Loren realized that since leaving the LAPD his questionable associations were not a coincidence. She became convinced—but could not prove—that whatever he was involved in, he had gone over to the dark side.

Loren kept telling herself that eventually he would screw up and she would be there to put him in cuffs. And that would be a disappointing day because she liked the guy. But circumstances changed people. Greed and money changed people. Sometimes circumstances, greed, *and* money proved a lethal combination, corrupting people beyond repair.

A couple of years ago, a case involving human trafficking was assigned to her unit. After months of getting nowhere, they received a tip that a ship coming into the port of Oakland was arriving with two dozen children locked inside one of the containers.

It turned out the cargo came into San Francisco, not Oakland, so the Bureau was late to the party. But upon their arrival, Loren saw a man who looked like Keller. He ultimately gave them the slip—although several hours later they got a hit on the BOLO she had issued: Keller was picked up on a traffic stop near San Jose International airport.

He denied involvement with the smuggling ring in any way, but Loren knew that could be total bullshit. It could have also been the truth, and they had no way of proving otherwise.

"Here we are again," Loren had said after walking into the interview room.

"Having an unscheduled chat?"

"You know what I mean. On the wrong side of the law. Affiliating with known felons."

"I take jobs. I usually don't know who I'm working for. I do my investigation and submit my report. I'm not saying that's the case here, but we're talking in generalities, hypotheticals."

"That makes one of us. Last time you assured me you hadn't done anything wrong. And yet we find ourselves in the same situation."

"Last time was nothing with nothing. You let me go. And even offered to have coffee with me next time you arrested me."

"I'm seeing a pattern develop. And I don't like it."

"Yeah, I don't like this pattern, either. You keep arresting me. And then letting me go. Can we go for coffee now?"

"*No*, we can't go for coffee."

"But you said you would, 'Next time I arrest you.'"

"I also said it'd better not happen again."

Keller shook his head. "Loren. You've gotten hard."

She looked at him a long moment, then said, "Only when it comes to you. You used to be better than..." She shrugged.

"Than what?"

"This."

And now, as she shook her head to bring herself back to the present, she feared that Keller was involved in a case in which Amy was the person of interest—if not the prime suspect. Beyond her confusion relative to what, and why, Amy was doing what she was doing, Loren did not understand the connection to Keller.

Given his rumored affiliations, this was not good news. Amy was in trouble many times over. And she was apparently dealing with dangerous people, likely without any idea of what she had gotten herself into.

Sitting here in her office was getting Loren nowhere. But what could she do? If she told her squad supervisor that Amy was her sister-in-law, she would be isolated and banned from participating in the case. Loren would be shut off from updates and information.

But it was only a matter of time before Hill figured out that she was related to Amy. How long until they made that connection was tough to predict.

One thing Loren was sure of: it would be measured in hours, not weeks. She did not have much time.

42

Keller made a list of area hospitals and then waited until the men searching for him left Starbucks. He got up, dumped his cup, and worked his way back to his Lincoln. There was an increased police presence as officers patrolled on horseback and in cruisers—but they were looking for a man whose physical appearance had changed. Keller walked right by two cops and they gave him only a cursory once-over.

He called around but despite his best efforts at subterfuge, he could only elicit information from one hospital on a young child arriving at the emergency department—a leading trauma center that was about five miles away. He tapped the address on his iPhone and Maps opened.

Twelve minutes later, he pulled into the lot and circled once, checking for security cameras. He saw none—which did not mean there weren't any—so he parked and walked into the ER with his head down and his jacket collar extended.

He took a seat in the waiting room and picked up a copy of *People* magazine. As he casually flipped through it, he observed the flow of staff and medical personnel. There were double doors that led to the triage area.

He surmised that beyond it lay the nurses station and the treatment cubicles. If he was correct, Robbins and Melissa were a mere twenty yards or so from him. But trying to get into, and past, triage might be a point of resistance—where any unauthorized individuals would easily be spotted—and stopped.

Keller set the magazine down and walked back outside to evaluate the exterior, in case there was an easier way in. The ambulance bay stood twenty feet to his left. He glanced inside the sliding doors and saw two male nurses near the entrance.

He returned to the waiting room. A man and his son rushed in a few minutes later, the teen bleeding profusely from his right thigh, which was wrapped in a soaked bandage. Personnel appeared and rapid-fire orders were exchanged. Someone grabbed a wheelchair—and Keller used the opportunity to squeeze past them into triage. No one was at the station—they were inside attending to the youth—but other staff members were working on patients in the nearby treatment rooms.

He avoided making eye contact—and did not dare stop and look confused as to where he was headed, as that invited attention and questions of, "Can I help you?" "Are you lost?" or challenges such as, "Who are you and why are you back here?"

He walked purposefully down the corridor, trying to catch a name or clipboard indicating who was occupying each of the rooms. He saw nothing—likely because of privacy laws. Always *something* to make his job more difficult.

He stopped at what appeared to be a break room with a sign that read, "Authorized medical personnel only." Keller interpreted that to include him. He entered and saw a coffee machine on the left, a wooden cabinet on the right. He pulled the latter open and found what he was looking for: a blue scrub top, EMERGENCY DEPARTMENT embroidered over the left breast.

He shrugged it over his head and although it was not a perfect fit, it did not need to be. He walked out, then grabbed a patient chart out of a slipcase beside the first door on his right. It was for a forty-two-year-old male, not a five-year-old girl.

Nevertheless, he took the clipboard with him and walked down the corridor.

Into the next treatment room.

43

When Brandon Ellis arrived home from the office, he was dog tired. The past several weeks his sleep had been fitful and short, maxing out at five hours on a good night. When he did finally get into bed, Christine's tossing and turning kept him awake.

But they were in the home stretch and he suspected—and hoped—that the pace, and stress level, would ease up once the IPO closed. He had a feeling, however, that though there might be a slight reprieve, the frenetic schedule would continue for the foreseeable future.

The unrelenting pressure had taken its toll on their marriage, for sure. But as he had counseled dozens of patients in the past, this was not unusual. High-performing careers demanded intellectual, emotional, and physical stamina. This left little for the "other" in your life—your spouse—who expected to be the *significant* other in your life, not merely a *generic* other, a secondary afterthought... if and when there was time.

Christine walked in ten minutes after Ellis—they often took their own cars to work so each could sit in on meetings the other one did not need to attend. They decided to have an early dinner because they had skipped lunch and were both running on fumes.

"I just want to crawl into bed," Ellis said as he fell onto the dining room seat. Jennifer, their housekeeper, quietly set a plate of Atlantic salmon with mustard asparagus in front of him. Christine unfolded her cloth napkin and then lifted a glass of whiskey to her lips as her own dinner, a rare prime rib with fingerling potatoes, was placed on the table.

"Drink a couple cups of coffee after dinner," Christine said. "We've still got a lot of work to do for tomorrow morning's meeting."

"Yeah." Ellis looked at the fish and knew it was delicious, but he was too tired to lift his hands from his lap and pick up the utensils. "Smells so good."

He took a deep breath and summoned the strength to reach for his fork when the door chime rang out, up and down the musical spectrum.

Christine closed her eyes and clenched her jaw. "This better be important."

They stared blankly at the table, listening as Jennifer dealt with the intrusion.

"Can I help you?"

"I'm Agent Hill, FBI. This is Agent Minh and Inspector Courtland. Oakland PD. We're looking for Mr. and Mrs. Ellis."

"That'd be Dr. and Dr. Ellis. I'll tell them you're here. May I ask what this is about?"

"No," Hill said. "You may not."

The Ellises exchanged a glance—and it was not one of comfort and endearment.

Adrenaline infused Ellis's bloodstream as he rose and tossed his napkin on the table.

A few steps later they entered the foyer, facing three men wearing dark suits.

Jennifer started to relay the information—but Christine cut her off. "We heard. Would you please keep dinner warm?"

"Yes, Dr. Ellis."

"Can we help you?" Ellis asked.

Hill did the introductions.

"What's this about?"

"We're here about your daughter."

"Follow us," Christine said, leading the way down the stone hallway to a room off to the right. They entered and she closed the door.

Inside was an oval table that seated six. They took chairs across from each other.

"What about our daughter?" Christine asked.

"We have information she's been kidnapped," Hill said.

"Really." She made eye contact with each of the men. "Who told you that?"

"We're not at liberty to say."

Ellis cleared his throat. "Your information is correct."

Courtland leaned forward and set both forearms on the conference table. "Oakland PD has no record."

"We didn't report it. We have a private inv—"

"Brandon," Christine said firmly. "That's enough." She turned to Courtland. "We're handling it."

"All due respect, Doctor," Hill said. "When dealing with a child, the police should be notified. Her life could be in danger."

"We were told specifically not to involve the police," Christine said.

Hill and Minh shared a look. Ellis was not sure what it meant, but apparently the two men did.

"Dr. Ellis," Minh said, "there someplace we can go to talk?"

Christine snorted. "What's wrong with right here?"

Minh kept his eyes riveted on Ellis, as if Christine had not spoken. "My partner needs to chat with your wife. Separately."

Ellis shifted in his seat. "Well, I—"

"Neither of us is going anywhere," Christine said. "You want to talk with us, this room is perfectly fine. If not, I've got our attorney on speed dial."

Courtland canted his head to the side. "Why would you need an attorney?"

"Honey," Ellis said, resting a hand on Christine's. "If they want to talk with us separ—"

"No, Brandon. It's both of us. Right here and right now. Or

not at all."

Hill cleared his throat. "Time's critical, so I'm not gonna haggle with you. Who told you not to involve the police?"

"The kidnappers," Christine said. "They called. They said we'd never see Melissa again if we called the police."

Ellis swung his gaze over to Christine. *What's she doing? Lying to the FBI? Or did Amy Robbins call and she and Lira didn't tell me?*

"Do you know who the kidnappers are?" Hill asked.

"No."

Hill looked at Christine a long moment. Ellis found it unnerving.

"Dr. Ellis, we have reason to believe you're not telling us the truth. Now I'm going to ask you again. Do you know who the kidnappers are?"

"I didn't recognize the voice. That's all I can tell you."

"Was the caller male or female?" Minh asked.

"Male. But I heard a woman in the background. She said something but the guy cut her off."

"Were you also on this call?" Hill asked Ellis.

"Just Christine."

"Any accents?"

Christine bit her bottom lip and she looked down, shook her head no. When she looked up, her eyes were teary.

Ellis placed a hand on Christine's shoulder. "This is upsetting my wife. Can we continue this tomorrow?"

"Like I said." Hill clenched his jaw. "In child abduction cases, every minute counts. So no, we can't continue this tomorrow. Unless you know who the kidnappers are."

"My wife already told you. She didn't know who called."

Courtland cleared his throat. "Any unusual, or identifiable, noises in the background? Fog horn? Train? Airplanes?"

"I wasn't really focused on that." Christine sniffled, her gaze on the table. "I don't remember hearing anything. It was a short call."

"Did he ask for ransom?"

"No." She looked at Courtland. "But he said he'd be contacting us again. He hung up when I asked to talk to Melissa."

"Has he called again?" Minh asked.

"No."

"Home phone or cell? Which did he call?"

Christine hesitated. "Home."

Courtland pulled out his spiral notepad and clicked his pen. "Do we have permission to look over your phone records?"

"We're dealing with a very sensitive financial transaction, Detective. With our business. So I'm sorry, that wouldn't be wise."

"We can debate the wisdom another time," Courtland said, jotting something down on the page. "You have caller ID?"

"We do. But it didn't have a name or number. It just said 'wireless caller.'"

"Do you have any staff that work for you?" Minh asked.

"You met one of them a few moments ago," Ellis said. "Our housekeeper. We've also got a gardener and an au pair."

Minh glanced at Christine, then turned his attention back to Ellis. "The au pair is the one we're most interested in. She's had the most contact with your daughter. We'd like to talk with her."

Ellis swallowed hard, trying to disguise his discomfort at misleading them. "She's not home."

"Where can we reach her?"

"She's out of town," Christine said, her gaze again dropping to the table. "On vacation."

"Dr. Ellis." Hill shook his head and hardened his features. "Lying to a federal agent is a felony. I strongly suggest you consider your answers. Once we walk out and confirm that you've lied to us, you're going to prison."

"There are things we know about this case," Minh said. "And when you contradict these known facts, it's easy for us to determine you're not being truthful."

Christine brought her head up and made eye contact. "She's on her way back to Germany for a vacation. That's all I know. We haven't seen her, so I assume she went. More than that I can't say. She's only an employee. I'm not her mother. I can give you her cell number if you want. Call her. Ask *her* where she is. And whatever else you want to know."

Christine rattled off the digits; Courtland recorded them in his notebook.

"We hope you help us find Melissa," Hill said as he pushed his chair back and stood up. "Anything you remember, call us." He handed her his card.

"But what about not involving—"

"We've handled a lot of cases like this. The kidnappers won't know we're working with you."

"Thank you," Ellis said.

Christine pulled a tissue from a box on the table and dabbed at her eyes, careful not to smudge her mascara. "My husband and I have had a long week. A long year. And now this."

"We'll do our best to get her home safely," Hill said.

AS THEY WALKED back to their vehicle, Minh glanced over his shoulder at the Ellis home.

"What do you think?"

Hill snorted. "I think she's lying."

"Definitely lying," Courtland said.

"Probably," Minh said. "Maybe. But not definitely. I don't find her super credible, but everyone processes stress in different ways. She might just be spooked because the kidnappers told her not to call us."

"But we know who the kidnapper is," Courtland said. "A woman, not a man."

Minh pulled out his keys as they approached their Ford. "We don't really know *what's* going on. Robbins could be working with someone. I'm not convinced a woman saddled with emotional instability and mental health issues can pull off such a successful kidnapping without help."

Hill opened his door. "Christine Ellis might not be credible, but it doesn't mean she was lying. Phone call could've been real. She may not have contacted OPD because of the threat."

"She said there was a woman talking in the background. If you believe her. We should pull her phone records," Hill said, "see who's called. Who she's been talking to."

"I doubt we have enough for a warrant."

Courtland shrugged. "Lying to a federal agent—"

"Isn't enough," Hill said. "We need some kind of probable cause that we're gonna find evidence of a crime in those records. Like complicity in the abduction."

Minh got into the car. "Besides, if *I'm* not convinced she was lying, how are you going to convince a judge? We know Giselle was given a ticket back to Germany. Ellis saying it was a 'vacation' is, at best, a white lie. I mean, she *could* be characterizing it as that. Could we really prove to a judge that Ellis didn't think Giselle was going to visit her family, or whatever, while in Germany? We'd be lucky to convince a judge of *anything*. And no way will he believe a young au pair over an accomplished physician with no criminal record of any kind."

Courtland thought a moment. "The mother's been victimized because her daughter's missing. If we're gonna victimize her again—by accusing her of being complicit and lying to the police—and then digging around her records—we'd better be right."

"Sure wouldn't play well in the media if we're wrong," Hill said.

Minh chuckled. "Understatement of the year."

"What about issuing an amber alert?" Courtland asked as he shoved the seat belt latch home. "If she's telling the truth about someone else being involved, that would be broadcasting the fact that she contacted the cops."

Hill chewed on that as he started the engine. "Damned if we do and damned if we don't. We don't want to get the girl killed if Ellis isn't jerking our chain. But if we *don't* act and he kills her, we'll be skinned alive for not issuing the alert."

"Better to err on the safe side until we know what's going on," Minh said. "Let's keep digging. Wait on the amber alert."

Hill pulled the shift into DRIVE. "Fine. But only for a day. I'm still not convinced she's telling the truth."

44

"Well that was upsetting," Ellis said.

After talking briefly with Jennifer, Ellis and Christine retreated back into the room, shut the door, and sat down at the conference table. "If we don't find that Robbins woman soon, we could be screwed."

"Let's not overreact, Christine."

"Overreact? If the FBI's on the case, how long do you think it'll be before the media gets hold of it?"

Ellis chewed on that a moment. "I see your point."

"And what if they go public with a press conference? If it goes on much longer, if there are no leads, they may do that. A plea to the public to keep their eyes and ears open."

"You may be right. This is not good." Ellis started looking around for where he had left his phone. "I need to call Angelo. I don't know what his people are doing, but they're digging a hole for us."

Christine let her head fall back, as if she were examining the ceiling. "We need to be more proactive."

Ellis found the device and started dialing. "Not sure what else we can do. We've got a skilled investigator on the case."

"Who doesn't seem to be getting the job done."

The phone rang three times before Lira answered. "I was just about to call you. Nora's got a request from the *Wall Street Journal* for a big piece in their technology section."

"Okay, but—"

"And they want Melissa there. For a photo shoot."

"Well that can't happen. Obviously."

"What's going on?" Christine asked, grabbing Ellis's arm.

Ellis moved the phone away from his mouth. "*Wall Street Journal.* Wants to do a story and photo shoot. With Melissa."

"Sonofabitch. The *Journal?*" She balled a fist. "That would be huge."

"I put her off," Lira said, "but I just wanted you to know. I told Nora to see if they can do it without Melissa, but—"

"We've got a bigger problem," Ellis said. "FBI was just here asking about her."

Lira groaned. "So they know."

"They know."

"How'd they find out?"

"Wouldn't say," Ellis said. "But—"

"Had to be the au pair."

"Isn't Giselle on the way back to Germany?"

"Ten o'clock flight," Lira said. "Driver's supposed to pick her up very soon. He should be on his way to your house. Is Giselle there?"

"No. Jennifer hasn't seen her."

"Doesn't matter. At this point, she's a nonissue. Now that the FBI knows, there's nothing she can do to hurt us."

"I gave the FBI her phone number," Christine said. "You deactivated her cell, right?"

"I took care of it," Lira said. "Vacation mode suspension. I didn't cancel the line because I didn't want it to look suspicious. They check, it'll match what you told them. She's traveling abroad, suspending service while she's gone."

"But what about the FBI? Christine and I are worried about—"

"Yeah. I'll talk with Bill Tait, see what can be done. But he warned me that these things can take time. As much as we don't want to admit it, if someone doesn't want to be found—and it looks like Robbins knows what she's doing—it might take longer."

Ellis rubbed his forehead with a clammy right hand. "Keep us posted."

"I know this is tough," Lira said. "But you and Christine have to hold it together. Keep focused on the prize. Leave the issue of finding Melissa to me."

45

Amy stood in the corner of the emergency department's treatment room 4 watching as the physician completed his examination.

She had been placed on a gurney and wheeled into an area and examined. Dehydration and acute stress reaction were diagnosed, and intravenous fluids were administered. Her right eye was twitching nonstop and made her self-conscious.

After consulting with one of the doctors, the nurse unhooked Amy. "You need to fill out the patient intake form," she said, giving her a clipboard with paperwork to complete.

"I'm so embarrassed," Amy said. "Sorry to put you through all that trouble."

"That's what we're here for. C'mon, I'll take you to your daughter."

When they walked in, the doctor was refastening Melissa's neck brace. "Okay Rhonda. Let's get a CT of the head and neck to rule out subdural hematoma or subarachnoid hemorrhage."

"No MRI?" Rhonda asked.

"With a five-year-old? She'd have to remain completely still for forty-five minutes."

"We can sedate her."

The doctor made a note in the chart. "I'm not going to sedate a child with a head injury."

Rhonda nodded. "And we need to monitor sleepiness."

"Exactly."

Amy was watching the back-and-forth like a patron watches a tennis match. "Is she going to be okay?"

The physician faced Amy, whose hands were shaking. She crossed them over her chest to steady them.

"I'm Dr. West. Your daughter's very lucky. If she'd fallen on the back of her head, she would've fractured her skull because there isn't much soft tissue there to absorb the impact. A fall on the face is better, so to speak, but it risks damage to the teeth or nose. Fractures or chips. Somehow, other than a forehead laceration, which will require stitches, she lucked out there, too. But the loss of consciousness indicates she's suffered a concussion and what I suspect is a hematoma on the top of her forehead, near the point of impact."

"Hematoma? A tumor?"

"No, nothing like that. Just some blood accumulating where she struck her head. Looks like it was a pretty bad fall. How'd it happen?"

"We were at the farmers market and a man grabbed her and ran and someone tried to tackle him and—" Amy's voice caught— "she flew out of his arms. I—I was frozen, I couldn't believe what I was seeing." She wiped her wet right cheek on her sleeve.

"We need to check with Child Protective Services," Rhonda said.

"Child—" Amy swallowed deeply. "Why?"

"Any time a child comes in with this kind of trauma, we're—"

"There's a police officer right outside, in the—in the waiting room. You can—you can talk with him. There were a ton of witnesses, not to mention the guy who tackled the kidnapper. Child Protective Services? Don't take my daughter from me, please. Don't traumatize her more than she's already been traumatized."

West placed a hand on Amy's left shoulder. "We'll confirm with the police. I'm sure it'll be fine. Don't worry, she's in good hands. We'll take special care of her. Okay?"

Amy managed a nod.

Rhonda unlocked the gurney and wheeled Melissa, with an assistant, out of the treatment room.

"We're going to run some tests," West said. "Once we have all that information, I'll have a better idea of what we need to do for her."

"When can we leave?"

"Well," West said with a lift of his brow. "That depends on the test results. Let's wait and see. Meantime, have a seat in the waiting room and I'll come get you once I've had a chance to look over her test results."

"Can I stay with her?"

"When she's in the scanner, you have to be in a separate area. So there's really no point. It'll be an hour at most, maybe less. And Nurse Rhonda has a little girl of her own. Your daughter's in good hands."

"And safe? That man, the one who tried to kidnap her, he's still out there."

"He won't be able to get past security into the emergency department. But I'll have someone ask them to be extra careful."

Amy nodded. She had pushed as hard as she could—but there was no point in creating a scene. However, she was not ready to talk with the officer. She had to get her story straight, find a way to prevent the police from checking her information until she could get out of town.

Rather than going back to the waiting room, where the cop was likely pacing, ready to question her, she went to the restroom...to hide. And think.

46

Loren sat at her desk, leaning back in her chair, staring at the ceiling. How could she not help her sister-in-law? How could she face Zach if he found out she knew what his sister had done and she said nothing to him? He would not buy the "need to know" bullshit the Bureau was famous for tossing around—sometimes warranted, other times used as a dodge when convenient.

She rocked forward and set her forearms on the file splayed out in front of her.

"You okay?"

She swung her gaze to the left, where Tran Minh had just returned to his desk. "Just thinking. Tough case."

"Got one of those myself."

"I'm gonna get some fresh air. Clear my head."

Loren waited until she cleared the building before she dug out her cell phone.

Zach answered on the third ring. "Uh-oh. You never call during the day. Everything okay?"

Not even close.

"Have you talked to Amy?"

"Not in a few days. Why?"

"Run over to the drug store and try calling her. Let me know if you get through."

"Drug store. Why—"

"Use the pay phone there. It's in the back by the bathrooms. Don't say anything to her about anything. Just call like you're checking in. Usual stuff. And don't tell anyone we're discussing this."

"I'm not sure *what* we're discussing. What's going on?"

"Just do it and call me back. If she doesn't answer, leave a voice mail that you wanted to touch base because you haven't heard from her in a while."

"Okay, but—"

"Don't tell her I asked you to call or that I'm worried about her. Or that you're calling from a public phone."

"You're obviously worried about her. Just tell me—"

"I can't. And I'm outside and it's cold and I don't have my coat, so hurry."

Loren had never smoked, but as she stood there, her emotions were all over the place—anger, sadness, confusion, fear—and made her fidgety. Holding something in her hand and sucking on it would be comforting. She laughed at the sexual innuendo and realized it calmed her nerves—for a moment.

Her phone buzzed seven minutes later. Loren nearly dropped it while fumbling to answer it with chilled fingers.

"No answer, Lor. I left the message you told me to leave. Now you want to tell me what's going on?"

"Hang out for another twenty minutes or so, then try her one more time."

"Wait. Lor—"

Loren hung up and closed her eyes. *Amy, what the hell are you doing?*

She paced, walking along Webster Street, the gloomy, darkening city doing nothing to lift her spirits.

What am I getting myself into?

She ran through the scenarios in her mind, trying to reason it out. But there was no good solution. For now, until she could get in touch with Amy, she could not make any assumptions as to what happened, why, or how. It sure sounded like her sister-in-law abducted a child. But Amy was a bright woman...troubled, yes...but could that really explain why she would do something like this?

Loren felt she knew the answer, though she was not a mental health professional—and she had very few facts. That the ones she *did* have were damning did not mean anything. It told her she had to get to the bottom of what was going on. Amass all the information and then she would know the motivation—and be able to assess whether a crime was committed.

Loren stopped, looked up at the multistory building to her left. A crime *had* been committed. That much she knew, regardless of what she could glean going forward. Denying that would get her nowhere.

She continued walking to Lakeshore Avenue, where she witnessed two men making a drug handoff—and thought of looking the other way. This was not uncommon on Oakland streets, but if she collared the guys it would consume the rest of the evening, prevent her from helping Amy, and solve nothing. She looked the one doing the selling in the eyes and said, "Drugs kill. They destroy lives. You wanna make a living? Get a goddam job."

The man flipped his head back, scattering the long dreadlocks onto his back. "Who the f—"

"*This* is who." Loren moved her sweater top aside and revealed her badge. Then she pushed past him and stopped by an electronics shop three blocks away where she paid cash for a burner phone with a clean SIM card that was not traceable to her.

As she turned it on—and saw it was partially charged—she shook her head at the irony of admonishing a drug dealer on engaging in illegal activity when she, a federal agent, was preparing to do the same.

47

Keller stepped into room 3 as a doctor and nurse swung their gaze toward him. Lying on the bed was a gray-haired woman. Keller opened his eyes wide in mock surprise, apologized, and backed out.

He stood outside number 4, hand on the knob. *Please let this be Melissa's room.*

He pushed the door open—and saw a father comforting a young teenager for what looked like a fractured leg.

Room 5 had a girl around Melissa's age—but brunette and clearly not her.

Keller continued on down the hall, checking one room after another...and coming up empty.

He cursed under his breath. Had Melissa been moved to another department for X-rays? Had she been released already? Could she have been processed and sent on her way that quickly? If they didn't need to run any tests, it was possible. But judging how she looked lying on the pavement, he was sure they would have done a precautionary diagnostic workup.

He returned to the break room and considered additional options: she could have suffered a fatal injury from the fall—in which case she would be on the way to a morgue somewhere.

She could have sustained a head injury or skull fracture—not surprising given the way she landed—that necessitated immediate emergency surgery.

Or he could have gone to the wrong hospital.

The brunette in room 5 could have been the girl he was told about when he called and spoke with the emergency department coordinator.

He leaned his buttocks against the counter and tried to reason a way forward. Robbins would likely not use her, or Melissa's, real name, as that could be tracked. If there was a law enforcement alert issued, she would be located easily—and quickly.

Keller pulled off the scrub top and put his own shirt back on, then fingered the badge in his pocket. He could seek out the administrator and ask if another young girl was brought in following an accident downtown.

But the police responded to the scene at the farmers market—so they would have arrived at the hospital around the same time as the ambulance. And they would have sought out the mother for questioning. Even faced with the threat of discovery, Robbins would not have abandoned the girl she believed was her daughter, the one for whom she had risked everything.

Yet there were no police officers here.

Keller left the badge in his pocket and headed for the exit. He needed to find the right hospital—because he likely did not have time to guess wrong twice.

48

Loren took the elevator up to her office, figuring she had at least five minutes before she got the return call from Zach. She grabbed the coat off her chair and glanced at her desk. Unfinished business stared back at her. She did not have time to play detective relative to her sister-in-law.

But family comes first. She made that pledge to Zach when they got married and although there were times when she could not keep that promise, this was not one of them.

"Hey Tran. I gotta run to my car for something. Be back in fifteen."

Minh twisted his mouth. "You just got back. We've got the Zemani case to follow—"

"Well aware. But it's a woman's thing. My period. And my pads are in the car. You really need me to explain?"

Minh held up a hand. "Nope. It's cool. TMI."

"Next time don't hassle me." She immediately regretted her tone, as Minh was a good guy and from his perspective, she was shirking her responsibilities. "You know what? I'm just gonna knock off. I'll try to come in early tomorrow and get a head start. Sorry for being testy. See you in the morning."

"You got it. Feel better."

If only it were that easy.

Zach called as she reached the elevator and informed her that Amy had still not answered. Loren thanked him and told him she was on her way home.

He was standing outside the garage as she pulled into the driveway.

"What the hell's going on?" he asked as she rolled past him.

Once the garage door finished closing, she slid her window down and said, "Get in."

He squinted in confusion, then ran around the front and fell onto the passenger seat.

"Lor, if there's s—"

"Amy's in trouble. And I don't know what to do to help her."

He swallowed deeply before answering. "What kind of trouble?"

"I'm not sure I should tell you. If I do, I'd be dragging you into a bad situation. Once you have knowledge of something, you can't unknow it."

"Obviously. But so what if I know?"

"She's done something illegal. Very illegal. So out of character I don't know what to think, what to make of it."

"Amy? Illegal? Give me a break." His eyes scanned her face. "You sure about this?"

Loren sighed and turned away from Zach, looked out the driver's window. "I have very few facts. I can't go into it without involving you."

"She's my sister. I need to know."

Loren chuckled. "Not sure this qualifies as 'need to know.'"

"Don't give me FBI speak. You get what I mean."

"I *get* that she's your sister. But I have to think of our family, too—our immediate family." She faced him. "Our boys."

Zach drew his chin back. "Now you're freaking me out."

"I'm about to do something that'll likely cost me my career and get me thrown in prison as an accessory."

"Jesus, Lor. What the hell's going on?"

"Just know that I'm trying to balance our kids' and my sister-in-law's well-being. And the two may not be aligned. Wish I could say I've got all the answers, that I know what to do here. But I don't. I'm flying by the seat of my pants, following my gut."

Zach's gaze wandered Loren's face again. "I trust your gut. And I trust *you*. Do what you can to help her."

"And what about you?"

Zach thought about that a long moment, his eyes darting back and forth. Finally he groaned loudly. "For now, keep me out of it."

Loren could only imagine how difficult it was for Zach to say that. While she had to admit that was her preference, it was important for him to reach that conclusion himself. If—or more likely, when—Amy was arrested, Loren's refusal to let Zach help her could destroy their marriage.

Now I just have to figure out how to reach Amy. And think of some way of getting her out of this mess.

49

Amy waited in the bathroom for thirty minutes, wishing she could turn her phone on. But she had little to no reception in the ER, so she shut it down to conserve the battery. She had no charger with her.

The door opened and the nurse she had seen earlier stepped in. "There you are. Dr. West has been looking for you."

"How's my daughter?"

"Come talk with the doctor," she said, gesturing for Amy to follow her. "And reception has been looking for you, too. There are more forms that need to be completed—this time for your daughter." She handed her a clipboard and pen, clearly assuming that Amy had already submitted the first set of documents.

West was writing in a chart when Amy arrived at the nurses station. "Ah," he said, setting the pen down. "Your daughter's doing fine."

"Where is she?" Amy asked, looking around the open department.

"Still in radiology. We're going to keep her here overnight for observation."

"Here?"

"In the ER. We'll watch her for twelve to eighteen hours. She definitely has a concussion but no apparent focal neurologic damage. A wet read of her scan shows a hairline fracture of her sphenoid bone. Not bad considering the impact. Could've been much, much worse. We're going to have orthopedics fashion a face guard to wear for a few weeks."

"A face guard? Like a mask?"

"Like the NBA players wear. It's clear, protects the facial bones."

"Is that really necessary?"

"It's a wise precaution. She's a young girl and young girls can be active. The swelling will subside over the next few days, the discoloration a week to ten days. She banged herself up pretty badly." He set the chart down, made eye contact with Amy. "We do this right, everything will heal up perfectly and she'll be good as new." He chuckled. "She looks just like you. Bet you hear that all the time."

"Yeah." Amy broke out in a cold sweat. "If only you knew."

"Anyway, it'll be a little uncomfortable with that mask on, but she'll get used to it. Assuming no neurological findings crop up during the next twelve to eighteen hours, you'll be good to go."

"Can I see her?"

"She's still in radiology. I'll have someone take you up."

The orderly delivered Amy to a room and told her to wait there. A couple of minutes later, a nursing assistant wheeled Melissa in.

"Be right back," the woman said.

Melissa's face—bruised, swollen, and abraded—broke into a distorted smile that brightened her face. "Amy!"

She jumped out of the chair and ran into Amy's arms. They embraced tightly and seconds later Amy realized that Melissa was crying. Amy leaned back to get a look at her. "What's wrong?"

"I was scared. I didn't know where you were. I was afraid you'd leave me. And that they'd call my mommy."

Amy pulled her close, gently cradling her head and stroking the back of her hair. She started to cry. "I'd never leave you. I'll always be here, no matter what. I love you, sweetie."

They both wept.

Amy realized she could never keep the promises she just made. Her tears of joy turned suddenly to ones of sadness, of loss. Because she knew her time with Melissa was drawing to a close. Today? Tomorrow? The end was coming soon. It had to. How long could she keep this up?

And just like that, Amy now had clarity. How she could have shut the logic of her situation out of her thoughts, her consciousness, for so long, was inconceivable.

"My mommy never tells me she loves me."

Amy drew back and looked into Melissa's tear-filled eyes. She understood the need to feel that your mother cared deeply for, and about, you. "I'm sure she loves you."

Melissa shook her head. "I wish you were my mommy, Amy. Will you be my mommy?"

Amy choked up and she was unable to speak. She forced her throat to relax, to let the emotion ease enough to say, "What about—what about your daddy?"

Melissa thought about that—but only for a matter of seconds. "We can visit him on weekends."

I'd take that deal in a heartbeat.

Whatever the case, Amy now knew—understood—that what she had done was beyond wrong. It was unforgiveable. The impact of her actions hit her full on, her impulsive act and subsequent inability to think it through leaving her woefully unable to fix what she had wrought.

Not that Melissa's living situation was ideal—or even tolerable—but she had now caused additional damage to the girl's life. It would be hard to get her home to her parents now without causing her substantial anguish—not to mention that any hopes Amy had of seeing her grow up were now dashed. Amy would undoubtedly be facing significant jail time...and maybe even a restraining order restricting or denying access to Melissa...even when Amy was released from prison.

Giselle could testify about Christine Ellis's abuse. If convicted, that would leave Melissa's father with custody. But if he was really involved in the clinic fire—and that seemed highly likely based on what Amy knew—he would go to prison himself for conspiracy to commit arson and theft of biologic property. That would leave Melissa...where?

Amy felt guilty for having set in motion a sequence of events that was going to bring to Melissa's life an awful turn of events with no good solution.

The door opened and the orderly reappeared. "C'mon, dear. The radiologist wants to repeat one of the films. Then we can get you over to orthopedics. You can wait in here if you'd like, Mom. Shouldn't be too long."

Amy drew back from Melissa. "Go on. This nice lady will bring you back to me soon as you're done. Okay?"

Melissa nodded. Amy ran her fingers through her knotted hair. "You need a bath so badly..."

"C'mon now," the woman said.

When the door clicked closed, Amy dug out her phone. She booted it up and called Loren—who answered on the first ring.

"Jesus Christ, Amy. I'm so happy to hear your voice."

"Same here."

"But call me back from a pay phone. Can you do that? Right now."

"Um...I'm kinda short on cash."

"If you don't have enough change, call me collect."

"Okay."

"Do it now." Loren gave Amy the burner number.

"May be a bit. I've got to find a phone."

"Call as soon as you can. But don't call me on my cell again and don't use your iPhone anymore. Shut it down and take the SIM card out. Talk to you soon. Love you."

With that, Loren hung up.

What was that about? Does she know about Melissa? How could she? No, it had to be something else.

Amy walked into the corridor but did not see any pay phones. Despite the ubiquity of mobile devices, she figured the hospital had to have at least one somewhere, in a lounge or waiting room—if nothing else, because there were places where wireless communications were prohibited due to equipment interference. But finding an opportunity to make the call—when Melissa would be left alone—would be a challenge.

As she tried to reason that through, the elevator doors opened down the hall.

And the San Luis Obispo police officer stepped out.

50

Keller pulled into the San Luis Obispo Medical Center emergency room parking lot. He had no verification that Melissa was taken here after the accident, but given the proximity to the farmers market, it was his second choice after the Sierra Vista facility.

A promising sign was the presence of a SLOPD police cruiser. While it was not unusual for cops to be at an emergency department, they would definitely be located wherever Melissa Ellis was taken.

It also added a wrinkle he was ill prepared to face: law enforcement. He was already on their radar—and although he had done a decent job of altering his appearance, was he tempting fate by walking into the lion's den?

If the police suspected their perpetrator might be a child molester or sexual predator, they would know he could be fixated on his target and would take moderate risks to continue his pursuit.

While Keller *was* fixated on Melissa Ellis—and he was willing to take moderate risks to get at her—it was to help, not harm, her. But his motivation did not matter if law enforcement was searching for him.

He sat in his vehicle, trying to decide if he should enter the hospital or retreat and wait for Robbins to emerge with the girl, then follow her. Assuming the police did not accompany her, he would force Robbins's vehicle to the side of the road, take Melissa, and head back to the Bay Area.

But did Robbins drive her car to the hospital or ride with the ambulance? He suspected the latter.

Of course, if the Ellises had not been dead set against police involvement, he could simply walk into the ER and explain to the cops that Amy Robbins had kidnapped the girl.

But that was not the case. Discretion was the reason why he was hired, the reason the Ellises were willing to drop five million dollars on his services to bring her home, without anyone being the wiser.

Keller checked his watch, then popped open his door and headed toward the entrance.

51

Amy slipped into the room and stood with her back against the door, heart beating hard and quick. Was the cop coming up to radiology to find her because the police in Oakland put out an alert about Melissa?

Or was his shift ending and he needed to file his paperwork?

She realized it was only a matter of time before the officer found her and asked the required questions. Delaying it further, and unreasonably so, would only draw attention to her if his interest was merely procedural and routine.

She pulled the door open and walked out into the hallway.

"There you are," the officer called a moment later from down the hall. As he approached, Amy saw that his name tag read, Nicholson.

"Sorry. We're still waiting for them to finish the testing. I've—I've just been a nervous wreck." She took a deep, uneven breath.

"I understand. I hope she's going to be okay."

Nicholson was in his late twenties, Amy figured. That may work to her advantage—not as seasoned, not as hardened.

He pulled out his notepad. "Let's start with your name and address and tell me what you saw, a description of the man who grabbed your daughter. I've got some pretty good input from the other witnesses, but this was an attack on you, so maybe you know him or have come across him before."

"I—no, I have no idea who it is. I was playing one of the musical instruments at the band's booth, and I turned around and—" her voice caught. "She was gone. I freaked. I caught a glimpse of this guy, from behind, carrying a girl. I saw her shoes, realized it was her, so I—"

"Hang on a second. Let's start with your name."

"Right. Sorry. Ada Robinson. I'm from out of town. I don't know anyone here. I took my girl because my boyfriend was—well, he was abusive so we got on a bus and we ended up here. I was in San Luis once, years ago. It's pretty."

"Where are you from?"

"North Dakota."

"And your daughter's first name?"

"Elissa."

He asked Amy the standard information, including date of birth, middle name, last name, social security number. "And your address?"

Fortunately, Amy had spent a few minutes researching and preparing the lie. "It's my boyfriend's place, 2300 46th Avenue SE, in Mandan."

"ID?"

"I—I think I lost my wallet when I was running after the guy. I had it out to pay for ice cream a few minutes earlier, and that's the last time I remember seeing it."

"Maybe someone turned it in. Check the market's lost and found."

"I will, soon as we get out of here."

"Anything else you can tell me? Identifying marks on the guy? Something strange that he said? Accent, unusual speech patterns?"

"I never got close enough to get a good look at him—let alone talk to him. Probably would've kicked him in the balls, not carried on a conversation."

That got a chuckle from Nicholson.

He clicked his pen shut. "Okay, Ms. Robinson. Hope your daughter's okay. I'm gonna get this info into the system. We'll do everything we can to catch the guy. Meantime, be careful in case he comes back."

"You think—you think he might?"

"Don't know enough to say. Could be lots of reasons why he went after Elissa. If it's personal, yeah, he might come back. I was him, I'd be long gone. But we've got no way of knowing. Want me to hang out here awhile? Are they going to release your daughter tonight?"

"They said they're keeping her overnight for observation. Broken bone in her face and a concussion. Fitting her for a mask as soon as we're done here."

"I can hang out for a bit till my shift's over. And I'll alert hospital security and give them a description of the perpetrator."

Amy smiled warmly. "Appreciate it. Thanks, Officer Nicholson."

"I'll find your daughter and maintain a post nearby."

As he disappeared down the hallway, Amy figured she had better find that pay phone now, while Melissa was still undergoing testing.

She left a message at the nurses station that she needed to make a call and would be back shortly. The man then directed her to the coffee shop one floor down.

52

Keller walked confidently by the registration desk and through the double doors, then up to the nurses station. He flashed his badge and held out his phone with a photo of Melissa.

"Have you seen this girl in the ER?"

The woman's face wrinkled in concern. A police badge had a tendency to do that to people.

"I—yes. But I can't disclose any information because of HIPPA ru—"

"That's fine. All I need to know is that you've treated her. She's the victim of a child abduction and I've been sent to retrieve her."

"The police officer already spoke to us."

"Where is he?"

"He went up to X-ray to talk with the mother."

"Great. I'll coordinate with him there. Thanks." Keller turned on his heel and walked straight out, not wanting to engage her in further conversation. He had all the information he needed.

Keller made his way around to the main hospital entrance and obtained a visitor's badge from the front desk. He followed the signs to radiology and took the elevator up two floors.

A moment later, he exited and made a single pass of the corridor when he encountered the SLOPD officer. Keller stopped and turned right, into the small waiting room.

The cop was fifteen feet away, standing with his back to him. He figured the guy was doing his duty—looking after the girl following an attempted kidnapping. But was this was a long-term assignment that continued after she was discharged, or just a temporary security posting while she was in the hospital?

He doubted law enforcement had an accurate description of him, so while there was risk in hanging out there, he figured it was worth the gamble. If she was being admitted, he would wait until the middle of the night when staffing was thin and others were asleep—and take her then.

He grabbed an issue of *Popular Science* off the table and turned to an article on the recently launched Chinese unmanned mission to the moon.

At the moment, time was on his side.

53

Loren was in the kitchen fixing dinner with Zach when her burner rang. She pulled it from her back pocket—drew a perplexed look from Zach—and answered it.

"I found a pay phone."

Loren glanced over at her husband, then walked into the garage. "So talk to me. Where are you and what's going on?"

"Right now, I'm in a hospital."

"Hosp—"

"I'm fine. It's—I need help. I've done a terrible thing."

"The girl?"

Amy was silent for a moment. "You know?"

"It's now a federal case. That's why I insisted on the pay phone."

"I hadn't heard anything on the news, so I figured they never called the police."

"They didn't," Loren said, coming up along the passenger side of her Infiniti. "The girl's au pair and Ellen, your boss, reported it to the FBI."

"Giselle." Amy sighed audibly. "I'm so sorry for what I've put her through. I'm sure she feels responsible. Wait, if they went to the FBI—"

"Yes." Loren leaned back against the car. "The Bureau knows who you are."

"Shit."

"Yeah, shit is right. What the hell were you thinking?"

"What do I do, sis? I—I didn't—oh my god."

"I could make a pitch to the Alameda DA's office for a deal. If you turn yourself in and Melissa testifies that she never felt in danger and that you took good care of her...I don't know, no guarantees. But it's the best—the only—option."

"No," Amy said, her voice uneven. "I want to keep you out of it. I've done a terrific job of screwing up *my* life. I won't do the same to yours."

"Soon as they realize I'm your sister-in-law, which is not too far off, they're gonna want to know why I didn't come clean right away. And then they'll investigate to see if I was complicit in the kidnapping and aiding and abetting a fugitive."

"But you weren't."

"I know that, and you know that, but sometimes perception is all that matters."

"So I can't turn myself in," Amy said. "There's gotta be another way."

"There's not. I mean, you can bring Melissa to the local police department and disappear. Really disappear. You'd have to leave the country."

"How would I even do that?"

"It's dangerous. And you'd be all alone. No contact with family or they'll find you. You're better off turning yourself in."

"What about Melissa? She can't go back to her mother. She's been abusing her."

"You know this?"

"Giselle told me. Sending her back home is...I don't see that as an option either. As for me, I should go to prison. What I did was wrong. I know that now."

"A good attorney can claim temporary insanity. With your history—"

"*You're* telling *me* about the law?"

"I'm not convinced you're thinking clearly."

"With my history a jury might just buy it. Either way, even if I get off, or get a light prison sentence—which I highly doubt—it'll be a huge story. I'll never climb out from under this. I'd have to change my name, move to another place where no one would recognize me. And I'd never see Melissa." She sighed again. "But I've made my bed."

"Want to tell me why you're in a hospital?"

Amy recounted the night's events.

Loren listened as she continued to circle her car. "I may know this guy, the one who's after Melissa."

"Know *who* he is, or actually know him?"

"Know him. Used to work with him."

There was a long silence, then: "That explains it. When he broke into my apartment and tried to take Melissa from me—" She cleared her throat. "He asked me about the family photo hanging in the dining area."

"He saw me. And you. He put it together. What'd he say? What'd he do?"

"He just left. I looked up and he was gone."

Interesting. "But if he's still after Melissa, he's probably working for the parents and wants to get paid."

"He's not wrong here. I did kidnap the girl."

"Hey. Don't say that in public."

"Shit. Sorry. I'm—I'm not used to doing this type of thing."

"I want you to buy a burner—a pay-as-you-go phone. Pay for it in cash. Don't sign up for service with your real name or use any identifying information that could be linked back to you. Follow me?"

"Yes, but that's expensive and—"

"You may be able to just buy a SIM card and put that in your iPhone. That'll be a lot cheaper. A little more complicated because you have to deal with compatibility between your phone and the network the SIMs use. The retailer may be able to help walk you through it, but the less contact you have with people the better."

"I'll see if I can figure it out."

The Amy of old could.

"But I've got no money left."

"You have any jewelry on you?"

"Just my wedding ring."

Amy had stopped wearing it years ago, so she brought it with her when she left her apartment—meaning the abduction might have been premeditated. *Jesus, Amy.*

"Okay, listen to me carefully. Find a pawnshop that's open late. Do not speed. Do not break any laws. Hock your ring and you'll have a decent amount of cash. Buy the burner with that."

Amy hesitated but then agreed.

"I know that's a big ask. But get a receipt. We'll pay the loan back when this is over."

Amy sniffled. "Thanks, sis."

"Do this ASAP, before the stores close."

"I can't leave until Melissa's discharged. Hopefully tomorrow."

Loren sighed. "Where are you staying?"

"Sands Motel. Under the name Ada Robinson."

"Okay, good. Be aware of your surroundings...people who may be following you, places where the police may be. Avoid them if possible. At some point soon they're going to get an alert. The locals may spot you."

"I'll be careful."

"Use the pay phone until you can get that burner. Call me on this number tomorrow morning to check in. I've got no way of contacting you, so if there's something urgent you need to know about, until you get a new phone, let's do regular check-ins. But no matter what, do not call me on my cell or Bureau phone. Just a pay phone or the burner."

"What about Zach? Can I call him?"

"No. No text or email either. All that can be tracked. Meantime, let me think about this, about what we can do. Call me back if you need something. I'll keep the burner charged and on me at all times. If I'm not alone and can't speak, I'll call you Charlie."

"Charlie. Got it." She managed a forced chuckle. "I feel like some kind of spy."

"Let's hope you're one of those spies who never get caught."

54

"I only heard one side of the conversation, but—my god—that was enough."

Loren pushed off the car and turned around. "Zach. What the hell? I came out here so you wouldn't hear me."

"I know. But I couldn't stay in the kitchen knowing you were talking to Amy. I had to know what's going on."

"You can't get dragged into this, too. One of us is enough."

"Who's Melissa?"

"Zach, please listen—"

"'No. This is my sister we're talking about. And she's obviously in trouble—lots of trouble. Now who's Melissa?"

"If I tell you—"

"I'll deny I ever knew. There's nothing connecting me to anything Amy's done."

Loren sighed. She led them back into the house. Telling him was a bad idea...but if she refused and Amy came out of this on the short end—which was highly likely—it would forever be a splinter in their marriage.

"Amy kidnapped a little girl. A five-year-old named Melissa."

Zach looked at her, mouth agape. "No. Doesn't sound like her. She'd never do that."

"I don't have time to debate this. She did it. That's not in question. She admitted it."

He started pacing. "I need to talk with her. This doesn't make any sense."

"Amy thinks Melissa is her daughter."

"What? She said that?"

Loren gave Zach a quick rundown of what she knew regarding the embryos.

He sat down at the kitchen table and stared at the empty plate. "Amy should turn herself in...with her history, she could get off lightly."

Loren took a seat across from him. "You're looking at this too clinically. This is your sister. She's been through way too much in her life. Too much tragedy."

"And you're projecting, looking at this emotionally."

"Damn right." Loren slapped the table. "This might be her child. Your niece."

"I get that."

"Losing Lindy destroyed her. If there's something—anything—that can save her, resuscitate her life, it's Melissa."

"But Lor..." Zach spread his hands apart, palm up. "Do I need to state the obvious? This is wrong."

"Is it?"

Zach laughed sardonically. "Yes—on so many levels. Jesus, Lor, what am I missing here? You're an FBI agent and I used to work on Wall Street. Which of us should have a better sense of right and wrong?"

Loren closed her eyes. "I know it's wrong. But it's also not." She stood up and started pacing. "It's...not black and white. Honestly, it's hard to figure out what's right and what's wrong here. And yeah, I'm not exactly unbiased. But I'm not a judge. All I know is what's in my heart."

"And in that woman's heart—what's her name? Christine Ellis? What's she going through, with her daughter missing—kidnapped? Wondering if her little girl is still alive?"

"I know, dammit. I know. I don't have a good answer."

"Yes you do. As an FBI agent, you know what's right here.

And it's not helping my sister get in deeper, with a child that's not hers."

"But it is hers. Hers and Dan's. That's the whole point."

"Do you know that? Do you really know that? Or is my sister delusional? You know her history of mental illness."

"Know it? I've lived through it." Loren put a hand to her forehead. "This is all fucked up."

"You have an obligation to arrest her. If *you* do it, it'll be easier on her."

Loren snorted. "Let me get this straight. You want me to arrest your sister?"

"Of course not. But you'll get in a world of trouble if you don't. And she's in trouble already, whether or not you sacrifice your life and career—and leave your children without their mother."

Loren sat down heavily on the couch. Coco came bounding over and leaped onto her lap. She rested her right hand on the dog's chest.

"You'll be throwing your career out the window. You wanted to be an FBI agent since you were fifteen. And we need to bring that girl home safely. Not to mention—"

"I can't do this, Zach. I just can't. Amy would spend years in prison—and if the jury doesn't buy the insanity defense, maybe the rest of her life. It'd be doing to your sister what tragedy failed to do. It'd kill her. Not physically, but emotionally. Permanently. She'll never recover."

"But what about this girl—Melissa? I mean, if she's not Amy's child, she's been kidnapped, taken from her family. If she really is Amy's, wouldn't Amy want what's best for the child?"

Loren sighed. "There's more to this story. The mother is abusing her. Not sexually but physically. Emotionally. I don't know all the details. And the father, because of his involvement in the clinic fire, will likely be convicted of conspiracy to commit arson, insurance fraud, and a list of other things prosecutors will pile on. Melissa will be without her parents no matter what happens with Amy."

Zach shook his head. "The situation sucks. There's no good

solution. But we've got to think of what's best for our family. Amy...I love my sister, but her tragedy has become ours. It's taken a toll on all of us. And now, to sacrifice your career, and potentially deprive your boys of their mother, not to mention being ostracized...that can't be the best option here."

Loren did not reply.

"Arrest her and we'll hire the best attorney in the Bay Area. That much we can do for her. Stand beside her, support her, try our best to lessen the blow, get her in a minimum-security facility. Hell, maybe it'll help her in some strange way."

Loren tapped Coco's rear and the dog sat up. Loren rose from the couch. "She actually wanted to turn herself in."

"Now *that* sounds like my sister."

"Yeah, whatever." She pivoted right and pulled open the garage door.

"Where you going?"

"For a drive."

"Now? It's late."

"I've gotta clear my mind."

"But what about dinner?"

"Smells good. Enjoy it. When the boys get home from youth group, tell them I'll see them later."

55

The nurse checked Melissa's heart monitor, then turned to Amy. "Not a lot of room in here. Is that cot going to work for you?"

"It's fine," Amy said. "Not sure how much sleep I'm going to get anyway. I'll probably lay awake the whole night watching her breathe."

The nurse chuckled. "I've got two kids. Completely understand."

When the door closed, Melissa turned to Amy. "What happened? Why am I here?"

"You don't remember?"

Melissa shook her head. "They said I had a bad fall."

"Remember the man who came to my apartment? He must've been following us. We were in the farmers market. Do you remember *that*?"

"The big bear." She laughed. "And the yummy ice cream."

"Right. After the ice cream we saw a booth with the school band. They were showing people how to play all their instruments. I sat down to play one, and that's when the man grabbed you. I ran after him and started screaming and some people saw what was happening and tried to catch him. They ran into him and you fell, hit your head."

She stared straight ahead, as if trying to recall those events. "Why does that man want to take me away?"

Amy sighed. She sat up in bed and crossed her legs. "I think he's working for your parents."

"Why?"

"They probably paid him to find you and bring you home."

Melissa thought about that. Then she looked at the ceiling. "I don't want to go home. I want to see 'Selle, but..."

"Why don't you want to go home?" Amy waited a moment but Melissa did not answer. "Is it because of your mom?"

Melissa glanced at the door.

"You're safe here. No one's gonna come in. It's just you and me."

The girl's gaze settled in her lap. "She's not nice. She...she gets angry, grabs my arm and it hurts."

"Do you tell her it hurts?"

"Yes."

"And she stops?"

"She squeezes harder. I cry and she squeezes more. I try to pull away and she hits me." Melissa's eyes teared over. Amy stroked her arm, swallowed deeply.

"When I want to watch TV after dinner she pulls me by my hair into my room. Tells me to go to bed."

"Does she ever read you bedtime stories?" Amy had to think there were *some* redeeming qualities to Christine Ellis.

Melissa shook her head.

Amy gently touched the side of her face. "I'll do what I can to protect you from that, okay? I don't know how, yet, but I'll figure something out."

The nurse entered and asked if Amy had finished the paperwork yet.

"Yeah," Amy said. She got close to the woman and said, in a low voice, "It's a little incomplete because I lost my wallet. We had to leave North Dakota pretty quickly. Boyfriend was...well, we were having problems. I lost my wallet downtown when that guy—when he tried to kidnap her." She handed over the clipboard and pen.

"I'll bring it to the administrator. If she has any questions, she'll come find you. She's gone home, so I'm sure she'll touch base with you in the morning."

As the woman was leaving, Officer Nicholson stepped in. "Well. Someone's looking better. I'm Todd." He sidestepped Amy and shook Melissa's hand. "Can you tell me what the man looked like? The one who took you?"

"She doesn't remember what happened," Amy said.

"I remember seeing the big bear. And I remember getting ice cream."

"He took her right after we got the ice cream," Amy said.

Nicholson crumpled his lips and nodded. "Okay. I'm sure it'll come back to you. When it does, we need to know everything you remember, okay?"

Melissa nodded.

He turned to Amy. "My shift's over, so I'm gonna take off. A detective will be by to get more information. At this point, it'll probably be tomorrow." He took out one of his business cards. "You think of anything, or if you see anything suspicious, you call me." He pulled out a pen and wrote something on the back. "That's my cell. I spoke with security and they said they'll hang around and keep an eye on your room." Nicholson chuckled. "I gave him some tips. Tricks of the trade I learned from a deputy US Marshal a couple of years ago. He was in charge of protecting witnesses."

"Thanks, officer. I appreciate everything you've done for us. You have a good night."

"You too, ma'am." He winked at Melissa. "Feel better."

"I already do. Lots better."

Nicholson hooked his belt loop with a thumb. "Now if we find the guy who did this to you, *I'll* feel a lot better."

56

Keller set the magazine down and watched as the flow of hospital staff thinned. Moments later, the officer headed toward the elevator.

He figured that meant one of two things: the girl was being released or the cop's shift was over. Hopefully both.

Keller made his way to one of the radiology rooms and flashed his badge at an orderly who was entering data into a computer. An image of an X-ray was on the screen to his right. "This girl," he said, holding up his phone with an image of Melissa. "She was having some diagnostic tests. Has she been released?"

"I'm afraid I can't give out any information on patients."

"Look, pal, I'm not interested in *medical* information. Nothing private. I'm working her case. Some guy tried to grab her from the farmers market and I'm in charge of catching him. I need to know if she's finished with her testing and if so, where she was sent. Was she admitted or released?"

The man frowned. "She had a scan and X-rays but we needed to repeat a couple of films." He clacked some on the keyboard, then said, "She was sent back to the ED. Staying overnight for observation."

"Thanks."

Keller used the stairs and reentered the emergency department, where he caught a glimpse of the officer walking out the doors.

He found the restroom and stepped into one of the stalls—his hiding place for the next few hours while he waited for the staffing to drop to overnight levels.

Once that happened, he would—carefully—go in search of his prey.

57

Keller's phone vibrated ten minutes later. It was a Bay Area number, but not one he knew. He answered anyway. When on a job, you never knew who might be trying to reach you with time-sensitive information.

"Kill the bitch."

Keller straightened up. "Who is this?"

"Christine Ellis. And I want you to get rid of her. I want Amy Robbins gone, out of our lives."

"Mrs. Ellis, we shouldn't be talking about this on the phone."

"It's *doctor*. And you're not here. I have no idea *where* you are. Are you nearby?"

"No."

"So this will have to do. Do you have reason to believe your phone is being monitored?"

"No, but still, it's bad form to—"

"Then don't worry about it."

"Look..." Keller walked out of the stall and checked to make sure no one else was in the restroom. "I have my orders and mission scope. And what you're asking is way outside that scope. Way, way outside it."

"If it's the money—"

"The money is fine—for what I agreed to do. Bring Melissa

home."

"And that's why I've increased your fee. I want results. *Now*, not next week. Not next month."

He cleared his throat. "Is Mr. Lira there?"

"No. And this does not involve him."

Keller scratched his head. "Dr. Ellis, my job is to bring your daughter home. I'm working on that. She's in the same building as I am right now. So just be patient and—"

"Patient. Patient, Mr. Keller? I've *been* patient. And my patience has run out. I want my daughter back and I want Robbins out of our lives forever. I don't want to have to worry that she's going to go to the media over her crazy delusions about Melissa. And I don't want sleepless nights. The only way to accomplish that—"

"Offer her money. Make her a deal."

"This isn't about money."

"Then talk to your attorney. Maybe—"

"You're not listening. Kill. That. Bitch."

"Dr. Ellis—"

"You're running out of time. She's jeopardizing a billion-dollar deal. Do you understand that? Can you comprehend that amount of money?"

Keller leaned his back against the tile wall. "Honestly, no. I can't. I'm not sure anyone can."

"If she talks to the media, posts things online, that deal is—"

"Right now, she wouldn't dare. But even if she would, I'm doing my best to make sure that doesn't happen."

"Your assurances are meaningless."

Keller cleared his throat. "Look, let me talk with Mr. Lira and I—"

"Fifty million."

Keller pushed away from the wall. "What?"

"I've deposited fifty million dollars in a Cayman account in trust for Mr. Tait."

"Dr. Ellis, my boss would never—"

"I already spoke to him."

"You what?"

"He's the one who set up the account. He verified the money is on deposit."

"I'm not comfortable with this."

She laughed contemptuously. "He thought you'd have a problem with it."

"He said that?"

"Not exactly. He said he might need to remove you from the case. And he assured me he'd take care of it, one way or another. So you've got a choice to make."

Keller stood there a long moment, absorbing this. "Dr. Ellis, why'd you call me?"

"Honestly?"

Keller did not answer. What is honesty to a person who would order an innocent woman murdered?

"You know what?" he said. "Doesn't matter." No doubt Tait figured a woman would have a better shot at convincing him to make Amy Robbins disappear. "Good-bye, Dr. Ellis."

Keller disconnected the call. He stood there staring at... nothing. Inside, he felt as empty as the bathroom.

Thirty seconds after hanging up, his phone vibrated again. It was Tait.

"Can you talk?"

"This is not a secure line."

"Call me back on the sat phone."

Keller cursed under his breath and left the hospital—hoping he could get back in—and dialed Tait.

"Yeah."

"Bill, you can't be serious."

"I take it you spoke with Christine Ellis. And that your answer is no."

Keller started walking the parking lot. "You knew what my answer would be."

"Yeah, I kinda did. But fifty million dollars is a hell of a lot of money to turn away. Hell, your twenty-five million cut would be enough to retire on. You could get out of this business, like you've wanted to do all along."

"Jesus."

"I don't want to lose you, but my sole focus right now has to be mission success. And that means getting the girl home safely and taking care of the woman. That's it. The rest—your retirement—we can discuss later."

"Bill...I was fine with bringing the girl back. But killing the mother?"

"Mother? What the hell are you talking about?"

"This is more fucked up than you know. The Ellises stole Amy Robbins's embryos from a fertility clinic in Boston. That's the girl Robbins abducted. Her own daughter."

Tait emitted a pained sigh.

"Mickey...you know how soldiers operate. They get their orders and they execute. Efficiently. No emotional involvement— or they make mistakes."

"And I was fine with my orders. But this...the Robbins woman lost her husband and daughter in a car accident. Her life has been torn apart. She deserves more. I can't compound an injustice by killing her."

"Take a few minutes to think about this."

"Retirement is great, Bill, but you've gotta enjoy it. And that means a clear conscience."

"Clear conscience? What the fuck is that? You fought in a war, buddy. You killed people. Innocent people. Who's got a clear conscience? I sure don't."

"This is different. And you know it. Killing an innocent woman—"

"Innocent? She kidnapped a five-year-old girl and took her on a road trip. And from what you told me, that girl's now in the hospital with head trauma. This was an open and shut case. If you'd done your job in the first place, they would've had Melissa Ellis back and Robbins would've continued on living her miserable life."

Keller could not argue with that.

"So if you really want to look yourself in the mirror, *you're* responsible. And either you clean it up or I send Sinbad."

Keller squeezed the phone. Sinbad lived up to his name, a case where irony was on full display. The man had a sadistic streak to him. He was lethally effective, a six-foot-five, three-hundred-pound steroid abusing psychopath who was not above torturing his victims before carrying out the job of killing them. As a result, Tait only used Sinbad on specific jobs.

"What about Dansbury? Or Greene?"

"Both overseas on cases. This is time sensitive. And Sinbad needs the work."

Keller groaned—internally. "I'll do it."

"Mickey. Take some time. An hour. Think it through."

"No. I'll do it. Sinbad...I couldn't live with myself knowing what he was going to do to her. He'd probably even do it with the girl standing there. I do it, it'll be quick and painless."

"Fine. But if you have any doubts, any at all, you need to tell me. Otherwise you'll screw up. We've had enough of that."

Keller clenched his jaw. "I got it, Bill. I'll take care of it."

He put his phone down and rubbed his temples. He needed to somehow separate Melissa from Amy so that her life was not marked by witnessing the murder of a loved one—and so that she did not become a witness capable of identifying him.

He closed his eyes and sucked in the cool night air, frustrated he was even thinking along these lines.

Sometimes life just plain sucked.

58

Loren was in bed, staring at the ceiling. After getting home, she spent some time poking around the internet researching the Ellises to get a sense of who they were, what their business interests were, and what was publicly available on Melissa.

Before embarking on that virtual journey, however, she went into paranoid mode by using a virtual private network to mask her internet connection, then scrubbing her browsing history with software that overwrote the deleted files nearly three dozen times with a Department of Defense algorithm. She wanted to leave behind no record of any connection to the Ellises.

There was very little recent information on them—their social media presence was limited to Facebook postings on infertility and articles having to do with their breakthrough genetic testing company. Their LinkedIn profiles contained more of the same, with the addition of education and work history and job postings they made over the years.

However, an old article in the *Mercury News* archive mentioned that Melissa was their only child, both sets of their parents were deceased, and Christine's only sibling, an older sister, had passed away in her thirties from a skiing accident. They had no next of kin.

Loren lay there another hour thinking. Zach was likewise awake. They both needed shuteye—Zach always rose at 6:00 AM when the market opened and Loren...well, she was going to be tired tomorrow. She did not foresee any sleep coming tonight.

Thirty minutes later, she said, "We can't do this."

Zach sighed. "Do what?"

Loren brought her eyes up to meet his. "We can't turn her in. And she can't turn herself in."

Zach groaned.

"I know. But what if the best attorney in San Francisco can't get her off and she goes to prison? Even if it's only five years. It'd be a death sentence for her."

Zach turned on his side toward Loren. "We've been through this."

"Who knows what'll happen to her in prison? One thing's for sure—she'll lapse back into depression. She was just starting to come out of it—because of Melissa. It brought Amy back to life again."

"She was making progress before she met Melissa."

Loren snorted. "Yeah, she got a job. At a bakery. Kneading dough. You're right, Zach. She was making *progress*. But we're talking about a Harvard educated, Stanford Law attorney."

"None of this was her fault."

"The kidnapping sure seemed to be premeditated—"

"Amy's not a kidnapper," Zach said. "She's not a criminal. She was the most honest person I ever knew. And then everything was taken from her."

Loren fell silent. She did not want to have this debate. This was one of those situations that they had little to no control over and arguing about it was not going to change that fact.

She hoped that when Amy called in the morning Melissa would be doing better and she would be able to leave the hospital. But then what?

The next thing Loren was aware of, Zach's alarm was dinging. She turned over and found that he was already out of bed.

Loren padded over to his office and saw him sitting at his desk, the computer screen filled with stock charts and real-time quotes.

She walked into the bathroom and started to brush, checking the burner phone to make sure she had not missed a call from Amy.

As she thought about what her sister-in-law's next moves should be, Loren realized she had made one miscalculation. In her effort to think of everything, she forgot something. Something really important.

Amy might have used her credit card in San Luis Obispo. The Bureau, with an identity attached to their kidnapper, would look for electronic traces of her whereabouts, and that included purchases involving the banking system.

Amy did not have much money left to her name. The medical and rehab expenses, psychiatrist and pharmaceutical costs drained her savings during the years she was unable to work—and state disability was wholly insufficient to keep her afloat. Even if she had planned the abduction ahead of time, it was unlikely she had much cash at her disposal to take with her.

Loren stood there staring at the bathroom mirror, thinking and not seeing. She refocused and spit, then rinsed. That's why she had no money left. She probably took whatever cash she had at home and when that ran out, drained her checking account. With her ATM card.

That, or she was forced to use her credit card. Either way, the Bureau would soon have access to those records. They would then parse her receipts and charges.

Loren got dressed quickly. She had two changes of clothes in the go-bag in her Bureau car, or BuCar, trunk—along with a couple hundred dollars—but she needed more to give her maximum flexibility.

She walked into their closet and opened the safe, withdrew the envelope where they kept the cash part of their earthquake preparedness backpack, and stuffed it into her purse.

Loren stopped into Zach's office and kissed the back of his neck. From the sound of his side of the conversation, he was on the phone with a trader.

He swiveled in his seat and glanced up at her. While simultaneously talking about option spreads for Apple, he gave her a nod. She blew him a kiss and mouthed, "Call you later"—then walked out before he could ask any questions.

It was better this way. He would not worry about her—about her doing anything stupid. For all he knew, she would be at work. And if anyone asked him where she went, or spent the day, he would truly have no clue.

Loren grabbed an awl from the tool pegboard, then fired up the Bureau car and headed for San Luis Obispo.

59

Brandon Ellis was seated at the conference room table, a venti cup of high octane Starbucks steaming by his right elbow. "Well that can't be right."

"Come again?" Angelo Lira was sitting across from him, paging through a PowerPoint presentation his assistant had prepared.

"Did you make a drawdown of fifty million dollars?" Ellis clicked and expanded the entry. "Electronic transfer."

"What account?"

"Capex."

"I don't have access to your accounts, Brandon." Lira squinted. "You know that."

"Yeah." Ellis frowned and continued clicking through recent transactions.

"So who else has access?"

"Christine."

"That's a large sum," Lira said. "Mind if I come around and take a look?"

"Says it was a wire transfer."

Lira moved behind Ellis and studied the transaction. "Yeah. To an international account. Not sure but might be Cayman Islands."

"Exactly right."

They looked up. Christine was standing in the doorway.

"Exactly right, what?" Ellis asked.

"Cayman Islands." She closed the door behind her.

"For what?"

"An investment."

Ellis and Lira shared a look. "Fifty million? An investment? That's our working capital for equipment and the lease we have coming due."

Christine waved a hand. "In a week, that won't be a concern. The money won't be missed."

They watched as she walked over to the table and took a seat opposite Lira. She folded her hands in front of her.

"What kind of investment?" Ellis asked.

"I'd rather not say."

"Christine," Lira said, "large expenditures—and this is way over the definition of 'large'—are subject to AIL Venture Capital's approval. We've gone out of our way to avoid micromanaging your business. But this—this requires a thorough explanation."

"Really, Angelo?" Christine laughed mockingly. "We're going to be swimming in money in seven days. What are we arguing about here?"

"We're not arguing." Lira clenched his jaw. "Everything we do, especially in the weeks before the IPO, is closely scrutinized. And a withdrawal of this magnitude—to some kind of offshore account in the Caymans—is highly suspect. Do I have to remind you the FBI is now asking questions about Melissa's disappearance? I need an explanation for this fifty mil right now or—"

"Or what?" Christine leaned forward, sliding her clasped hands forward on the conference room table. "What'll you do? Report me? Get angry? Threaten to pull out?" She lifted her left hand and held up one finger. "First, you're not going to report me to the FBI or SEC because your billion dollars will evaporate before your eyes." Two digits. "Second, it's too late to pull out." Three. "You can get angry. Yes, that you can do."

"Oh, I'm already angry."

"Christine," Ellis said. "What are you up to?"

"I used our funds wisely. And I did something you should've done from the beginning," she said, looking intently into Lira's gaze.

"Dammit," Ellis said. "Enough playing games. What'd you do with the money? You may not have to tell him, but you need to tell me."

Christine slapped the table. "Fine. You want to know? I put it in trust for Tait Protection. I increased the fee."

"We already paid them five million dollars to bring Melissa home," Lira said. "What on earth could cost ten times that?"

"Making sure we don't have a problem. After the FBI came calling, I realized we needed to take this up a notch. What we've been doing isn't working. There are risks that need to be managed. Risks that *should've* been addressed from the start."

Lira and Ellis shared a perturbed look.

Then Lira turned slowly to Christine. "Tell me you didn't do something stupid."

"Hiring you. *That* was stupid. No, I just made sure nothing could come back on us. I was looking out for you. And us."

Lira's eyebrows rose. "You put out a contract on Amy Robbins?"

Christine cocked her head. An admission without verbal confirmation.

"Oh my god," Ellis said. "Christine, please tell me Angelo's wrong."

Christine turned away and let her gaze roam the walls.

"Jesus Christ." Ellis dropped his head into his hands. "This isn't happening."

"Christine," Lira said, his voice soft yet confident. "You need to call it off. We can't do this."

"*You* can't do it. That's why *I* did."

"You may've thought that was a good idea, but trust me. It's not. Let my guy do his thing, get Melissa back safely. Robbins won't come forward. She can't because she committed a felony. She abducted a young girl. She'll go to prison. Plus, she doesn't know anything about the IPO. She's not going to try to extort us. And even if she does, again...she committed a serious crime."

"Your guy needed extra motivation," Christine said. "Five million wasn't getting the job done and there was no time to hire someone else. So I gave him forty-five million other reasons to bring Melissa home—and make sure none of this comes back on us. Ever."

Lira got up and faced the wall, put his hands on his hips, and closed his eyes. "Brandon, I'm going to touch base with Bill Tait and see about calling this off."

"When the job's done," Christine said, "the fee automatically gets paid out of the trust account. Even if I try to cancel, which I can't, the fee still gets paid."

Lira pulled out his phone. He punched in a string of numbers and then left the room while it rang.

Ellis sat there staring at Christine. "I'm sure you thought this would help, but...I don't even know where to begin. How could you do this without checking with me first?"

"Because you would've had a problem with it. Just like you do now. This way, it's done. Sometimes it's better to do something and ask forgiveness later."

"Forgiveness is a good word. But you'll have to talk to Father Jensen, because if Keller kills that young woman, I won't be able to forgive you."

Christine sat back. "Well, what do you know? My husband has grown a set of balls. If you'd had those a few years ago we wouldn't have needed those embryos from John. Could've avoided all this hassle."

Ellis's face pimpled with perspiration. "Christine, I don't understand what's gotten into you. You were never like this. I...I don't know you anymore."

The door opened and Lira walked in. His expression was hard, his features angular, his face red as he looked at Christine. "I hope you realize what you've done."

Ellis stood up. "What happened?"

"I couldn't cancel it. Like she said, in contracts like this, there's no buyer's remorse."

"Let them keep the money. Tell them the Robbins woman's not to be harmed."

"Really, Brandon? I didn't think of that." Lira rubbed his forehead. "I did my best. But they've got procedures in place for a reason. Once Tait gives the assignment to the operative, he may not be able to reach him until he completes the job. So right up front it's made very clear that the order is noncancelable."

Christine shrugged. "Like I said."

"Did he even try to reach the guy?"

"There are other reasons," Lira said. "I couldn't argue with him. But even if I could, he wasn't in a listening mood."

Ellis rubbed the back of his neck. "So now what? Do we warn Amy Robbins?"

"Hard enough trying to find her to get your daughter back," Lira said. "'How are we gonna find her to warn her? The person we've hired to find her is now the one who's trying to kill her. Even if we could contact her directly, if you were her, would you believe us? I mean, how would we know someone's trying to kill her unless we're the ones who ordered it?"

Christine stood up and walked toward the door. "Two men in the room and the only one with the balls to do this was the woman."

60

Amy awoke before Melissa and brushed her teeth using the care kit the hospital had given her. It was only 7:30 AM, so she surmised the administrator had not arrived yet. But she would soon—and Amy would likely be her first stop.

While Amy was washing her face, Melissa stirred. "Where am I?"

"In the hospital. Remember?"

"Yeah," she said, rubbing her eyes with two fists.

"How'd you sleep?"

Melissa blinked a few times and looked around the small room. "The nurse was mean. She woke me up."

"It's her job to check on you. You had a concussion so they're just being careful."

"What's a con-cushion?"

"When you hit your head, your brain gets bounced around a little bit. Like when you drop an apple and it gets a bruise. It'll be all better in a few days."

Melissa's eyes opened wide. "We have to stay here?"

"They'll let us leave soon. Hopefully today. Then we'll take it easy. No jumping out of airplanes for a while."

"Jumping out of airplanes?" she sung. "That's silly."

"Yeah, sometimes I get silly. Hey, I've gotta go make a phone call. Can you wait here for a few minutes by yourself?"

"Yes."

"Okay, sweetie. I'll be back as fast as I can."

Upon leaving the room, Amy scoped out the vicinity. She saw only a handful of people milling about—nurses and a few technicians. Quiet morning in the emergency department. She notified the security guard that she was stepping out for a few minutes, and he assured her everything would be fine.

Amy made her way over to the same pay phone she had used yesterday and dialed the burner number Loren had given her.

"Hey sis."

"How are you?"

"Tired but fine."

"And Melissa?"

"She just woke up. Doctor hasn't been by yet. But I'm going to have to answer to the hospital's office manager. I put bogus info on my intake paperwork but I'm sure they're gonna want some kind of insurance information."

"There's no good way out of that one. But it may be moot. You've gotta get out of there."

"When?"

"Now."

"What? Why?"

"I assume you used your credit or bank card for gas or a hotel?"

"Motel. And yeah, for gas, too. I didn't have much cash—"

"The Bureau can track your electronic transactions and as soon as they get the warrant—which they may already have—they're going to zero in on your location."

Amy glanced around the coffee shop. People were beginning to file in to get their breakfast java and muffins. "I can't leave if it's not safe for Melissa."

Loren was silent.

"Some things are more important than ourselves."

"Amy, you could be arrested. In an hour, two, three...I just have no idea. They'll coordinate with the local police, who'll put out an APB. And an amber alert. I'm surprised they haven't issued one already. Once that happens, all eyes and ears, traffic cams, and surveillance cameras will be looking for you."

Amy squeezed her right eye closed, trying to still the twitch. "I understand the risks."

"And if they find out about the incident downtown at the farmers market, it'll take them *seconds* to draw the line between that and the woman and young girl at—where are you?"

"SLO Medical Center. And let me ask you this. If you were in here and Devin or Daniel had a head injury, would you check him out of the hospital against doctor's orders?"

"No."

"Well this is my daughter and I won't jeopardize her life. I'd do anything for her, just like you would for your boys. If I get arrested, then so be it. Like I said, maybe that's what I deserve anyway."

"I'm just worried about you. Which is why I'm on my way there. I should be in SLO in about three hours."

"For what?"

"Everything. Anything."

"But I don't want you to—"

"That point you just made about Devin? Well that's how I feel about you. Family comes first. I lose my job, I'll be upset. But financially we'll be fine."

"And if you're thrown in jail?"

There was a moment's hesitation, then: "You'd better get back to Melissa. Are you using the same name at the hospital?"

"Yes. Ada and Elissa Robinson."

"See you soon, Ada. Remember what I said. And watch your back."

61

Jimmy Hill hung up the phone and called to Special Agent Tran Minh two cubicles over from his. "Yo, Tran. We got us a problem. Conference room."

"Mountain know?"

"He's in San Francisco today."

Mountain was their nickname for Child Crimes Squad Supervisor Zeke Bailey, a six-foot-four college lineman-turned-FBI agent after a compound leg fracture prematurely ended his NFL career.

Minh set his phone down and followed. They walked through the maze of hallways and entered the large rectangular conference room. A long table with padded leatherette seats dominated the space. An oversize flat panel was mounted on the far wall, with a robust camera system on the right designed to work with the secure video teleconference system.

Hill grabbed the remote—and quickly set it down. "Wrong freakin' one. Like my house. Five clickers and I never know which to use. All I wanna do is turn on the damn TV and veg on the couch." He pressed a button and the system booted up. They took seats and within seconds two men and a woman were staring back at him: Special Agent in Charge of the San Francisco Field Division

Bennett Jackson, Assistant Special Agent in Charge Dahlia Scott, and squad supervisor Bailey. For some reason, putting Mountain on a television screen, even if he was only a dozen miles away across the bay, made him seem less threatening.

"Sir," Hill said, "I found some disturbing information on the Melissa Ellis case. The abductor, Amy Robbins, is related to one of our agents."

"Which one?" Jackson asked.

"Loren Ryder. Her sister-in-law."

"And where's Loren? Why isn't she on this call?"

Hill looked down. "First, this isn't her case. Far as I know, she has no clue about the two women who reported the girl missing."

Jackson spread his hands. "That's assuming her sister-in-law didn't tell her."

"Assuming that," Hill said. "However, Loren didn't come into the office this morning. She left me a voice mail telling me she was heading down to Monterey to interview a couple of witnesses on the Wyatt case."

"Did you call her?" Bailey asked.

"I did." Hill bit his bottom lip. "Went straight to voice mail."

Scott and Bailey shared a look of concern.

"Do we have reason to believe Loren is involved in this abduction in *any* way?" Bailey asked.

"No sir. But I haven't had any time to look into it. I just found this out ten minutes before I messaged you."

"Okay," Jackson said. "If you don't hear from her by midafternoon, use all necessary measures to find her. Put out a BOLO with local PD and CHP. I want to take her at her word—we all do—but we also have to keep our eyes open in case she's involved in this abduction. So just because she told you she was headed to Monterey doesn't mean she is."

"Of course," Hill said. "But I can't imagine Loren having anything to do with this."

"Me either," Minh said.

"I hear you." Jackson looked over at Scott and Bailey, who both nodded. "We agree. But at the same time, we don't want to get caught up in an OPR inquiry a month from now answering tough questions as to why we didn't take appropriate action," he said, referring to the Office of Professional Responsibility—the Bureau's internal police.

"I'll be back in the office in an hour," Bailey said, "in case anything breaks."

They covered some additional details, then signed off and Hill and Minh returned to their desks.

"I'm gonna be real pissed if Loren's wrapped up in this," Hill said, stopping in front of his chair. "Do you think she heard me talking about the case? Heard her sister-in-law's name and..."

"And what?"

"I don't know. Went to warn her?"

Minh thought a moment. "Find Loren and we may find her sister-in-law and Melissa Ellis."

"Okay, here's the plan. Draw up an affidavit for the warrant. If we need to search her house or car, I don't want to lose any time. Then take Mr. Ryder's finances and phone records. I'll dig through Loren's desk and dive deeper if we don't hear back from her."

"This sucks," Minh said.

Hill stepped across the "aisle" to Ryder's cubicle. "I feel dirty. Like I'm looking through my wife's phone, emails, photos. You know?"

"Hope she's innocent. And I hope she understands why we're doing what we're doing."

"She'll understand," Hill said. "But she still won't like it. Not one bit."

62

As Loren approached Soledad, she began doubting her decision to leave Oakland without stopping by the office. It was not a question of *if* the Bureau discovered the connection to Amy, but when. Because of its inevitability, she felt it was smarter to leave before they detained her. Once they did that, they would question her for a prolonged period, then monitor all her communications, movements, and case work.

She would have to ditch the burner because having it on her would immediately raise suspicion that she was doing something that was not above board.

The more she parsed it, she figured they could also take a different approach: absent convincing evidence of collusion, they would treat her as a colleague helping them make sense of something that appears—on the surface—disconcerting.

They would question her first, without telling her why, and once they had her answers and time lines and whereabouts locked in, they would explain why they were asking.

When Loren then expressed surprise at Amy's rogue behavior, absent any direct evidence of contact between them, they would surreptitiously monitor her, hoping Amy would call, text, or email her.

After the initial round of questions, she would go to the bathroom, remove the SIM card from the burner and flush it down the toilet, then wipe the handset to remove her fingerprints and DNA. She could dump it in the water as well—the older iPhones were not sealed and the motherboard and chips would be ruined—but finding an expensive device submerged would raise red flags and, given the context, point directly to her.

The better move would be to merely hide it somewhere en route to the bathroom or leave it behind in the stall when she returned to her desk. It would take a day or two for them to find it—and it could not be traced back to her.

However, the phone call Amy made to Loren's cell would be a problem. It only lasted a minute, but she needed to be prepared to explain it.

Loren was about ninety minutes from San Luis Obispo when she exited at Soledad, a four-and-a-half-square-mile farming community off the freeway nestled against the Gabilan Mountains. Known for the Spanish mission, Nuestra Señora de la Soledad that dated to 1791, the town sat in the Salinas Valley, the "salad bowl of the world"—one of the most economically productive agricultural regions on the planet.

She found a secondary road and pulled to the side, then dug around in her go-bag and removed one of the old wigs she had used while undercover. It was in decent condition and transformed her from a brunette short hair style to a strawberry blonde with shoulder-length waves. She looked in the rearview mirror and fluffed the locks, making sure the positioning was correct and that it obscured her darker strands.

Next, Loren removed the colored contact lenses from their case and hoped they were not bathing in bacteria-laden fluid. She had been good about changing the solution periodically but forgot and went longer than was probably smart. They made her hazel eyes a deep sky blue.

She got out, removed the awl from her purse, and drove it into the thinner rubber between the treads of the left rear tire. It took some perseverance, but she penetrated the surface deep enough to hear the rapid release of air. She got back in the vehicle and drove it a half mile until the rear end fishtailed, leaving telltale sway marks in the surface dirt.

Loren shoved her two-way radio and magnetic light cube into her go-bag, then got out and started walking toward the nearest house. After passing numerous orchards, she came upon a residence. She did a quick assessment from the road, then moved on. Three more homes and a mile and a half later, she saw something to her liking. She went up to the front door and knocked.

A Hispanic man in overalls with a dirt rag in his hands appeared behind the screen. "Yeah?"

"I need a car and I noticed the Ford on the side of your house."

"You *need a car*? Señora, do I look like Avis? I'm busy."

"I only need it for a few days."

He grabbed the wood door to close it. "Go rent one."

"I'd rather give *you* the money." She held up a few hundred-dollar bills. "Cash. Tax-free."

He stopped, eyed her, then pushed on the screen door and it swung open with a metallic squeak. He stepped out onto the porch.

"And you wanna use one of my cars?"

"I do. The one covered in a thick layer of dust. I figure you don't drive it much."

"Oh yeah?"

"Yep."

His gaze rode up and down her body. It made her uncomfortable, but it was not the first time in her life a guy had done that.

"How about a hundred a day?"

"Estas demente. How about two hundred a day?"

"Cash? How about I find another car." Loren turned and headed off the porch.

"One-fifty."

Loren turned and faced him. She thought a moment. "How's it run?"

"Good enough. Engine works. Don't burn oil. Needs brakes."

"They work?"

"Señora." He laughed. "They'll stop the car, if that's what you're asking."

"Fine. One-fifty a day." She looked down at the bills in her hand and started to count.

"Two-day minimum. And a five-hundred-dollar deposit."

"The car itself isn't worth that. How 'bout I just buy it from you?"

"'Cause I got a kid who'll be driving next year."

Loren pursed her lips, then nodded. "I'll give you three days in case I need it longer. And the deposit." She held out the money and he reached for it. "Get the keys and let's start the thing up. Then I'll pay you."

"Already got 'em in my pocket."

"What's your name?"

"Gomez. You?"

"Nancy."

They walked up to, and around, the vehicle. It was an old navy Ford Crown Victoria, the kind most police departments used. If it was in better condition, it could be mistaken for an unmarked vehicle. That was a big reason for knocking on Gomez's door.

It had tinted windows—not surprising given the intense central California sun—and started up fine, if a little rough. Sounded like the muffler needed to be replaced, too. But the idea was to have an untraceable set of wheels while she retrieved Amy and Melissa—and this would do.

Then...well, she had not figured that part out yet. But leaving her BuCar on the side of the road in Soledad gave her some cover in not being in the same place Amy was when, or if, the FBI or local law enforcement found her.

Loren handed him the cash and tossed her bag inside.

"You got any ID?"

"Sorry," Loren said, "Not with me."

"Didn't think so."

"Look, Señor Gomez. This is a trust-based transaction. You trust me?"

Gomez looked her over. Again. "Don't know why I should, but sí."

"You look like the kind of guy I can trust. And yeah, you can trust me." She stuck out her hand and he shook it.

Gomez was counting the cash as Loren got in the car. She adjusted the seat and pulled the ratty restraint across her body. She blew the dust off the instrument panel, then drove away.

63

Amy asked a staff person at the registration desk where the nearest pawnshop was. A quick Google search found one nine miles away. Amy had a sense that the area where it was located was questionable—not as safe as the rest of San Luis Obispo—but that's generally where such businesses set up shop.

She returned to the room and found Melissa watching *WordGirl*. Ten minutes later, Dr. West walked in.

He made small talk while he examined Melissa and scribbled some notes in the chart. He flipped the pages, compared test results, and nodded.

"Everything looks stable. You had a good night, young lady." He turned to Amy. "There's no progression of neurological signs or indications of an intracranial bleed. At this point, I think you're clear to take her home. We'll give you a list of instructions and things to look out for."

"Thanks, doctor."

West clasped the chart against his chest and looked at Melissa. "You have any questions for me?"

"Nope."

"Great. Then you get this." He reached into his lab coat pocket and pulled out a small stuffed animal: a rabbit with a pink stethoscope around its neck.

"For me?"

"For you." West handed it to her and shook Amy's hand. "Call us if you have any questions."

Fifteen minutes later, they were walking out of the room when Amy heard someone calling after them.

"Hold it! Don't go anywhere."

Amy turned to see a middle-aged woman shuffling down the hallway.

"I need to discuss the insurance information with you."

Amy opened her mouth to speak—but nothing emerged. She stood there, frozen, thinking only that had they left thirty seconds earlier, she would have made it outside without incident.

64

Hill turned to Minh and leaned back in his chair. "Zero activity on Loren's cell. No calls, no texts. No outgoing emails."

Minh finished typing a sentence on his keyboard. "Not a good sign."

"Definitely not. Makes me think—" Hill stopped and waved a hand. "Gotta stop jumping to conclusions. But things are not trending in the right direction. She hasn't responded to any of our attempts to contact her. Sure looks like she shut her phone down to keep us from seeing where she is."

"And there's no good reason for that."

Hill sat forward. "How about tracking her two-way? Have we ever done that?"

"Not sure. Check with Timo."

Timo was Tim Gates, one of the technogeek special agents the Bureau set loose in cyber to hack, crack, and track the devices criminal enterprises employed.

"While I do that, I think it's time to issue the amber alert."

"On it," Minh said.

Hill took the elevator down a floor, tapped his key card, and navigated the hallways to the large cyber room. Desktop PC towers sat at stations along both sides of the room, as well as on a central countertop.

"Timo." Hill held out his fist. Gates looked at it a second, then touched it with his.

"Got a question you're probably asked every day."

Gates pushed a pair of wire-rimmed glasses up his nose. "Okay."

"Can we track our Bu radios?"

"I'm *not* asked that question every day."

Hill scratched his forehead. "No, I realize that. It was a figure of speech."

Gates looked at him. "Oh. Right."

"Buddy, sometimes you scare me. You need to get out of here, interact with real people."

Timo glanced around at the computers. "Why?"

"Never mind. I don't have time to get into that. Can we track our Bureau radios?"

"Short answer is yes. It's possible to triangulate *any* radio device. But there are some things you've gotta keep in mind."

"Like what?"

"Like it depends on the strength of the signal, the area of transmission, and how long the radio has been transmitting. Cell phones are a great example of this—the proximity and number of cell towers around it are key. Not very close, too few towers, and we can't get a good fix on the location. Another problem is that Bu radio communications are all encrypted. If one is lost or stolen, the encryption codes are all changed."

"It's not lost or stolen. But what if she's turned the radio off?"

"Who's 'she'?"

"Loren."

Gates physically drew back. "Why would you need to find Loren? She okay?"

"Look," Hill said, "I know you're fond of her, but we've got an abducted child case. She might be AWOL. And she may be involved."

"That doesn't make any sense."

"It's her sister-in-law. She kidnapped a young girl."

Gates scrunched his brow. He started moving the fingers of his right hand at his side, as if he were playing the piano. "And Loren's gone off the grid?"

"Yes."

"So you want to track her radio to find her."

"Now you're getting it, Timo."

"Well." Gates picked up a screwdriver and bent over one of the partially disassembled towers. "If she's turned the device off, no chance. Can't track it. If it's not putting out a radio signal, there's nothing to find and therefore nothing to triangulate. Is the radio off?"

"Don't know. If she's trying to go dark, she likely shut it down. But what if she turns the radio back on?"

"If she turns it on and leaves it on—and we see the signal—and if she's near some towers, then yes. I should be able to locate her. But it'd have to be a pretty important reason to search for it. It'd take a lot of Bureau resources to do it."

"Kidnapped girl. I'd say that qualifies."

Gates looked up at him. "All our cases are important."

"Can't argue that, but—"

"You've worked with Loren for years. You really think she's capable of aiding and abetting a fugitive?"

Hill worked his jaw. "Family's very important to her. No idea how she'd react. I mean, not sure what I'd do if it were *my* sister-in-law. How would you react?"

Gates turned back to the screwdriver. "I don't have a sister-in-law."

Hill chuckled—but realized Gates was serious.

Gates pulled his gaze from the tower. "You think Loren's sister-in-law is dangerous? Is she violent? Is the child in danger?"

Hill bit his lip. "Don't know. The woman has a history of mental illness, so she's unstable. Still gathering info to get a better picture of what we're dealing with. More than that I can't say. Yet."

Gates sighed. "Okay then. Get Mountain to sign off. He does, I'll do my best to locate her radio the second it goes live."

"On my way to ask him right now."
"Keep me posted," Gates yelled after him.

65

Loren stopped by the gas station on Soledad Canyon Road to fill up and get a car wash. The vehicle was so filthy it would attract attention, begging some wise guy to scrape his finger in the dust proclaiming, "Clean me."

As she headed south on 101, keeping the speedometer needle pinned to 65, she made a mental note to tell Señor Gomez that the sedan needed new shocks, too. At times it felt more like she was navigating a small sailboat across a choppy ocean than driving on a paved road.

As she was leaving the car wash there had been some chatter on the FBI radio about the amber alert and BOLOs for Amy and Melissa, but no indication that law enforcement knew they were in San Luis Obispo—or anywhere in central California, for that matter. She only kept the radio on for two or three minutes, not wanting to take a chance they were tracking it. She knew that was no easy task—and if they had not yet made the connection between her and Amy, she was being needlessly paranoid. But that was far better than guessing wrong.

Multiple times she checked the burner, willing it to ring—and hoping that, because of the spotty reception, she had not missed a call from Amy.

She anticipated reaching the SLO town center in early

afternoon. And when she arrived, the question of where she would go—and what she would do when she got there—gnawed at her.

Loren tried, unsuccessfully, to stop thinking about what her colleagues were up to. She felt awful keeping them in the dark. From their perspective, they were only doing their job.

Loren laughed into the dead air of the car. She was now a conspirator, breaking the very laws she had spent her career fighting to uphold. How did that happen?

She felt deeply conflicted, a sense of unease that could not be reduced to words. But she had to remain focused. Family came first, just as she had told Zach. She was closer with Amy than any of her siblings. And Amy was in trouble.

Despite Amy's emotional and mental health issues these past several years, she was a bright and loving individual. She would never do something spurious and she would never do something that would cause harm to a young girl. If she took the extraordinary step of kidnapping Melissa Ellis from her family, Amy must be convinced that Melissa really was her child.

But did that make what she did *right*?

And was she truly mentally stable?

Loren clenched her jaw. She had put everything on the line to help Amy. She could not let doubt creep into her thoughts now. She had to see this to the end...and if Amy was not in a healthy state of mind, she would arrest her. After all, Loren was not doing this to aid and abet a criminal. She was helping a family member in need, to ensure that Melissa was being properly cared for, and to assess Amy's emotional fitness.

That's what she had to believe.

As the miles melted by, she realized she was gripping the steering wheel so tightly that her knuckles were white. And her speed had inched past seventy-five.

Loren took a deep breath and slowed to sixty-five. She had no registration and did not want to be recorded as being anywhere outside of Soledad in any official database, so the last thing she needed was to get pulled over by California Highway Patrol.

She turned on the car radio to relax and found a station playing '70s soft rock. She sang along to Billy Joel, Elton John, and James Taylor—until she heard herself say, *"The closer you get to the fire the more you get burned..."*

66

Amy was holding Melissa's hand as the woman approached. "I'm sorry, I've got to get her home."

"I understand. If you can just give me your insurance card, I'll run a copy and send you on your way."

"I lost my wallet when people started cha—" She leaned in close to the woman's ear. Her name tag read, Barbara. "When people started chasing the man who'd kidnapped my daughter. Sorry, it was traumatic enough. I don't want to talk about it in front of her. Nightmares."

The woman gave Melissa a half smile. "I understand."

Amy leaned back. "If you give me your contact info, I'll call or email you with everything you need."

Barbara curled her mouth into a snarl. "Much as I'd like to accept that, honey, I've got a responsibility to the hospital. And if I let every Jane and Alice get a pass who claimed she lost her wallet, we'd have to close our doors."

"Barbara, you can check with the police officer who was standing guard by our door last night. Officer Nicholson. He'll verify everything that I'm saying. You send me a copy of the bill and I'll make sure it gets paid."

Barbara scrutinized her face. "Can I trust you, dear?"

"Absolutely." Amy held out her hand. Barbara thought a moment, then shook. "Give me your address and I'll send you a copy of the bill."

"Address is on the intake forms. Send it there. I'll get it."

Amy had every intention of paying the bill—somehow. Melissa was, after all, her biological daughter. How she paid it, and when, would have to wait for another time. Right now, she had to get out of there.

"And I *am* going to call Officer Nicholson. Have a seat in the waiting room until I can reach him."

"Which way is that?"

"Through those double doors," Barbara said with a nod to her left.

Amy gave Melissa's hand a gentle squeeze and they started walking down the hallway.

"What did that lady want?"

"She wants me to pay the bill."

"But you don't want to?"

"I do want to, because it's the right thing to do. But...it's complicated. I'll have to send them money later."

"My daddy can pay. Call him."

"Great idea, sweetie. I'll take care of it. No worries."

They entered the waiting room, where a large security guard was standing.

"Barbara told me to make sure you had a seat over there."

Of course she did. "Great. Thanks." Only it wasn't great. Given what Loren had told her, any interaction with law enforcement was fraught with danger, as they would have been notified that there's a woman and a kidnapped girl somewhere in the area. And she happened to be the woman they would be looking for.

Amy stood up and held out her hands. Melissa extended her arms and Amy lifted her against her body.

"Okay, honey, we're going to leave."

"But the man said to wait."

"He did, you're right. But he doesn't know what's best for us. I do."

Amy paced back and forth, then waited until someone asked the security guard a question. He turned—and Amy walked out the sliding doors. She immediately hung a right and walked along the building's exterior. A surveillance camera was mounted on a light post to her left, and another to the side of the brick facing just above her head.

Amy needed to get out of range of their lenses. She stepped off the sidewalk and into the lot, squeezing between the parked vehicles.

Her heart was slamming against her chest wall, her breathing getting labored—from both stress and the work of carrying Melissa.

"Where we going?"

"Not sure," Amy said between gasps. "To find us a ride...back to our room...I guess."

Wilton Road, the street that bordered the hospital, was just ahead. *Can I make it before the guard realizes I left?*

Loren found an opening in the bushes planted along the property line and turned right along the sidewalk. Vehicles zipped past them, headed north and south. She turned and faced the latter, shifted Melissa onto her hip, and held out her right thumb.

Several cars later, a man in his early twenties slowed and pulled to the curb. He rolled down the window and craned his neck to make eye contact. "You need a ride?"

"I do, my SUV broke down and I need to get back to our motel. It's only a few miles. The Sands."

"Yeah, no problem. I know the place."

Amy pulled open the back door and helped Melissa inside the Hyundai. She buckled the belt and pulled it tight.

Amy breathed a sigh of relief—yet she could not help but think that more danger awaited.

67

Keller spent the night in his Lincoln camped out in the emergency department parking lot, leaning on his years doing surveillance as a detective and, before that, lying in the muck in the middle of Bumfuck, Nowhere, as a member of the 1st Special Forces Operational Detachment—Delta, colloquially known as Delta Force.

Compared to that, sitting in a luxury vehicle with climate control and heated leather seats was nothing to complain about.

He perked up when he saw a woman who looked like Amy Robbins holding a girl who appeared to be Melissa Ellis walk out the sliding doors. He started the engine and headed toward that area of the lot, but he had to be careful: he was now in range of the security cameras.

He drove to where he had seen them—but they were no longer there. He rubbernecked and caught a glimpse of Robbins's blonde hair bouncing on her shoulders as she navigated the spaces between the cars.

Keller accelerated and swerved down an aisle of parked vehicles, but as he neared he saw them squeeze through a line of low-trimmed hedges.

"Shit."

He thought of getting out of the Lincoln and pursuing them

on foot, but what was he going to do when he grabbed Melissa? Run away again? That did not work out so well the first time.

He sped toward the exit of the lot, braking hard to avoid an elderly couple shuffling through the aisle with tennis-ball tipped walkers. Keller glanced in his rearview mirror, then over his shoulder, attempting to locate Robbins.

As soon as speedy Martha and spry Ed cleared the way, Keller hung a right onto Wilton.

68

Keller scanned the road—but did not see Robbins or Melissa. He slowed and looked in the rearview mirror, then glanced left and right. Nowhere to be seen.

But that was impossible. They did not have their car here and they were on foot—which meant, in the absence of taxis, they took an Uber or Lyft...or hitchhiked. In a college town, an attractive young woman with a little girl would not have difficulty getting a ride.

Keller pulled out his sat phone and called Martinez. "You see any activity on Robbins? Cell phone?"

"Hang on a second." A moment later, he returned to the call. "Nothing. And no electronic transactions on credit or debit."

"Okay, thanks."

"Lose her again?"

"All's good." *Asshole.*

He hung up and headed to the one place he knew she might go—her motel.

When he arrived at the Sands, he backed into the spot, affording him a view of their door. He no longer could wear his disguise, so he was now at greater risk.

He checked his watch, then reached behind the passenger seat and extracted a black nylon 5.11 messenger bag. Nestled inside the concealed quick-draw compartment was a suppressor that he could attach to his Glock—and a .22 Ruger. He chose the compact pistol because it was small and quiet and efficient if you wanted to dispose of someone at close range. It was also clean—unregistered—with the serial numbers ground down to the base metal.

His plan was to grab Melissa, inject her, and then dispose of Robbins. He would put the do not disturb sign on the doorknob, then call in a Tait cleaning crew to efficiently dispose of the body and scrub the room of blood and forensics.

Although he did not want to kill Robbins—for a plethora of reasons—doing so would make it feasible to retrieve Melissa here. With Robbins out of the way and Melissa drugged, his egress would be quiet and uneventful. No drama.

Just guilt. The guilt would have to be reconciled later. Right now, he needed laser-like focus on the mission.

Efficiency, not emotion.

Keller checked the Ruger and got out. He casually glanced around as he crossed the parking lot and strode to the door. There was a peephole lens, so he could not knock and impersonate motel staff unless he kept his head down and hoped she did not recognize him. She had only seen him once, under extreme duress.

Years ago he had taken a one-day LAPD course on witness and victim memory retention during bank robberies and other violent events. In such situations, people generally had poor recollection because their visual fields narrowed and their body produced a flood of hormones—glucocorticoids—that calmed them so they could function. But these chemicals also destroyed neurons in the brain, affecting their ability to store the incident in long-term memory. Their emotional output was more completely retained than the facts of the occurrence.

Keller was hoping that would be the case here.

He dropped his chin to his chest and knocked on the door. "Assistant manager. Please open up."

Nothing. He waited a few seconds, then rapped on the painted surface again. "Open up. Assistant manager."

He glanced left and right. No one was nearby. A maid was across the way, about forty yards from where he was standing. She was busy with her cart and did not appear to be paying attention to what he was doing.

Keller waited another fifteen seconds then tried to get a look inside through the curtained window. The room appeared to be dark.

To keep from arousing suspicion, he walked back to his vehicle, cursing silently, concerned that Robbins would not be returning to the motel. He closed the door, took a deep breath, and let it out slowly.

Patience. Tough to master but vital to practice.

69

Amy turned in her seat to face the young man. "You a student at the university?"

"Cal Poly. Yeah. Engineering."

"Good field."

"Thought about pre-law, but my dad talked me out of it."

"Your dad sounds like a wise man. I'm Amy." She immediately realized she had used her real name.

"Brad."

"Hey, Brad—would you mind making a detour? I have to get over to a shop in Diablo Canyon."

Brad scrunched his face. "Not a great neighborhood."

"I know. I figured it'd be okay during the day."

He nodded thoughtfully. "Yeah. Probably true. What's there?"

"Pawnshop."

Brad eyed her, then swung his gaze back to the road. "Buying or selling?"

"Selling. I need the money."

He stole a look at the clock on the Jeep's dash, then said, "I've got a class in forty minutes, but I can drop you off and head back. It'll be close, but I should be able to make it."

"Appreciate it."

"And what's your name?" he asked, looking in the rearview mirror.

"Melissa."

"You look like you took quite a fall."

"She did," Amy said, jumping in. She had no idea what Melissa would say about who Amy was, and why she was hundreds of miles from home. "We had an altercation downtown and—well, she got banged up pretty good."

"Cool mask."

Amy turned and glanced at Melissa.

"Thank you," the girl said.

Brad got on the freeway and Amy engaged him in a discussion of his coursework and fraternity life. About twelve minutes later, he exited the freeway.

"Never been to a pawnshop," Brad said.

Amy chuckled. "Me either. Don't quite know what to expect."

"You have a way to get home? I don't feel real good about just leaving you here."

"We'll figure something out. Call a cab or something."

"Uber?"

"Or Uber," Amy said with a laugh.

"I'll wait as long as I can."

"I don't want you to miss your class."

"It's a test, actually."

"Then I definitely don't want you to be late. I'll be as fast as I can. But if you need to leave, just go."

"You sure?"

"You're a nice young man, Brad. I appreciate you looking out for us—and for giving us the ride. Yes, absolutely. Don't worry, we'll be fine."

He pulled up in front of the building that housed Diablo Pawn & Loan and craned his neck to take in the barred windows above the store. "I'll hang out here as long as I can."

"If we're not back in time, good luck on your test." She gave him a smile, then got out and helped Melissa from her seat belt.

Amy pulled on the shop's door—it was locked—and then a

buzzer sounded followed by a metallic click. She gave it another try and it swung open. She ushered Melissa in first and made her way past aisles of stuff—knickknacks, decorative antiques, small kitchen appliances. A wall of flat panel televisions, Zippo lighters, acoustic and electric guitars, fishing tackle boxes, lawnmowers... and locked display cases of jewelry.

But the signs caught her attention:

$ We Pay $Cash for Gold $
No Cash Refunds
Smile Shoplifters You're on Camera
If You Don't Buy It Today, It May Not Be Here Tomorrow
Buy A Gun, Commit A Crime, & You're Done

Melissa squeezed Amy's hand. "Why are we here?"

Amy drew Melissa close, an unconscious desire to shield her. "I need some money, so I'm going to see if this store will buy something from me."

"That's silly. Stores are where *we* buy things. Not sell things."

For a fleeting moment, Amy grinned. But a door opened and a man with greasy, slicked back hair and wearing a pair of soiled canvas cargo pants stepped out of the back room.

"Hep ya?"

Amy cleared her throat and started twisting the ring on her finger. "Yes. Yes, um, I need to, um, pawn this." She had taken it after they had returned to her apartment, figuring a *married* woman with a girl would attract less scrutiny if the police were looking for her—or she might amass less attention from potential witnesses who saw her in passing. It was a silly assumption, but people were funny that way. Sometimes small details made a big difference.

He gestured at her left hand and he held out his right. "Lemme see."

The thought of this guy touching her was not particularly appetizing, so Amy slipped the band off her finger and hesitated before giving it to him. This was her last tangible connection to Dan. And she was in a sleazy central California neighborhood selling it to a pawnshop. *What the hell am I doing?*

Then she realized that *Melissa* might be the most important thing she had left of Dan. A living, breathing part of him. His daughter. That mattered so much more than an inanimate object, regardless of how symbolic and filled with memories the ring was.

"I'm Buck," the man said as he pulled a jeweler's magnifying lens over his head and examined the ring. "Hmm. You Amy?"

Amy swallowed hard. She had forgotten about the inscription on the inside of the band. "Yes."

"Original owner."

"Yes."

"Got any papers with this? Insurance appraisal? Purchase receipt?"

"I—no, I didn't think to bring them. I should've."

"Woulda helped." He swung his head over his left shoulder. "Yo. Charlie. Git up here a minute."

The back door opened again and Charlie, a man fifteen years Buck's senior with a mane of wiry silver hair, emerged.

"Need an appraisal." He handed over the jeweler's loupe and Charlie took the ring over to a work area on the shelf behind the countertop.

Amy kept her eyes on Charlie. She had no reason to distrust him, but at the moment that single piece of jewelry represented everything of value she had. She needed the money.

"What's a—a—praisin?" Melissa asked.

"When someone figures out how much something is worth," Amy said absentmindedly while turning and looking out the front door, where she could make out the front bumper and fender of Brad's car. "Any chance we can speed this up a bit?"

"Nope," Buck said. "Tell me. You lookin' to hock it or sell it?"

"I want it back. It's—" Amy stopped, not wanting to say too much in front of Melissa. She had told Giselle that she was not married, and she did not know if Melissa had been listening. But Amy did not want to get caught in a lie. Everything with Melissa was based on trust. "It's got a lot of sentimental value."

Buck nodded as if he empathized with her. But she was under

no illusions. He was a businessman looking to make money off her. And if he put cash in her hand right now, she would be fine with that.

Charlie came over and said, "It's real. Had to estimate the weight based on diameter and depth. I'd say it's one and a half carats, VS1 clarity, excellent cut, round brilliant. Color's an F. And a 14-karat gold setting. Needs a cleanin', but good condition."

Buck stepped back and lowered his ear to Charlie, who made a few comments. Buck turned back to Amy and handed her the ring. "I can give you five thousand. Twelve percent interest. If you ain't claimed it in ninety days, I'm gonna sell it."

Amy swallowed. She needed the money but did not want to part with the keepsake. And three months...who knew where she would be then. Zach could come and claim it, pay the loan and the interest. He would do that for her.

"I'll take it."

"Thanks, Charlie. I'm gonna write us up a contract." Buck reached for a pad of pages filled top to bottom with fine print and filled in a few numbers. He took a photo of the ring in Amy's hand and slid the paperwork over to her for her signature.

Given her training, Amy had never signed anything during her adult life without first having read it. Until now. She grabbed the pen and swirled her name as the front door buzzer sounded.

Amy and Melissa swung their gazes behind them.

In walked four men. Their arms were covered in tattoos and they were dressed in loose fitting jeans and sleeveless T-shirts.

"Boys," Buck said. "How you doin' today?"

"Not too good," one of them answered.

Amy drew Melissa against her and handed the contract to Buck. "Here you go."

"Gimme a minute boys," Buck said. He scooped up the papers and nodded to Amy. "Be right back."

The four men spread out inside the store, each going down a different aisle and lingering. Amy glanced up at the large convex surveillance mirrors to see what they were doing.

"Here ya go," Buck said. He held out his hand and Amy gave

him the ring. Buck gave her a copy of the agreement and then opened a small metal strongbox. He asked how she wanted the cash.

Amy cringed and glanced up at the reflection of the men. "Twenties," she said in a low voice.

"That's gonna be a real thick wad," Buck said, not doing anything to mask his volume. "Two hundred fifty twenties. Not sure I have that many here."

"Give me what you've got. Rest in fifties or hundreds."

Buck made a show of counting the bills into her palm. She wanted desperately to check on the four men but needed to be sure he paid her the correct amount.

"Amy," Melissa whined, "I wanna go. I'm hungry."

"Okay, honey. You've been very patient. We'll go get something in a minute."

As soon as Buck finished, Amy shoved the stack into her purse and pulled the strap over her head.

70

L oren was getting nauseous being bounced around by the Ford's poor shocks, but she was only a couple of miles from her exit.

As she prepared to get off the freeway, she hoped that her assumptions were correct. She figured that if Amy were still at the hospital, she would have used the pay phone to update Loren since Loren had no way of finding, or contacting, her. That left only one other option: the Sands.

If Amy was not at the motel, she would swing by the hospital. That carried more risk because any contact with people and witnesses could place Loren in SLO, narrowing her hopes of getting out of this whole—with her career intact.

At the moment, that was only a secondary concern.

She exited 101 and looped around, following the GPS instructions on her burner phone. She pulled into the Sands' rectangular parking lot.

There would be no badge flashing here—her goal was to find Amy and Melissa quietly and without confrontation.

Those hopes suffered a blow when she saw a man who bore a strong resemblance to Keller backed into a spot no more than thirty yards away.

He started his car and pulled out, headed right. Loren followed, wondering if it *was* Keller or if she had him on her mind and was thus imagining it.

He went over a speed bump and exited the lot, turning left on Garfield Street. Loren did likewise. They continued through the middle-class residential neighborhood, the driver giving no indication he was concerned about the vehicle behind him—or was even aware of it.

A block later, he hung a right onto Graves and then swung a quick left onto Abbott. His speed increased.

So much for him not being aware of her presence. It likely *was* Keller. Had he seen her face? Or did he realize she was shadowing his random maneuvers?

She reached over to the passenger seat and gathered up the light cube, then rolled down her window. It grabbed the metal roof—a magnet to steel. She switched it on and Keller accelerated.

Well that wasn't supposed to happen.

She followed him under the El Camino overpass along Grand Avenue and sped up—the old engine downshifted with a two second hesitation and then a loud roar—and she closed the distance between them as she came up alongside his driver's side rear door.

But the Lincoln had a large engine, and Keller punched it up to seventy-five along the straightaway and widened the gap once again.

They sped along Grand, going way too fast for a quiet area like this. As the road curved left, Loren saw the signs for the university approaching. She could not continue a high-speed pursuit though a college campus. Keller knew this.

Despite his shady work for Tait Protection, he was not one to risk hitting, and killing, an innocent person.

She had to believe that, at his core, Keller was still the same person she had worked with. She *wanted* to believe that. But it was not something she could count on because, truth was, she had no idea. And when you affiliated yourself with a company like Tait, sooner or later you were forced to make a decision that tested your moral base. You either succumbed to money or you preserved your scruples and got out.

Keller was still with Tait, which was disturbing. However, he had a longtime relationship with Bill Tait, so perhaps that bought him an exception. Perhaps not.

Business was business.

And that was what bothered her most.

AS KELLER CLOSED ON the location of large student housing buildings on the right, he realized he had made a tactical error. Because he did not know the area well enough, he found himself on a college campus. He should have pulled a 180, but that could have allowed Ryder to block his path.

This was not much better.

And by now she had radioed in and other agents or cops would be responding.

With few choices, he pulled to the curb in front of a line of parked cars and got out of the Lincoln. He walked briskly down the sidewalk and, after having traversed a block, glanced over his right shoulder. Ryder was pulling in front of his vehicle and angling it so that it was pinned in—just in case he circled around and returned to it. So that option was now eliminated.

This was not turning out as he had planned. He took off running.

LOREN GRABBED HER radio and sprinted down the street in pursuit. He had a decent lead on her, but she was a runner and had endurance on her side. She had no idea what his fitness level was, but she recalled that he had been in the military, Special Forces if she remembered correctly—and he still looked to be in shape.

No matter what happened, she was not going to be the first one to shut it down. She was determined to outrun him in time and distance, so the only thing she had to be sure of was that he did not find a way to disappear between cars or inside a building.

"Mickey," she yelled. "Stop."

A few students who were walking and riding bikes in the area swung their gaze in her direction.

From her years of training and fieldwork, Loren almost yelled "FBI"—but caught herself: she didn't want to draw anyone's attention to her identity. Absent security cameras, there would be no definitive proof of her presence on campus. If she remained careful.

"Mickey...please, I need your help."

71

Amy glanced up at the mirror, where the men were watching her.

She was more than uncomfortable—but tried not to show it. In court, she had never been one to back down. She assumed that attitude now, hardening her brow and jawline, making eye contact and holding it. Amy hoped that conveyed the right message.

She took Melissa's hand and turned toward the exit. "C'mon, honey."

"Can we eat now?"

"Yes," Amy said, keeping her gaze steady and in front of her. "Great idea."

One of the men stepped out of the adjacent aisle near the entrance. He looked Amy over, nodded acceptance—as if to say, "Nice piece of ass, you'll do"—and then pushed open the door for her.

Amy muttered "Thanks," and passed right by him, Melissa corralled against her left hip, as they exited to the sidewalk. Brad was gone, which was not surprising given how long the transaction had taken.

She turned right, not wanting to look lost or confused, and started walking. They pressed the crosswalk button and waited for the white icon to proceed. She took those seconds to casually glance around and take in the shops in the vicinity. If there was a place to eat—a café, a restaurant, even a dive—they would head there to use the phone to call a cab.

Her hearing was focused behind her, listening for any steps or movement. She was concerned about the four lowlifes in the pawnshop—but perhaps Buck, who seemed to know them, told them to back off. It would be bad for business if word got around that people were robbed after coming out of his store with cash.

Off to their right, about a block away, was an old, red neon sign advertising pizza.

Perfect.

As soon as the light changed they crossed and headed for the parlor. Once inside—an interior that did not disappoint, as it was as dilapidated as the exterior—Amy ordered a couple of slices and cold drinks, then asked to use the phone.

The man—who looked to be in the same condition as his restaurant—made a face, like she had asked a major favor. "Phone's for business."

"This is important. I need to call a cab." She gestured at Melissa. "My daughter needs a nap."

The guy frowned, then handed her the receiver and stretched the old, greasy and coiled cord across the counter. "Number?"

"Do you know a local cab company?"

"Normally no, but there's one's got a number that's all threes. Always thought that was stupid, but guess it works." He dragged a finger around the dial—Amy had never seen a rotary phone in person—and the call connected.

She ordered the taxi and asked for the food to go.

Five minutes later the man opened the horizontal oven door and slid the two warmed slices onto a couple of paper plates, then put them in a paper bag.

By the time they walked outside, the cab was pulling to the curb. They got in and Melissa immediately pushed the plastic mask from the hospital off her face, then grabbed at the package to extract the pizza.

"San Luis Obispo," Amy said to the driver. "The Sands Motel."

72

Keller was winging it, always a dangerous proposition but sometimes unavoidable. It was something he had done all his career—when his unit was in the shit and their backs were against the wall in some third world country or when an unstable perp had unexpectedly taken a hostage.

Sometimes it worked out. Sometimes it did not.

Most were life-threatening situations. And usually the other guy got the worst of it.

But this was someone he cared about. It was different.

Could he shoot Ryder if he needed to?

That was a question he could not answer until the pistol was in his hand and his finger was on the trigger. For now it was tucked into the small of his back, to the left of his spine and nestled against his kidney.

Fight or flight.

At the moment he was fleeing. But that could change in an instant.

"Mickey...please, I need your help."

Keller slowed, then turned and faced her, his right hand behind his back. "Don't come any closer."

Ryder broke her stride and allowed her momentum to carry her forward several more feet before dropping her speed to a walk.

"That's enough. Right there."

"Or what? You gonna shoot me?"

"Do we really need to find out?"

Ryder stopped.

He noticed that she was wearing her old undercover wig. And blue contact lenses. Why? It surely wasn't for him. "What do you want?"

"I need to find my sister-in-law."

He chuckled inwardly. *That makes two of us.*

LOREN WAS ABOUT THIRTY FEET away from him, meaning she did not need to shout, but their exchange was loud enough that they had attracted a crowd. Campus police would be responding shortly if this escalated. She did not want that—and she imagined Keller did not, either.

"What makes you think I know where she is?"

"Seriously? Let's be honest with each other. Can you do that?"

"Always have been."

"Good. Then where is she?"

Keller sighed, then pivoted toward the gawkers. "What're you looking at?" he said to them. "Don't you have classes?"

A few walked on, glancing back over their shoulders because they sensed something juicy was about to happen. One had his cell phone out and pointed at them.

Shit. She turned her body slightly, subtly, to reduce the quality of his angle. And the wig and contact lenses could provide some cover if she had to deny the images were of her.

Then again, if they kept calm there would be nothing of interest to film. It would end up deleted rather than uploaded.

Keller was likely thinking the same thing because he took a deep breath to calm himself. "Amy and the girl were at SLO Medical Center. I lost them after they left."

"You lost them? Doesn't sound like you."

"Tell me about it." He chuckled. "I went to the motel because that's the only other place I knew about. That's when you showed up."

Loren advanced on him slowly. "And why are you even here?"

"I thought we were being honest with each other."

Loren bit her bottom lip. "Fine. That girl. It's probably Amy's."

"I know."

"You know?"

"I was hired by the parents to get their daughter back."

"And?"

"And I did my homework. I put two and two together, extrapolated a little, and reached some likely conclusions."

Loren stopped about ten feet away. "And you're still trying to bring Melissa back?"

"It's my job. I can't pass judgment. I'm paid to—"

"Bullshit. You? Not passing judgment?"

"I know, right? Part of the problem I have with this job. But I need it. I don't have a wealthy spouse."

Loren let the dig roll off her back.

"It's a lot of money. Can't turn it down. Besides, I say no, my boss'll just bring someone else in. And trust me—I know the guy—that definitely won't be in your sister-in-law's best interests."

"And your job. To bring Melissa back?"

"Like I said."

"But Amy is a loose end. With the IPO, billions at stake, how can they take the chance that she won't talk? Even an unfounded report could tank the offering. Too much money involved."

"I know. Just let me bring the girl back and everything'll be okay."

Loren canted her head to the side. "*Okay?* Christine Ellis abuses her daughter."

"You have proof of that?"

"And the Ellises conspired to commit arson and insurance fraud. They're going to prison."

Keller did not reply.

"Unless Amy is taken care of," Loren said. "Eliminated. And then there'd be no one to report it. No one with any proof."

"All I know is I've been paid, very well, to bring Melissa home.

That's my job. I gotta do my job."

Loren had crept forward to the point where they were now almost a normal talking distance apart. Most of the onlookers had dispersed. At the moment, they were two adults having a conversation—an odd one that started off with a foot chase but had devolved into something seemingly civil.

"Mickey," Loren asked gently, "what happened to you?"

"Don't look at me that way, Loren."

"What way is that?"

"Disgust. Disapproval."

"If the shoe fits."

"You've got a habit of judging me."

"Don't give me a reason and I'll stop judging you."

"That's not fair. Working for Tait Protection isn't what I wanted to be doing, but the situation presented itself. And you do what you gotta do, you know?"

His smartwatch vibrated. He twisted his wrist and glanced at the display: "BT" was calling. Bill Tait. *Great timing, pal.*

Loren reached behind her back and pulled out her handcuffs with her left hand and her Glock 9mm with her right. She kept the pistol at her side, at the ready...just in case. "I *do* know. And that's why you're under arrest."

"Under—are you crazy? I haven't done anything wrong. I'm a private investigator trying to find a missing child so I can bring her home. Since when is that against the law?"

"Put your hands above your head, where I can see them."

He did not move.

KELLER THOUGHT ABOUT running.

If he was going to collect on the payout, he could not get stuck in a police station answering questions while Amy left town with Melissa. He might never find her again—or, with time getting short, Tait would lose confidence in him and dispatch Sinbad.

None of those were acceptable.

But something about this interaction with Ryder seemed wrong. It did not smell like she was there on official Bureau business. She could have worn the disguise so that he would not recognize her from a distance. But she was here without a partner and without backup anywhere in the vicinity.

That said, she was a federal agent and officially or not, she still had the authority to arrest him. And he was carrying an illegal weapon.

Once you got into the system, all sorts of things could bubble to the surface from your past. While he considered all that, Ryder had snapped the cuffs on his wrists.

73

Hill's phone rang. He lifted it as he read a file. "Jimmy Hill."

"It's Timo. Tran's not answering his phone."

"He went to take a leak. Why?"

"Potential break on your case."

"*Which* case?"

"Robbins. I'm sending you a video. We got a hit on a traffic cam, facial recognition. Lots of false positives. I need a confirmatory ID before I alert local PD."

Hill navigated to his email and found Tim Gates's message. He opened the attachment and watched the looping clip.

"Whoa. Yeah. Not only is that Amy Robbins, that's Melissa Ellis. The girl. She's got some kind of—what is that, a mask?"

"That's my guess. Maybe a disguise?"

"Maybe. Where is this?"

"Diablo Canyon."

"Where the hell's Diablo Canyon?"

"Just outside San Luis Obispo."

"And yes, Loren turned on her radio. Was only on a couple minutes. I took me awhile but I triangulated and it was coming from Greenfield, a few miles south of Soledad."

"Soledad. You sure?"

"Lots of mountains around there," Gates said. "And service is spotty, so I'm *fairly* sure. Not guaranteed. Somewhere near there. That's what took me so long. More than that I can't do without diverting a lot more resources. Mountain signed off on this, but that's all you're gonna get. She turns it on again, we're not gonna know. I won't be 'listening.'"

"No, no, this is great. I'll alert SLOPD about Robbins and the girl. Good work."

"Computer algorithms. All technology. I had nothing to do with it. The facial rec—"

"Dude. Dude. Not important. We can talk about that later."

Hill hung up, called SLOPD and forwarded the traffic cam capture, gave them the location, and set the wheels in motion. He thought about calling the FBI's Los Angeles Division office to request two agents, but figured they would be dispatched from the Santa Maria Resident Agency, which was a great deal closer. He phoned them directly.

Minh was returning to his desk when Hill jumped out of his seat, grabbing his FBI windbreaker in one motion. "We got a hit."

"A hit? On Robbins?"

"Yeah, Timo just called me. Traffic cam, facial recognition. Positive ID. And we got a ping on Loren's radio. Near Soledad. Grab your stuff. We're going to San Luis Obispo."

"Us? Aren't they coming out of...that would be LA."

"Santa Maria RA. But this is our case. And it's Loren. I want to be there to find out what the hell's going on, look her in the eyes."

"Soledad's about an hour and a half, two hours from SLO, depending on traffic. You really think that's where Loren's headed?"

"Yep," Hill said as he started down the corridor toward the elevators. "I'd put money on it."

74

"Mickey Keller, you're under arrest for impeding a federal investigation. Obstruction of justice. And impersonating a police officer."

He closed his eyes as she patted him down and extracted a suppressed handgun.

"What the hell's this for?"

"Protection."

"With a suppressor?"

"Quiet protection."

"Mickey." She shook her head. "Registered?"

"Negatory."

Loren switched on the radio. There was chatter but nothing that interested her.

She tugged on the handcuffs to lead him back toward her car when a thought occurred to her. She stopped suddenly. "Was I right? About Amy being a loose end that needed to be eliminated?"

Keller shrugged. "Ask the Ellises about that. They're the ones threatened in your scenario."

"I'm just saying. A suppressed .22. Quiet protection or quiet aggression?"

"Key concept here is *quiet*. Don't wanna get stuck in a police station answering questions."

"And yet that's exactly what you'll be doing."

"Curious, Loren. Who's arresting me, an FBI agent or a concerned sister-in-law?"

A chirp came over the Bureau radio. "Suspect Amy Robbins located on traffic cam. Melissa Ellis in her company, does not appear to be in distress. Last seen getting into a taxi."

Loren froze. "Shit."

The dispatcher provided the address, then said, "Agents en route. Local PD being notified. Attempting to contact cab company to determine driver's destination."

Loren gave Keller another tug and they started moving quickly toward her car. She did not want to leave the radio on but did not see a choice. She had to know what was going down.

This was worse than bad. The Bureau would have dispatched agents from the Santa Maria Resident Agency, about thirty to forty minutes away.

But San Luis Obispo police would be pulling over Amy's cab a lot faster than that—or snatching her when she got out.

And Loren had no way of warning her.

75

Amy and Melissa had finished eating their pizza when the driver's phone rang.

He pulled the device off the holder to the left of his windshield, where his GPS was telling him to maintain his course for another mile and a half.

"Yeah, bro. Whassup?"

The man listened a moment, then said, "Sands...Yeah, in SLO." He was quiet, then said, "Yeah, I got it. No, that's fine. About three minutes... Nope." His eyes found the rearview mirror, where Amy was looking. He moved his gaze back to the road. "Okay, I can do that."

He hung up, then placed the handset onto its magnetic holder.

"Everything okay?" Amy asked as she repositioned Melissa's mask.

He kept his focus on the road ahead. "Just my boss. He checks in on me coupla times a day. Annoying, but he's the boss, ya know?"

Amy had no reason to suspect anything untoward, but the exchange, and the driver's reaction, were a bit off. Her experience reading jurors' body language gave her reason to become suspicious. And Loren had once told her that a little paranoia can be a good thing.

Well, she was now properly paranoid. Problem was, there was nothing she could do about it, short of getting out of the cab. They were almost at the motel, but she decided to follow her gut.

"Pull over."

"Huh?" The driver glanced at her in the rearview mirror. "We're not there yet."

"I know. This is good. Stop the car."

"Are we here?" Melissa asked, trying to sit tall to see over the seats.

"Yeah. Couple of blocks away."

He pulled to the right and stopped at the curb in front of La Cuesta Inn motel on one side of the street and the Apple Farm boutique hotel on the other. A gas station stood on the opposite corner.

Amy would try calling Loren from there. Unless she had stopped somewhere, she should have arrived in SLO by now.

"Twenty-two dollars."

Amy dug into her purse, shielding all the cash and extracting two bills. "Sorry, I don't have anything smaller."

"How much you want back?"

"Keep five."

The man pulled out his wallet and started counting off the money, but he kept glancing up, peering out the windows.

"You know what? Keep the change."

"Wow, thanks. Need a receipt?"

"I'm good." Amy sat forward in the seat and grabbed the door handle. In that instant, a police cruiser became visible, approaching at high speed. And its light bar was lit up.

76

Loren yanked on the handcuffs, pulling Keller along, as they neared her car. They had run farther than she thought during the foot pursuit.

She put Keller in the backseat and got in.

"Really?" He looked around and snorted. "This isn't a BuCar," he said. "You're rogue. Protecting Amy. That's why you're wearing a wig and colored lenses."

"Shut up, Mickey. You're under arrest, in federal custody. That's all you should be concerned about."

Loren started the Ford, turned the light cube on, and screeched a U-turn on the two-lane road. She increased the gain on her radio and sped toward the Sands Motel.

"Suspect in a white taxi," the dispatcher said. "License plate seven niner kilo tango zulu five two. Stopped at 2074 Monterey Street. Police cruiser approaching. FBI ETA twelve minutes."

"Would be good if you just let me go," Keller said.

"And why would I do that?"

"Tarzana."

Loren did not respond—but she was all too familiar with the reference. It went back several years to her early days with the Bureau. Keller was still with the LAPD and they were working a case together. Something happened...or more like went wrong because of Loren. And Keller had her back, saving her an embarrassing—and potentially career altering—disclosure.

He was calling that chit due. And now Loren had a decision to make.

Or was it a threat? He would come clean and she would lose her job because she failed to divulge it to her squad supervisor—and even worse, because she filed a false report. She could be prosecuted.

As Loren sped down Grand, she reached out and switched off the light cube and pulled it into the car. She still did not want to be identified as law enforcement—because that would mean revealing herself and being placed at the scene.

However, if she had Keller in custody, she could always argue that he was the focus of her efforts and the reason for her trip to SLO. No one would buy that, of course. While she had breached procedure, they could not prove she deliberately went dark—or so she hoped.

However, OPR would look to make a lot more trouble for her. How much? At the moment, she did not even want to consider it.

She hung a left onto Monterey—where she saw a police cruiser approaching the white taxi. And in the backseat of the cab sat her sister-in-law.

Shit, Amy. Now what are we gonna do?

77

Amy froze. The police had somehow found them. She had her left hand on Melissa's, her right on the doorknob. But it would make no sense to run. Melissa would not understand—but *would* have the crap scared out of her. She did not want her to grow up thinking the police were bad.

"Honey, I have to be honest with you."

Judging by the expression on her face, Melissa knew something was about to happen—and it was not going to be good.

Amy took both her hands in hers. "Your parents don't know you're here with me. I didn't tell them. I didn't tell Giselle. They've been looking for you. I did a bad thing."

"But I was having fun."

"I know. I was, too." *Well, except for the stress. And the mental anguish.* "I'm sorry for lying to you. That was wrong. All of this was wrong."

"Then why'd you take me?"

Amy looked up and the police car was getting close. She did not have much time.

"This is too hard to explain, but I think I'm your mother and I was just trying to do the right thing—"

"But how could you be my mommy? I have a mommy."

"Like I said, it's too hard to explain. When you get older you'll

313

understand."

Amy realized she was making a confession in front of a witness—the cab driver, who was staring at her in the rearview mirror. But she did not care. She was never going to see her daughter again. She knew that now.

And there was so much to tell her.

Yet there was no time to say it. And how does she make a little girl who just turned five understand science, technology, and the nuances of profound loss and severe mental anguish?

"You're probably not going to remember me when you get older. I don't remember much before I was ten years old. A few scattered memories when I was six or seven." She laughed through tears as she fought to keep her composure. "But I hope one day when I get out of prison I can find you and we can be friends."

The two police officers were approaching the taxi with their handguns drawn, one on either side of the cab.

Melissa saw the men and grabbed Amy's forearm, pulled her close. "I don't want you to leave me!"

Amy's eyes teared up and her voice broke as she spoke. "I know, honey. I don't want to leave you either."

"Who's going to take me to the zoo to see the elephants and bats?"

Amy could no longer keep the tears contained and she started to weep. "Oh, I'm so sorry, baby. I should never have done this to you."

Melissa looked to her left at the officer, who was yelling something through the window. She squeezed Amy's arm harder.

Amy forced a smile. "Giselle will take you to the zoo. I'm sure if you ask her she'll make it happen." She looked at the cop outside her window, then at Melissa. Tears were rolling down both their cheeks.

"C'mon, sweetie. It's time."

78

Loren pulled to the curb half a block away. Frozen.

She slammed an open hand against the steering wheel. "Shit. Shit. Shit!"

"You've gotta help her," Keller said. "She doesn't deserve this."

"What am I supposed to do? Bust in there with guns blazing?"

"That'd be suicide by cop."

"So what am I supposed to do? She's seconds away from being taken into custody."

"Obviously, you have to get her *out* of custody."

Loren laughed sardonically. "How am I going to do that?"

"*You're* not going to do that. I will."

"And why would you do that?"

"I've always liked you, Loren. Respected you. And yeah, although this case didn't start out this way, looks like I ended up working for the bad guys. But after I found them the first time, when I could've grabbed Melissa and left...I found out about all the shit Amy's been through. The car accident, her family...the arson at the clinic."

Loren watched as one of the cops gestured at the window. He wanted Amy to open the door. "What do you have in mind?"

315

"First, remove these." He twisted in the backseat to reveal the handcuffs.

Loren snorted.

Keller groaned. "Dammit, Loren. We don't have a lot of time here."

"What do you plan to do?"

"Gimme a minute. I'm working on it."

Loren pulled out her handcuff key. "We don't have a minute."

79

Loren figured they actually had about *seven* minutes before the agents from Santa Maria arrived. But it could be five. Or nine, depending on traffic, lights, and a number of other unrelated issues. She had to work fast without appearing rushed or stressed.

She was both.

Loren put the light cube back on the roof, then headed for the SLO police officer who was taking Amy into custody. The other was talking with Melissa. With Keller behind her, looking official enough in his dress shirt and disheveled sport coat, she held up her creds, her fingers partially covering the name—the badge glinting in the late afternoon sun.

Keller had reasoned that with a federal warrant, the local cops did not want the jurisdiction. Their role was simply to assist the Bureau with taking her into custody. Arresting her would entail paperwork and court appearances on a case to which SLOPD had little connection. They had no need to mirandize or question Amy.

There was, however, one potential flaw in Keller's plan: depending on the timing of how things unfolded, the Santa Maria agents would contact SLOPD. If Hill or Minh had relayed their suspicions of what Loren was doing, along with her physical description—and if dispatch had time to relay that information to the officers—despite the disguise, the cops might suspect this was Loren. And that would not end well for her.

The only good thing is that they would know immediately if the officers had already been briefed.

"Maura Rader, FBI. This is my partner, Michael Collins. Thanks for covering for us. Got here from Santa Maria as soon as we could."

She avoided eye contact with Amy but felt her sister-in-law's gaze boring into her.

"Ray Richards," the officer said with a nod. "Not a problem."

"Appreciate you having our backs," Loren said. "Tough one to find. Thank goodness for facial rec technology." She forged ahead, relieved—for the moment—that Richards and his partner had not been alerted. Of course, a crackle of the radio could change that.

She quickly handed Amy off to Keller so that she would be the one to deal with Melissa. Since Melissa had seen Keller in a very stressful situation, it was hard to judge how she would react—freak out, not remember him, or register fear but not know why. For that matter, Amy probably had the same initial response—but she might recall that Loren told her she used to work with him.

The officer brought Melissa around the back of the taxi and Loren met her there, doing her best to use her body to block the girl's view of Keller.

"Hey," Loren said, "thanks again."

"You got it." Richards turned and headed back with his partner to their cruiser.

"Let's get the heck out of here," Loren said.

They led Amy and Melissa to Loren's Ford, now a dozen feet away.

"What's going on?" Amy asked.

Loren opened the rear door. "Everything's fine, but we don't have much time."

Amy and Melissa got in. Amy found Melissa's buckle and shoved it home with a click.

"Where are we going?" Melissa asked. "Why did the policemen

leave?"

"Good questions," Amy said. "These are policemen, too."

Loren started the engine and turned to give Melissa a wink and then pulled out and hung a right onto Garfield Street.

"We're going back to where you left your car," Loren said. "It's only a half-mile or so away."

Amy leaned forward in the seat. "Something tells me you're not here as an agent."

"If I was, you'd be on your way to the county jail."

As Loren approach Keller's Lincoln, she elbowed him. "Get in and be ready to go. I'm gonna wipe this thing down."

"The adventure continues," Keller said. "Follow me, ladies."

"C'mon," Amy said, unbuckling Melissa. She gave Keller a wary look as they got out of the Ford.

Loren found a rag on the floor and dragged it across the steering wheel, the door, the dash, the mirror...anything they might have touched. She then got into the Lincoln's front passenger seat.

Keller hung a U-turn and glanced at Loren. "Now what?"

"Nice and slow," she said. "Obey all traffic laws. We've got another hour before it's dark. If we can make it to nightfall, we stand a better chance of not being identified."

"And then what?"

"We're headed to Soledad. I've got my Bureau car there. I'll check in and then head back to the office."

"And me?" Amy asked.

Yes. What about you?

"And Melissa?"

"One thing at a time," Loren said. "I'll figure it out on the way to Soledad."

THEY ARRIVED IN Soledad as a dusky steel blue sky faded to black like a movie that had come to an end.

Loren had done a lot of thinking along the way. Melissa fell asleep in Amy's lap. Amy stared out the window at the inky landscape, not knowing what the future would hold.

Keller occasionally checked in with Loren to see if he could be of some help. "Run some ideas off me," he said as they approached the exit.

"There's no perfect solution," Loren said.

Keller laughed. "There never is. But how do you define perfect?"

Loren held out her hand and raised a finger with each point. "Amy is not prosecuted. Melissa doesn't end up in an abusive environment—" she glanced over the seatback to make sure the girl was still asleep—"and her parents do time for all the crimes they committed, including arson, insurance fraud, and theft of personal property. I remain an agent in good standing. And you get your money."

Keller shook his head. "Nope. No one solution that'll accomplish all that."

"And I have to somehow get that car I left in SLO to Señor Gomez," Loren said.

"You've got more important things to deal with," Keller said. "The police will find it—if they haven't already—and will be returning it to Gomez once they're done processing it."

Loren pointed toward the freeway. "Get off here."

As Keller looped around and followed her directions to the disabled BuCar, Loren turned on her Samsung.

"What are you doing?"

"Trying to salvage my career." She called Hill and waited while it rang.

"Jesus Christ, Loren. That you?"

"Yeah. Been a hell of a day. Got a flat when I pulled off the freeway for lunch, then fell in a ditch and, I dunno, I think I hit my head and lost consciousness. Just came to, it's dark out."

There was a pause of hesitation. Then, Tran's voice: "Your phones were off all day, Loren."

"Left my iPhone at home. Samsung battery must've died. Not sure. I got back in the car and plugged the thing in. It booted up and I called you."

An awkward silence ensued.

"You guys still there?"

"Yeah," Minh said. "Here. You, uh, you okay?"

"I'm—probably could use some food and water. Got a splitting headache. And I've still gotta change the flat. Or call road service."

"Where are you?"

"Soledad."

"We're only about forty-five minutes off your twenty. Get in the car and rest. We'll change the tire."

Forty-five minutes? Holy crap. "Thanks guys."

She hung up and let her head fall back against the headrest. "That did not go the way I planned."

Keller chuckled. "What *has*?"

"My colleagues will be here in forty-five minutes. Maybe less."

"Then we'll be long gone by then." He pulled in front of her Ford and Loren and Keller got out.

She sighed deeply and looked out into the darkness. Fields were out there somewhere, but at this time of night the topography was formless.

She swung her gaze to Keller and saw that he was holding a handgun. And it was pointed in her direction.

Loren looked over at Amy, whose view was blocked by the BuCar.

"Mickey, what the fuck?"

"Loren. I'm real sorry. I respect you a lot, despite our differences over the years. Everything I said earlier was sincere. But I have to take the kid. It's my job."

Loren snorted. "Seriously? You'd bring the girl back to an abusive mother?"

"Not the way I want this to go down, but there are other considerations. Personally, I don't think the parents are gonna be around. Like you said, both will be going to prison."

"And then what?"

"Amy could petition the court, or however it's gotta happen, to adopt her."

"Amy. Adopt a child? Given her history of mental illness? There's no way a judge would go along with that. They don't know her like I know her. She's a fantastic mother. Melissa—Melissa saved her life. If there was one thing that could heal the pain she's experienced, it was another little girl that she and Dan created."

"Look," Keller said. "I'm not a judge, I'm not a jury. Hell, I'm not even an officer of the court anymore. I've got a private client. And my job isn't to hold a trial out here in the middle of freakin' nowhere."

"Don't forget who I am," Loren said. "I'm a federal agent and you're holding a gun on me."

"Yeah, well, I'd never forget that. But don't you forget how this goes. It cuts both ways. Anything happens to me, there's always Tarzana."

Loren ground her molars. "So I let you ruin my sister-in-law's life. Or I arrest you—and we both lose our jobs."

"You'd do time. A lot of it. Me?" He shrugged. "Who knows. My boss has a lot of money and even more contacts in the federal government."

"Mickey, you're still under arrest. And my partners will be here very soon."

She held up her right hand and exposed her Glock. "Looks like we've gotta make a deal. Let Amy and the kid go and I'll let you go, look the other way."

"You don't know how to do that. Pardon the expression, but it's not in your DNA."

"It's my idea. As hard as it is for me to do this, I made the offer. Take it or leave it."

Keller's gaze roamed her face.

"Please. Mickey, I'm asking you as a sister-in-law. As a mother. As a former colleague. I'm asking you for a favor."

"A favor?" He laughed. "That's a five-million-dollar ask."

They locked eyes. Loren swallowed hard. "A what?"

"A lot more, if it costs me my job."

"No one will ever know you had her and let her go."

Keller bit his bottom lip so hard he drew blood.

Loren reholstered her Glock. "I trust you."

"Then you're crazy."

"I know who you are at your core. And I know you're going to do the right thing here."

Keller closed his eyes. "Dammit."

"Obviously I can't ever replace the money you'll be out. And my god, is it really five million?"

"My cut's fifty percent, but yeah. That's what they paid." Keller took a deep breath. "Actually, it *started* at five. Christine Ellis upped it to fifty."

"Million?"

"Provided I bring Melissa back safely *and* kill your sister-in-law."

"You're shitting me."

"When I said I ended up working for the bad guys, I wasn't kidding."

Loren studied his face. "Do this for me and I'll forever be indebted to you."

Keller scoffed.

"C'mon, Mickey. Assuming I keep my job, that's worth a lot." He holstered his sidearm. "Even if I fail here, my boss won't give up. They'll send in someone else. They *will* get the girl back. And take out Amy in the process. Christine put the hit out on Amy." He waited a beat. "She paid. It's not rescindable."

"Then I need your help."

Keller laughed. "That's—that can't happen. If I have any hope of keeping my job, I can get away—maybe—with *walking* away. But aid and abet you? Today was...inexcusable. I let my emotions and feelings get in the way of doing my job. Whether it's you or me, cop or agent, that can't happen."

"She'll have to disappear."

"Amy? With a young girl?" Keller shook his head. "Even the Marshals Service has difficulty with witness protection when children are involved. How's Amy gonna do it by herself?"

"She'll have to make it work."

He snapped his fingers. "Unless...Butch Thurston. WITSEC."

"WITSEC? No way would—"

"He retired from the Service. He owes me. Might be willing

to get Amy and Melissa new identities, place them in a small town somewhere under assumed names. Faux WITSEC. Maybe even better than real witness protection. No paperwork. But no monthly stipend, either."

"Zach and I can take care of that. We'll hire Butch, pay him a salary to look after them. A few years, who knows?"

"It'd have to be untraceable. Cash, small amounts."

"Of course."

He thought a moment. "The Bureau will never let this go."

"No," Loren said. "Probably not. What about your boss?"

"Once the IPO goes through—or falls through because they're arrested and convicted—Tait may let the whole thing drop."

Loren glanced at her watch. "We need to reach some kind of deal here."

Keller lifted his brow. "If you're willing to foot the bill and if Butch is willing and able to do it, it could work."

"Call him. Ask."

"And the rest?"

"We'll figure it out. But we're running out of time. Call Butch. If he's not on board we're screwed. No way around it."

Keller pulled out his phone and dialed.

80

Ten minutes later, Loren opened the Lincoln's rear passenger door. "Hey sis. How you doin'?"

"What was that all about?"

"Nothing. Nothing to worry about."

Amy squinted disbelief.

Loren placed a hand on Amy's forearm. "Everything's gonna work out."

"What does that mean?" Amy asked, studying Loren's face. "How?"

"Barring a major flub by the assistant US Attorney, Melissa's parents are going to prison. They'll be out of the picture. Melissa would go to a foster home. She has no next of kin." Loren laughed. "Except that's not really true, is it? She's got you."

"What are you saying?"

Loren looked at the sleeping girl, her head comfortably resting in Amy's lap. She was in that kind of very deep slumber when kids can sleep through almost anything. "We're arranging for you to be given new identities. Someone who used to do this for the Marshals Service will be relocating you. We'll get you set up at a hotel tonight. Tomorrow a man named Butch Thurston will come and pick you up. Listen to everything he says. *Do* whatever he says. Don't question it. You and Melissa will start

325

new lives together."

Amy's eye began twitching uncontrollably. "Where?"

"Don't know. And I can't know. Somewhere safe."

"But what about you? And Zach, and the boys?"

Loren pursed her lips. "There's a cost for this, sis. And that's the price. No contact with us. For a while. How long, I don't know. The statute of limitations in California for kidnapping a child younger than fourteen is six years.

"But kidnapping on a federal level is much more serious—there's *no* statute of limitations. Charges can be filed at any time following the crime."

"That means I can never come home, can never see you guys again."

"We don't know that. Using intermediaries, Zach and I will try to find a way out of this for you. Maybe an attorney somewhere will have a novel approach. But that's—"

"Wishful thinking."

Loren moved her hand over Amy's. "We won't give up hope. And you shouldn't either." She gave a squeeze. "In the meantime, you get to make a life with your daughter." Loren laughed quietly. "Never thought I'd ever get to say that to you."

Amy allowed a smile to spread her lips. "I know." The grin evaporated. "But the Ellises? You really think they're going to prison?"

"I do. But Christine is a vindictive bitch. I'm not sure she'll admit defeat. That's another reason why I want to make sure you're safe."

"If the feds can't find me, I doubt anyone Christine hired could, either."

Loren looked into Amy's eyes with intensity. "I would not make that assumption, sis. That's why no contact means no contact. No emails. No text messages. No photos in the mail. No social media posts. Don't log into *any* of your existing accounts. Nothing. One mistake could be all it takes, because people will be listening. It's too risky. Your cover gets blown, if you're lucky enough to escape, you and Melissa will have to uproot and leave, start over again."

Amy wiped a tear from her cheek. "Okay."

"When things calm down, I'll get in touch with Butch and he'll get word to you. It could be a year, probably more before you hear from us." Loren touched the side of Amy's face, then gave her a hug. "You've gotta go now. My partners are on the way and they can't find you here. Mickey's gonna take you to a safe place."

She looked left, out the window. "He's—are you sure I can trust him?"

Loren could not help but laugh. "Yeah, I trust him. I've known him a long time. It's complicated. *He's* complicated. But at his core, he's a good guy."

"Okay."

"Okay. You take care. I love you." She dug out the burner and gave it to her. "I'll have Zach call you on this sometime tonight. Then give it to Butch to get rid of."

Amy nodded. Loren stole one last look at Melissa—at the niece she might never get to know—and closed the door.

81

oren had removed the wig and contact lenses. Keller would dispose of the former, while she tossed the latter into the adjacent farmland. She had done some good work with that disguise, but the time had come to retire it and part company.

Because Loren had told Hill and Minh that she had fallen into a ditch and lost consciousness, she had to make it look believable. After Keller drove off, Loren bent down and grabbed a handful of dirt and rubbed it into her blouse and pants. She mixed a little with saliva and smeared it on her cheek and then gathered some branches off the adjacent field and scraped them across her face and neck to increase the believability of her story.

She capped it off by smashing a rock against the side of her skull. It hurt and raised only a modest bump...but it was enough to bolster her depiction of the intervening "lost" hours after going off the grid.

Loren had just gotten into the Ford when her Samsung rang. It was Hill. "Ryder."

"Where you at?"

She gave him instructions on how to get to the road. "I'm on the left shoulder. The car with the busted back tire."

Two minutes later, their BuCar pulled up alongside hers.

Loren got out to greet them.

"Man, you look like shit."

She managed a smile. "Do me a favor. My head's killing me. You see anything?"

Hill parted her disheveled hair and turned on his phone's flashlight. "Yeah. Looks like—" he touched the spot and she jumped— "a nasty little bump."

"Must've gotten it when I fell. Now I know what a bruised apple feels like." She nodded at her disabled vehicle. "How long you think it'll take to change the tire?"

"Ten minutes," Minh said as he pulled the jack out of the trunk.

"Would one of you mind driving my car? I don't think I should be behind the wheel."

"You wanna go to the hospital?" Hill asked.

"Honestly, I just want to go home. See my husband. I have any problems, he can run me over to the ER."

"Okay, have it your way."

Loren lay down in the back and tried to clear her mind while Minh and Hill worked their magic.

They were on the road shortly thereafter, Hill chauffeuring Loren and Minh driving his own vehicle.

"So did I miss anything in the office today?"

"Just your sister-in-law."

"She came by the office?" Loren pushed herself up. "What'd she want?"

Hill glanced at her—but in the darkness Loren could not make out his expression.

"You don't know?" he said.

"Know what?"

"San Luis Obispo PD had her and the girl in custody, but Santa Ma—"

"Hang on a second. What girl? San Luis—what're you talking about?"

Hill pulled over and swiveled in his seat to face her. "The five-year-old she kidnapped."

Loren looked at him, doing her best to register confusion—

and shock. Not having any acting experience, she had no idea if she was being convincing—or overdoing it. She tried to keep her focus, determined to play a role, while not letting her face betray her. "Jimmy, if this is a joke, it's not funny. My sister-in-law has been—"

"A fugitive."

He proceeded to explain what they knew, Loren dropping her chin to her chest as she absorbed the information. She subtly shook her head a few times in disbelief.

When he finished, Loren made eye contact. "She's suffered terrible emotional and mental anguish ever since her husband and daughter were killed in that accident, but this doesn't sound like her."

"She never said *anything* to you about Melissa Ellis? About planning to...take her?"

"She never said anything to me about even thinking about doing something like this. I—I would've talked her out of it. Obviously." She looked out the side window. "My god, Amy..."

"Santa Maria RA sent a couple of agents, but when they arrived on scene, Amy and the girl were gone." Hill looked hard at her. "Story I got was that two individuals impersonating federal agents took custody."

"Two people? What—how—"

"One of 'em had creds and a badge. And knowledge of FBI procedure."

"Who was it?"

Hill chuckled. "He didn't read the name on the creds, but the woman identified—"

"Woman? A female agent?"

"Yep. Said her name was something like Maureen Rader."

"Do we know who that is?"

"No one in the Bureau, that's for sure."

"Did he give us a description?"

"Blonde, blue-eyed, about your height and build. Same age, too."

"Did they put out a BOLO?"

Hill laughed. "Oh yeah they did. SLOPD chief is pretty pissed."

"And what about the other guy?"

"Six feet, thin, charcoal hair. Wearing a dark sport coat. A few years older than you."

"So they've got nothing."

Hill's eyes darted left and right as he scanned her expression. "Pretty much. Found a car matching the description of the one the fake agents were driving. Parked a mile away in a motel lot. No prints other than the owner's. But only in a few places. None on the steering wheel or gearshift. Like the car had been wiped down."

"And the owner?"

"Not involved. Lives in Soledad. Not far from where we picked you up. Tran's on his way there to talk with the guy right now."

Loren swung her gaze over her left shoulder. Minh's vehicle was nowhere to be seen. "Hopefully he gives us a better description than blonde and blue-eyed." *Damn. One mistake I made. No, two. My latents could be on the bills I used to pay Gomez.* But Gomez might just report the car stolen rather than being accused as an accessory to a crime. More importantly, he would not risk having to turn the money over as evidence.

"Has my husband heard from Amy?"

"You haven't talked to him?"

"I only called you. I was kind of out of it. Still not thinking clearly."

"Call him now."

He would ask what happened, not knowing that Hill was in the car with her. "I'll just talk with him when I get home. He'll know something's wrong by my voice. I'd rather tell him what happened in person, so he can see I'm okay."

Hill did not reply—but Loren knew that he doubted her story. What did she expect? The real test would be when she faced her squad supervisor. He would not pull any punches. Nor would the Office of Professional Responsibility.

Loren closed her eyes and rested against the door. Those were battles for another day.

82

Loren awoke to a hand shaking her. "We're here."

She opened her eyes and squinted against the streetlight. "Where?"

"Home," Hill said. "*Your* home."

"Oh, man." She sat up and grabbed the dashboard to steady herself. "Fell asleep."

"I noticed."

"Sorry I wasn't better company."

Hill chuckled. "It's okay. You had a tough day." Loren yawned deeply and shook her head, popped open the door. She was surprised she had been able to nod off—but she had been up a good part of the previous night and felt drained from all the stress-induced adrenalin flowing through her bloodstream all day. Despite the nap, she was exhausted.

Hill pulled the keys out of the ignition and took the Ford fob off the ring and handed her the rest. "I'll take your car home. Maybe Zach can drive you to work tomorrow?"

"Yeah, sure. No worries. Thanks for doing this."

Hill eyed her. "I admire your commitment to family. Just want you to know that."

Loren hesitated. She studied his face, then got out.

As Hill drove off, she sat down on the cement steps by the

front door and took several deep breaths. Her night was not over—not by a long shot.

She reflected on the plan she had set in motion with Keller before Hill and Minh arrived:

Keller called Christine Ellis's cell phone.

"Mr. Keller," she said. "You have news for me?"

"I've got your daughter. And I've got Amy Robbins here."

Loren, channeling Amy, cried out—restrained, but frantic. "Please, let me go."

"Wire the money, Dr. Ellis. Once I have confirmation from Bill Tait that the funds are in our bank account, I'll pull the trigger."

Loren gave it all she had: a pained "No!" escaped her throat, right into the phone.

"I'm logging in." A few seconds later, Christine said, "I'm ready to release the funds."

"Do it."

"You do it first."

"Dr. Ellis," Keller said firmly, allowing a tinge of anger to color his voice. "If you want your daughter back and Amy Robbins out of your life, hit that button. Now."

"It's done."

"I'll call you in one minute."

He dialed Martinez in cyber. "Manuel, I need confirmation that Christine Ellis has released the funds."

"Released? You completed your mission?"

"Manuel—yes or no. Is the money in the account or not?"

"Yes. Just came through."

"Great."

He clicked off and called Christine Ellis back. "I'll bring Melissa to a neutral location later tonight. I'll text you the coordinates for the handoff."

"And Robbins?"

"Thought you'd want to hear it for yourself." He brought Loren close. "No," she said, doing her best to plead convincingly. "Please d—"

Keller fired his pistol. It echoed in the quiet distance.

"We're done for now, Dr. Ellis. Watch for my text. Come alone. Anyone

with you, I'll know and Melissa and I will leave. Don't be late."

He hung up, mere minutes before Hill and Minh were due to arrive in Soledad.

LOREN CHECKED HER WATCH. By now Keller had texted Christine Ellis the location for the meet. She entered her code into the wireless garage remote and it rolled open. She got into Zach's Mercedes and started the engine.

Zach walked out of the house and stared at Loren through the windshield. She blew him a kiss and then backed out. She had to give him credit. He understood the gravity of the situation and did not try to stop her.

Loren parked the car several blocks away in front of a Thai restaurant she frequented and walked to the lake, keeping aware of her surroundings to avoid any nefarious types looking for trouble. She found a bench and sat for an hour in the cold, thinking about the day.

Thinking about Keller and Butch Thurston. And Amy. And Melissa.

It was almost 10:00 PM when she got up and made her way along the trail toward the boathouse. It had closed hours ago. There were no cameras in the vicinity.

Ten minutes later, a woman traversed the path that circled the lake. Loren watched for others—but per Keller's admonitions, there was no one else with her.

Loren walked out into the dark courtyard and came up alongside Christine Ellis. The woman turned and saw Loren—and surprise registered on her face. "Who are you?"

"Keller couldn't make it. He sent me instead."

"That doesn't answer my question."

"I'm your friend or your enemy, depending on how our discussion goes."

Christine squinted confusion. "And what exactly would make you my friend?"

"Back off. Forget about Melissa. Do that and the police will never be told about the arson and theft of Amy and Dan Robbins's embryos."

"I don't know what you're talking about. I just came here to get my daughter back. She was kidna—"

"Kidnapped. Yeah. I know all about it. And I know all about Mickey Keller and Tait Protection and the hit you put out on Amy Robbins. I also know how you like to knock your daughter around. That's called child abuse."

Christine's eyes narrowed further. Her jaw tightened.

"So here's how this is gonna work. You're going to get on with your life. You will not see Melissa again. You will not ask about her. You will not pursue Amy Robbins."

"Who the hell are you to threaten me?"

"Someone who knows an awful lot about you."

Perhaps Christine's eyes had adjusted to the darkness, because her brow lifted and her chin rose slightly into a subtle nod, as if sudden realization had slapped her in the face. "You're Amy Robbins's sister-in-law, the FBI agent. I've done my research, Agent Ryder. And Robbins *is* going to prison. And I *will* be getting my daughter back."

"I've got evidence of the fifty million you paid for the contract to kill Amy. And I can produce a witness willing to testify to that. In addition to what you did back at Hutchinson's fertility clinic with the fire, you're never going to see a dime of your IPO. But you *will* have a long-term reservation waiting for you at a cozy federal prison. Unless you do what I said."

Christine studied her face. "You're bluffing. If you had all that 'evidence,' you'd have shown up with a dozen cops and arrested me. Instead, you came to make a deal for your sister-in-law. So I don't think you're in the driver's seat here, Agent Ryder."

"Think whatever you want. I came to make a deal and give you an easy out." Loren reached to her belt and removed her handcuffs. "You'd obviously rather go to prison. Fine with me. That works, too."

Christine pulled out a pistol and held it in front of her. In the dark, it looked like a subcompact Glock, perhaps a G43. She looked comfortable with a firearm in her hand. *Too comfortable.* Loren surmised she had a concealed weapon permit because of where she lived and worked, which likely included attending nighttime meetings. And such a certification came with significant training.

Even if Loren were able to draw and shoot Christine before Christine got off a shot, Loren would have to report the discharge of her weapon. It would be easy for the Bureau to connect the dots as to why Loren was there.

"What do you think you're gonna do with that?"

"I'm going to renegotiate our deal. With more favorable terms."

Loren tilted her head. "I'm listening."

"Bring my daughter back in the next hour and we won't press charges against your sister-in-law."

"So you can continue to abuse Melissa? Not happening. Find another punching bag."

"That's none of your business."

"As a law enforcement officer, as a concerned citizen, as a mother—and a decent human being—it absolutely is my business. You're not getting your daughter back, no matter how you look at it."

"So I guess we've got nothing to discuss."

Loren had to agree—but she was not the one holding the pistol. They were standing only three feet apart. Even the worst shot would find it hard to miss. Loren had only one option.

"You're not really going to kill me," Loren said.

"A few years ago, I would've agreed with you. But money does strange things to people."

Loren could not argue with that—so she had to act. She swung her gaze over Christine's left shoulder and shouted into the darkness. "Melissa, no. Stay back!"

Christine spun around to look. It was a deke Loren knew the woman would not be able to resist. Loren rushed her, forcing Christine's forearms into the air. Christine stepped back and tried to bring the Glock down toward Loren's face. They were now in a wrestling match—and Loren had no doubt that Christine Ellis was going to pull the trigger.

Loren grunted and groaned, focusing all her energy on her forearms. She abruptly jerked down hard while twisting, torquing Christine's left wrist. It buckled and Loren forced the Glock toward Christine's face, pressing the end of the hard barrel against Christine's pink lips, squeezing the delicate skin against her front teeth.

They were both leaning over at about ninety degrees, refusing to give in. But pain was a powerful motivator. And the lips were one of the most sensitive parts of the body.

Christine's eyes filled with tears, the agony clearly reaching unbearable levels.

She opened her jaw to scream. Loren shoved the tip of the pistol into her mouth. And fired.

Christine instantly went limp and slumped like a dead weight toward the pavement. Loren staggered sideward and landed on her right hip, covered in blood spatter. Her face, her jacket, her hat.

She shook off the shock of the moment and got to her feet, then retrieved the fallen Glock. Her ears were ringing but her mind was back in control.

Since Loren would have no way of explaining her presence at the lake late at night without going through standard Bureau arrest procedures—if she could even make the case she was there to apprehend Christine Ellis—she had to erase all traces that she had been there.

She used the inside of her jacket to wipe the pistol clean of fingerprints. She then put the weapon back in Christine's hands, making new latents on the handle and the trigger. The forensics would not make sense, but nothing would implicate her.

That done, Loren glanced around. All was quiet. She made her way to another dark area of the lake, putting distance between herself and Christine Ellis's body. Using handfuls of filthy water, she washed the red spatter from her skin as best she could.

She removed her socks and used them to dry herself, then shoved them in her pocket. She turned her windbreaker inside out, hiding the blood evidence, and walked home, a twenty-minute journey. When she arrived, she punched her code into the garage door opener and a minute later she was disrobing, inserting the stained clothing into a Hefty bag. She used bleach-soaked rags to wipe down her skin, which was a less than pleasant experience.

As she finished, the door to the house opened and Zach stood there sniffing the air like a hungry canine. "What the hell is going on? I smell bleach. And...why are you naked?"

"I'm not naked."

"Don't avoid the question. What's going on?"

"Nothing you need to know about," Loren said as she gathered myriad items from the shelves and placed them in a shopping bag. "But if anyone asks, after Hill drove me home, I *stayed* home. We ate a sandwich and talked. Kids asleep?"

"Of course. And why again are you standing there in the cold garage with no clothes on?"

"Can you run up to the bedroom and get the sweatpants and shirt in the Salvation Army bag in my closet?"

"So you're not gonna answer me."

"Nope. Just get me the clothes, please. I have to go back out."

Moments later, Zach returned with the apparel—along with Coco and her leash. "I know you don't want me going with you, but there's no reason why *she* can't. It's late."

Loren sighed. This was a concession she could make for Zach's sake. She pulled a baseball cap over her hair, took the dog's lead, and left.

Fifteen minutes later, after making a stop for Coco to pee, she was standing in one of the less desirable areas of Oakland. Coco seemed to sense the potential danger, as her ears were erect, her gaze darting left and right, her posture weight-forward. Acute readiness.

Loren poked a hole in the Hefty bag and set it inside a rusted, beat-up metal dumpster. She squirted a stream of lighter fluid inside, then lit a match and tossed it onto her bloody clothing. The material caught fire and burned. She wanted to leave but waited to make sure the flames did not spread. When the apparel had completely turned to ash, she pulled out a small bag of potting soil and smothered the simmering powder.

Loren moved another garbage bag atop the detritus and closed the lid, then gave the leash a tug. "C'mon, girl. Let's go get daddy's car."

83

Loren parked in the garage, removed Coco's harness, and took a deep breath. She walked into the house, where Zach was waiting for her. He embraced her and they stood there in each other's arms for a long minute.

He leaned back to examine her face. "Wanna tell me what that was all about?"

"Doesn't matter. I'm home."

"I've been worried about you. And Amy."

"Amy and Melissa are fine."

Zach pushed away and held Loren at arm's length. "Where are they?"

She handed him a slip of paper. "Call her, say good-bye."

"Good-bye?"

Loren peeled off the sweatshirt and tossed it over a kitchen chair.

"Where is she? Where's Melissa? And what does good-bye mean?"

"I can't tell you where they are. They're going dark."

"Dark. What the hell does that mean?"

"For lack of a better term, unofficial witness protection. A retired US Marshal who used to run the WITSEC program is gonna set them up in a place. We won't have any contact with them."

Zach searched her eyes. "No contact? For how long?"

"I don't know. We'll have to see how it goes."

Zach turned away and began pacing the kitchen. "I don't understand. This isn't my world, Lor. I buy and sell stocks. I don't—"

"The Bureau isn't going to let the case go. The statute of limitations on kidnapping is six years for California. Federally, there's *no* statute. I'll have to find a defense attorney who can be trusted. But everything needs to die down before I try something like that."

Zach stopped and faced Loren. His eyes were red.

"We'll probably be under surveillance for a long time. We can't risk any kind of contact with her. Okay?"

He looked up at the ceiling. "So she's a fugitive."

"Yes."

"How long?"

"Don't know. A few years. Maybe more."

"Jesus."

"It was the only way." She could not tell him about Christine Ellis. For a lot of reasons—most of which, he would never look at her the same way again. For that matter, she would never be able to look at *herself* the same way. It was self-defense, yes—but not reporting it, not being honest with Mountain, Hill, and Minh from the beginning...had previously been unthinkable. But she did it for family. That's what she kept telling herself during the short drive home with Coco, when she finally had a moment to reflect.

Zach sat down heavily on the couch. Coco jumped up and lay down alongside him as Zach unfurled the piece of paper. "This is Amy's number?"

"For tonight."

Loren looked at Zach. It was difficult enough for *her* to process this...she had no idea how her husband, a stranger to this life, would handle it.

She noticed an envelope on the table from Advanced Genetics. "When did this come?"

Zach looked up. "Looks like a couple of days ago based on the postmark. I went by Amy's mailbox this afternoon on the way back from the market."

"The DNA test Amy sent in." Loren sat down beside Zach and handed it to him. They both stared at it.

"Should we open it?" Loren asked.

"*Should* we?" Zach repeated mockingly. "You—the woman who couldn't wait until the boys were born to find out their sex? You made the doc tell us as soon as he did the ultrasounds."

"I just want to make sure we're on the same page with this."

"Yes, we should open it." He handed her the letter. "*You* should open it."

Loren bit her bottom lip. "What if Melissa's not her daughter?"

"You mean her biological daughter? Does it matter?"

Loren slipped her thumb nail under the flap—and then stopped. "If Melissa's not hers, do we tell her?"

"I'm not gonna tell her unless she asks. But you know what? I think she already knows. She doesn't need a test. She doesn't need computerized verification of what's in her heart."

Loren withdrew her finger. "So don't open it?"

"Hell *yes.*" Zach reached for the envelope, but Loren yanked it away.

She ripped off the end and pulled out the DNA report. She flipped the pages to get to the conclusions.

"Thank God." Her eyes found Zach's. "Melissa's our niece."

84

Amy and Melissa sat down on the bed inside the Sunbelt Motel room. It was an economy inn off the freeway a few hours from where they bid good-bye to Loren. Originally an old truck stop, the facility had seen few upgrades over the years and now served as overflow temporary housing for the migrant community during central California's wine-growing season.

Keller dropped them off at the curb and waited for them to go inside before leaving to visit the local Walmart a few miles down the road with a list of items to pick up for the next couple of days, including a car seat.

As instructed, Amy secured the door with the deadbolt and swing bar lock. It looked strong and unbroachable.

Melissa was still half asleep, having been woken from her nap only minutes ago.

"Where are we?" she asked, rubbing her eyes with a fist and having a tough time of it because of the plastic mask.

Amy sat on the edge of the bed beside her. "This is where we're going to sleep tonight. And then, tomorrow, we embark on a new adventure. Just you and me."

"Really?"

"Really." She wiped Melissa's bangs from her eyes. "You don't have to go home."

"Promise?"

"Promise. We're going to find a new place to live."

"What about 'Selle?"

Amy took a deep breath. She had thought there would be some questions about why they were doing this. Maybe even some concern over not seeing her father. Perhaps those would come later. Tomorrow. The day after.

And perhaps not.

"She won't be able to join us. I'm sorry."

Melissa looked down, seeming to process that. She reached out to pull her closer, but the bump in the adjacent room caught her attention.

Amy jolted upright and listened.

"What was that?" Melissa asked.

"You heard it too?"

Melissa nodded silently.

Amy bit her bottom lip. The noise could've come from the unit next to theirs. But that's not what it sounded like.

It sounded like someone landing after jumping. Someone big.

Coming through a bathroom window.

85

Keller had pulled out of the lot and used his sat phone to call Bill Tait on the way to Walmart.

"Bill," Keller said, maneuvering the handset to his left ear to facilitate reception.

"Mickey. Tell me it's done."

"All's good on my end. I assume Martinez told you we got the fifty million?"

"He did."

"You got some proof for me that Robbins is taken care of?"

"Yeah, like I said, it's all good. Just gotta return the kid tonight. Gonna meet the mother, hand her over."

"I know, Christine Ellis called me."

"Great."

"But I need to give our client some proof. Peace of mind. Satisfaction."

"I had her on the phone when I...took care of it."

"She told me that, too."

"Okay."

"She spent fifty million, Mickey. We owe her tangible proof. Where's the body?"

"Gone. I took care of it. Bill, what the fuck's the problem

here?"

"I want to make sure nothing comes back to bite us in the ass. I don't want unhappy clients. Unhappy clients make problems."

"She's not goi—"

"And this was a really difficult thing for you to do. But you seem to have put it behind you. Very easily. Too easily."

"Yeah, well, like you said. Fifty million's a lot of money."

"I don't want you to take this personally, but I tried calling before. When I didn't hear back, I sent Sinbad to check up on things, make sure everything went according to plan."

"Sinbad?" Keller licked his dry lips. "When's he due here?"

"Already there. Sent him yesterday. An insurance policy in case you got cold feet. Told him to hang out nearby in case we needed him."

Keller felt a lump in his suddenly parched throat. *Holy Christ.*

He hung a left—cutting across traffic—and barely missed hitting an oncoming truck.

"Where exactly did you send him? Oakland?"

"No. Where you are. I had Martinez track your signal. He's at the Sunbelt Motel right about now."

Keller pushed his foot to the floor and the car downshifted.

"Mickey. Mickey, you there?"

Keller disconnected the call and powered off the phone. His heart was beating a forceful, irregular rhythm against his chest wall. His breath was short, his vision narrowing.

Get hold of yourself, Mickey. Get there alive.

86

Amy got up from the bed and walked over to the bathroom door. She rested her right ear against the painted wood surface and listened. No movement, no breathing, no running faucet.

She thought about ignoring what she had heard, but if there was one thing she had learned about her years of depression, ignoring something and hoping it would miraculously disappear was a highly ineffective approach.

They had to get out. Just in case.

She turned toward Melissa—and felt the breeze of the door flying open behind her. She spun and saw an enormous man standing there. He reached forward and snatched her shirt with a thick fist and pulled her inside, whipping her head back. Amy opened her mouth to scream but his other hand clamped down across her lips.

"Quiet," he said in her ear. "Or I'll kill the girl."

Amy's eyes bulged at the mention of Melissa. She forced her gaze to the extreme left and saw Melissa cowering against the headboard.

"Be quiet or I'll kill your mother," the man said in a restrained, though menacing, tone. "Understand?"

Melissa started to cry but no scream emerged from her throat.

"Understand?" he growled, baring his teeth like an animal.
She nodded comprehension, her gaze locking on Amy's face.
"What do you want?" Amy asked.
He bent his neck and brushed his wet lips against her left ear. "I want you."

87

Keller threw the Lincoln into PARK and left the front door open as he ran toward the motel room. He shoved the key card in, got the green light, and pushed. It opened an inch—and caught. Amy had done as he had told her. The swing bar lock was thrown across the top of the jamb.

Under normal circumstances, his was the worst approach one could use to breach a door with an armed felon potentially inside. But these were anything but normal circumstances: a young woman and her daughter were likely in the company of a psychopathic killer.

Keller pulled his Beretta, leaned back, and smashed his right shoulder into the wood door. It splintered and flew open.

He landed off balance at the side of the bed and saw Sinbad, all six-foot-eight of him, huddled over Amy on the mattress nearest the bathroom.

Melissa was cowering against the headboard inches away from Keller. Duct tape was wrapped across her mouth and around her neck, arms strapped behind her back.

Keller shifted the Beretta to his left hand and gathered Melissa against his body with his right. He pulled her off the bed and shoved her out of the room—all while keeping his gaze, and gun, on Sinbad. "Wait outside, Melissa." Keller leveled his pistol at Sinbad's head. "Get off her."

Sinbad rolled backward, off the bed, Amy tucked tightly against his body—much as Keller had done with the girl. Sinbad was holding her up, her head against his, her feet dangling a foot off the ground, a rag doll at the whim of its owner. Like Melissa, her mouth was taped shut, her wrists fastened together.

"Fuck off, Mickey. If you'd done your job, I wouldn't be here."

"I've got this," Keller said, trying to avoid an escalation.

He kept his handgun trained on his target—but who was he kidding? There was no way he could shoot. Sinbad was holding Amy's head against his.

"I'll take care of her," Keller said. "That's my job. What I'm being paid for."

"I'm getting paid, too. And my job is to clean up your mess, do what you don't have the balls to do."

Amy's eyes widened and she cried out—a weak moan against the tape.

Keller had only one option—other than backing off, which was not going to happen—and that was to confront Sinbad physically so that he had no choice but to drop Amy. She might then be able to run out of the room and get somewhere safe with Melissa.

Keller did not know if Sinbad was armed, but Sinbad was a guy who liked killing with his hands, not guns or knives. He would likely not draw his weapon even if he was carrying.

Yet despite Keller's martial arts training, a physical confrontation played to Sinbad's strengths, literally: the giant had several inches and a hundred pounds on him.

Keller made eye contact with Amy, then lowered his Beretta and fired off two rapid shots, striking Sinbad in both ankles.

The killer let out a guttural yell and dropped Amy as he fell to his knees. Amy scrabbled away, clambering awkwardly across the beds.

Keller pulled out a knife and sliced through her bindings. "Get Melissa and get in the car."

He holstered his pistol and stepped closer to Sinbad. "I told you I was gonna handle this."

"Fuck you, Mickey. You've lost your mind. Not to mention your job."

Keller brought his boot back and swung it squarely into Sinbad's jaw, like a placekicker sending a football fifty yards downfield toward the uprights.

Sinbad's head snapped backward and his eyes rolled up into his head. His torso slumped into the doorjamb.

As he stepped into the cold night air, Keller heard sirens. A couple of people were in the dark parking lot, keeping their distance.

He got into the car, where Amy and Melissa were huddled together in the back. "We're gonna be driving for a bit while I find somewhere safe for us to stay."

"Who was that?" Amy asked as she got Melissa situated.

"That," Keller said with a chuckle, "was my ex-colleague."

He pulled out of the lot and entered the freeway, then looked at Amy in the mirror. "You two okay back there?"

Amy held Melissa against her body as she stroked the child's hair. "You okay, Missy?"

Melissa nodded but kept her chin down. Keller had a feeling the girl was going to need some time to process all she had been through the past few days...perhaps even some counseling. But for now, they were both safe.

Keller turned on the satellite handset and dialed Tait. "Bill, have Martinez get a fix on Sinbad's cell. He's back at the motel and needs medical care."

"Mickey. This is not—"

"I don't have time to debate this. I've gotta catch a flight." He turned off the device, then powered down his personal iPhone. As soon as they found a place to stay, he would destroy the SIM card and replace it with one of the new ones he kept with him for situations such as this.

As he accelerated to the speed limit, he felt good about what he had done but was fairly certain that Sinbad was right: he'd probably be looking for a new job.

88

The following morning, Loren did not wait to be called into her boss's office. She knocked on Zeke Bailey's door.

"Come in."

She stepped inside.

His face drooped at the sight of her. "Close the door."

Loren complied—knowing that a private conversation in such situations was never a good sign.

"Take a seat."

She sat. "Any news on my sister-in-law?"

"Maybe I should be asking you that."

Loren drew her chin back. "Not sure what you mean."

"Loren. Can we talk honestly?"

"Always, sir."

"Hill filed a report last night at..." He consulted something on his desk. "One o'clock. In the morning."

"It was a late night."

"Yeah, that's what it sounds like." He lifted a thin sheaf of papers from his desk. "Just to be clear, your sister-in-law, who lives a half mile from you, abducts a young girl and you suddenly go off the grid for twelve hours?"

"Was it that long?"

"Close enough."

"I got a flat t—"

"Flat tire. Yes, Hill mentioned that in his report." He paged to the right spot and followed the words with an index finger. "You fell into a ditch and lost consciousness for several hours. And your cell battery went dead. Around 10:00 AM? Does that sound right?"

"Something like that, yes. Must've forgotten to charge it the night before."

Bailey nodded slowly, maintaining eye contact with her the whole time. "Uh-huh. And your radio? You turned it off."

"I don't remember doing that."

"I bet you don't." He shook his head. "And during the hours you were unconscious, lying in a ditch, your sister-in-law was spotted near San Luis Obispo, only about ninety minutes or so from Soledad, where you had that flat tire, dead phone, and unfortunate trip and fall."

"Yes sir."

"Well that's awful convenient."

"Convenient?" Loren canted her head left. "Sir, don't take my word for it. Have someone in the office check my phone records, email, text—"

"Don't talk to me like I'm an idiot, Loren. I know how to work a case."

"Sorry sir."

He leaned across the desk and extended his thick right index finger. "If we find anything, *anything* placing you near San Luis Obispo, you can kiss your career good-bye."

"Understood," Loren said. "I'd expect nothing less."

"No," he said slowly. "That much I believe. You're a damn good agent and I'd hate to have you throw away everything you've worked for. Just to help out a family member."

Loren took a deep breath. "You know, there are worse things in life than making sacrifices for family. Hypothetically speaking, of course."

"Yeah." Bailey narrowed both eyes. "Hypothetically speaking. You better hope we don't find anything because if we do—"

"If you do, you'll have my badge, my creds, and my gun, within the hour." *But not my integrity. Or my family.*

Bailey maintained eye contact a long moment. Loren stared back, not willing to give in to him. Finally he leaned back in his seat and pulled a document from the stack to his right. "There is one other thing that hit my desk this morning. Know anything about Christine Ellis?"

Loren glanced at the ceiling, searching it for a moment. "Which case?"

"Same one. Mrs. Ellis is Melissa's mother. Melissa is the girl your sister-in-law abducted."

"Okay."

"She was found dead at the lake."

Loren leaned forward. "Dead?"

"Apparent suicide. Or murder. Not sure yet what the hell happened. Ate her gun. Looks like some bruising on the lips, like the barrel was forced against her teeth."

"Whose gun?"

"Hers. She had a concealed carry permit."

"Hmm. Was she depressed?"

"OPD just started investigating. But as you know there aren't many cameras around the lake."

"No eyewitnesses?"

"Nothing yet. OPD said they'll share whatever they get." He sat forward again. "Where were you between 9:00 PM and 1:00 AM?"

"I was...in the car with Hill. He dropped me off...I don't know, sometime around 9:30 or so. I was with my husband after that."

"He'll corroborate?"

"I'm sure."

Bailey nodded but held her gaze a long moment.

"Are we done here, sir?"

"For now."

Loren nodded. "Thank you, sir." She rose and walked out, headed for her cubicle.

89

Having transferred Amy and Melissa to Butch Thurston the following morning in Bakersfield, Mickey Keller had much to think about going forward.

Did he still have a job? Did he still want to have that job?

Would Sinbad be coming after him? Would he have to spend the rest of his life looking over his shoulder, jumping at every errant sound in the dark?

Keller sat down on the bar stool in Sherman Oaks and ordered a beer, even though it was still early afternoon.

He reached over and grabbed a handful of nuts and popped them in his mouth. As he chewed, he realized there was one thing that required zero thought. He rooted out his iPhone and dialed.

Richard Prati answered immediately. "Who is this?"

"It's Mickey. Got a new cell number. And I've got a tip for you."

"Any of that info on the fertility clinic fire pan out?"

"Sure did. That's what I'm calling about. Remember it looked like arson? It *was* arson. And I can give you the perpetrators and connections. Pretty amazing story. High profile."

"I'm listening," Prati said. "Go on."

"I've got a couple of conditions."

"Conditions," Prati repeated. "Like what?"

The bartender set the beer on the counter in front of him.

"You've gotta leave me out of it. And I want immunity."

Prati groaned. "I'm not liking the sound of this."

"Do those two things and I'll give you a good case. I didn't do anything wrong here. I wasn't even involved. That's not why I want immunity. The implications could endanger my employer and my career." *Assuming I still have an employer—and a career—to protect.*

"Then why do you want immunity?"

"Because the people you're going to arrest are very well capitalized and vindictive individuals. They'll try to cut a deal by dragging me through the mud. But they'll be lying and it'll have nothing to do with the arson."

"I'll have to talk with the AUSA."

"Call me back."

Keller drank his beer, the dark porter rolling over his tongue, the alcohol relaxing his taut shoulder muscles. Tossed back some more nuts. And then his phone rang. He had been lost in thought—and consequently lost track of time—but figured it couldn't have been longer than thirty minutes.

"AUSA is reluctant to agree to your terms without more information as to what we're dealing with, but I vouched for you and she's given me a lot of leeway."

"Okay."

"Based on our relationship, I'm going to give you what you asked for. Please don't make me sorry. Because it'll be the last time."

Keller took a long, deep breath, then closed his eyes. "When you're done hearing what I have to say, you'll realize who the bad actors are in this equation. And that I've been the good guy."

He went through the story, blow by blow—minus a few details.

"What happened to the woman and the girl?"

"No idea. But this case isn't about them. They're basically background noise."

"And you want me to—"

"Arrest the couple. And the owner of the fertility clinic in Boston, John Hutchinson. Arrest Dr. Hutchinson first, then get him to roll on the Ellises. Hutchinson gets a reduced sentence but loses his medical license. And those two bastards, the husband and wife, will live out the next few decades in federal prison. Conspiracy to commit arson, conspiracy to defraud insurance companies, conspiracy to steal biologic tissue."

Prati sighed. "Sounds intriguing, I'll give you that."

"Trust me. It's a solid case. You'll come out looking like a hero."

"You know that's not what makes me tick."

"No. But it never hurts. So, we got a deal?"

"Deal. Give me their names."

Keller grinned. Finally—a case where he got to do something constructive. Positive. And, most importantly, help put bad guys behind bars.

Just like the old days.

90

The Indiana summer sun was beating down on the ribbon that stretched across the small storefront door of Lindan Bakery. Ramie Spector shielded her eyes as she sliced through the taut nylon with a pair of scissors, the ends snapping back as if being freed from each other.

In a sense, she and Melissa, now Missy, had also been freed—from the burdens of their prior lives—as they embarked on a new journey together.

In the six months that had passed, Ramie had taken the $75,000 that Zach had given her, untraceably through Butch Thurston, and signed a lease for space and equipment. She printed promotional materials that were distributed to area businesses, residences, and caterers and invested in a website for online ordering.

Ramie had figured that if she could build the business modestly enough to employ a handful of people, including a manager, she could devote afternoons and evenings to Missy as her daughter matured through childhood, teen hood, and adulthood.

She had learned from her prior life that a career was important, even vital, in providing for your family and establishing personal self-fulfillment, but it exacted a high price when it became all-consuming. Ramie lost her family once. She did not want to risk having her second chance pass in the blink of an eye.

As fortunate as she felt, Ramie still had moments where she would be overcome with sorrow. While the clinical depression was gone, the years of medication a bad memory, she knew the deep sadness over the loss of her family would never leave her. She took solace in knowing that in Missy, both Lindy and Dan would always be nearby.

The ups and downs, challenges and obstacles, sorrow and elation were part of life. Intellectually, Ramie knew that—but more importantly, she had come to realize that in order to appreciate the good, she had to summon the strength to defeat the bad. She had done that and—with the help of her little girl— had survived.

That afternoon, when Ramie picked her up from school, Missy was excited to tell her mom all about her day. After talking nonstop for five minutes, she paused long enough to make a request.

"Of course, honey. What would you like?"

Ramie figured Missy would want to go out for strawberry ice cream. Or to a zoo or find some ducks to feed. Yet it was something completely different—and wholly surprising. She wanted to go to the bakery to make a loaf of bread.

Pumpernickel.

ABOUT THE AUTHOR

 Alan Jacobson is the award-winning, *USA Today* bestselling author of fourteen thrillers, including the FBI profiler Karen Vail series and the OPSIG Team Black novels. His books have been translated internationally and several have been optioned by Hollywood.

Jacobson has spent over twenty-five years working with the FBI's Behavioral Analysis Unit, the DEA, the US Marshals Service, SWAT, the NYPD, Scotland Yard, local law enforcement, and the US military. This research and the breadth of his contacts help bring depth and realism to his characters and stories.

For video interviews and a free personal safety eBook co-authored by Alan Jacobson and FBI Profiler Mark Safarik, please visit www.AlanJacobson.com.

You can also connect with Jacobson on Instagram (alan.jacobson), Twitter (@JacobsonAlan), Facebook (AlanJacobsonFans), and Goodreads (alan-jacobson).

NOVELS AND STORIES BY ALAN JACOBSON

Alan Jacobson has established a reputation as one of the most insightful suspense/thriller writers of our time. His exhaustive research, coupled with years of unprecedented access to law enforcement agencies, including the FBI's Behavioral Analysis Unit, bring realism and unique characters to his pages. Following are his current, and forthcoming, releases.

STAND ALONE NOVELS

False Accusations > Dr. Phillip Madison has everything: wealth, power, and an impeccable reputation. But in the predawn hours of a quiet suburb, the revered orthopedic surgeon is charged with double homicide—a cold-blooded hit-and-run that leaves an innocent couple dead. Blood evidence has brought the police to his door. An eyewitness has placed him at the crime scene, and Madison has no alibi. With his family torn apart, his career forever damaged, no way to prove his innocence and facing life in prison, Madison must find the person who has engineered the case against him. Years after reading it, people still talk about his shocking ending. *False Accusations* launched Jacobson's career and became a national bestseller, prompting CNN to call him, "One of the brightest stars in the publishing industry."

The 7th Victim (Karen Vail #1) > Literary giants Nelson DeMille and James Patterson describe Karen Vail, the first female FBI profiler, as "tough, smart, funny, very believable," and "compelling." In *The 7th Victim*, Vail—with a dry sense of humor and a closet full of skeletons—heads up a task force to find the Dead Eyes Killer, who is murdering young women in Virginia...the backyard of the famed FBI Behavioral Analysis Unit. The twists and turns that Karen Vail endures in this tense psychological suspense thriller build to a powerful ending no reader will see coming. Named one of the Top 5 Best Books of the Year (*Library Journal*).

Crush (Karen Vail #2) > In light of the traumatic events of *The 7th Victim*, FBI Profiler Karen Vail is sent to the Napa Valley for a mandatory vacation—but the Crush Killer has other plans. Vail partners with Inspector Roxxann Dixon to track down the architect of death who crushes his victims' windpipes and leaves their bodies in wine caves. However, the killer is unlike anything the profiling unit has ever encountered, and Vail's miscalculations have dire consequences for those she holds dear. Publishers Weekly describes *Crush* as "addicting" and New York Times bestselling author Steve Martini calls it a thriller that's "Crisply written and meticulously researched," and "rocks from the opening page to the jarring conclusion." (Note: the *Crush* storyline continues in *Velocity*.)

Velocity (Karen Vail #3) > A missing detective. A bold serial killer. And evidence that makes FBI profiler Karen Vail question the loyalty of those she has entrusted her life to. In the shocking conclusion to *Crush*, Karen Vail squares off against foes more dangerous than any she has yet encountered. In the process, shocking personal and professional truths emerge—truths that may be more than Vail can handle. *Velocity* was named to *The Strand Magazine*'s Top 10 Best Books for 2010, *Suspense Magazine*'s

Top 4 Best Thrillers of 2010, Library Journal's Top 5 Best Books of the Year, and the *Los Angeles Times'* top picks of the year. Michael Connelly said *Velocity* is "As relentless as a bullet. Karen Vail is my kind of hero and Alan Jacobson is my kind of writer!"

Inmate 1577 (Karen Vail #4) > When an elderly woman is found raped and murdered, Karen Vail heads west to team up with Inspector Lance Burden and Detective Roxxann Dixon. As they follow the killer's trail in and around San Francisco, the offender leaves behind clues that ultimately lead them to the most unlikely of places, a mysterious island ripped from city lore whose long-buried, decades-old secrets hold the key to their case: Alcatraz. The Rock. It's a case that has more twists and turns than the famed Lombard Street. The legendary Clive Cussler calls *Inmate 1577* "a powerful thriller, brilliantly conceived and written." Named one of *The Strand Magazine*'s Top 10 Best Books of the Year.

No Way Out (Karen Vail #5) > Renowned FBI profiler Karen Vail returns in *No Way Out*, a high-stakes thriller set in London. When a high profile art gallery is bombed, Vail is dispatched to England to assist with Scotland Yard's investigation. But what she finds there—a plot to destroy a controversial, recently unearthed 440-year-old manuscript—turns into something much larger, and a whole lot more dangerous, for the UK, the US—and herself. With his trademark spirited dialogue, page-turning scenes, and well drawn characters, National Bestselling author Alan Jacobson ("My kind of writer," per Michael Connelly) has crafted the thriller of the year. Named a top ten "Best thriller of 2013" by both *Suspense Magazine* and *The Strand Magazine*.

Spectrum (Karen Vail #6) > It's 1995 and the NYPD has just graduated a promising new patrol officer named Karen Vail. During the rookie's first day on the job, she finds herself at the crime scene of a woman murdered in an unusual manner. As the years pass and more victims are discovered, Vail's career takes unexpected twists and turns—as does the case that's come to be known as

"Hades." Now a skilled FBI profiler, will Vail be in a better position to catch the offender? Or will Hades prove to be Karen Vail's hell on earth? #1 *New York Times* bestseller Richard North Patterson called *Spectrum*, "Compelling and crisp...A pleasure to read."

The Darkness of Evil (Karen Vail #7) > Roscoe Lee Marcks, one of history's most notorious serial killers, sits in a maximum security prison serving a life sentence—until he stages a brutal and well-executed escape. Although the US Marshals Service's fugitive task force enlists the help of FBI profiler Karen Vail to launch a no holds barred manhunt, the bright and law enforcement-wise Marcks has other plans—which include killing his daughter. But a retired profiling legend, who was responsible for Marcks's original capture, may just hold the key to stopping him. Perennial #1 *New York Times* bestselling author John Sandford compared *The Darkness of Evil* to *The Girl with the Dragon Tattoo*, calling it "smoothly written, intricately plotted," and "impressive," while fellow *New York Times* bestseller Phillip Margolin said *The Darkness of Evil* is "slick" and "full of very clever twists. Karen Vail is one tough heroine!"

Red Death (Karen Vail #8) > *Hawaii. Home to picturesque waterfalls. Pristine beaches. And a serial killer who proves as elusive as the island breeze.* When Honolulu Detective Adam Russell encounters the body of a woman in her sixties—the second in recent days to inexplicably die of what seems like natural causes—he reaches out to renowned FBI profiler Karen Vail. But even for someone as fluent in the language of murder as Vail, this case is hard to read. Lacking a profile, Vail and Russell pursue an offender who asphyxiates his victims while leaving behind a clean tox screen and no signs of trauma. Perhaps most terrifying of all, if the deaths appear natural at first glance, how many victims have already been overlooked? The queen of FBI thrillers, *New York Times* bestseller Catherine Coulter, calls *Red Death* "A unique and imaginative plot filled with witty dialogue and page-turning intrigue."

The Hunted (OPSIG Team Black #1) > How well do you know the one you love? How far would you go to find out? When Lauren Chambers' husband Michael disappears, her search reveals his hidden past involving the FBI, international assassins—and government secrets that some will go to great lengths to keep hidden. As *The Hunted* hurtles toward a conclusion mined with turn-on-a-dime twists, no one is who he appears to be and nothing is as it seems. *The Hunted* introduces the dynamic Department of Defense covert operative Hector DeSantos and FBI Director Douglas Knox, characters who return in future OPSIG Team Black novels, as well as the Karen Vail series (*Velocity*, *No Way Out*, and *Spectrum*).

Hard Target (OPSIG Team Black #2) > An explosion pulverizes the president-elect's helicopter on Election Night. The group behind the assassination attempt possesses far greater reach than anything the FBI has yet encountered—and a plot so deeply interwoven in the country's fabric that it threatens to upend America's political system. But as covert operative Hector DeSantos and FBI Agent Aaron "Uzi" Uziel sort out who is behind the bombings, Uzi's personal demons not only jeopardize the investigation but may sit at the heart of a tangle of lies that threaten to trigger an international terrorist attack. Lee Child called *Hard Target*, "Fast, hard, intelligent. A terrific thriller." Note: FBI Profiler Karen Vail plays a key role in the story.

The Lost Codex (OPSIG Team Black #3) > In a novel Jeffery Deaver called "brilliant," two ancient biblical documents stand at the heart of a geopolitical battle between foreign governments and radical extremists, threatening the lives of millions. With the American homeland under siege, the president turns to a team of uniquely trained covert operatives that includes FBI profiler Karen Vail, Special Forces veteran Hector DeSantos, and FBI terrorism expert Aaron Uziel. Their mission: find the stolen documents and capture—or kill—those responsible for unleashing a coordinated and unprecedented attack on US soil. Set in Washington, DC, New York, Paris, England, and Israel, *The Lost Codex* is international historical intrigue at its heart-stopping best.

Dark Side of the Moon (OPSIG Team Black #4) > In 1972, Apollo 17 returned to Earth with 200 pounds of rock—including something more dangerous than they could have imagined. For decades, the military concealed the crew's discovery—until a NASA employee discloses to foreign powers the existence of a material that would disrupt the global balance of power by providing them with the most powerful weapon of mass destruction yet created. While FBI profiler Karen Vail and OPSIG Team Black colleague Alexandra Rusakov go in search of the rogue employee, covert operatives Hector DeSantos and Aaron Uziel find themselves strapped into an Orion spacecraft, rocketing alongside astronauts toward the Moon to avert a war. But what can go wrong does, jeopardizing the mission and threatening to trigger the very conflict they were charged with preventing. *New York Times* bestselling author Gayle Lynds said *Dark Side of the Moon* is "the thriller ride of a lifetime...a non-stop tale of high adventure that Tom Clancy's most ardent fans will absolutely love!"

MICKEY KELLER SERIES

The Lost Girl (Mickey Keller #1) > Amy Robbins suffers a tragedy no one should ever endure: the loss of her young daughter and husband in a deadly accident. Mired in a depressive fog, her successful career vanishes—followed by her life savings and the will to live. But while biding time in a dead-end job, she stumbles on something that upends everything—and lays bare a disturbing truth at the heart of a tragic lie. With fixer Mickey Keller attempting to take from Amy the last hope she has for a return to a normal life, her sister-in-law—FBI Agent Loren

Ryder—squares off against Keller in a heart-pounding climax that will leave you wondering who are the good guys and who are the bad. In the words of Rizzoli and Isles' creator Tess Gerritsen, "Jacobson expertly ratchets up the tension and shows us that the most courageous heroes are those with everything to lose."

SHORT STORIES

"Fatal Twist" > The Park Rapist has murdered his first victim—and FBI profiler Karen Vail is on the case. As Vail races through the streets of Washington, DC to chase down a promising lead that may help her catch the killer, a military-trained sniper takes aim at his target, a wealthy businessman's son. But what brings these two unrelated offenders together is something the nation's capital has never before experienced. "Fatal Twist" provides a taste of Karen Vail that will whet your appetite.

"Double Take" > NYPD detective Ben Dyer awakens from cancer surgery to find his life turned upside down. His fiancée has disappeared and Dyer, determined to find her, embarks on a journey mined with potholes and startling revelations— revelations that have the potential to forever change his life. "Double Take" introduces NYPD Lieutenant Carmine Russo and Detective Ben Dyer, who return to play significant roles in *Spectrum* (Karen Vail #6).

"12:01 AM" > A kidnapped woman. A serial killer on death row— about to be executed. Karen Vail has mere hours to pull the pieces together to find the missing woman and her abductor—before it's too late. In a short story that reads like a novel straight out of the award-winning Karen Vail series, *USA Today* bestselling author Alan Jacobson sets a new standard for short form fiction.

More to come > For a peek at recently released Alan Jacobson novels, interviews, reading group guides, and more, visit www. AlanJacobson.com.

ACKNOWLEDGMENTS

It's impossible for writers to know everything about each topic they explore in their novels. I rely on experts to fill in the holes in my knowledge base and to educate me on those things I know little (or nothing) about. With that in mind, I owe thanks to the following experts:

John Bennett, special agent in charge, FBI San Francisco Division, for providing me with hours of insight as well as a detailed overview of the Bureau's work in child crimes, including the procedures and protocols it uses in finding these offenders.

Martha Parker, special agent, FBI; Agent Parker is the FBI Academy's child abduction program coordinator and the Bureau's foremost expert on crimes against children. Her review of the manuscript, and correction of my procedural flubs and terminological errors, was invaluable.

Mark Safarik, supervisory special agent, senior profiler at the FBI's Behavioral Analysis Unit (ret.) and principal of Forensic Behavioral Services International, for his assistance with FBI-related protocols and approaches, and for reviewing the entire manuscript for accuracy.

Jon Chinn, special agent, FBI, San Francisco Division, Squad CY-2, for assistance with Bureau radio technology and cell phone tracking.

John P. Cooney, special agent, Bureau of Alcohol, Tobacco,

Firearms, and Explosives (ATF), for reviewing, and correcting, my chapters pertaining to the arson and fire investigation procedures.

Jillian Manus, Managing Partner of Structure Capital, a Silicon Valley early-stage venture capital firm, for reviewing the manuscript relative to IPO procedures and the many SEC-mandated rules that govern such investing vehicles. Owing to her previous career in Hollywood as a development executive and literary agent, Jillian has a keen eye for story and loves to pull out the red pen and edit; as a result, her input on *The Lost Girl* went beyond the LifeScreen IPO.

Bennett Leventhal, MD, Deputy Director of Child & Adolescent Psychiatry and professor at University of California, San Francisco, for brain injury information and the diagnosis of, and clinical approach to, Melissa's injuries.

Tomás Palmer, cryptographer, one of the guys who fights for justice, honor, and the American way by thwarting cyber criminals in the public, private, and governmental space, made sure Keller's tech-related ventures were accurately conveyed.

Rhett Bratt, vice president at Charles Schwab (ret.), for an early overview relative to venture capital, angel investing, and the IPO process.

Davina Fankhauser, president of Fertility Within Reach, for explanations, ideas, and resources regarding GPD, fertility, and IVF.

Deb Phillips for answering my initial exploratory inquiries regarding Lake Merritt.

Jacquam Blue, sales associate, and **Darrick Barnes**, director of sales development, Shane Company jewelers, for assisting me with the pawnshop's approach to valuing Amy's wedding ring.

Bill Tait, for supporting this project and providing us with a terrific name befitting his character. Likewise, **Steve and Leslie Johnson**—whose namesake characters don't make an appearance in this novel, but whose beloved Coco *does*.

My longtime editor, **Kevin Smith**, who was once again instrumental in orchestrating the various notes to help make the

369

symphony melodic. My copyeditor, **Chrisona Schmidt**, who has also accompanied me on many of my literary trips to novel land while cutting unnecessary words, striking those well-intentioned (but superfluous) commas, and making the manuscript CMS-compliant.

My good friend **Mark Share**, for lending his sharp eye and proofreading skills.

My agents, **Joel Gotler** and **Frank Curtis**, for negotiating what needed to be negotiated and for keeping me out of trouble.

Annie Maco, graphic designer, for going above and beyond the call of duty in cover design. Her artwork provided a fresh look and some very creative concepts that previous designers had never explored.

The dedicated team at Suspense Publishing for their stellar work in getting *The Lost Girl* to you, my readers. Special thanks to **Shannon** (creative director) and **John Raab** (CEO and publisher), two of the most genuine people in the industry. Likewise, **John Hutchinson** and **Virginia Lenneville** of Norwood Press sit atop the publishing world in terms of individuals authors prefer to work with. (Contrary to his namesake in *The Lost Girl*, John is actually a pretty decent guy.)

My wife **Jill**, who conceived the idea behind *The Lost Girl*. I love writing and reap the benefit of seeing my creation reach fruition. Jill experiences the hard work I put in (and on the business side, the stress and frustration I endure) and for that deserves a medal. Perhaps even a ruby encrusted medal!

CPSIA information can be obtained
at www.ICGtesting.com
Printed in the USA
BVHW041655260721
612926BV00016B/455

9 780578 916088